Carolina

The boy can take no more. He is lost. He is desperate. his wrecked family—his abusive father, his religion-besotted mother, and the family hovel, his home of sixteen years. He must escape the unrelenting grind of poverty and the life-sucking mire that is the slums of Petersburg.

The gaming parlors hidden away in the magnificent hotels of downtown have lured him like a moth to a dark night's fire. Within two quick decades, he has amassed a fortune. Even so, he is haunted by a vague emptiness. He has long believed life must have meaning and feels a great destiny awaits him. With the flip of a card, Samuel Elwyn Biggs has won an undeveloped expanse of land in North Carolina from an aged and obviously "consumptive" man who no longer cares that he is dying and cares even less for the possessions he spent a lifetime accruing. With the winnings, Sam's life is changed forever—his destiny has arrived.

Sam is intent upon establishing a plantation with his new holdings. He finds his neighbor, Hesper Griffen, owner of the plantation to his north, is mentally ill and an alcoholic—and one sickness feeds the other. For years Griffen has ruled the countryside into which Sam has arrived with a frenzied and deadly tyranny. He has long felt the abandoned land which Sam now owns is rightfully his. Determined to crush the interloper, he violently confronts Sam but quickly learns the newly arrived stranger has no fear of him and that his brand of retaliation is not only aggressive, but extreme. Thus, a war erupts between the two men. Neither fears the other and neither will back down.

Emmett Detwyler, Sam's neighbor to the south is also, a wealthy and respected plantation owner. He, too, has little use for Hesper Griffen. With an agenda of his own, he befriends Sam and becomes his mentor. With Emmett lives Rose, a mysterious and beautiful young woman. She is not Emmett's wife, nor is she his daughter. The two are devoted to each other.

Sam and Rose fall in love and wish to marry, but she continually forestalls the wedding—there are secrets that must be told. Secrets that hint of incest and sexual aberrations. Secrets that can ruin lives.

And there are many wrongs which must be righted.

. . . poverty, wealth, love, threats received and retaliations paid, . . . things we can control . . . sometimes. Finally a strong storyteller has arrived.

Books, Books, and Books

You might put it down, but not for long . . . there's too much waiting.

The Monthly Reviewer

d. v. murray uses a clever style to address a difficult problem. How far would you go to protect someone you love? A forceful retaliation? Maybe even murder? He delivers the options and the shattering final decision.

David Shuster

This new voice has prepared a literary feast . . . my stomach growled and my mouth watered for more . . . then he opens the door to the banquet.

The Book Writer's Group

Native son and new author, d. v. murray exposes a dark and sinister underbelly of the "beloved" Antebellum era of the Old South. Carolina gamble was hard to lay aside.

The Raleigh Post

Master story teller, d. v. murray builds the story into a roaring storm of love, hate and revenge . . . and leaves the reader seeking shelter with the turn of the page.

Richmond Daily

The family saga, an almost lost genre has been brought back for us to enjoy. And enjoy it you will! Pages filled with intriguing plots and a bevy of varied personalities—from the strong-willed to the mentally ill, will keep you reading and reading.

Ellen Gettings Smith, author, "Hell's Broken Family"

Just as your eyes become gritty from reading, a new plot appears . . . and you must continue.

Darrell Quinn, Author, "Snake Eye Joe"

Carolina gamble
by d. v. murray

Published in 2009 by Wild Pony Publishing
                            9611 Amberwick,
                            Houston, Texas 77031

Dwight V. Murray
Carolina gamble
Wild Pony Publishing
ISBN: 978-0-615-23732-9
Library of Congress Control Number 2008934797

About the author

The author, Dwight V. Murray was born and raised in the part of North Carolina in which this riveting family saga is set. As a youngster, he found a badly rusted sword in a nearby woods. All that remained was the guard, the tang and four inches of the original blade, the balance of which was missing and lost forever. He was told by his history teacher it dated from the Civil war. He has been on a journey since that day. He has held fast to an abiding interest in all things antebellum and all things involving the American Civil War. His interest in that long gone era has taken him to the great National and Memorial Battlefields and to the bloodied fields of smaller skirmishes. He has walked across those hallowed fields of destruction. He has heard the weaponry of war sing its dreadful songs. He has felt the loss of loved ones, the pain of the wounded man, laying alone, cast aside much like the broken weapons of war that they were. He has seen their suffering. He has seen their dying.

Those excursions imparted upon him a desire to tell the stories of those Americans, the warriors, and the men and women who stayed at home and prayed for their loved ones. There will never be enough said about the heroism of the warriors—those Yankees, and those Rebels.

His stories are based upon legends and part-truths. But oddly, the one thing each story has in common is, in reality—they are all true. Every bad and unimaginable thing was committed during those terrible four years, thence, even the legends and the half truths must, in fact—be the truth—such was the magnitude of the American Civil War.

The icon of the deep south, the huge multi-columned mansions are still plentiful in the area in which he was born and lived. The occasional artifact of a war which nearly divided the United States of America can still be found.

And everywhere, there are the ghostly reminders of that long ago time.

Acknowledgements

I would like to thank all those who helped me with this story. First and foremost, my wife, Judy. She kept me on track. Secondly, my son Ryan for his graphic skills. Next, all the members of our writer's group for their critiques. Thanks Griff, thanks Lauren, thanks Steve and all of my friends who agreed to read the story and be honest with me with their criticisms and/or praises. A very special thanks to my editor, D. J. Resnick of KD Writers Service whose patience and suggestions proved invaluable.

Carolina gamble
by d. v. murray

Carolina gamble
by d. v. murray

Prologue

He pulled the chair from under the table, and spinning it around, threw his leg over the cane-bottomed seat. Crossing his arms on the headboard, he leaned forward. Wearily, he rested his stubbled chin on his arms and stared at the items on the table. In the near-dark of his hotel suite, a beam of moonlight, combined with the pale, orange glow from the whale oil lamp, barely lit the surface of the table before him. He ignored the loosely stacked piles of money held in place with novelty brass paperweights and studied the stained and aged envelope. The rust colored remnants of a long ago wax seal reminded him of dried and crusted blood.

His confidence fading, he longed to look at the contents again. What would he do—what could he do, if the folder did not hold the prize the old man told him it did?

Samuel Biggs reached for the thick, brown file and turned up the wick of the lamp. Careful not to complete the tears in the frayed edges, he opened the fragile folder and retrieved the stained paper from within. He folded back the top flap and in the yellow glow of the room he searched for the Great Seal of the State of North Carolina.

He held the paper near the globe of the lamp. Yellow needles of light streamed through the circular pattern of pin holes left decades earlier by a clerk's seal press. Beneath the perforated artwork, he read the words: Deed of Title. Again, he agreed with his previous assessment. It did look real, but he was quick to remind himself, he'd never seen a Deed of Title. He returned it to the table and continued to study the age-worn certificate before him. It does look official, he thought.

An excitement began to build within him. He felt the longed-for change in his life was near.

His eyes burning, he wiped at the moisture building in their corners from thirty-six hours without sleep—thirty-six hours during which thick cigar smoke had engulfed him and the aged gentleman who had handed the envelope to him. The soft tissues around his eyes had turned into a swollen and reddened mass, leaving his vision strained. His eyes had suffered enough for him to suspect the authen-ticity of the intriguing document. Only time would tell if his opponent was the skillful liar many had warned him he was.

If it contained what he was told it did, no wonder sleep evaded him. But he dampened his growing excitement by acknowledging he may have been deceived. Sam was confident the elderly man knew others had tried to cheat him. Yes, the man was old, but certainly not a fool—he would have been aware of the repercussions for cheating Samuel Elwyn Biggs.

I'll stop by the accountant today, let him look at it, he prom-ised himself.

And yet, again, he unfolded the deed and carefully read each line a third time. Finished, he returned it to its folder, stood, stretched and blew out the lamp.

Exhausted, he lay naked and sweating, upon the massive bed. It was late in the night—or early in the morning, depending on whether one was a day person or a night owl. Samuel Biggs was a gambler—he worked at night.

He tossed and turned. "The hottest night of the year," he com-plained. "Too tired to sleep, too hot to try." The flimsy curtains hung limp and motionless by the opened fourth floor window.

His suite at The Excelsior, Petersburg's finest hotel, was small but it served his purposes adequately. It was expensive, but well worth the money to be close to his work—the poker tables two floors above. He'd played poker for years and found his skills profitable, so money was never an issue.

Tonight, a seed had been planted. His future, he thought, might be there on the table, inside that aged brown folder laying next to the pile of money.

With the night fading, his thoughts kept returning to money;

money not even counted secreted away in a cash box hidden deep within the bowels of the hotel's basement. Now, it seemed, he had something more to add to his growing wealth.

Goddamn, I'm a landowner, he thought, incredulously. He lay there, thinking of possibilities.

The first tinge of pink from the rising sun colored the walls of his room. Finally, he felt sleep approaching. His eyes grew gritty as he slipped into the void between barely awake and barely asleep. Old memories began to gather and they formed into dreams of his childhood. Soon he watched his past.

***

With a plank pallet serving as his bed, Sam lay with his eyes closed, pretending to be asleep. His arm ached from the night before, after his drunken and angry father stumbled through the cabin's door and violently threw him aside.

Violence was his father's typical reaction to yet another of his fruitless meetings.

His mother scurried across the room, busying herself getting her husband's dinner on the table.

With the rising of the sun, he heard the rustling of bedclothes and the ill-mannered grunts and moans of his hung-over father. The sheet used as a make shift partition did little to muffle the inevitable curses of his father condemning the previous night's investors' stupidity. Lately, his meetings had grown progressively longer and less productive. His drinking grew with the longer hours and his violence increased with the drinking.

An irony, thought the boy—alcohol craves violence, violence craves alcohol. He could not understand how the need of one always led to the need of the other.

He lay there, his ears attuned for the telltale whispers warning him of the mood his father was in. Lately, his father's drinking had hardly ceased. So in his good hand Sam held tightly to a butcher knife, pilfered from the kitchen.

Tired of living in fear, he'd often asked his mother why God would let such meanness exist. Her answer, always something about how God acted in mysterious ways, served more to appease her inner turmoil than his own.

That night, his arm aching, hatred flooding his heart, he

stopped praying to his mother's God. Nothing good had ever come of her one-sided conversation with the man upstairs, and nothing ever will, he reasoned. So he simply whispered, "God, I'm telling you, if he bends over close enough to me, I'm going to shove this knife clean through him."

At first, when Sam was much younger and his parents' marriage seemingly happier, his father thought himself a businessman in the growing town of Petersburg. In reality, he was anything but. Always full of money making ideas, he busied himself explaining in great detail the workings of his latest plans to anyone he could corner with promises of liquor and ale. When the drinking funds ran out, so did his potential investors.

And in those happier days, Daniel Elwyn Biggs seldom was a loud, obnoxious, or mean drunk. An easy drunk, a quick drunk, but not necessarily a cheap drunk and never on his scouting and selling nights. Nor was he one to hold his liquor. He slurred his sales pitch before the third round of drinks was served. With his failures came less effort and an ever-increasing need to drink.

In his mind, Sam could see his father ordering still another round of drinks for the potential investors and hear his slurred voice interrupted by the waiter, "Pardon me, but what did he say?"

And always, one of the new potential investors answering, "He said more drinks and keep 'em coming," as they slapped each other's back, and laughed at their good fortune.

The man had devastated the poor, but happy family it had once been.

Sad memories surfaced, too; those of his mother struggling to roll the limp, drunken man over in bed; sometimes onto the dirt floor where he had slowly slumped, so she could search through his pockets for coins which might have survived his cost of doing business.

His mother, Harriet Sager McMurphy Biggs, had been a pleasant and patient wife. Sam thought she was beautiful—the most beautiful of all his friends' mothers. Now, years later, he knew that was merely a rite of passage; all boys thought their mom was by far the prettiest of all women.

But in truth, a brown tow sack of red potatoes could edge her out of the running for the prettiest of anything.

Her husband's slovenly manner had driven her toward the solace of religion—the lure of which filled her with promises of serenity and happiness. She was enraptured with a preacher's interpretation of what God expected of a Godly wife. She never complained to her husband about his inability to make a living for the Biggs family.

Whenever needed, and it was, often, she hummed hymns so God could not hear her wish the man she'd married would just go off and die.

He didn't know his father very well—just well enough to know he didn't like him and had little use for him. The man could be cruel and often proved it by back-handing his son and his wife. For that matter, he felt little for his mother, either. She'd never rushed to his aid to save him from his drunken father.

Once upon a time, he'd felt sorry for his mother's dire living conditions, until he realized people could change their lot in life if they wanted to. She didn't want to, not really, or she would have.

They, neither of them, seldom picked him up to hug him—to love him, and when they did yank him from the floor, it was to smack him on the ass because he had found a coin and made the mistake of thinking he could keep it for himself—kind of like a secret.

But a boy, always alone, morose, lost in thought, had to find something with meaning; if only because he'd managed to keep on living—and thinking. He'd shut his eyes, ears and heart to his parents. It wasn't hard to do; never shown love, love for others was foreign to him.

The family cabin was not one of those shacks down by the river which were rebuilt time and time again after each flood washed them away. Those were the homes, temporary homes, albeit, of the really poor, those really down and out. No, theirs was more substantial; planks over logs, newspapers serving both as insulation and window shades, a dirt floor, soft enough to feel like carpet, and a fireplace that came with its own guarantees; it'd cook your front parts while your ass froze solid; it'd burn more wood than you could find to feed it . . . and the big one; it'd burn your shack down someday.

Leaving the confines of the hell-hole he called home, Sam liked to explore. With each passing city block heading into the town center, the dwellings became larger and more pleasing to his eyes.

Six blocks due north of the family hovel stood houses built by master carpenters and skilled tradesmen. Constructed of sawnwood and kiln-dried brick, painted with real paint instead of the chalky whitewash which ran off the outside wall each time it rained, made them even more intriguing to the curious boy.

And two blocks north of those were similar houses, these equipped with a side barn and a hitching rail for horses. These were the biggest and finest of all the buildings in Petersburg.

And what a sight they were. There was nothing like this in the Petersburg Sam was familiar with.

Where's the newspaper that's stuck in the windows to keep the flies out in the summer and the heat in during winter? Even the stables—the people who lived there called them what? Carriage houses? They were palaces compared to the toilet he lived in.

They had large barns with lots of Negroes working in them. On the entryways sat beautiful black carriages, trimmed in red or gold, and the occasional white carriage trimmed with gold leaf, and each always harnessed to two huge white horses.

Of course, not everyone had such lavishly equipped homes or lifestyles, but to the impressionable boy, as far as he was concerned, everybody from there all the way to downtown had a black carriage drawn by two white horses.

And those little iron darky boys stuck in the ground at the end of the drive? What do they mean? he wondered.

He decided the only way things around these parts could possibly get any grander was if somehow he could live in one of those fancy houses with the carriage and horses and the little iron darky boys with feet encased in the packed dirt.

And yet, another place existed. He'd seen it from afar—dreamed of exploring it. Downtown. To think he'd ever be allowed into one of those huge buildings was preposterous. Just to be a guest in one of these fine homes—hardly likely.

The streets of downtown Petersburg proved to be Sam's schooling. When he reached sixteen, he'd long since grown tired of his life and his family.

He was smart and learned quickly. His mind was like a huge clay jar; when things got in, they stayed. His constant search for knowledge implanted in him the desire to better himself.

He had grown tired of hearing people laugh at his pa and tired of people talking about how his ma must be a nun, maybe a saint even, given her ever growing display of devotion to all things Godly;

thereby, ignoring the husbandly.

Sam felt like a growth on the family; something which existed only to use up space and food.

He pushed aside his meal, which once again consisted of boiled potatoes and burnt cornbread—burnt because Mom was off in dreamland smiling her imbecilic smile, thinking about the Lord, and the preacher's latest promises.

Cornbread burns easily when you ignore it.

He was convinced his parents thought he should feel honored to be named after one of his forefathers, a man who supposedly enjoyed an unspecified notoriety for his warlike tendencies back in the fatherland, Ireland; always going on with their Sir Elwyn this and Sir Elwyn that.

Frustrated with their single-mindedness, in anger he said, "This is America. Or do you still wish you were back in Ireland? Do you think anybody here gives a good goddamn if grandpa ran around wearing sacks tied at his waist, killing people?"

His father had lunged at him, angry over the show of disrespect for his beloved ancestor and once again, demanded he leave.

Sam started planning his escape from the wrecked family and the collapsing hovel.

Elwyn was about as close as anybody could get to such names as Delbert, Clyde, Herman, or suchlike, and still not be laughed at behind his back just because he was burdened with such an ill-sounding name. He knew those foolish enough to chide him with Elwyn were going to get a good thrashing—that, he knew for sure.

After twenty or so beatings he'd delivered to some of those disagreeable souls, folks learned he was a thin-skinned young man who most certainly did not like being called Elwyn. His closest friends, of which there were never many, not even in the best of times, could not and would not call him Elwyn.

Tired of it all, the constant bickering and his father's excuses for the lack of money, he walked over to the peg next to the door which held his one good coat and one good hat, and put them on. The other two people that lived there, the ones who liked to be called Ma and Pa, asked him where he thought he was off to. They heard his answer, but didn't understand.

"Anywhere but here."

Sam rented suitable quarters in the center of Petersburg and devoted himself to forgetting his past. The rented room, clean and freshly painted, furnished with a bed and one chair, impressed him greatly.

He studied the thickly woven rug on the planked floor, fearing he may have been put into the wrong room. The rug alone was worth more than the shack he'd just moved from.

He studied the streets, watching finely dressed men wearing pinstriped suits and stove-pipe hats. His mind started to bend toward the finer things in life.

He ran errands for the big men of Petersburg, and studied them as he did. He sought to ingratiate himself to such men, figuring some of their wealth and power would rub off on him. And he found he was right. Within a few busy years, Sam had become a man to be recognized by his uptown peers. He quickly acquired properties and interests in others' businesses. With wealth came leisure, and with leisure, came poker.

***

He was a tall man, handsome, well proportioned, trim and fit, easy to spot in a crowd. He was well muscled and agile. He wore his brown hair stylishly long; breaking over his ears and the collar of his coat. He often combed it with spread fingers—a boyish habit, but something the young ladies found endearing. A straight thin nose accented his chiseled face. A thick, unruly mustache required constant trimming. The young ladies liked it, also, so he willingly put up with the bother.

His dark blue eyes were penetrating. They could hold a woman in place while he approached her. He carried himself with an air of importance—something else the ladies admired.

Although he shaved closely each morning, he appeared to need yet another by mid-afternoon. And as irony would have it, a darkly shadowed face served him well. His dark brooding face intimidated many of his opponents at the tables, but attracted women.

He was known for his lack of a sense of humor, his quick temper, and a willingness to fight at the drop of a hat. Some men are like that. Besides, it was common knowledge that gamblers, Men of Fortune, could hardly afford a sense of humor.

In spite of their father's orders to stay away from him, the young ladies of Petersburg's high society sought him out to accompany them to the city's many soirees and festive events.

And fathers can not constantly watch their daughters.

***

Sam's life became one big poker game. High stakes, low stakes, it didn't matter. The enjoyment was in the winning. Win large, win small, but win. Sam wasn't a lazy man, nor was he a card-cheat. He was good at cards—he hardly needed to trick or cheat.

He no longer gambled so much for the money as he did the pleasure. He did at first; he needed money like everybody. But after years of poker, he had an excess of money. He played now to keep himself sharp.

With a childhood spent in poverty, which brought with it the inevitable ridicule and taunts, Sam needed to best his fellow man and winning was now his reward; money, a pleasant side benefit. Money bought him friends. Winning bought him respect and respect bought him into any game he wanted to be in. He was a winner. Now people wanted to try him—test him—and beat him at his own game.

He'd put away enough money to last a lifetime—two life-times. And Sam had just made the poker play of his life, a gamble so large his whole life was now changed.

Chapter One

The massive door to the Excelsior's Gentlemen's Club suddenly swung open. Through the doorway, walked an aged, gray haired man, dressed in a white summer suit. Behind him, the gaming parlor's security guard stared nervously past the man blocking the doorway, distress shadowing his face as he attempted to apologize to Mr. Reardon, the Club's treasurer and the night's acting manager, for the man's intrusion.

"Speak of the devil," said Jake. Tapping Sam's shoulder, he pointed toward the door, "That old son of a bitch ain't dead, after all. Look." Sam Biggs turned as a gray haired gentleman entered the room. All eyes in the room followed the man while he searched for and found a seat not far from the table where Sam sat playing cards. It was a pattern he'd followed religiously month after month, but Harold S. Ledbetter had not been present at the last two month's poker games.
It had been a pleasant two months for the Club's members.
Murmurs spreading through the room told the old man he was not welcome. Harold already knew that, and he didn't give a damn.
Finding his seat, he raised his arm and snapped his fingers at the night manager. With two extended fingers, he wiggled them with a come here motion.
Mr. Reardon, irritated by being summoned in such a manner, reluctantly approached the man.
"Get me a drink," ordered Harold S. Ledbetter.
The manager's face reddened with anger, but he graciously held his tongue. He stood erect and motioned for the bartender to bring the old man his drink.
"Compliments of the house, Sir. Welcome back."

Tonight, Harold Ledbetter seemed slowed as if by sickness or the burden of age. Usually immaculate in appearance and personal hygiene, his gray hair was unkempt, his face pale. He needed a two day's growth of stubble removed from his flabby cheeks and hanging jowls. In sharp contrast, he wore a perfectly cleaned and pressed white summer suit. A monogrammed handkerchief, trimmed in red, stuck from his jacket pocket.

The musty, unpleasant odor which often accompanies the elderly, gained him extra room as members sought seating elsewhere.

He sat watching Sam.

"Thinks he's that good, does he? Wait till I get through with the arrogant bastard," the old man muttered. If anyone overheard and cast a look of disdain at him, Harold S. Ledbetter would either ignore it or sneer at them.

Suddenly, lung ripping coughs erupted from his throat—consumption killing him. He removed his handkerchief and wiped at his mouth. Pulling it away, he spread it open just enough to see what he already expected—yellowish phlegm, turning pink with blood.

"Goddamn it," he mumbled and stuffed the handkerchief back into the pocket. Yet he continued to watch the game from his vantage near Sam's table. Every move Sam made was stored away in the old man's mind. Slowly, he eased himself up to the edge of the crowd beginning to gather around the table. He was becoming restless and agitated and he intended to be next in line to challenge Sam Biggs.

As usual, his tendency to think aloud and belittle those around him confirmed he was loathsome, but he did not concern himself with what others thought—he was there to watch Sam play cards. He'd been doing that a lot since being granted membership in the Club. Sam too, had watched the old man's card games.

Fair is fair, he thought.

Each now confident he understood the other, longed to challenge him from across a poker table—both thinking they had something to prove.

Sam thought the man skillful and hoped he would prove to be a worthy challenger. After years of playing hand after hand of poker with men who barely understood the game; men who seemed anxious to give him their money, he longed for a confrontation with a formidable enemy.

He knew the man was ill-tempered, often rude to the other members of the Club, but such personality faults were of little concern to him. He'd spent his entire life with obnoxious, loudmouthed people.

He liked the fact Harold Ledbetter was extremely wealthy and confident in himself. Both were good traits to possess, but each could lead to foolish mistakes and Sam would use those mistakes against him.

His gut hinted tonight would be the night Ledbetter would challenge him.

Sam watched with amusement as the man toyed with his drink. Although the man nursed his drinks at first, he would start drinking heavier and heavier as the game wore on. When he did, the old man's demeanor would change—it always did. Sam knew that, also. Few of his opponents ever noticed the more they drank, the less he did.

Nor was he surprised when the elderly man became angry at not being able to buy into the game. Sam could tell he thought it a sign of disrespect for his age or a lack of proper respect for who he was. On his face, a smirk of superiority implied . . . Am I not one of the wealthiest plantation owners in all of North Carolina? Not to even mention land holdings considered too large to farm successfully? He laughed at the fact that with all his holdings, he was worth more than all the hicks in the room put together.

Like Sam, he had money to play with and money to lose. How often he thought of the irony of being so damned wealthy and now about ready to die.

Still, he was a winner, everybody else losers—losers, all of them.

"Especially you, Sam Biggs," he mumbled, not caring who heard him.

Sam watched the old man's rheumy eyes. They held contempt for everybody in the room. But it seemed he particularly did not like Sam. Sam thought that was fair, also; he did not particularly like the old man.

He watched as the man's superior attitude grew along with his drinking.

Sam was tired, but he had to play all challengers—all comers—an unspoken rule of the Club. His current opponent, a young man, drunk or unskilled in the game of poker, perhaps both, seemed determined to keep losing his money to Sam. The game could not last much longer; not with the man's glass nearly emptied and his money nearly gone.

Soon the hoped-for last hand of the game was on the table.

Sam had worked the table down to himself and the young challenger. Almost two thousand dollars lay in front of the two men. An enormous amount of money, but such large hands were not uncommon; not in this Club.

Play out the last game and fold up shop; that's all Sam wanted, but Ledbetter was determined to get to the table. Sam hoped the elderly man would become too drunk to stay or too tired to wait for a seat and leave.

But Sam knew he would stay; drunk and tired. It wasn't about the money. He understood the man was determined to give him a good thrashing, thereby proving himself superior.

The poker games had been held monthly at the Excelsior for over a decade. It was an exclusive, members only Club, located on the uppermost floor and the players watched over by hired security. No one could enter the room without a sponsor. But being granted entry as a guest did not necessarily allow you to sit in on a game. No one could sit at a table unless he had deposited the required amount of money in the Club's guaranty account. As simple as that—no deposit—no game.

Most of the members, not all, were of the elite of Petersburg's society; lawyers, prosperous plantation owners, and businessmen from varying walks of life.

"Let me at that cocky little son of a bitch," the old man muttered and gagged from yet another fit of coughing. The elderly man was tiring. He looked tired—dying tired, even.

All eyes were on the two players. Tension mounted. Ledbetter was not about to leave the room. The other members crowded the table, awaiting the inevitable war. Sam Biggs had the cards; he had the game. What he wanted—what he needed, was rest.

Seeing Sam's victim was about to fold, the man pushed forward, positioning himself to be the next in line for the chair soon to be vacated.

Sam flipped his hold card, a six of diamonds, and covered the three spread upon the table before him. The room gasped, but quickly quieted. All men of honor. Membership rules. No cheering for one player or jeering of another allowed. Men with enough wealth to play if they chose and lose if they did. A small matter—these men could make up lost money in their sleep.

The defeated opponent jumped to his feet, his face contorted with anger, ready to accuse Sam of cheating or trickery—needing to save face. He wisely withheld his accusations, and throwing his chair in frustration, he stormed from the room.

An elderly man who coughed occasionally into a soiled white handkerchief—an intoxicated man who cast contemptuous eyes at Sam and the men standing around him—a man that had a dying look about him, pulled up the vacated chair and sat down.

Arrogantly, he threw a large bundle of money on the table. Sam stared at Harold Ledbetter, and smiled at the feeble attempt to intimidate him.

Seven hours later Samuel Elwyn Biggs' last opponent ever, rose from his chair and asked for the Club treasurer. Harold Ledbetter had a debt to pay, a huge debt.

Chapter Two

Samuel Elwyn Biggs crossed the Virginia State line on a well-used dirt road serving as a direct link between Petersburg in Virginia, and Weldon in North Carolina. Heading toward the site of his most recent acquisition, five-thousand acres of undeveloped land, he had in tow all his earthly possessions, a mixture of hired hands and four slaves—all new to him. The hired hands were happy to have found work, even though it meant uprooting their families and moving to North Carolina. Good jobs were scarce in Petersburg. The slaves had no choice.

His arms grew heavy from the constant batting away of insects. Gnats swarmed by the millions in large, dark and dancing masses, looking like ghostly, evil specters swaying to and fro above the roadway—so thick one could easily think he might have heard, Go back . . .Go back.

Gnats clustered in the corners of the eyes of the men, women, their children, and their animals, nearly blinding them all. They crawled into ears and nostrils.

Deer flies, sometimes called Three-Corner flies because of their triangular shape, announced their approach by the annoying buzz they emitted. With bodies as big as a dime and a bite that could raise a welt the size of a nickel, a traveler was wise to wear long-sleeved shirts or light jackets, even in the dreadful heat.

Every creature was about its business; gnats sucking moisture from the corners of eyes; deer flies darting in for quick mouthfuls of flesh or blood—man or beast, little did it matter which—they were crazed by the smell of both.

"Every square inch of this God forsaken swamp's full of something that wants to eat me or suck me dry," he mumbled, slapping at his neck.

A water moccasin fell from a tree branch into the swamp, splashing noisily six feet from the hooves of his mare.

Sam was afraid of only two things, poverty and snakes.

"Whoa, whoa," said Sam, as the startled mare, covered with the red mud of the soggy toll road, danced to the side. The mare's fiery eyes opened wide, her nostrils flared, showing her fear of the passage. He patted the animal's neck, and whispered soothingly to calm her.

He'd won the horse at a poker game. His opponent, a horse breeder from England, had lost his money and staked the magnificent animal to cover a reckless bet. The highly strung horse, a result of years of cross-breeding of the best of horses found in the eastern states, quickly became Sam's most cherished possession.

She stood, her chest heaving, her back and rump twitching to warn off gathering flies, as her tail swished furiously to warn away new arrivals. A thing of beauty, she was sixteen hands tall, with a massive chest, broad shoulders and firmly muscled quarters. Her coat was coal-black and shined when the sun fell upon it just so. A long mane fell loosely from her neck and it needed to be curried.

The Englishman called the coal-black mare The Queen of England. Sam thought the name fitting, but gave her a new one— something less regal. Affectionately, he called her Queenie.

The barely manageable road which led into the foreboding swamp had all but disappeared. Still the same dirt road, but with seepage from the swamp, it was sinking into itself, and becoming impassable.

The roadway no longer provided pleasant views to comfort the weary travelers. Gone were the wide variety of plants and flowers in hues of every color; and the wildlife; the rabbits, the squirrels, and the occasional mother deer with her fawns. Some of it pretty, some of it ugly, but all of it interesting.

The passage became dark and gloomy; the noon sun unable to filter through the heavy growth. The road continued south through a tunnel of dark gray cypress trees, heavily laden with massive clumps of bluish-gray moss. Someone called it Spanish Moss but didn't say why. Others laughed at him as if he was showing off a supposed wisdom.

What happened to the fields full of all kinds of flowering wild plants? Where are the deer with their fawns? Is this an omen of things to come? Sam dared to wonder. Only the occasional raccoon or opossum would show itself—hissing, growling, and baring razor sharp teeth to the trespassers. Wild hogs with tusks five inches long stood their ground, feet planted solidly, warding off creatures which might lay claim to their muddy wallows.

How comforting the tall pines, now far behind them had been; the forest floor carpeted in thick pine needles.

Weary riders led the way on their horses. Those walking behind; tired and worn, were battered by the clumps of moss which released myriads of insects that made their homes within the tightly woven masses. Hair and clothing crawled with unnamed insects. An acrid, bitter smell, emanating from the moss, assaulted the senses. The air, thick with humidity, was hard to breathe.

A veritable hell, this road into Carolina. Somehow it managed to stay afloat as it wended through the dark brackish water.

Horses and mules wheezed, straining every muscle to carry or pull their heavy burdens while sucking the wet, thick air deep into their lungs. White foam dripped from the mouths of the huge animals while sweat flowed down their muscled bodies in a vain attempt to cool the massive beasts.

Permeating everything was the overpowering odor of rotting vegetation, rancid swamp water, and the soured sweat of men and animals—gagging lungs that already hurt from sucking at the thick air.

"Well, this is a pretty fine corner of hell," mumbled Sam, stroking Queenie's neck. The occasional hand lettered sign said they were still on the Weldon-Petersburg Road.

"Petersburg wasn't all that great," Sam said to his horse, "but if this hog-trail is anything to judge by, Weldon's got to be uglier than a pig's ass. Don't you reckon, old girl?"

She nodded her head vigorously. A passer-by would have thought the horse understood her master.

Even so, the existence of the recently built road, although heavily rutted and sinking into itself, was a Godsend to him. With all of its faults, it was still the most direct route and certainly better than hauling wagons filled with everyone's possessions through the tangle of the woods.

Sam and his people were tossed like rag dolls due to the lack of maintenance of the thoroughfare.

"If they had no intention of keeping up this part of the road, why the hell did they build it through this goddamn swamp? How's about I give Your Highness a break?" Sam said to himself, as much as to the black mare, and slid from her back.

"Reckon they ever scrape this goddamn road?" he grinned,

subconsciously feeling eyes upon him as he continued the conversation with his horse.

He held up his arm to stop the caravan.

"We've got to stop. This damn road's going to kill us and the horses. Let's rest for a bit. Come on, Little Missy," he said, as he led the mare to the abundant grass growing at the edge of the road.

The slaves huddled closely together, their faces showing fear of the strangeness of the dark and foreboding swamp. They were oddly relieved to now be the property of a man who had literally won them in a card game. They didn't know what won meant and they didn't care. Whatever it meant—they knew they were still going to be slaves. But at least they were long gone from the gray haired, crazy old coot who used to beat them all the time.

"It sho be strange how little our skinny asses be worf' to dem white peebles 'less we be out in dem fils," said one of the slaves—the others agreeing. Being a slave was a concept they understood.

"White peebles—damn, dem be sum crazy ass sum'bitches, yo acks me," said one of the Negroes. "But at least we doan got's to Yas Suh and No Suh that old gray haired devil no mo'." Their memories of the meanness of Harold S. Ledbetter were fresh.

If one could hear and understand their muffled comments, he would have overheard, "I be a hopin' dat man be dead'r dan hell."

Another would try to outdo him, adding, "Lawd A'Mitey. I be a hopin' he be dead an' rot'n way lac ah old dead dawg an' he be gitt'n et up by dem wile hogs what libs in de woods."

With that came gleeful laughing.

To what was becoming a source of amusement, another said, "If dat sum'bitch be ah lay'n on de groun' ah burn'n up, I be a piss'n in my britches fo I hep put out dat fire."

That was followed with Amen's and Praise de Lawds and more laughing. They all agreed they hoped he was dead; and that some people did not deserve to live—too goddamn mean. Died in his sleep or got himself killed or something. They didn't care how he got dead. Dead was dead and that was a good thing as far as Massa Ledbetter was concerned.

They had no idea of what to expect from their new master, Massa Biggs. To them, all white people were devils and none had souls. Things couldn't get worse for them; there was just no way. Based on past experiences, they were sure there would be more beatings. After all, the man up in front of them was one of those white devils and they were darkies. They could handle the beatings; hell— they expected them. Nigger beatings had seemed like high sport to the previous master. "But please, Lawd, no mo ah dem dare darky kill'ns," they prayed. They could hope and they could pray, but they knew they'd find out, one way or the other.

Chapter Three

No more Aces. No more Kings. No more burning eyes and swollen sinuses from heavy cigar smoke. Lately, it seemed cards, money and drinking had a way of evolving into problems. It was time to get out of that life. Time to quit living on the jagged edge; knowing he would win the hand, but also knowing the man sitting across from him might be broke enough, mad enough, or drunk enough to pull out his pistol and shoot him dead. He wasn't afraid to die. He'd never given it much thought. He was tired—tired of it all.

He'd had his close calls; reminders of how quickly things could change. A knotted scar on the back of his hand, compliments of another loser who had become more careless and angrier with each drink, reminded him there were always risks. Everything about life was a risk.

After the man called Sam, demanding to see his hand, Sam reached to flip his hold card. A boot dagger was driven, hard and fast through his hand by the drunken challenger—pinning both hand and card to the table. His blood flowing freely, Sam nearly swooned from the burning, intense pain.

The club's guards, one on each side, shoved small derringers against the man's temples. Both ears were grabbed firmly as someone said, "Whoa, hold up friend." A hand reached forward and carefully pulled the dagger from the table, and gently lifted Sam's hand and placed it on a towel. The same hand flipped the hold card face up—and once again—Sam was the winner.

The drunken fool sobered rapidly and started trembling.

The guards eyed the blood dripping from Sam's sinewy fingers. "What do you want us to do with him, Mister Biggs?"

Seldom a heavy drinker, Sam quickly downed two shots of bourbon and as his stomach burned, the searing pain in his hand eased. He looked at the man, and flexed his fingers to see if they worked. They hurt like hell, but by some miracle, they did still work.

Determined to frighten the man, and without raising his voice, he answered, "Kill him. Just don't do it in here. Take him down to the basement."

His cold, hard stare convinced the man pain and death awaited him. He renewed his whimpering. The point had been made.

The Club did not need that kind of publicity. To be sure his advice would be heeded, Sam added, "Mister, you've made all your own bad luck. You're a poor drinker and an even worse poker player, but I'm going to let you win something tonight. You just won your life back. We could get the town law up here, but I don't think we want that, do we fellows?"

The two guards shook their heads.

"Why don't you get on out of here and don't come back."

Seeing the man's fear growing, he added to make sure he stayed away, "Your sponsor's got some explaining to do. If I were you, friend, I'd stay clear of him, too. Some of these fellows are going to be mad at me for not letting them kill you. That's what we usually do to assholes like you. Maybe I should. You really need to remember drinking and cards don't mix well for you."

Newly sobered, the man choked back a building sob. "Yes Sir, Mister Biggs. Thank you, Mister Biggs," and fled from the room.

***

That last game—the game with Harold S. Ledbetter . . . what a game it had been. Sam had beat him good and won a huge prize. He'd been told by the man what he'd won, but just barely, and that poorly described in a drunken stupor.

Harold S. Ledbetter died within a fortnight of the poker game. He was buried in a church cemetery and nobody had shown up, except the undertaker and the preacher; one of them to do the planting, and the other—well, it was his calling.

***

Sam's winnings lay to the south. He'd never even been in North Carolina before and he didn't know whether he had really won big or lost big at the card game. But soon, he would know.

The ride south on the Weldon-Petersburg toll road ended at a small town located at a nondescript intersection of the north and southbound road he was on. Weldon lay seventy miles below Petersburg, just inside North Carolina's state line.

Weldon's main street was bustling—a flurry of activity. The

buildings were basic, each filled with the kinds of businesses required for growth and the town appeared to be prospering. The town hall was a board and plank structure. It, too, simple and basic. Next to it, rising from the ground, a new foundation of concrete, stone and brick for a larger courthouse confirmed the steady growth of the young city and the promise of good things to come.

The town radiated a feeling of possibilities. The people in the street and those on the planked sidewalk watched the group as they rode through the town. Stares of curiosity from the townsfolk bothered no one.

Mules pulled wagons loaded with all types of farm produce. Most were loaded with mounds of tightly bound tobacco. It was that time of the year. Harvest time. An acrid odor of the cured tobacco followed wagons rolling toward unseen docks.

The travel weary men and women gazed at the clean, bright shops filled with all manner of things. They wished for the leisure to stroll past and window-shop, but their tired bodies had beaten them down and looking at each other, they knew they were a road-dirtied lot. Weldon and the window-shopping would have to wait.

The camp needed to be erected before it became too dark to do so. The night would be spent in a new camp, hopefully the last of the road camps, and just west of Weldon. Sam was told of suitable spots in which to camp. If they left early in the morning, they should be able to make it to their final destination before nightfall. Bone jarringly aware good roads were scarce in this part of the world, he hoped better roads awaited him and his people.

Shadows lengthened, the air cooled, and darkness chewed at the light of the day.

***

Sam called for Henry Atwell, the first man he had hired. He believed Henry to be honest and ambitious. He needed a good man to be the General Manager of the new plantation which he intended to develop and Henry seemed to be such a man.

Matt Davis was told to join him and Henry, also. He'd hired Matt shortly after Henry, and since Matt would be second in charge to Henry and serve as the plantation's overseer, he wanted the two to learn to work together. Sam had few concerns about the others he'd hired. They would do as they were told, so the group was sent ahead to find a campsite, Henry and Matt leading them.

The least of his concerns were the four slaves. Already confused and frightened by the recent changes in their lives, they would follow timidly. He suspected Ledbetter had treated them harshly and they would be wary of their new master. He'd watched them closely on the trip south. Unsure of what was happening, they seemed to readily accept their new lives.

He was hungry for information about Weldon and his new holdings. He informed Henry he would stay in town for a while, but he'd be along soon.

He was pleased to find that the Roanoke River flowed past Weldon. North of the city and at the city limits was a privately owned small dock and pier. He had been assured the owner, a Mister Brantley, was an honest and fair man.

The dock and pier were large enough to service all the farm goods delivered to it. Warehouses were filled with tightly bound tobacco and bales of cotton ready for shipping. Sam stood aside, watching the hustle and bustle of loading and unloading wagons. Large and small crates filled with all manner of goods being transferred into the freight wagons of the local mercantile served as proof the area was well-suited for farming.

By the dock's owner, he was told the Roanoke River was wide enough and deep enough to float small cargo barges. The size of usable barges was really dependant upon the rain. The God-forsaken swamps above Weldon provided enough run-off to keep the Roanoke River flowing and therefore, no trading season had ever been ruined because of a lack of rain.

From the swamp, the Roanoke meandered wildly, snaking its way toward the Atlantic Ocean. As it drank in the waters of the great Dismal Swamp, it grew in width and depth. Heading southeast, it widened until it was of considerable size. It joined with other streams and together they began their long search for the Albemarle Sound. Every port in the world could be reached from the sound; therefore Sam Biggs' goods had a very large market available, indeed.

"So far," Sam mused, "there seems to be more good going for it than bad.' He nodded his head. "It might work."

Walking Queenie back toward the center of the small village, he watched people gathering in front of Weldon's mercantile. An object being greatly praised by a yapping barker sat in the street by the edge of the sidewalk. Farmers, well dressed businessmen, bankers wearing dark visors, the town butcher identified by his bloodied

apron, women carrying recent purchases, and an assortment of children, were held as if in a trance by the skilled sales pitch of the
barker; a man determined to part with a huge black machine. His desperation to be shed of it showed in his eyes.

Sam climbed the wooden steps leading to the mercantile's
covered porch. He recognized it as one of the new steam-powered
machines he had been reading about in Petersburg.

There it stood, its tall, black smokestack adorned with three
gleaming brass bands. He never ceased being impressed by the pure
genius of the modern American people. He shook his head in amaze-
ment. In awe, he thought, How can anyone even think up such a machine, much less build something like that from scratch—something
out of nothing? He'd seen the machine in the illustrated magazine articles he'd browsed through during the slow days back at the Excelsior.

He recalled the trip long ago, when he'd ridden one of the new
railroad machines which had a larger version of the same engine up
front. It towed people along in long wagons outfitted with wooden
benches and handrails. The trip had been as uncomfortable as hell and
he dreaded the return trip home.

The big engine pulling the train was called an Iron Horse; a
logical name, he thought, amused. The trip was only from Petersburg
to Baltimore, not far, less than two hundred miles on iron rails. The
trip took eight hours—horseback would have taken three days of hard
riding.

He was fond of the white summer suits worn by men of
wealth, just as he and many of the other passengers on the little train
wore that day. His first and last train ride had cost him an expensive
ticket, a bruised rear-end and a very expensive white suit.

In anger, he wondered why no one had warned him that it was
the dirtiest, smokingest and steam-spewingest machine in the world?
It could not have been a secret. The suit was beyond cleaning, and
covered with cinder-burned holes, it was left worthless, a rag fit only
to be thrown away.

"There is no way this piece of shit child's toy will ever catch
on," he said to fellow passengers disembarking at Baltimore.

They all agreed it was a novelty of the rich, each massaging
their rears; sore from the roughness of the ride, and waving their
hands behind them, they dismissed the machine as pure folly. They

stumbled off to hire horse drawn and spring loaded carriages fitted with cushioned seats.

He grinned when he saw a gentleman that was so soot covered he was almost as black as the Negro man-servant escorting him. The grin disappeared when he remembered he, too, had been on the same train.

Disgusting way to travel. Interesting, though, he thought.

Still, he had been mightily impressed with the raw power the machine was capable of, recalling the unbelievable tonnage the little train was able to pull.

The engine in front of the mercantile was not at all an attractive machine, but it wasn't as ugly as it appeared from a distance. Attempts had been made to dress it up. Strategically placed bright red trim and polished brass rings added to the smoke stack gave it a touch of elegance.

Here, in Weldon of all places, was a steam-powered machine that had a practical use and little in common with the childish toy train. He knew it was a sawmill, at least that was what it was called in the books he'd read and the pictures he'd seen. A sawmill powered by steam. Damn. Who would have ever thought of such a thing? Unlike the fire breathing, smoke belching, cinder spitting, worthless child's toy he had ridden to Baltimore, before him stood a money-maker for a man that had timberland. He had timber, and he had a lot of ideas.

But he did not want to make himself known to the town folk scattered about, so quietly he acquired further information from the salesman who had been bragging about the big, black, brass and red trimmed machine. He knew the machine would be his, but there would be a proper time to claim it.

Trying to hide his desperation to be done with the huge machine, the salesman said, "Best not wait too long, friend—this here beauty ain't gonna' last long."

Sam remained noncommittal with the overly anxious barker. Old habits kept him playing his cards close to his chest.

Nearly too dark to read the street signs, few that there were, it was time to leave for the camp. The town's inhabitants had started lighting their rooms and businesses with their oil filled lamps. The pungent odor of the burning whale oil hung in the air like a morning's cool mist. Up ahead, the street lights—all six of them, were aglow as if to assure safe passage to the few people still on the streets and sidewalks; yet, they only threw out little more light than a full moon.

He was not fearful of his own safety. He never felt dressed in the morning without slipping the small Colt revolver he called the pocket cannon, into a small holster sewn inside the vest and under his left arm. Religiously, he thumbed the nipples on the revolver before he stored it into the hideaway pocket. It was a habit—a good one. The small brass firing caps seemed to fall off easily, but they were all there, clamped on tightly.

Most of the townspeople he rode past on his way west to the camp paid little attention to the stranger in their midst. Others acknowledged him with waves of the hand. A friendly gesture which he returned.

Riding past the most brightly lit business, coming from deep inside, were all the familiar noises he had been around most of his adult life. Noises that could only come from a gambling hall—memories of loud boisterous laughing, yelling, swearing and the annoying plinking of a cheap piano. A loud and off-key attempt by an obviously drunken woman was destroying what could have been a pretty song. He thought it odd how alcohol could make the piano and the singing sound so much better, if you drank enough.

But those days were gone. It had been well over a month, closer to two, since he had played that last hand. The hand, which in fact, was responsible for him riding past this very spot.

Long desirous of a new life, he was like a man who awoke one morning and decided to never drink again and found it easy to stick to his conviction. It was finished—his gambling done. He neither missed the drinking nor the poker. He had grown tired of living on the edge.

He did, however, think it ironical that ending one type of gambling had pushed him toward the largest gamble he would ever make in his life.

Chapter Four

He rode toward the night's camp, unsure of where it had been set up, but he was not overly concerned. He knew it would be up ahead, and close by.

For the first time since an early breakfast, his stomach growled. He hoped a warm meal would be awaiting him upon his arrival. Such a meal would serve two purposes; one being to fill his stomach and the other, to see the nature of his hired hands and the slaves. A non-requested hot meal would tell him much about his choice of people.

With a light tap of the reins against Queenie's neck, she stepped forward. His thoughts were of the events of the day, which, all in all, had been re-assuring to him. Ahead, he heard the quiet camp noises. Steaming pots of food hung over a dying fire. A larger, communal fire burned near the wagons while men sat, leaning against wagon wheels, smoking and drinking coffee.

They're good people, Sam thought. I hope I can live up to their expectations. He would try, but knew the work ahead would weed out those that did not belong or the ones who just couldn't make it.

Uncle George, one of the recently acquired slaves, was the first to see his master ride into the camp. At the high end of middle age, George was fifty-five, maybe sixty. The slave was unsure of his age or where he'd been born. He knew he'd lived on five different plantations—Ledbetter's being the last and by far the worst. He was still in good health and carried himself with a quiet dignity Sam admired in a man who had never been offered any dignity because of the color of his skin.

George rose from the camp stool. Approaching his new master, he tugged at his worn shirt, carefully peeling it away from his back. His eyes squinted, and his face contorted with pain as he grabbed the reins of his master's horse.

Sam saw the pain the dark skinned man tried to conceal.

"Massa, I sho be glad dat yo is heah. We'uns was a gitt'n a mite worried. I be a fetch'n yo some vitals iff'n you is redi. Git'em while dey's still hot."

"What's wrong with your back? Here, turn around."

George did as he was told. Sam lifted the ragged homespun shirt, stained by leakage from untreated infections, and stared at an odd pattern of dark and ragged scars interlaced with festering welts cut deep into the slave's back. Ledbetter's cruelty spoke for itself. The evil of the man lay exposed in varying degrees of healing; some of it healed into long knotted ridges, others weeping clear fluids and the worst of the cuts, crusted with dried blood and yellow pus. George winced when Sam touched a recent slash with his finger.

"Ledbetter do that to you?"

"Yas suh," the slave replied, his voice a whisper. George did not look at his new master.

It seemed to Sam, George was ashamed of something he had no control over and by remaining quiet, the dark skinned man was apologizing for being born black.

"Matt," he called out. Matt stood and walked toward him. He had been hired as the overseer of the plantation which Sam hoped to develop.

Matt would now prove himself to his boss. What kind of man was he? There were only two types of overseers—the kind that hated slaves, but loved the power the position implied, or the kind who cared more for the slave than the power.

Sam watched Matt's face closely. He needed to see the reaction on the overseer's face when he lifted George's shirt. He needed to know the kind of man Matt was.

Shock registered on Matt's face. Sam was relieved by the reaction.

"Have you ever seen anything like this?" asked Sam, pointing at the handi-work of Harold S. Ledbetter.

"No Sir. Don't reckon I have. Something like that'd be hard to forget."

"None of that, ever," stated Sam, his eyes blazing with anger. "You ever see anybody do that to one of my people, you bring him to me. For every cut I see, I'll slice three exactly like them, into their own backs."

The veiled threat registered with the recently hired field boss.

"Get one of the women to see to this man's back. Now." Sam demanded. "Check those other three, too."

George had never been defended by anyone and he was embarrassed that he'd been the center of attention. Oddly, he felt befriended,—and by of all things, a white devil.

Henry approached Sam to inform him of all that had happened since they left Weldon. Henry was a large man, not well educated, yet he was conversant in a manner which belied his lack of education.

Sam was impressed by Henry's demeanor when he'd first met him. The man exuded a raw ambition. He was a family man, soft spoken, with a wife and two young boys. The boys were ten and eleven years old and they would someday be an asset to their father; thereby, the same for him, and in the not so far off future, judging from their size.

Henry's wife, Sara, a woman of considerable girth was, according to Henry, an excellent cook and her size proof enough for Sam. He allowed the large woman to appoint herself as the sole cook for the entire trip and found he had no desire or need to replace her.

Henry spoke casually about the evening's events. He and others had scouted the nearby area, asking questions of the countryside which lay ahead. Sam liked their initiative and their growing anticipation pleased him.

He thought it wise to lay over a few days to use a bit of precaution. There was no set deadline to prevent it. Perhaps a quick foray into his holdings would be wise. If anyone awaited them, wishing them harm, they could find other, safer roads for the remaining trip.

He told Henry to choose one of the slaves to help with the camping and the pack mules needed for the trip.

The group was restless, weary of the continuing march south. Henry's enthusiasm was contagious and it was vital he remain as enthused as before. Many within the group felt they could approach Henry easier than Sam. Sam knew this and it did not offend him.

During the afternoon's ride through Weldon, food purchases and other necessities had been loaded into yet another wagon which Sam had purchased, along with a team of mules. He suspected Weldon would be the last town of any size in which to obtain needed goods before they arrived at their destination.

Unsure of what lay ahead, it was a good location to rest. If additional supplies were needed, a trip could easily be made back into Weldon before they started the final portion of their ride.

He, Henry and one of the slaves would leave in the morning as soon as everybody knew what was expected of them during his absence.

"Uncle George," shouted Sam, "Come here." George promptly dropped the harness he had been repairing.

"Yas Suh, Massa Sam" he replied. Stepping over a wagon tongue, he headed toward his master.

George wore a cleaned shirt, now freshly stained from a recently applied poultice of turpentine, coal oil and onion. The slave's face showed less pain than it had before. Sam stepped away, up-wind of the pungent odor of the salve spread upon the man's back.

"You feel any better?" he asked George, lifting a corner of the stained shirt. He was genuinely concerned for the man he owned.

"Yas Suh, I does," he answered, still staring at the ground.

"Keep it clean and get that poultice changed every day. I told Matt to make sure that woman who put that poultice on you stays at it until you get better. It's working, but it's sure got a smell to it, don't it?"

"Yas suh, it do. Dat's why I be walkin' away frum it all de time," he grinned. "It be a bit rank, and it's a mite hard to outrun,"

"You'll be fit as a fiddle in a few days," Sam said. "Henry and I are going to ride ahead and inspect the new holdings. Henry wants Willie to go with us. You reckon that boy can handle the job? He can cook some, can't he?"

"Yas Suh. Dat Willie, he be a good boy, Suh. He knows a lotta' stuff. But sum'times he be's ack'n lac he ain't got nary a thought one in his head so he doan gots to do no work."

Sam laughed at George's observation.

Willie looked about twenty years old. He was a strapping young man, but Sam was unaware Willie saw things through the eyes of a twelve year old.

"George, you help with the other Negroes. Keep them in line and tell 'em to keep this camp clean. And the livestock; make sure they take care of them. Now George, I've been watching you closely and I think you are a good man. I'll be counting on you to help me out here. Get everybody up and gathered around for breakfast at six in the morning."

The new Master presented a puzzle to George. How come he keers how I be a feel'n? he wondered. He be a white man and I be black as a chunk a coal. How come he doan' know dat? He doan be nuff'n a'tall like all dem udder white peebles.

But he liked the kind man. He turned away, hiding his wide toothy grin, hoping his new massa would not think he'd become up-pity from the praise he had given him.

Sam awakened earlier than usual. He'd slept little, anxious to see his land. Henry had stoked the cook fire, and started a large pot of coffee atop the grill. Soon, Sara and Henry joined Sam and Matt for their first morning coffee.

George watched Willie, making sure he loaded the gear prop-erly. No white man had ever told him he was a good man, and George was zealously trying to prove to his new master he was worthy of the praise and trust which had been afforded him.

While the group gathered, Sam did a tally of the people ven-turing into the unknown with him.

In addition to Henry and Sara and their two boys, another fam-ily who had joined him was the Privets, consisting of Joseph, his wife Delma, a mountain of a woman and a young daughter, Annabel. Beau was the older of their two sons and the other boy was called Blue for some unexplained reason. The boys were heavily freckled and each had vibrant red hair, turning orange.

Hired for his extensive knowledge of growing tobacco, Privet would be a great asset. The man was impressed with North Carolina and when he'd been hired he'd told Sam, "That's the best land in all of America for growing tobacco. People all over the country want that Carolina grow'd tobacco."

Matthew Davis had been a plantation overseer for the previous decade. He was no longer a married man—he'd lost his wife three years previously and decided there was no way he would ever find a woman who could replace her. He readily admitted he'd found a bot-tle instead and courted it, plus many more for a while; but after he'd ran out of grief for his lost wife, he'd run out of thirst for liquor. His children were grown and scattered, leaving him no hindrance to ac-cepting the job if such were offered. Sam liked the man and offered it to him.

A blacksmith, reportedly the best in Petersburg was hired next. Robert L. Dayton was fifty years old and also unencumbered by family. Most considered the man an artist with iron. Sam was delighted when the blacksmith accepted his generous offer. Blacksmiths were held in high esteem for their mechanical abilities, as well. And Sam considered the employment of Mr. Dayton essential for his success. A blacksmith and a mechanic. A pretty good deal, he thought, two for one.

James Motley, a seasoned lumberman was hired soon after. Much as with Henry, Sam sensed an air of driven ambition about the man. He'd been told timber was a huge part of the holdings he had acquired. Since there was a growing demand for saw-milled lumber, equaling or exceeding the demand for tobacco, cotton and corn, all over the eastern coast, Sam intended to be a major supplier of building materials, also.

Four young men were hired to perform all the heavy jobs requiring strong backs. Brothers Zachary and Walter, were the younger of the four, and both still at the awkward age when they were no longer boys, but not yet men.

Twin brothers, Harry and Doyle Bailey, were hired for their strong bodies, as well. The two were only a couple of years older than Zack and Walter, but they had passed fully into manhood and Sam sensed the two brothers were desirous of learning a trade.

He watched as the group assembled before him. He sensed all of the people with him were like children, counting on him for everything. Hardly a one of them had ever been twenty miles from their birthplace, including himself, except for the toy-train ride to Baltimore. They had no idea of what to expect; what lay around the next corner or the next bend, and that, they had in common with Sam. They were his responsibility and he knew it.

He thought it ironic only a few weeks before, his life had been all about himself and now in front of him stood men, their wives and children, dependant on him for everything. He dreaded telling them he wanted them to stay in the camp a while longer. Sam longed for new ways to ease their burdens and worries, but he had offered all the moral support and encouragement within him. He would not lie to them, nor would he add to their fears by laying his worries and doubts out for them, as well. All he could do now was encourage them to stay the course.

As they gathered before him, the light from the fire cast a pale orange tint upon their faces. On many, he saw concern. He said, "You all know by now, I'm going ahead with Henry and Willie. There have been no threats or discourtesies extended to any of us. I think we have been well treated by people who do not even know us. So don't start looking for trouble behind every tree or rock. My concern is, I know little about the routes we have to take, or were told to take. That's my fault, not yours. But bear in mind, we did have good, accurate reports of all the roads between Petersburg and Weldon. Well, that section over the swamp was kind of a mess, but we got through it alright, didn't we?" he smiled, recalling the tortuous road. "But they sure as hell ought to blow it up now that we're done with it."

The group laughed, nodding their agreement. Their memories of the tortuous road were still fresh.

"My knowledge of the area west and south of us is limited. Like most of you, this is as far south as I've ever been. So we are going to ride ahead and look things over ourselves. Henry and Matt said some of you are concerned about the lack of welcome from folks who came through earlier. I'm sure no ill was intended by any of those people. To me, it seems they're only curious about us. The folks I met in town were all pleasant. Remember, we are the strangers here. Besides, you could use a few days rest. Once we determine a safe passage for the wagons and livestock, we'll be back. So quit with the worrying."

To further assuage their concerns, he added, "Not only will we know the best roads to use, but we'll probably need to go back into town for things we don't even know we need yet. Maybe get some sweets for the young ones. Matt, you'll be in charge of everything while we are out exploring.

"All you folks pitch in and help out. No one is to leave this camp. Having said you should not worry, being smart and cautious is another thing. You have all the provisions you need. Do not leave the camp and do not invite a soul into this camp."

His face grew stern. "Harry, you and Doyle are to switch off with Walter and Zack keeping an eye open at night. Take this key. The chest under my seat has five guns in it. I'm not going to go into what I expect of you if you need those guns—you'll know. Enough said about that. If you are more than ten feet from that chest, you lock it.

"We hope to be back in three days, quicker if we can," he said, ending the longest conversation he had ever had with them as a group.

With the morning light, he mounted Queenie. The mare snorted and pawed at the ground, and seemed anxious to get under way. Swinging his leg over the saddle, the wind lifted the corner of his jacket, revealing a Colt dragoon revolver of considerable size tucked into his waist band. Looped onto the pommel, a big bore rifle hung, tied into place with a leather strap.

Henry fell in behind his boss. He too, was well equipped with a similar-sized rifle and a fourteen inch knife stuck in his belt. He refused the offer of a similar Colt, explaining if he had to use two hands to shoot something so large, it might as well be his rifle.

And lastly, the slave boy, Willie. Slaves carried no weapons— an unspoken law of the land. Instead he held on to the reins of the two mules loaded with the camp gear and provisions the three needed for their trip.

Without further instructions, Sam tugged at the reins and guided Queenie onto the road.

***

Sam hoped there would be a public house at the nearby West-land Crossroads; an inn, or maybe a tavern. He was unsure of the directions given to him regarding the route he should take. He thought when a man giving directions is scratching his head in a manner which left you doubtful of his own knowledge of the area, maybe it behooves you to seek clearer directions from someone who lives closer to the area into which you're heading.

In the distance, a small building sat back off the road, deep in a grove of old oaks. Might be anything from a house to a tavern, maybe even an empty shack, Sam thought. He was pleased to find it was a tavern and that it had customers at such an early hour.

He dismounted and threw the reins over the hitching-rail and motioned for Henry and Willie to lead his horse and their mounts over to the side of the tavern and wait for him in the shade.

"I'll go find out how to get wherever it is we're going. I won't be long."

He entered the tavern, moving slowly, his eyes adjusting to the dimly lit room.

"Hello, and welcome stranger," boomed the voice of a tall and very overweight man standing behind a counter lined with jugs and cups, an indication while it was an eating establishment now, later it could be easily converted into a tavern. "Can I git y'all sumpt'n teet?"

Sam puzzled over the strange phrase, but after breaking it down, he understood . . . something to eat.

The man held a spatula in one hand and a pot of steaming coffee in the other. "We got sausage and fresh eggs and the best buttermilk biscuits this side of Raleigh. Might be the best in the world, but I ain't never been no further than Raleigh." His laughter boomed and his stomach bounced. "And, the Missus here, she might just be the best cook in all of North Carolina. Don't you reckon I'd know?" he added, rubbing his protruding belly, and again, broke into renewed laughter. "Y'all want some coffee? The Missus just made some fresh."

"No, but thank you for your kind offer. I'm about coffee'd out, but I would appreciate some directions, if you don't mind. Sam Biggs' the name. I'm new to this area."

The man stepped around the counter, wiping his hands upon a lightly soiled apron, and extended it to Sam.

"I'll be glad to hep' if I can, Mister Biggs. Name's Webb Denton and that's my Missus, Elvira. Me and the Missus been 'round these here parts fifteen years, going on damn near twenty, or sumpt'n like that. I reckon we'd know this area as good as any of the folks here 'bout. That y'all's camp back yonder? So where y'all off to, Mister Biggs?"

"I'm on my way to a place called Brinkleyville. We'll be going past as far as Ringwood."

"Well," said the big man, "that's the Brinkleyville road out yonder. Y'all just go on down it 'bout three, four miles. Ain't much left of Brinkleyville, though. Three, four buildings 'bout all, if they ain't fell down yet."

Webb continued, "Three miles or so past Brinkleyville go right on the Ringwood road and head west for 'nigh on a mile. Maybe some less, not much though. Then there'll be a 'nuther road what leads off to the south again. Don't go down that'un unless y'all wants to end up in Fort Harwood. That road goes through part of old man Detwyler's plantation. That old coot put up a toll road some years back. Ain't there now, though. Done turned back to field by the plow. Go on past his place and you'll see Ringwood."

Webb started laughing again as if thinking of a new story. "Old Detwyler tole everybody that road was his'n and he'd do whatever the hell he wanted to do wid it." He was still laughing as he drank coffee from his cup, dribbling it onto his large belly.

"Folks 'round 'bout these parts, them what remember the old days, say it was just a big joke for him. Probably was—he sure as hell didn't need no more money. Him and that Griffen fellow, that's the man what owns that land just over yonder across the road; them two's 'bout the richest landowners 'round these here parts. Seem's like there's bad blood 'tween 'em. Goes back a long time, too. Don't know what it's all 'bout. Don't much give a shit, neither. Live and let live, I always say. They stay clear of one another like the other'ns got the scabies, and I stay clear of both of them."

Sam was eager for the directions, eager to get under way, but he found the man personable and entertaining.

"Detwyler ran so many people off that road wid him a charg'n that toll of his'n, the county people had to git after him. What wid Fort Harwood not gitt'n their fair share of farm stuff to sell, seemed like there was gonna' be some killings up this way and most likely it was gonna' be old Detwyler gitt'n the killing part done to him. And all over a damn joke.

"Well anyways, just look west and y'all see the roofs of three buildings up ahead. But like I said, they mighta' fell down already. Ain't much of nothing else there, neither."

He shouted back into the kitchen, "Hey Vi, ain't that where Elmer and Dorrie live at?" If his wife answered, it was drowned out by the clanging and rattling of pots and pans in the kitchen.

"Well, them's the O'Reillys. They some nice old folks. That boy of theirs' works for that Detwyler fellow. Believe his name's Isaac."

Sam thanked him and told him he was much obliged and headed for the door.

"Oh Sir, don't mean to bother y'all or noth'n, but y'all need to be kinda' careful from here on down to that there Brinkleyville cross-road. What wid that darky boy y'alls got wid you, it'd be best y'all keep your eyes open. On the right side of that road is the Griffen place. Y'all be riding past his land clear down to Brinkleyville.

"Sum'a his darkies done run off on him, and he's got a heap of slavers out looking for 'em. Could be some trouble . . . most likely not. Griffen's 'bout as mean as a water moccasin trying to get out of a fight wid a cotton hoe. Don't reckon he'll start nothing, but I sure wouldn't want to be one of them runnin' darkies when them slavers catch up wid 'em, though. Griffen's 'bout as crazy and mixed up," tapping his temple with his finger, "as a bag full of busted up walnuts. Know what I mean?"

Webb's information had given Sam more to think about than directions. Looks like my land is directly between two old rascals. They sound like they musta been some disagreeable sons of bitches back in the days. Well, it's none of my affair, Sam reminded himself.

"Henry, that man in there told me we need to keep our eyes open—something about the fellow who lives down there being crazy," he said, pointing towards the west.

He relayed Denton's directions to Henry, more conversation than necessity. Choosing his words carefully, he told Henry about the runaway slaves and reminded him to stay alert.

Willie became visibly shaken by what he'd overheard.

"Massa Biggs, I sho' would lac to goan back to de camp wid dem udder niggers and Uncle George."

"Stop that fool talk. You are not going back anywhere. Henry, I want you and Willie to stay close up to me. There's not much of a chance we'll even see anybody. Regardless, stay close up on me."

Sam had never owned a slave until he'd won these four. But a man couldn't live in Virginia almost forty years without knowing the rules for whites and the rules for slaves were at odds with one another.

If, in fact, there were runaway slaves about, Griffen would have already put notices in the Weldon paper and the Fort Harwood paper, too. Announcements would be posted near and far—nailed to posts, nailed to trees—to attract men who hunted down runaway slaves for a living and returned them to their advertised owners. Upon delivery, the owner would pay the slaver a handsome bounty for each slave caught.

Slave catchers wore the lowest of the lowlifes who earned their living doing jobs no one of decent morals would do. Calling them white-trash was being excessively complimentary. They were nasty to look at and nasty to the nose. They were offensive in conversation and drunk when not sleeping. They would beat the hell out of any white man who got in their way and would kill a Negro, if he did not call them Sir. They viewed Negroes as hardly more than mules, creatures without souls. A runaway—was nothing more than a paycheck.

Slave hunters seldom knew the owner who had advertised for their service. It didn't matter to them who the runaways belonged to. What did matter was the man doing the asking better have the money when the slaves were returned to them.

Sam saw Henry was as aware of the slave hunter's bad nature as he was. He reasoned Willie had heard horror stories about how runaway slaves were treated by such men. Wisely, he felt further discussions within earshot of the frightened slave would cause him to faint dead away and fall off his mule.

"Henry, I want you to fall back to the rear. Anybody who sees Willie with us might get to thinking that boy is a runaway, but if they see him between us, they'll ride on by. Now let's get going. It should take an hour or so to get to our property. Keep your eyes open."

The road was not only well used, but well maintained. The ditches on each side of the wide lane were dug deep and drained well. There was no standing water to stagnate and start stinking or to serve as breeding ponds for mosquitoes.

All the available field space was being used to its fullest. The cornfields ran from east to west, the rows arrow-straight. They were planted so far into the distance, none of the men could tell where the cornfields ended or the sky began.

The tobacco fields were as large as the cornfields. The harvesting finished, the stalks now stripped of leaves, awaited the plow to turn them under.

Cotton neared full bloom. It would be another five to six weeks before it was ready to be picked, usually after the first hard frost. When the bolls burst open, the fields would appear to be covered by a hard winter snow.

A mile distant, a clearing by the roadway indicated an intersection. Arriving at the barren spot, Sam found what he expected; the grand entrance to the plantation home of Hesper Griffen. Both sides of the roadway leading off of the county road and back to a very large mansion, were shaded by the low hanging branches of very big and very old oaks.

"Impressive as hell, ain't it?" he asked Henry.

Chapter Five

The men showed only a passing interest riding past the entry to Hesper Griffen's magnificent mansion. Sam had been the guest at dozens of such places; the impressive dwelling was nothing new to him. Henry, earlier in life, figured nothing as grand as this was likely to come his way, but maybe some day, now that he'd been hired as Sam's General Manager, he and his family might end up living on such a place.

Knowing the possibility of danger existed, Sam kept an eye on Willie. He'd begun to think the slave childlike—more child than man—and the innocence of the slave drew him to the Negro.

Groups of slaves worked the fields near the road under the watchful eyes of Hesper Griffen's overseer. Willie watched them toil. He was as curious of them as they were of the three men riding past. He waved—a childish effort to be friendly. Of the field slaves who did make eye contact with the riders, none would hold it long, and none returned his friendly wave, but all were quick to avert their attention from the travelers back to the man towering above them on horseback. The overseer shouted orders, followed by warnings, and they quickly returned to their tasks. He braced a long rifle on his hip. In his other hand he held tight to the horse's reins and a long braided leather whip, and purposefully ignored the men as they rode past.

"Massa, dat man on dat horse skeers me. He sho do looks lac a bad man, doan he?" Willie asked.

"Don't bother those field hands. It's none of your affair," said Sam. "You and Henry close up a bit. Let's get on our way."

Fifteen minutes later, Henry broke rank and joined his boss at the front.

"Sam, you see those men back there at the edge of the woods?"

"Yes. I don't know who they are but I suspect they're watching us. Reckon they're interested in Willie. With all the runaways down this way, those sonsabitches are liable to make a move on us. Keep your eyes open."

Sam felt for the big Colt. Assured it was there, he said, "Listen to me carefully. See that rise in the road up there, and that overhanging rock at the top of the hill on the right hand side? Looks like the road's going to make a curve to the right. Here's what I want you and Willie to do.

"When we get to the top of that hill, as soon as I can jump off, grab my reins and you two ride on another hundred feet or so. Watch me . . . I'll tell you when to stop. Get the animals off to the left side of the road. If there's a clearing big enough, get 'em in it. Don't try to hide 'em. I want those fellows to see you and the animals. Hand all the reins to Willie. Grab that big bore of yours and get on the far side of the horses.

"Make it look like you're checking its shoe or something; minding your own business. Hide that gun close so you can get it the second they look back at me—and they are going to look back at me—you'll know when to grab it. Here, take these reins and get on down there."

Using the overhanging rock, Sam concealed himself. When the two reached the clearing, he motioned for Henry to stop. Henry did as he was told and slid off of his horse. Even Sam could not see the long rifle Henry had drug off and hidden away.

Watching for the riders coming from behind, he pulled the big revolver from inside his coat, cocking it as he did. He fingered at the firing caps, making sure they were still in place. He laid the gun across his arm as the two riders rode into view. The two intently watched Henry and Willie below them. Sam saw their tension mounting. He knew they were thinking, Where's that other fellow, the big one?

Before they could spin around and look for him, he stepped onto the road behind them.

He shouted, both to scare them, to gain the upper hand, and to make sure Henry pulled his rifle to his shoulder. "Hey. Assholes. Now, real slow-like, look at me. You two have just made some big mistakes. Your first was slipping up on a man minding his own business. The second was you two shit-birds turning to see who's yelling at you. Now, real careful like, look back down that road. My man down there's real good with that gun and I'm so close, I don't have to be any good. But you make one wrong move I'm going to put a hole through your head so goddamn big a turkey buzzard can fly through it.

"Henry, get up here, quick. Don't take your gun off that fellow on the far side. I got this one covered."

Knowing the two were in no hurry to get themselves killed, he added. "Take your gun and stick it in the seat of that man's britches. If he makes one goddamn sound—if his horse even farts, give him a second asshole, you hear me?"

The intensity of his boss' orders frightened Henry.

"Yes sir, boss," he answered.

Willie made himself scarce, sliding down behind the horses and mules and like a squirrel, he darted behind the largest tree he could find.

"Why are you two following us?" Sam asked. "You," he said to the taller of the two men, "What's your name?"

"Name of Buck Ellis, Sir," the tall lanky man answered.

Sam looked at the man on the far side of Buck.

"Yours?"

"LeRoy, LeRoy Jones."

The hammer on the Colt clicked loud and hard as Sam thumbed it to full cock.

"Well, Buck, LeRoy, the two of you look like you got caught with your britches down. Both of you look hard at the end of this barrel. Big bore, ain't it? Now look back up at my eyes. I look a little nervous, don't I? I'm going to ask you some questions and you need to tell me the truth. You don't answer me quick, I'm going to figure you're thinking up lies. And if I think you're lying, I'm sure as hell going to kill you. I'd rather be scared and alive than dead and you hauling ass out of here."

Buck was the first to do as he was told.

"Suh, can y'all aim that cannon a little over that way, sum? We works for Mister Griffen. We keeps an eye on folks 'round these here parts. There's been a heap of trouble out this way what with all them darkies what's been running off like they is. Not only from Mister Griffen's place, but from a bunch of them other big places 'round 'bout here, too."

"Go on," said Sam, impatiently.

"We was told by the boss man to watch out for any darkies what comes through here, no matter who they's with. Your darky looks kinda' like one of them offa' his place. You know how all them darkies looks alike, don't you? But he ain't one of Mister Griffen's slaves. No Suh. I can see that, now."

The men had begun to sweat. "What with three of his darkies running off, we was jus' doing our job when y'all come along with that boy y'all got with you. All we was trying to do, was ketch up with you and see if that boy's your'n, or not.

"An' Suh, that Mister Griffen we works for is a bit tetched in the head, if you knows what I mean. He doan put up with nobody not doing what he tells 'em to do. He tell us to be a lookin' out for them darkies, that's 'zactly what we's gotta do. We looks at 'em all. We don't mean no offense to you. We jus' doing our job, see? 'Fore we could ask you anything, you done throw'd down on us. That's the truth, I swear to you, ain't it, LeRoy?"

Leroy failed to answer.

"Where are those other two fellows we saw with you, the two with the dogs?" asked Sam.

Sensing the last question was directed at him, Leroy answered, "We don't hold no truck with no trash-ass people like them. They's scum of the earf', they is. If they'd come up on you, them ole boys woulda' tried to sic their dogs on you. They were on Mister Griffen's land and he don't like that nary one bit. Every time one or two of them darkies gits to running, that trash starts a show'n up an git's to sniffin' out the bounty money and they don't keer how much or how they gits it, neither. We tole 'em to git on down the road—that we's in charge of all the slave ketch'n on this here place. So they took off wid them dogs of theirs." Leroy shifted nervously and stared at Buck, hoping he would help with the conversation.

"Suh, ever single word we done tole y'all is true and we's sorry if we made y'all mad. We don't mean no harm. We was jus' gonna' ask to see that nigger's papers."

"You fucking idiots came within a whisper of getting your asses shot clean off your bony little legs," said Sam.

The color returned to the men's pale faces.

"You need to find a new kind of work. You're not too good at what you're doing. That boy does belong to me. I don't know who this Griffen fellow is, and what's more, I don't give a damn."

Lifting the barrel of the big gun, he pointed it squarely at LeRoy. "You tell him how happy you are you don't have two ass-holes. Make sure you tell him I'm coming back through here on this very road and that I'll shoot him dead before I show him any papers on that Negro of mine. If he's the law around these parts, he'd better have papers of his own to show me, or else he can kiss my ass. Fuck it. Tell him anything you want to. Get outta' here."

But quickly, the inevitable warning, "If I do find you two anywhere close to me in the future, I'm going to think you might be wanting to hurt me and my friends here, so listen up real good. I like them a whole lot more than I like you and I'll kill you deader than a rotting dog. Got that?"

Buck and LeRoy spurred their horses and galloped away.

***

"Sam," said Henry, his eyes as large as saucers, "I ain't never seen nothing like that. Would you have really kilt them fellows?"

Sam looked at Henry and answered, "You don't know, do you?"

"No, Sir, I don't."

"They don't either and that's what's important.

"Willie, get on out from behind that tree. Let's get on our way."

***

The three continued south; no one talking. Conversation's what we need, thought Sam.

"Let's ride a bit longer, at least get away from here. I think we can get to our land around two this afternoon. We'll stop there and grab a bite to eat. Henry, you think you can shoot us a rabbit, maybe a squirrel?" Henry nodded and checked the road behind them.

"Don't worry about those two back there. They're more afraid of us than they are of that Griffen fellow. They'll want no part of us," said Sam.

"Hell, Henry," he chuckled. "Sometimes, I even scare me. I was hoping we'd find our neighbors a bit more friendly, though. We'll see how it goes. It's not likely everybody around here is like those two."

Henry remained quiet. He was not in the mood for small talk, casual or otherwise. So Sam tried to occupy his mind with the business at hand. There was a lot the three of them had to see, but soon the sameness of the timber-filled woods, the barren fields, the dirt road and the heat of the day caused him to think of the strange events that led him here.

***

It had been a long night, actually two nights and one day, perhaps the longest game he'd ever played at one sitting in the Club.

Desperately tired, Sam stooped, and collected the money on the table. He watched Harold Ledbetter push his way to the chair just vacated.

"Hold up. Not so fast," the elderly man snarled. He threw a fistful of money on the table. "I'm next."

Sam responded, "Sir. It's late and I'm tired." Hoping to not offend anyone, he said, "Perhaps another night."

The man exploded into a fit of anger. "Mister Biggs or whoever the hell you are, do not condescend to me. I bought into this game and I've been waiting all night. You'll play me and the only way our game will end is when either you or I have lost our guaranty. I've deposited a small fortune into my account. How about you?" he asked sarcastically. "Can you cover my bets?" Impatient, he asked, "Are you ready to play cards or not?"

Taken aback by Ledbetter's rage, his self-praising, superior attitude, and his attempt to belittle him, Sam held his temper.

"Sir, if you think I was being rude or condescending, you are badly mistaken, and you will hardly receive an apology from me. I do not know how much you put in your guaranty. However, I'll not flip another card until you and I both know if my deposit is, as you say, large enough. I don't give a damn who you are or how loud you shout, I am stopping the game long enough so you can see that I do, in fact, have your bets covered."

"Then play cards, goddamn it," shouted Ledbetter, his face red, his anger building. He slammed a fist onto the table.

Sam stared at the man and smiled. That infuriated the drunken man.

"You asked me a question and you're going to get your goddamn answer," said Sam.

Beckoning the night's manager, he said, "Mister Reardon, not knowing the size of my worthy opponent's guaranty, I am obliged to ask, am I able to cover old Harold's," he chuckled, thumbing back toward the obnoxious man, "deposit?"

Mr. Reardon grinned and answered, "Mister Biggs, Sir, enjoy your game."

Sam pushed aside the shot of bourbon he referred to as his show liquor, a shot that he had been nursing for over an hour, and requested coffee and lots of it. Black.

Ledbetter, made no attempt to hide his disdain of Sam, or any of the Club members, for that matter.

"Ante up," he snarled.

Sam placed the deck of cards upon the table and stared at the man across from him. Purposefully continuing to irritate the old man he said, "Harold, your bets are covered—and like he said," pointing at Mr. Reardon, "mine, too. So you want to play cards, do you? What about no limits? Alright with you? Not scared are you? Put whatever you want on the table, I'll match it. I want all your money. I want every goddamn thing you own and I will take it all away from you." Then he sneered at his opponent, an exaggerated sneer, knowing it would push the drunken fool deeper into his mounting rage.

He knew an angry man could not think clearly and the contempt on Sam's face forced the old man to throw onto the green-felt table top the largest ante ever at the Club. He went deep for one final twist of his sharp as a knife tongue and chuckled loud enough for the old man to hear. The laugh, full of sarcasm and derision, mimicked Ledbetter's laugh—and it rattled the gray haired man.

The game continued with the higher stakes for the first few hours and slowly began to rise. The man reacted to Sam's defiance of him as he expected he would.

Harold S. Ledbetter's actions proved he thought everybody present was beneath him, and Sam would use this to help the intoxicated man self-destruct. Angry and distracted, the old man was not playing as skillfully as prior to his outburst. Sam had waited for him to reach the level of sloppy drunkenness in which Ledbetter was positive he could do no wrong; totally unaware of how careless his playing had become. He misread his cards and bet huge amounts of money. He had become so drunk he was losing count of his losses while gleefully praising himself each time Sam knowingly folded a winning hand.

"What's the matter, boy? Can't handle it?" He smirked.

"Luck's turned—you're cleaning me out," said Sam, baiting him.

The simplicity of the comments and the exaggerated look of worry on Sam's face fooled none of the bystanders, each enjoying the show immensely.

Sloppy became sloppier. Ledbetter was slowly falling apart. "Harold, old fellow, you wanted this game. You've got it. You're mine," Sam muttered under his breath.

The game ended just as Sam Biggs knew it would. He had
beaten the man—slaughtered him—bled him like a hog. Ledbetter's
nonchalance at losing such a fortune surprised Sam. On the table lay
at least two hundred thousand dollars and a title for land in North
Carolina.

Ledbetter arose from his chair, tipped his hat to Sam and
slurred, "You have been a worthy opponent Sir, and I may have un-
derestimated your skill with the cards. Nevertheless, you are now in
possession of a goodly amount of my money and a large piece of my
land. Will you arrange another game in the near future?" and before
Sam could answer Harold rose to leave, and as he did, added, "I bid
you good night, Sir."

Sam stood, stretched, and muffled a yawn. He was glad the
night was done. He looked at Harold S. Ledbetter.

"I will not lie to you and tell you I've enjoyed your company,
for I have not," said Sam. "I find you an unpleasant and boorish fool.
I am not going to tell you I would like to play cards with you again,
either, for I do not, and I will not.   And you didn't underestimate me,
you overestimated yourself.

"I can count the money in front of me. I know closely how
much is there. What I don't know is the size and worth of that Carolina plantation you've bragged about so much—and now lost to me. I
must insist you remain until I can have your claims verified.

"Mister Reardon. You know the guaranty rules, do you not?
May I ask if Mister Ledbetter's losses are covered in full by his deposit? And if so, are they ready for my inspection?"

"Yes Sir. Mister Ledbetter has covered his losses and all of
his guaranty is ready to be presented to you." Sam nodded his head,
and the treasurer brought him the paper work for his review.

"You, Mister Ledbetter, are required by the same house rules
to stay here upon my request, until I am satisfied with your full pay-
ment. Now, sit down and shut up."

The old man did sit as he was told, but much to Sam's chagrin,
he promptly fell asleep.

***

Henry's mind was in turmoil. He had seen a new side of his
boss; an impressive, but scary side. There were a lot of things he
wanted to ask, but for now he thought it best to think things through

for himself. He would talk to his boss when the man was calmer.

He began to review the past events. That man's as scary a fellow as any I've ever come across, but me and the missus done throw'd our lot in with him. I believe he mighta' kilt both of them fellows if me and Willie hadn't been there with him, but she ain't never gonna' hear about what happened back there. If he ever scares her as much as he did me, we're gonna' be on that pike to Petersburg quicker'n a rabbit out-running a dog. Well, at least he seems to have calmed down a bit. I sure, by God, hope so.

Willie had not uttered a word to Henry, Sam or the mules. His fright was like that of a child reprimanded by a stern father. Occasionally, Sam and Henry would hear low mumbling from him.

The man-child had seen bad things people could do to each other; violent, cruel things, especially between white men and darkies. After the first runaway slave beating he'd seen his former master administer, Willie was the last slave on earth who would ever run off.

"I ain't nebber gonna' run off, ebben if de Good Lawd tells me to. Nah suh, not ebben if he gots sum chain cutters in he's han's. Lawd A'Mitey, I sho be a hopin' dat man's no ways nere as mean as he ack's likes he be." He prayed aloud, not aware or concerned if others heard him.

Adding to his discomfort, the two men with the slaver dogs were constantly on his mind. Any rustle in the woods scared him so badly he would stiffen with fear. "Iffen dem slaber dog mens cum up on us, I sho be hopin' dat Massa Biggs gits he'self 'tween me and dem dare dogs." Lifting his eyes toward the Heavens, he continued his prayer, "an Lawd, if Massa Biggs gots to kills dem two mens, Suh, please tell him to shoot dem debil dogs fo he sen's dem mens to you fo dere judg'n day, Amen."

***

Sam studied the crude and fading surveyor's maps as he rode along. He guessed they were nearing the Brinkleyville Crossroads. He had no idea of what to expect but recalled the tavern keeper had mentioned a store with an old building next to it on the right. Across the road, another building stood awaiting its certain death. A similar ramshackle building nearing collapse, stood on the southeast corner. None of the buildings had been occupied for a very long time.

"Henry, I don't reckon that man back at the tavern gets down this way too much."

"No Sir. Don't look like it."

Sam, pointing southwest, toward the far corner of the intersection, added, "As far as you two can see, all the land over there across the road is our land, and somewhere out there," he said, sweeping his arm across the expanse, "we'll build our new homes. Now, let's see if we can find us a creek to camp by."

Chapter Six

Following a wagon path worn through his property, Sam found a clearing near the edge of the creek where he had expected it. The ground was clear of most of the undergrowth and the little remaining was quickly removed. The surrounding oaks, thick with leaves mottled with color, would provide shade for the remainder of the afternoon. He longed for a bath in the clean, clear water. The site was edged with a stand of luxuriant green plants flourishing along the creek.

"Let's set up our camp here," said Sam.

"If I see a rabbit or a squirrel, do you still want it for dinner?" Henry asked his boss. "What about a deer? If I see a small one, you want it instead?"

Lost in thought, Sam didn't answer, but laughed when he heard Willie mumble, "I sho wont's yo to shoots it."

Sam nodded his approval. "Either one'll be fine."

To Willie, he said, "Go and get those mules quiet. Fill their nose-bags with corn. If Henry does see a deer, it'll be half way to Weldon before he pulls that mile long gun of his out.

"You both know what you got to do. Henry, go get us dinner. Willie, get a fire going and start making coffee. Get the beans soaking, too. If Henry doesn't shoot anything we've still got enough salt-pork for tonight and tomorrow. We"ll need to turn-in early. I want to be off and at 'em at first light. Willie, you take the early watch; Henry, you get the midnight watch. Wake me up at three."

He stood and looked back in the direction from which they had come. "There's right at five thousand acres we have to get the lay of. You two know about as much as I do about this place and that ain't much. Some of it's going to be farming land; about half from what I was told, and the other half, timber. We got two, maybe three days rations. I want to see most of our land even if it's only from a distance and that'll take some riding. What we see is sure as hell gonna' tell us what we're about to get ourselves into, won't it?" he paused, considering the most important thing of all, water.

"I'd like to find a good place to start building on. But a good supply of water's the key. Something more than that creek. As slow as it's flowing,' he said pointing at the creek, "I believe it'd get stagnant too easily. So give me your ideas," he said to Henry.

"Willie, that goes for you, too. And don't worry, boy, I ain't going to eat you."

For the first time, Willie looked at his master differently. With his fear diminishing, a grin appeared on his dark face.

***

Sam rode back to the Brinkleyville crossroads to search for the iron rod indicated on the surveyor's map. He thought the likelihood of finding such a small object remote, at best. Rusted and long gone, the logical assumption.

He scaled the map to find the center of the intersection. Stepping over the ditch, he saw a cracked and splintered signpost lying in the ditch. He stood the post up, careful not to complete the near collapse of the loose planks, and fit the post into the jagged portion jutting above ground level. The whitewashed, arrow-shaped planks with fading names of nearby towns, were barely readable. The shaky arrows pointed off into various directions, and afforded him a better sense of the lay of the land.

The town of Battleborough lay southeast; Arcola to the west, Westland Crossroads to the north. After visually determining the center of the crossroads and considering roads could be altered by nature and man's traffic, he reopened the map and scaled the distance again. Sam knew he was at the northeast corner of his holdings.

If I walk southwest, straight as an arrow thirty feet or so, I might step on that spike, he thought. Careful of rocks, debris, briars and snakes, he stepped across the shallow ditch. At thirty feet, he stooped to the ground and studied it for hidden secrets. He kicked at the brown grass and loose leaves, exposing the fertile soil beneath.

"What do you think?" he asked Queenie. Long ago he had playfully assigned human qualities to his beloved horse and the mare nodded its head vigorously while Sam laughed at her showy display of enthusiasm.

"Okay." He pointed to the ground, and playfully asked, "Here?"

The sun did it's best to assure the balance of the day remained hot. Sam kicked, pushed, pulled and cursed at the overgrown and slowly expanding area at his feet. Soon, he removed his riding jacket, and lay it aside. Shortly, his vest followed. Folding it, he placed it on top of the jacket, making sure the pearl handle of his pocket revolver was within easy reach.

After ten minutes of clearing the heavy growth of weeds and briars, he grabbed a brown, rust encrusted object which seemed as determined to stay put in the ground as he was to pull it out. He'd found the boundary spike and with the heel of his boot, he kicked it back into the ground the half inch it had lost to his efforts.

A rush of confirmation swept over him. With Westland Crossroads due north and the boundary spike where he thought it would be, and adding in the ill-repaired sign post, he knew he faced his property. No longer was it an abstract thing, but something real, something solid. He spoke aloud, "There it is, Queenie. This is where it all starts, girl."

He stood, one foot in his past, one in his future. He knew his life was changed forever.

He rubbed his hands with dried blades of grass and leaves, managing to only partially clean them. The sharp, serrated edges of the dry saw-grass cut into the meaty side of his palm. A trickle of blood fell to the ground—his ground. He looked down at the dark spots at his feet as the blood soaked into the loose soil. He gazed south and westward, and overwhelmed by the beauty before him, he gave no thought to the blood at his feet.

He picked up his vest and jacket and put them on. The day was still too warm for them, but his concern was more for the location of the revolver than the heat.

Hearing the slow, steady tromp, tromp, tromp of a horse approaching, he looked north toward Westland Crossroads. His hand wrapped around the grip of the revolver. From the dark, thick woods emerged a large and muscled stallion, white as a cloud, and ridden by an elderly man. Queenie, upon seeing the big stallion, pawed at the dirt, snorted and threw her head wildly from side to side.

The stallion pawed at the road and fought against tightly held reins. The white haired man sat high and arrow-straight, fighting to hold his mount at bay, and strained to get a better view of the stranger—the man kicking and digging at the edge of a ditch. When he saw Sam looking at him, he jerked hard, warning his horse to remain still, and continued to stare.

Sam felt something sinister, something menacing about the man—nothing a person could see or touch, but more a feeling of malevolence. He watched the man and waved a greeting to the stranger. He guessed the man's age at early to mid fifties.

The man's eyes never flickered and continued to hold their hard threatening stare. He cupped his hands around the pommel, refusing to acknowledge the friendly wave. With the slightest of movements, he reined the horse around and rode back into the tree-darkened, black throat of the road, and away from Sam.

"Well now, that was different, wasn't it, Queenie?" he asked his horse.

Sam, officially now Master Sam Biggs, a man of sustenance, walked back toward the night's camp with his mare in tow. He felt differently about the land he'd crossed over twice before. He was walking on his own land and it felt good. But he felt something else, too. He felt a stranger's eyes burning into his back.

"Massa," said Willie, "I's a 'bout red'i to cum an fetch yo. I gots dat coffee biled up and I's fix'n sum'a dem fritters you be lik'n so much."

Sam traded his jacket for the plate of fritters. He sat on a small folding stool as Willie brought coffee and extra hot corn-fritters to him.

"Henry back, yet?"

"Nah Suh, nots yet, Suh," replied Willie.

Sam and Willie sat eating the hot fritters. Suddenly, the boom of Henry's gun, followed by a rolling echo, raced toward them. Startled, they both jumped.

Willie looked at Sam and asked, "You reckon Henry got us ah deer, duz you?"

"Well, if he was shooting at one, it's dead. If he didn't hit him, it probably fell over dead out of fright. I know I damn near did." He could see Willie picturing the scene in his mind, and he too, decided it painted a funny picture, and the two laughed.

Sam licked the sugary glaze from his fingers.

"Not bad. Sara better watch out, Willie, you might give her a run for her money," he jokingly said to the slave. The boy's broad smile said he liked the tone of the words, but his eyes indicated he had no idea what his master meant.

They looked up as Henry rode into the camp. Across the horse's rump lay the carcass of a deer. Willie ran to meet Henry, asking, "Did chew shoot dat dare deer, or did cho' skeer him to deaf?" and once again burst into laughter.

Confused by the odd question, Henry looked at Sam and silently mouthed the word, "What?"

The deer was field dressed. All that was necessary was for Sam to tell Henry which cut of meat he wanted Willie to cook.

Henry continued, "I could have shot a mess of wild hogs, big ones, too. There was a bunch of 'em back there in those woods, but I figured we're all about pork'd out—I know I sure as hell am. There was a lot of game down in those lower woods," he said, pointing south. "This whole place has a left alone look to it. Right smart bit of work to get through all that brush and bramble, though. There's a heap of rabbits and squirrels. We'll have some good eating when we do get back here and get settled in."

Out of Willie's hearing, Sam told Henry about the white-haired man on the big white stallion. He told him the man seemed strange and overly interested in him.

"Stay on your toes," Sam said.

Henry and Sam relaxed as Willie started cooking. They all needed rest. Sam dozed off. Too soon, Willie nudged him awake, handing him a plateful of venison, biscuits and beans.

"There's nothing under God's sun taste's as good as a fried venison steak after days and days of that salt-pork," said Henry as he held out his plate for more.

"Fried tree bark might," laughed Sam, agreeing.

The men were nearing exhaustion. The effort of eating seemed a task, but fresh venison made it a pleasant one. Willie wrapped a biscuit filled with venison and stuck it into his pocket, cleaned and put away the cooking utilities and fell asleep. Henry had fallen asleep within minutes, his snoring proved it a much needed sleep.

At three, Sam began his watch. He bolstered himself, drinking plenty of strong black coffee.

Early morning, still dark, a booming explosion roared down from the woods near the intersection, shattering the night's silence, its rumbling echo magnified by the quiet of the dark night.

Henry jumped to his feet, grabbed his hat and gun and slid over next to Sam. "What the hell was that?"

Sam knew what it was, but why would anyone do such a thing? he wondered. He lifted his dragoon and told Henry to go back to sleep. He let Willie sleep and nudged him awake at five-thirty. Willie was awake before Sam could step away from him.

"Okay Willie, let's get after it. I'll feed the animals and get everything I can ready for our ride," Sam said. He took one of the two remaining bladders of water and poured enough for a cursory bath.

Willie saw his new master was preoccupied. That was as far as his concerns went and he started mixing the biscuit dough. Soon he asked if he should awaken Henry.

"No, let him sleep a few more minutes." He wanted a short time alone to think, the blast from the night, fresh on his mind. He knew someone was telling him they were not welcome.

With breakfast ready, Sam shook Henry awake. Finished, they mounted their animals. Henry and Willie fell in behind Sam and they started their second day of exploration.

If he could believe the descriptions of the holdings provided by a very drunk Harold S. Ledbetter, they should be able to ride west three miles and still be on his land.

Off to the north rose a high hill. Compared to the gentle rolling swales around them, the hump seemed large and out of place.

If it wasn't too damn hot for these animals to handle it, we ought to ride up there. Probably'd be able to see everything we need to see. Maybe next time, Sam thought.

They skirted the hill and continued west. The land remained similar to that which surrounded Petersburg, neither overly scenic nor unpleasant to look at. With no hills rising in front of them, the hill behind seemed even more out of place.

His holdings appeared to be equally divided into tenable land and timber. Farm land, covered with shrub growth of thick brambles and blackberry briars, would require considerable work but the land could be recovered for planting.

Rabbits sprang from one tangle of thick brush and briars as the horses trampled their dens and warrens, and dashed off to the nearest similar tangled mass, never to be seen again. The forests were thicker, filled with luxuriant and huge trees.

"Old growth, Ledbetter called them," Sam said to Henry. The old man had not lied to him when he had bragged about it being full of trees which had never been cut down. Until now, Sam hadn't known whether the man lied or stretched the truth, but he'd suspected he was capable of both.

Pines and oaks stood in stands so large and thick, a man could spend months inventorying them. They had passed dozens of such areas in the past hour alone. Walnut and pecan trees, not as plentiful as the oaks and pines, were scattered throughout the groves. Cypress trees grew along and out into swampy areas. He began to think of the sawmill in Weldon.

"Just think," Sam said to Henry, "every tree on this place has a use and a customer waiting to buy it. Furniture makers, boatyards, carpenters, bridge builders; hell, even those little toy trains everybody's carrying on about, need thousands and thousands of ties to support their rails. And that's not to mention the firewood that toy uses.

"We ought to set up a sawmill right in the middle of these pines and start cutting firewood and rail ties for those toys before the novelty wears off. Railroad ties got to come from somewhere and it might as well be from us." The different uses for his timber were mind-boggling. The sawmill was as good as delivered, and the sooner the better.

They exited the woods at a nondescript road heading north and south. Not a building or living soul could be seen, but far away, two loaded wagons headed south and away from them. There were no fresh wagon tracks on the road beneath them—proof that the wagons had not passed from the north. And that could mean only one thing—somebody was using his land.

He rode his horse across the dirt road, and into the cooling shadows cast by the canopy of trees on the far side.

"What do you think those folks are up to, Henry?"

"Stealing, I'd say."

"We'll find out soon enough," responded Sam. "From here, we're still heading west. The next road, the Arcola-Ringwood Road is the western boundary of our land. Arcola's a short ways up to the north. Not much there, that's what the innkeeper back at Westland Crossroads said. He didn't have much praise for it; acted like it was a little wild or something, so keep your eyes open wide 'till we get there and leave. When we head south we'll start circling back toward Ringwood. Maybe we'll look for the southwest corner spike on the way. Henry, you and Willie look for signs of a creek or a river. I like this area, but we've got to have water."

"Sam, look out yonder, " said Henry, pointing to a ribbon of green trees wending through a far-away valley. "See them tree-tops? See how green they are? They got all the water they need . . . lapping it up from the creek they're growing along side of. If we go down there, you'll find one of them creeks you got us looking for."

"Damn, Henry, I do believe you're right. Good job. But for now, we'll keep heading west. If it is a creek, it's not liable to change its course by afternoon."

***

Hour after hour of the unchanging scenery, the trees, the briars, the brambles, and the barren clearings began to wear upon the men; the monotony tiring them as much as the heat of the day.

Suddenly, they emerged from the trees and onto the road leading north to Arcola and south to Ringwood. Arcola's buildings, a mile distant, were barely visible.

Sweat trickled down their cheeks and began to stain their collars.

"Let's ride up there; check it out. Maybe we can get some food. I sure as hell wouldn't push away a nice cool beer, either. Would you, Henry?"

Sam saw the slight reflected in Willie's eyes.

Willie's head hung low. He knew there were white men's things and slave's things, but he was curious about white men's beer. The reins for the pack animals were wrapped tightly around his hand and soon he busied himself braiding the frayed ends.

"Don't worry, Willie. I'll get you a cool drink of root beer if there is a tavern up there. You ever had any root beer, Willie?" Sam asked.

"Nah Suh, but I heer'd 'bout it." the boy answered. He mumbled to himself, "What Massa Sam gonna' think if I gits drunk frum dat stuff? All I ebber heer'd about dat root beer is wen yo drinks it, yo feels good, but sum'times yo fall down." It seemed strange to him— the falling down part, but it did not curb his curiosity. Stranger yet, was how it was made out of tree roots—but that's what Henry said, he thought. He'd bought into his friend's joke and laughed hard at the confusing statement.

"I sho doan see how dey can make dat stuff outta' dirty tree roots," he mumbled, "but I sho 'nough wants sum.'

***

In front of one of the few buildings stood a hastily rigged hitching rail, partially covered with bark and pine beetles racing from one slab of bark to another. Thrown around the rail with careless abandon, were the reins of two mules and four horses. The other businesses suffered from a lack of customers.

Above the door, a crudely painted window, covered with childish strokes and cheap paint, listed the liquid menu available inside. Passing years and gravity struggled to rip the panes of glass from their rotted window frames. A lopsided bottle emblazoned with three x's confirmed hard liquor was available. The thick, cracking paint of dark, heavy mugs filled with beer, topped with overflowing, frothing foam, a lopsided glass with amber colored sassafras, and a glass filled with lumpy curdled buttermilk, diffused the passage of the sunlight through the amateurish brush strokes. A hand-painted sign hung askew above the window. The ragged workmanship of the sign and the crudely painted window was a harbinger of the poor quality and service inside Shorty Jackson's Tavern.

Sam and Henry dismounted.

"Get some of the oats out for them, Willie, and give 'em corn. Keep them out of the sun as much as you can and don't let 'em bust a gut with too much water, either. Henry will bring you out your root beer in just a minute. If anybody tries to talk to you, don't. Understand?"

Sam and Henry grabbed their guns and entered the darkened tavern. They could not see the people staring at them, but felt hard eyes burning through them. People are curious, thought Sam. He chose to ignore the stares, yet he remained cautious. He and Henry laid their weapons aside, but within easy reach. A strong smell of pipe tobacco and the rancid, odor rising from the spittoons scattered about the room attested to the fact the men with the inquisitive eyes liked their tobacco; chewed, sniffed or smoked.

An offending stench of stale beer mingled with the sweat soaked bodies of men, past and present. A makeshift counter, supported by oak barrels at each end, served as a bar top. Slowly, their eyes grew accustomed to the dark room and they saw they remained the center of attention.

He and Henry sat patiently as a short, fat man, his soiled apron an indication that he was the bartender, stood talking to men sitting around a table near the rear of the room. The man occasionally turned from the men to see if his new customers were still at the bar and without acknowledging them turned back to the table, and rejoined the conversation.

"Barkeep" said Sam. "How's about some service over here?" his tone, loud enough to be heard, yet he was ignored.

"Barkeep," a second time—louder, but to no avail. Sam's eyes narrowed as his face blushed with a tinge of red.

"Now that's about as rude as hell, ain't it?" he said to Henry. "Let's go." He and Henry stood and grabbed their guns.

The squat man hurriedly rushed back to the makeshift bar top. "Sorry, Gents. Business, you know?"

Irritated, Sam added, "That sign outside says Shorty Jackson's Tavern? You Shorty Jackson?"

"Well, yes Sir. That's me," answered the bartender, wiping his hands in his dirty apron.

"Then you're not taking care of business very well, are you?"

"What can I git y'all?" Shorty asked, knowing he'd just been reprimanded.

Sam ordered two tankards of ale and a glass of sassafras root beer for Willie. Before the bartender could pull the tap and fill them, Sam asked for and was handed the mugs. He withdrew a clean white handkerchief from his vest pocket and wiped purposefully at the dusty mugs. The insulted bartender held his tongue and filled them with dark ale. He sat the ale in front of the two new customers and while smirking at Sam, he exaggerated the cleaning of Willie's glass.

"Clean enough?" he asked sarcastically, and filled the chipped glass with dark root beer.

"Cleaner than the mugs," Sam answered.

Henry's heartbeat quickened as he thought another battle was about to start.

Sam asked the bartender if Henry could take the glass out to Willie.

"Sure Mister, as long as y'all leave a half-dollar on the bar here 'til I see my glass again."

Sam glared at the man. "Let's see. You want me to give you a day's pay to use one of your glasses? That's what you're saying, right?"

The bartender diverted his eyes from the intimidating stranger.

Knowing he frightened the man, Sam forced a smile and said to him, "That's fair enough, and I thank you kindly."

Men gathered around scattered tables slowly faced back to each other and continued their muffled conversation. Sam heard the name Griffen mumbled—the same name the tavern keeper in Westland Crossroads had mentioned and the same name the peacekeepers used to prove their supposed authority over the road's traffic.

"Shorty, you fat bastard," was shouted across the tavern. "Get your lard-ass over here."

Shorty stepped from behind the bar and headed toward the men. A whispered conversation between Shorty and the men gathered around the shadowed table, floated back to Sam and Henry. It was obvious they were the objects of the mens' curiosity. Shorty nervously watched Sam and Henry. He lifted his finger, indicating he would return in a moment.

Sam and Henry drank their ale and asked if there was food available. The tavern owner brought out three beef sandwiches, each wrapped in white, coarse butcher's paper, dotted with tiny black specks. Sam scraped at the specks and was glad to find they were part of the thick paper and not what he had suspected—fly droppings. Pulling back the thick slabs of dark bread, they sniffed the beef, expecting their senses to be assaulted, but the meat was fresh and smelled edible. Two more tankards of ale were quick to follow, and another glass of root beer for Willie. Laying another half dollar on the bar, Sam smiled at the barkeeper. Henry took the root beer and sandwich out to Willie.

Grinning as he returned, he said, "You are not gonna' believe this. Willie's drunk. Damnedest thing I've ever seen."

The two finished their sandwiches and beer. Henry retrieved the second emptied glass from Willie and took it back into the tavern. Sam handed the glass to the bartender and held his hand out for the required deposits.

"My friend and I, and our boy out there are heading toward Ringwood. Would you be so kind as to help us with directions?" he asked the bartender.

Instead, the bartender responded with a question of his own, "What's y'alls business in Ringwood?"

Taken aback, Sam's brow lowered, and his eyes darkened. "Mister, my business is pretty much just that, my business, and I suffer fools poorly."

The bartender eyed Sam warily and decided he'd best watch what he said to the strangers standing before him.

"I'm sorry. I ain't got the right to ask y'all such a question. It's just there's been some unsettling problems 'round 'bout these here parts, what with some darkies running off from the Griffen place. Ever' time it happens you can't believe the trash-ass people what comes to these here parts looking for them running niggers." He coughed nervously, cleared his throat, straightened his suspenders and ran a greasy hand though his thinning hair.

Sam's eyes twitched and his jaw clinched at the term trash-ass, but the bartender did not seem to notice.

"They stirs up all kinds of trouble, what with their drinking and swearing. You can hear them beating those goddamn dogs they use for hunting them runaway niggers down wid all night long, just to keep 'em mean. They already so damn mean they'll try to kill any- thing what gits near 'em."

Sam locked the man with his hard stare. "We are heading down to Ringwood. Will you give me directions, or not? I hold no truck with any of those people you are worried about, and it offends me that you may be calling me trash."

The bartender quickly apologized to Sam and Henry. "Nah Sir, that ain't what I meant a'tall. Nah Sir, ain't no way. But a lot of strangers do come through our little town." And pointing south, he added, "Y'all take that road right out front, where y'all have your boy and them horses and mules standing and go on down that way. Ride on for about three miles 'till y'all gits to a bridge what goes over Swift Creek."

Seeing a way to buy back into the good graces of the man be- fore him, he offered further unasked for advice. "Y'all be careful down there; some of them slavers and that other riff-raff likes to set up their camp down under the bridge. If they're there, they'll probably be drunk'ern hogs eating watermelons what's near gone bad. When they been drinking, they're meaner than the devil himself. Y'all might want to keep them guns up close. They see that darky y'alls got wid you, they's gonna' be wantin' him, especially if they's good'n drunk. Griffen'll gib them boys two, three hunnert dollars for some of them runaways. And some of them niggers ain't runaways, if you knows what I mean."

Shorty paused, licked his lips, forced a smile. The bartender had Sam's attention and preferring that to his wrath, he continued, "Y'all head on down souf' past that there bridge, and the road will head off to the east. Go on around that bend for another one, two miles and y'all be in Ringwood, or what's left of it. That place ain't doing near as good as Arcola here's a doing. But it's the next place on down that way."

Trying to appear affable to the strangers before him, the short, fat bartender asked, "What's this world coming to? All we's trying to do is keep an eye out for things what's unusual. You understand, don't you Mister? I didn't mean no harm askin' where y'alls off to.

"Why, jus' this mornin' a coupla' old man Griffen's peace-keepers come through here and said they got jumped by some strangers, highway men they called 'em. Both of 'em said all they was doing was jus' moseying along, mindin' their own business, when they got held up and robbed down on the road right out in front of Mister Griffen's place."

Sam and Henry stood to leave, but still irritated, Sam touched Henry's arm, signaling him to stop. It worked. He and Henry turned toward the bartender.

"I thank you for your help, but it seems to me that somehow I'm now included in these troubles you speak of. That's something else I'm getting a bit tired of. Does everybody in this part of North Carolina treat people passing through like they're evil, the outcasts of society? Are you people so weak-minded that you believe the lies people like Buck and LeRoy tell you."

Shock flashed across Shorty's face. He hadn't mention any names. Immediately, upon hearing the two names, the tavern keeper's eyes proved he knew he had insulted the men again and it frightened him.

"That's who you're talking about, right—old Buck and Leroy?" asked Sam. "Have you even considered they might be the trash people you keep going on about? Peace-keepers telling lies, now there's a twist. They might be your friends but those two are liars. I know. We were the ones who were rode down on by those two lying bastards. We didn't rob them of one goddamn thing."

Sam continued, "But I'll show you how I stopped those thieving bastards from stealing my boy and killing me and my friend here, while they were about their peace-keeping." Sam reached into his riding jacket and pulled the big revolver out and laid it on the bar top. The bartender stepped away, sure he'd just sold his last beer, ever. Henry, as if learning from watching Sam, aimed his musket at the men sitting at the tables. They were quick to lay their hands upon the table, palms down.

Sam continued, "We rode into this slop-jar of a town minding our own business. All we wanted was food and drink and very simple directions. All we got was an unpleasant reception. I don't much like assholes like you looking down your nose at me. I can handle it, but I don't like it. Somebody lying about me is another problem. I reckon I can handle that, too. Somebody trying to steal my man away from me is one more problem. I sure as hell wouldn't like that and I'll kill 'em dead for trying it. Now, I want to leave here on friendly terms—if there are any friendly folk around these parts. All the land across the road, from here all the way to Ringwood and back east of here, clear up to Brinkleyville, is mine. I'm the new owner and your new neighbor."

The bartender looked confused—startled. He glanced over at the men sitting at the table, and back at Sam; his eyes narrowed. "What'd you just say? That land belongs to . . . " and wisely let the question trail away.

"You heard me. I'm your new neighbor. You treat me proper, like a friend next time we meet, and I'll do the same to you. Now, in spite of the fact I'm not in an overly friendly mood toward you right at the moment, I want you to give old Buck and LeRoy a message. You'll do that for me, won't you? Tell 'em this, and don't mess it up. I told those two idiots that if they decided they wanted to chase me down, I'd give them reason to rethink their position. So you tell them I think they are way too close to me and I'm getting a mite skittish. You think I'm a mite skittish, don't you?"

The tavern keeper nodded; his thick jowls shaking. He was at a loss for words, and badly shaken, he foolishly said, "I usually charge two bits per animal for that water out there, but you being a neighbor and all, well you can have it. No charge."

Sam threw a dollar on the table. "No thank you." He heard mumbling coming from more than one man as the door swung shut.

He and Henry stepped out of the tavern. "What you think all that was about, Sam?" Henry asked.

"Well, I don't know for sure but it caused him concern, didn't it?"

Chapter Seven

They gathered up a drunken Willie, two horses, the pack mules and crossed the street to a whitewashed building, Arcola's dry goods store. The building was as old as the neighboring buildings, but it stood out. Recent repairs made it the only one worth whitewashing.

"Let's go see if we can get a few more things, depending on what they got," said Sam, as he walked toward the store.

Passing Willie, he looked at the snoring Negro and shook his head.

"Willie said the corn meal and flour was only going to hold out for another day or so, so let's not take a chance. How about you, Henry? You need anything?"

"A couple twists of chewing tobacco. A bag of Virginia Heathen brand smoking tobacco'd be good, too."

"Ain't it amazing what two glasses of root beer mixed with a helping of simple can do to a person?" asked Sam, shaking his head when he looked at Willie.

"Well, I do believe those were his first two beers ever. I just hope he doesn't wake up with a hangover," Henry laughed.

"Stay out here with the animals and the little drunk, I'll be out in a few minutes. Just keep your eyes on that tavern. Ain't nothing liable to happen, but watch it, just to be sure. Those fellows ain't at all sure what just happened in there, but I'll tell you . . . that bartender's got his dander up. Don't figure nobody'll come out and strike up a conversation with you, though."

He walked into the dry goods store and gave a cursory look at the store's sparsely stocked shelves.

If Arcola's all this prosperous, Ringwood must be in one hell of a mess, he mused. He was amazed anyone could stay in business with so little stock. He walked around the small store gathering items Willie and Henry both had mentioned, along with a few things which might come in handy or add variety to their meager camp meals.

A few links of smoked sage sausage, a heavily spiced ground pork stuffed into washed out hog intestines and smoked to help it keep, were welcomed for quick snacks. Inquiring of dried fish, he was told there was a handful of smoked herring left.

"Try it first. Might be gone to ruin," warned the clerk.

Sam bought a dozen eggs and a spring lock-top jar. He broke the eggs and drained them into the jar. Scrambled eggs and sausage for breakfast—can't get much better than this, he thought.

He was obsessed with finding fresh greens. He craved collards, mustard or turnips, cooked with a slab of bacon. The greens would help hold scurvy at bay. He wasn't exactly sure what scurvy was, but the name alone made him dread it and not want it. He took enough for a large meal. It would have been nice to buy more but what wasn't cooked would not keep in the late summer heat.

Sam walked over to the store's one window and stood to the side, hidden from view of anyone who might be watching him and his men. Shorty Jackson, the bartender, rushed through the door of the tavern, buttoning up a clean shirt, and headed toward the town's stable. Soon his horse burst through the stable door and he spurred the animal towards the Griffen plantation.

"Now what?" Sam mumbled.

Small groups of men looked in the direction of the store, murmuring among themselves, trying not to be obvious. Leaving the tavern, some of the patrons stopped at the swinging doors and looked warily in both directions. They drew up short upon seeing Henry and Willie in front of the dry goods store.

Sam reached into the candy jar and grabbed a fistful of five-for-one-penny rock candy.

"For my men," he said, aware the owner was watching. So intrigued was he by Willie's reaction to root beer, he could hardly wait to see what Willie would say when he told him the root beer flavored candy could be carried around in his pockets and all he had to do was put it in his mouth and suck on it.

"Good day, Sir. Name's Sam. Sam Biggs. May I inquire of your's?" he asked the clerk and extended a friendly hand.

"Name's Lonnie. Lonnie Johnson. Lonnie's good enough. Just plain Lonnie," and facing his wife, added, "This here's my wife, Mattie."

"My pleasure, Ma'am," said Sam, and removing his hat, he nodded toward Lonnie's wife.

"Please tally this for me, Mister Johnson."

"Mattie, run that up for Mister Biggs. Will you?"

Lonnie was a rail-thin man, slightly balding and wore a thick, bushy mustache as if it would distract attention from his receding hairline. His dark indigo apron was dusted with flour. He dropped the flour scoop back into the opened barrel, brushed flour from his hand, and extended it in greeting.

Mattie's was a pale, drawn face. A tight thin-lipped smile, each end curving downward said she was wary of strangers. She nervously brushed at loose strands of prematurely gray hair and unable to look Sam in the eyes, she appeared leery of the new customer.

She pulled at her limp and fading dress, then smoothed it in a vain attempt to resurrect the long lost beauty of the new dress it had once been.

Sam and the store clerk each shared pleasantries and walked out onto the covered porch. Sam liked the man and felt his store could be a well located business for him in the future, but it was thin on supplies. Maybe things will improve for them, he thought.

"Seems like a nice enough fellow, that Lonnie," Sam said to Henry. They rode south toward Ringwood.

The ride was quiet, the summer heat building, the day not yet unbearable. Sam began to think of the past few day's events; some nice, some not so nice. A lot of information about his new holdings had been garnered and more still awaited him. Shaking his head in disbelief, Sam told Henry to poke Willie in the ribs and wake him up.

"Not too hard. If that boy is half as drunk as he thinks he is, damn fool'll fall off that mule and get himself trampled to death, for sure, and I don't know how to pitch a tent."

Willie woke with a start. He appeared lost. He had no idea where he was.

Henry greeted him with "Morning Willie, how was your nap?" Willie did not answer, but snuck a furtive glance at Sam.

The day grew hot and sticky. The animals were lathered from the heat and their loads. Evaporating sweat left long lines of drying salt on their heavy coats of hair. Sam was anxiously looking for the bridge over Swift Creek, wanting to find water for the animals and shelter from the sun. Finally, far down the road, he saw railings on each side of a bridge. He pulled back on the reins of his horse and motioned for the other two to join him.

"Either of you see anything out of the ordinary down there?" he asked. "Keep your eyes peeled for smoke, horses—anything that's not supposed to be there. Henry, get your gun up close to you. I don't think nobody's up there. Just be ready, in case. Hammer it to half cock."

Willie fell back with the mules and sawed at the reins, pretending to get the stubborn animals moving.

"Get your ass up here," Sam shouted at Willie.

"Yas Suh, I's cum'n."

Within walking distance of the bridge, they dismounted. Beneath the bridge, clean, clear water reflected the rays of the sun. "Creek's sure got the wrong name, don't it? Swift Creek. Which way is it flowing, anyway? It'd have to speed up to come to a stop," he said to Henry and the two men chuckled.

He motioned for Henry to head to the far side of the bridge while he walked to the left. Both men held their guns out and ready. The bridge was fifteen feet wide; wide enough to provide plenty of covered space under each end for man or beast. They carefully climbed down the sides of the bridge and slowly pushed their gun barrels into the darkened recesses.

Sam shouted to catch any person hidden away in the dark cavities by surprise. With no one responding, they inched forward. Henry shouted "Whoa," as a frightened cow ran headlong at him. He jumped back as the cow ran past and deep into the woods along the bank of the creek.

"Cow scared the shit out of me," said Henry. He glimpsed toward Willie in time to see Willie jump in alarm and hide behind the mules.

Sam and Henry climbed back up and told Willie to bring the animals up.

"Nobody's down there," Sam said to Willie. "Take those animals down to the creek. Let them drink all they want. Cows or something's been using that shade down there to cool off. Ain't none too clean. Smells to high Heaven, but they need water."

Sam felt his tension easing. He did not want a confrontation with slavers or anybody, for that matter, but he knew he had to be ready for it if it came. Based upon the events of the past two days, he expected more trouble to come along and strangers could be beyond the tree line training their guns on them now.

So far, there seemed to be a surplus of trouble everywhere they went. He felt as if he had been sitting on the sharp edge of a razor for the last few days, and the stress was beginning to cut into him. The animals drank their fill and moved over to graze upon the thick and sun burned grass. The stink of the place was overpowering. "I was hoping for at least a breeze, but I haven't felt one yet. Let's get back in the woods."

Easy access to the shaded woods was obtained by a well-worn animal trail running alongside the creek bank. It was wide enough for Sam and Henry to ride along side by side. They entered the woods and their day improved. No longer did their eyes ache from the constant glare of the sun, nor did it feel like their flesh was searing off. The woods seemed less confining and the air less stale than before.

The temperature in the woods dropped noticeably. The animals no longer suffered from the weight of the summer heat on their backs. Everybody began to feel refreshed, although they had only stopped at the bridge for a quarter of an hour.

The monotony of the dirt road had a numbing effect on the senses, tiring them easily. Not so with the creek side trail. Each huge oak was of interest. Each bend of the creek explored. The creek was flowing no faster, but to Sam's pleasure, it flowed no slower.

"The only place I've ever seen cleaner water, or slower water for that matter, is in a well," he said to Henry.

Without knowing what to expect from each bend of the creek, or knowing who or what might be hidden away and watching from heavy thickets, Sam cautioned Henry and Willie to keep a close eye on all they saw.

The oak groves looked as if they were maintained by caretakers—nature at its best. The occasional flood kept the soil beneath the looming oaks washed free of debris, leaving it covered with white sand. Thoroughly shaded by thick luxuriant foliage, lesser plants could not find root and grow. The oaks maintained sole ownership of the sandy soil.

The width of the creek varied greatly; hemmed in by outcroppings of boulders, or damned wide and deep by windfall trees and stumps.

The riders pointed at fish darting away from the creatures looming above them. Alligator gar, sunfish as large as a big man's hand, silvery bass and turtles of all sizes continually rippled the water.

Beaver slapped the water with thick, flat tails as muskrats muddied the creek, diving under the washed-out bank.

The bottom was as clean as the sandy soil beneath the stand of oaks. Rocks and gravel seemed to be within an inch of the surface, although the depth was three feet or more.

"I could get used to this," Sam mumbled, enjoying the seclusion of the forest.

"If we find a place closer to the road up ahead that runs up toward Brinkleyville, and if it's as pretty as this, maybe a bit larger, we might have found us a place to build our houses."

Henry nodded.

Rested and refreshed, Sam encouraged the men to ride further. Willie and Henry agreed, both anxious to see more themselves.

Henry touched Sam's arm. "Look over there by that stand of pines. You see what I see? Count 'em, there's eleven white tails and six wild hogs. They act like they own this place, don't they? I never saw such a sight."

The men stopped and watched the wildlife.

Neither have I, thought Sam.

Eastward they rode, north of and parallel with the Ringwood road. Soon they arrived at the Brinkleyville and Lewisburg-Raleigh Road which divided his holdings into two distinct portions, both nearly equal in size. Sam pulled back on the reins, stopping the mare in the center of the wide dirt lane. He stared at the broken surface of the road beneath him, studying it.

"You see something different about this part of the road? Different than when we crossed it this morning back up yonder?" Sam said, pointing north.

"If you're talking about how hard it's been used, yes, I do. Looks to me like somebody's been running some mighty heavy freight and a bunch of mules through here," answered Henry.

Sam nodded and continued examining the road's surface.

"Whoever it is, they're not going very far up that way." He pointed toward the area where they had crossed the same road three hours earlier. "There wasn't any wagon tracks up there."

He pointed at the shallow tracks left by empty wagons and the deep ruts left by heavily loaded ones.

"They're coming in empty and leaving loaded from somewhere between here and where we crossed it at noon. That means one thing. Somebody's doing something I'm probably not going to be very happy about. They're stealing from us, Henry."

Henry looked discouraged. "You reckon there are any decent folks in these parts, Sam?"

Sam tugged Queenie's reins and rode up the far bank and dismounted. Henry followed close behind. He dropped Queenie's reins, and picked up a twig. Twirling it aimlessly, he looked north and south on the road.

"I haven't seen but one thing worth stealing all yesterday and today—timber. If they're stealing from me with not so much as a howdy, that kinda' makes me mad."

They crossed over the torn up dirt thoroughfare and continued through more of the same countryside. Soon they emerged from the woods and onto the Ringwood road. Looking eastward, Sam saw three old buildings, all on the far side of the road.

They were poorly built cabins, with small lean-tos or shabbily built rooms barely attached, and only one of the cabins was occupied. From his vantage he could not see the everyday porch items; chairs, hanging water buckets, dippers, or the flower trellises common on southern porches.

The only proof of occupancy was a towering patch of sweet corn on the late side of the ripe season. The whole of the side yard had been plowed into a garden by whoever lived there.

Cornstalks towered above their heads. Most stood tall and straight, proud of their bounty, while others fell, their backs broken at mid-stalk, no longer willing to hold the heavy ears of corn up out of the dirt.

The poles used for the string beans and the tomato vines were nearing collapse, also, from the weight of the under-harvested, over-ripened vegetables they bore.

"These folks must have some mighty green thumbs and hardly no appetite," said Sam. Henry agreed with the waste he saw.

The other two shacks were just that; tumbled down cypress planked hovels, windows long broken out, doors hanging from rusted hinges and other doors completely missing. The roof, filled with holes from missing shingles had long since been worth repairing, although old planking was scattered haphazardly over holes of varying sizes. One of the missing doors had been used to patch a collapsed section of considerable size.

"Probably using that shack," Sam said, pointing to the sturdier of the two remaining shacks, "to put up some hay, corn, maybe some salt-pork, and dried tobacco. Be a waste to put effort in tearing them down, nature's already hard at it."

With no traffic to be seen in any direction, they let the animals close up and choose their own pace. Nearing the cabin that appeared to be occupied—the one with the garden—Sam noticed the occasional cloud of bluish-gray smoke wafting above the waist high weeds blocking their view of the porch.

He smelled the strong, bitter odor of pipe tobacco and next, he saw a sun-bleached bonnet from which loose strands of gray hair blew freely in the light breeze. An elderly woman rocked back and forth in an age-worn chair, shading her eyes with both hands, in an attempt to block the glare of the afternoon sun. The clickety-clack of the curved oak runners of the rocking chair complained of the poor quality of the splintered porch flooring.

They rode up to the opened gate—opened because it lay col-lapsed in the weeds of the yard. Sam called out, "Afternoon, Ma'am. How are you this fine day?"

She was in no hurry to respond, especially to strangers with a Negro in tow. Sam knew the three of them were being sized up by the woman. That's what I'd do, too, he reasoned.

The three riders watched her as she watched them. She did not trust strangers. Sam and Henry understood that and were not of-fended.

"Middlin, I 'spose," she answered.

Sam asked if they could water the animals.

The old woman looked at the three men, held up her hand, stopping them in place. "Y'all jus' stay right there fer a minute," and in a loud, gravelly voice yelled, "Elmer, git your gun and stick it out here on these folks, you hear me old man?"

From inside the cabin, Sam heard a man's gruff answer, "God-damn it, woman, what the hell you want now?" A flint-lock double-barreled shotgun snaked through the doorway and pointed straight at Sam Biggs.

"Afore y'all come any closer, that old man's 'bout as crazy as a mule-kicked dog. If any y'all makes a move that skeers me a little bit, it gonna' skeer him worser. An' that's libel to turn into sumt'n y'all ain't gonna' like. Just sit right there 'till I knows who y'all is. What y'all doing with that running Nigra of Mister Griffen's? Well, go on, start talk'n."

Sam raised his hand to his hat, slowly removing it. He hoped the old woman would see its removal as an act of respect, and prayed the old man behind the shotgun would not view it as an overly quick movement.

"Ma'am, we are heading to Fort Harwood and I have gravely misjudged the distance to the Fort Harwood road. Is it somewhere up this way? I thought we'd be near it by now."

Sam started to slide off Queenie.

"Mister, y'all dun been told to stay put once. I'm gonna' say it again, stay up on that horse. Now, that's two times. Don't reckon I can do my numbers no higher than that," said the white-haired man holding the shot-gun, both barrels still sticking straight out.

Sam regained his seat.

"We're thirsty and tired and so are our animals. We mean you and this fine lady no harm. I would be pleased to give you money for water."

The eyebrows of the old woman arched, and the barrels of the shot-gun dropped accordingly.

Always comes down to money, Sam thought. And before the gun would drop to a non-lethal level, Sam explained the presence of Willie to the old lady.

"That Negro boy back there is my valet. Willie's been with me for years; he's a little slow up here," he said, tapping his temple. "You don't have to worry none about him. He's so afraid of white folks, while the mules are drinking he'll sit by that fence over there, won't you Willie?"

The man-child stared at the ground, and continued to draw stick figures with a twig. Nodding his head, he answered, "Yas suh, Massa."

The old man stepped through the doorway, his gun no longer pointed straight ahead, but down toward the foot-traffic worn grass. The chickens scratching and pecking in the yard, scattered—they'd seen the gun before.

He was dressed in faded and tattered bib overalls; buttons long since lost and one shoulder strap flapping loose. His head and face were covered with a thick mass of tangled, snowy white hair. Snow white, with the exception of brown strains—tobacco juice—running downward, one on each side of his mouth. He spat out a copious amount of brown spittle toward the end of the porch.

Now, that was nasty, Sam thought, careful not to let the man see disgust on his face.

"Ain't no valley round 'bout these here parts. What you mean, that there darkie's a valley nigger?" asked Elmer, as he eyed Sam suspiciously.

Sam thought the comment amusing, and stifling a building laugh answered, "No Sir. Willie's my valet, you know, a personal servant, just for me. He takes care of me."

The old man whispered to his wife, "Got us a fancy pants man, huh?" and added, "Don't reckon I know that word. Mother, four bits, that 'bout right?"

"Git on over to the well and git all the water y'all wants. Daddy, go on back in the house and git the tea; it's as cool as the well water and tastes a mite bit good'r."

Sam and Henry dismounted and walked over to the gray-haired lady. He reached into his jacket pocket for the half dollar.

"Fergit about that. I jus' wanted to see what kinda' metal y'alls made out of. Tea's free, too."

She laughed aloud, thinking of the old man's valley nigger. "Elmer, you 'bout as dumb as a stick a far wood, sometimes."

Sam, again stifled a chuckle.

"Ma'am, my name is Sam Biggs. Me and my friend, Henry, are on our way to Fort Harwood to do some business. Thank you for your kindness. We'll not bother you long."

The old woman introduced herself to Sam and Henry. "My name is Dorrie, Dorrie O'Reilly. Tain't no bother. The old man there's Elmer. We been knotted up fer nigh on fifty years, ain't that 'bout right, Elmer?"

Elmer grunted.

She added, "Take that Nigra a glass of tea. Git on with it, and don't you skeer him none, neither."

Elmer entered the shack to get another glass for Willie.

She turned to watch Willie. "Your valley Nigra," and pausing to chuckle, said, "don't say much, does he?"

Sam touched his temple, to make sure she knew he was talking about Willie and not her husband, said, "He's a bit slow up here."

But instead, she replied, "Oh. Elmer, nah . . . he ain't crazy. Not crazy crazy, but he did git his brain-bucket kicked good'n hard by one of Mister Detwyler's mules. But he so hard-headed he hurt the mule's foot." She burst out laughing. Sam could see she was fond of her mule-kicked husband. "Thought he was gonna' die off on me, but no, there he is, still in the way. Oh, Mister Detwyler's the man what owns these shacks.

"That road y'alls a look'n fer is on the far side of that hill. Head off to the right. Fort Harwood's about six miles down. They dun built them a great big courthouse a few years back. Y'all be able to see that dome what they put on it sticking way up in the air 'fore y'all gits 'bout two miles this side of Fort Harwood. Heard in the mornings when the sun hits it, it looks like a big old silver moon rising up outta' the woods. Sun on one side, moon on the other. Now there's a picture, ain't it?"

Sam agreed with the observation and told her they would look for it.

"They needs that big courthouse, too, what with all them low-lifes what lives in that there town. Fools built it outside of town. Said town was gonna' grew out to it. Never heard such foolishness.

"Me and him," pointing at her husband, "used to live down yonder close to Fort Harwood. That town's a 'bomination, a regular Sodom and Gomorrah, yes sir," she continued.

Sam enjoyed listening to Miss O'Reilly. However, he took the opportunity when it arose, to head the conversation in the direction he needed it to go.

"Miss O'Reilly, Ma'am? We couldn't help but notice there's a right smart amount of cotton and corn back up the road. Looks like there was a mighty good crop of tobacco, too. This place yours?" he asked, already knowing the answer.

"Do me an' that old man look likes we got's any money? Like I dun said, this heah place belongs to Mister Detwyler. He lives over yonder in the big house," she said, pointing east, again.

"Well, he ought to be mighty proud of himself," said Sam, smiling.

Dorrie O'Reilly's face glowed as she started providing the information Sam wanted.

"All y'all see is Mister Detwyler's land, 'cept them woods on the other side of the road. Don't know who owns that no more. Used to be some old man what was richer dan God, but he ain't been 'round fer years. Might be dead fer all we knows."

Sam knew the answer to both of her comments, but said nothing.

With frail arms, flabby pale skin dangling underneath each, she pointed in all directions. "Everything on this side of the road y'all see, both directions, all that's Mister Detwyler's. Our boy Isaac's been work'n fer Mister Detwyler fer nigh on twenty years; more, maybe. Isaac's the one what grows all that stuff. Y'all seen he does a right fine job of it, too. Don't he? Mister Detwyler's kept him on all this time 'cause he so smart 'bout growing stuff.

"He don't treat them Nigras bad, need'r. He ain't never hit nary a one of 'em, an' I dun tole him, I'd knock his head off worser than that mule dun his Pa, if he ever clobbers a one of 'em. He went and asked Mister Detwyler if we could live up here in this old shack.

"Isaac keeps an eye on us. Sometimes, Mister Detwyler comes over and sits with us fer a spell. He's a good Christian man, ain't he Pa?"

"He do love the lord," her husband answered.

If he asked too many questions, Sam feared the O'Reillys would become suspicious of him, but he needed answers about the torn up road they had crossed. He needed to phrase his questions carefully.

"Is the road to Fort Harwood going to be in any better shape than the road that comes out of the north, back there about a half mile? Who in the world tore it up like that?"

"Yes Sir, they dun an tore up that road you talkin' 'bout all the way to Hades and back. Come right by here they did, with them big wagons, three of 'em." Miss O'Reilly paused and drank from her glass, "And ever one of 'em had eight mules a pulling 'em. They woulda' tore up that road out yonder jus' as bad, if it weren't used so much."

She brushed away bothersome strands of gray hair and continued. "It gits a lotta' use, that road does. Keeps it packed down hard. Gim'me a road what's used a bunch and there won't be nere as much dust, no sir, ain't that right, Pa?"

Elmer grunted and nodded his head.

"You'd think it'd be the other way around, wouldn't you?" she asked. "That road down to Fort Harwood won't be torn up; it git's a lot of use, but not that heavy kind. Y'all be fine. Them fellers leading those mules went on east toward Battleborough; they didn't go down to Fort Harwood."

"Three wagons? What were they hauling that takes so many mules to pull them?" No other way to ask—just ask it.

Miss O'Reilly, still not suspicious of his questioning, answered. "Them trashy people from the other side of Fort Harwood, they's all kin sum'way to that Griffen fellow what owns all the land over by Brinkleyville Crossroads."

Again—the name Griffen.

"They comes up here 'bout two, three times a year and cuts down some of them trees back in yonder what's got that purty wood in 'em when you bust 'em open. Most always it's them walnut trees. They drags 'em all the way down to Battleborough; then from there they git on that toll pike and head on down to Tarboro."

Amazed at the amount of information he was getting, Sam decided she was enjoying her chance to talk with strangers and he wanted her to continue.

"They gits them walnut trees down to the Tar River and sells 'em to a furniture making man. Hear tell, they makes heaps of money offa' them trees. Me? I don't want no money I'se got to steal things fer to git. That's jus' plain wrong, like the Bible say. Ain't it Pa?"

This time Elmer nodded, then grunted..

"Who is this Griffen fellow you mentioned? And you say the ones cutting those trees are this man Griffen's kin?"

"Mister Griffen owns most everything on the other side of them woods and that land what lays on 'cross the road, about four miles past, or so. How old you say he is, Pa?"

"Old enough not to be doing the stuff he does," answered Elmer.

"He comes by here ever so often," said Dorrie, her eyes hard to read. "He be riding that big fancy horse of his'n and talking to he'self. Now that's a sight to see." She burst out laughing, exposing teeth darkly stained by tobacco. "He be answering he'self too, like he's two people. Man's tetched, I tell you.

"Y'all watch out fer him, he ain't no good. Y'all see an old man talking to he'self and riding a big white horse, same color as his hair, turn 'round and find 'nother road to git on down if you can. Ain't that right, Elmer?"

Sam thought of his encounter with someone who sounded like the man she was describing. He knew it was the man everybody kept talking about.

He wanted to know more about the people who were stealing his lumber, so he asked another question to get her talking again.

"You say his kin from Fort Harwood are cutting lumber that doesn't belong to them? Why doesn't somebody stop them?"

"Everybody 'round these here parts dun tole the law people in Weldon and Fort Harwood. They knows them folk down at Fort Harwood is the ones what's stealing off that land," answered Dorrie. "They jus' don't wants to talk to old man Griffen 'bout it. He makes a heap of money offa' them trees, he'self. He's already got more money than most all the folks 'round these here parts put together. I 'spect he spreads a mess of that money 'round them law people up there in Weldon and down yonder in Fort Harwood, too, so they'll keep their blinders on and leave this part of the county alone," she said, tapping her corn-cob pipe against the porch post, and scraping at the char inside the bowl with a nail sharpened on a brick.

"Everybody knows he's behind the stealing. Tain't not one soul never tried to ketch 'em a cuttin' and a haulin' 'em off, neither. That man would steal the ticks' off a dog, he would," she said, as she packed a fresh load of tobacco into her scraped and cleaned pipe.

Sam took the opportunity to beg his leave.

"Miss O'Reilly, you and Mister Elmer, have been very kind and generous to us. I would very much like to visit with you two fine people when I come back through, God willing, and if you would be so kind as to extend an invitation to me."

The O'Reillys welcomed him to stop by whenever he wished. "We ain't gonna' go off too fer. Me and the ole man's jus' gonna' sit here and wait fer the good Lord to send his chariot to fetch us."

Dorrie pointed toward the side yard. "Y'all take some of that stuff in the garden, if y'all wants to." They both chuckled and waved goodbye to the three strangers.

Chapter Eight

Sam had deceived the O'Reillys—telling them he needed to go to Fort Harwood. Not a good way to start with a new neighbor, he thought. It ate at him, he'd meant no harm, but he was not ready to tell people why he was riding though. There would be a right time for that.

"It's amazing what folks'll tell you if you let them do the talking, ain't it?" he asked Henry.

"Seems like it."

After riding out of view of the O'Reillys, he said, "If we head back that way," pointing north, he said, "we should have to ride less than a mile before we find our creek. That's what the map says. We'll set up an early campsite when we get to it."

Seeing a large grove of oaks ahead, he said to Henry, "It should be cooler back in there." Upon finding the hoped for creek, he reined Queenie to a stop and dismounted.

"Willie, get those mules up here. Get 'em unpacked. We'll pitch here for the night. Henry, give Willie a hand. Both of you start setting up camp and cooking. I'm going to ride down the creek a ways."

He needed a bath and a break from the constant braying of the mules and the nerve-wracking, clanging and rattling of the burdens strapped to their backs. He needed time to think.

The stream remained clear but widened as Reedy Creek flowed into it from the North, nearly doubling the width of Swift Creek.

"Well, I'll be damned," he said aloud, admiring the beauty of the area.

The map showed the map-maker's crude and simplistic efforts to sketch-in their memories of the creeks and roads. And not accurately, Sam noted. But he possessed the knowledge of how he could make the most of the tenable portions of farm land and the timber.

Dismounting, he threw the reins loosely over Queenie's neck. She thrived on contact with her owner. She would not stray. Sam sat upon a log blown over by a storm.

Only the northeastern portion of his land remained to be explored. They would rest tonight and continue toward their previous camp on the new day. With luck, they would finish their exploration by late afternoon and head back to Weldon, earlier than planned

"What I'd give to sit for a bit—right here on this log. Drop a line and fish," he said aloud to his horse. The mare nudged him, an effort to comfort him—or beg for a lump of sugar. He dug into his pocket and held out a lump for her. She nudged him for another.

The calm and quiet of the woods and stream lulled him toward sleep. His eyes began to feel gritty. He closed them to ease the strain and fell into a much needed sleep.

The one sound he'd dreaded since his encounter with Griffen's men the day before, startled him—the roar of a gun racing from the direction of the camp, and that followed by loud shouting—the words indiscernible.

Henry would not have fired his musket for more game, we've got more than we need, he thought. Something's wrong. He ran to his horse. He grabbed the pommel of the saddle. The mare reared. With the mare's front hooves high in the air, he pulled himself into the saddle. Spurring the animal and pulling hard to the right, he sent the horse racing toward the camp.

***

Busy with their chores, Henry and Willie did not hear the approach of the two slave catchers. The steady chopping of Henry's hatchet drowned the noises the Slater brothers, Red and Daryl, made as they crept forward.

Red eased around the large oak which hid him from Henry and Willie. Henry had leaned his musket against the tree's trunk, but camp duties required him to leave the safety of the gun.

Red grabbed the musket and fired it into the air. Henry and Willie spun in his direction. Red pointed at Willie, an order for Daryl to head toward the slave.

The horses and their dogs were staked back down the trail but could be quickly fetched.

Red shouted, "Hey you, old man," speaking to Henry, "git your sorry ass on the ground, do it quick. Put your hands behind your back."

Daryl slammed into the slave, knocking him to the ground. Moaning and stunned from pain and fright, Willie lay unable to flee, unable to fight.

"Goddamn it Daryl, git his hands behind him. Cinch him up."

Daryl quickly grabbed a pre-tied noose from inside his filthy shirt and in a matter of seconds, Willie was hog-tied—hands and feet bound together behind his back. Red slipped a similar knot over Henry's hands and legs. Next he picked up the powder and shot bag and reloaded the musket. Freshly loaded, he stood it back against the tree. An empty musket was nothing more than a club to him.

Sam dismounted far enough away from the camp to not be seen and slid into the creek. The banks were filled with thick, lush vegetation, and hid him from view. His fear of harm to either Henry or Willie was far greater than his life-long fear of snakes. He pulled his bags of powder, shot and caps and hung them around his neck. Each hand held a loaded and cocked revolver.

Carefully pushing aside the thick foliage at the edge of the creek, Sam watched as the struggle unfolded.

He heard Red shout, "Daryl, you stupid asshole, git your god-damn gun out and cover both of these fucking idiots. That boy ain't gonna' go nowheres, so you watch this slave stealing son of a bitch over here real close. I'm gonna' go git the dogs."

Daryl did as he was told. Red was back in less than ten min-utes with two muzzled dogs tugging hard against their leashes and anxious to get about the work they had been trained for.

Sam held his fire, he needed the two brothers together.

Red staked the two dogs securely within inches of Willie. Na-poleon and Rufus strained against their stakes—slobber dripping from their muzzled mouths, their eyes wild with anticipation.

Willie's fear increased upon seeing the crazed animals digging their paws into the ground, straining hard at the deeply driven stakes. While praying for the stakes to hold, he wet himself.

Sam knew Willie was incapable of registering the muzzles and that all he would see were the dogs' mouths—their lips stretched taunt, exposing long sharp teeth.

Sam smelled the dogs from his vantage below the edge of the overgrown creek bank. Their stench permeated the air.

Red's frenzied shouting worked well for Sam. Climbing si-lently up the bank, he crawled into the thick undergrowth and snaked toward the camp. He was within killing range of the unsuspecting men, close enough to hear the red haired man say to the younger one, "Git us some of that coffee they got over there. If there's any food, grab it. I'm gonna' ask this nigger stealer some more questions."

Red stood above Henry. In his hand he held a greasy chunk of the still warm venison.

"Where's that big talking son of a bitch that was with y'all? He lit out on you, didn't he? Where'd y'all git that nigger?"

The rustle of reeds on a windless day caught Henry's eyes. Fingers pulled apart the lush overgrowth on the river bank. Henry saw Sam motioning to him. He was frightened, but he knew advantages had changed, not much—but enough.

"I asked you a question, you dumb-ass bastard," shouted Red, as he kicked hard into Henry's chest. Pain roared through Henry, but he said not a word to the man. Red kicked him again.

"Daryl. Get over here and help me untangle Napoleon's and Rufus' chains."

He turned back to Henry. "This'll help you talk. Daryl, git that muzzle offa' Rufus and stake him down by his feet," motioning toward Willie. "That dog gits himself a mouf' full of darky meat, old deaf and dumb here'll talk . . . talk until I have to tell him to shut up or shoot him, one or the other. Why is it folks got to be so fucking hard-headed when they got a gun stuck in their face?"

Frightened of his brother's rage, Daryl did as he was ordered.

His vision fading, Henry watched Sam and prayed for him to tell him what to do. Sam nodded slightly to his right, hoping Henry would understand he was to roll to the right, at least far enough to give him a clear shot at the man standing above him. Searing pain rushed Henry toward unconsciousness, but he understood and rolled to his right.

Sam's Colt roared and Henry felt the renewal of pain when Red Slater fell dead on top of him. A mist of red rained down upon the two men.

As the blast of burning powder from the big Colt rushed past him, Daryl released the muzzle from the dog's head. He stood quickly, fearing for his own life, and sought a direction in which to flee. The jaws of the excited slaver dog clamped tightly on Daryl's inner thigh and groin.

Daryl screamed. Pain contorted his face. He shoved his hand into the dog's mouth, and with the other, pounded the animal's face, eyes and nose. The dog merely added pressure to secure its mouthful of groin and hand.

Nearing shock, Daryl watched Sam Biggs step into the camp. His eyes pleaded with the man holding a smoking gun in one hand and a cocked smaller version in the other.

"Mister, please, please get Rufus offa' me."

Sam walked within ten feet of the man with the dog hanging between his legs. He mused at the absurdity of a four legged ball and chain. He was aware there was another dog to his left, struggling at its stake and that it desperately wanted to join the fight.

Sam stepped close to Willie and cut the ropes knotted behind his back. "Willie get up. Slow now, keep your eye on that dog at your head. Don't worry. If he makes a move for you, I'll kill him dead. Now move, move."

Willie did as he was told, and seeing Henry lying on the ground under a dead man, he rushed to him and pulled the red-haired bleeding mass off of his friend.

"What do you want me to do? Help you out with those dogs?" Sam asked the trembling and sobbing Daryl.

"Please help me."

"Alright, you got it." He walked up to the muzzled dog firmly staked to his left. The dog rushed at Sam. So fast did it leap, its head snapped back and foaming spittle splashed onto Sam's legs as the slack of the chain played out.

"Will this help?" He placed the barrel of his gun through the muzzle and forced the barrel between gnashing teeth. The Colt exploded and kicked into the air. The taunt rope yanked the dog backwards as the rear of Napoleon's head disappeared. The dog crumpled, his legs folding under him.

Sam stared at the quivering man, hatred growing in his heart. Daryl was overcome with fear and the pain of the dog still clamped to his inner thigh and hand.

He pocketed his revolver, grabbed the musket leaning against the tree and fired it into the air, rendering it of no use to anyone.

"You fools going to kill my friend and take my man, were you? Were you going to come looking for me, then? Kill me, too? Hand me that gun. That belt knife, too."

Daryl struggled to pull the revolver and knife from his belt and handed them to Sam.

"Willie, grab that gun from him," pointing at Red, "and check him good for a knife, too."

Sam threw the collection into the creek.

He turned back to Daryl. "What can I do for you?" Daryl looked at Sam and tilted his head and eyes toward the dog.

"Please," he groaned.

Sam ignored the pleas. Saying nothing to the man, he returned to Henry. Henry was rousing from his pain-induced sleep, his face contorted in pain.

Sam bent down to him and said, "Henry, hold on. Me and Willie are going to get you out of here quick as we can. Don't go back to sleep. Willie, get him some water. Throw a blanket on him and make him a pillow.

"Henry, you gotta' trust me. You'll be alright." Henry's eyes rolled back while he slipped into a dark place, void of pain.

Sam walked back to the whimpering slaver.

"I'll help you, but you're going to help me first. Who are you two working for? I know it's hard to talk, so if I'm right, just nod your head. Understand?"

Daryl nodded.

"That Griffen fellow put you up to this? You and that piece of shit over there? Going to steal Willie, were you?"

Daryl nodded again.

"You two been after us since yesterday? Hoping to make a little money with my man Willie, were you? Tell me something, you piece of shit, what good is money to a dead man?"

Daryl sobbed loudly, "Please, for Christ's sake, Mister. Please have mercy. I'm begging you."

Sam's anger grew within him. He sat on a camp stool Willie had previously set out. He stared at the man standing before him. Fearing his humanity had deserted him, he realized he could kill the man in front of him as easily as the dog he'd just shot.

Daryl never took his eyes off of his possible savior.

"Let me think on this," he said pulling the powder and shot bag from his neck and reloading the spent cylinders of his revolver. From his soaked trousers, he removed a pocket knife. He sat across from the man and tortured him by slowly whittling a twig.

After what must have seemed an eternity to Daryl, Sam stood, folded the knife and dropped it into his pocket. He smirked at Daryl and stuck the barrel of the big Colt into the dog's mouth.

"Bad Rufus," he said, and pulled the trigger. The dog's head exploded in a spray of red and gray. Two of Daryl's fingers joined the profusion of blood and gore. The dog and Daryl Slater dropped to the ground.

Sarcastically, Sam asked, "That feel better?"

Daryl pulled himself into the fetal position, cupped his bleeding hand with the other, and folded both to his chest. The crotch of his trousers were soaked with blood.

Regaining a hazy consciousness, Henry moaned.

"Henry, you feel better?"

Henry grimaced, "Boss, if them horses come back through here again, will you please shoot either me or them?"

Henry's attempt at humor lifted Sam's spirit. "I'm going to get you out of here. Can you hang on until I can rig the mules with a sling to carry you? I'll take you back to the O'Reillys and then head down to Fort Harwood to get a doctor for you. You'll hurt for a while, but we'll get you fixed up. I promise."

Sam looked at Willie and said. "Go get those mules."

Willie came back with the mules and Sam handed him the camp axe.

"Cut down two saplings, each a little longer than two mules lined up nose to tail. Straight ones and skin the limbs off. Get back as quick as you can." Using "inch" or "foot" would have been wasted, but Willie knew how long a mule was.

Willie ran into the woods, searching for two thin and straight saplings.

Sam grabbed a rope and started tying together a harness to throw over two of the mules' backs.

Willie drug the two saplings behind him as he entered the camp.

He and Sam slipped them into the harnesses strapped on the mules. Sam ripped the tent cover off the camp poles and together he and Willie rigged a stretcher for Henry.

"This is going to hurt, Henry, but we've got to get you up on that sling. Think you can you handle it?"

Gritting his teeth and holding his chest tightly with his arms, Henry answered, "Ain't much choice, is there? Let's do it."

Although loaded with great care, he passed out again from the unbearable pain. Blood appeared at the edge of his lips—broken ribs cutting into lungs. Sam told Willie to hold the lead mule's reins tight and grabbing the balance of the tent canvas he covered the dead man where Willie'd dumped him after he'd drug the body off Henry.

Second thoughts led him to lift the canvas and throw the two dogs on top of the dead man.

Looking at Daryl, his hate growing, he considered leaving him bleeding and crying on the ground. Let him die, he thought, but he couldn't, that wasn't in him. Instead he grabbed a camp towel, walked over and shook the man back from unconsciousness.

Daryl groggily looked at his three-fingered hand and nearly passed out again. Sam jerked his arm into the air and wrapped the towel around the bleeding finger stubs—the towel snagging on shards of bones protruding through torn and bleeding flesh.

"You make one noise, you complain one time, you are deader than a rock, you son of a bitch. Now you grab your horse and that mule. We are going to take that man for help, and you're going along for the ride, pain or no pain. You fall off, that's where you'll die."

Daryl opened his mouth to beg Sam's mercy, again. Sam slapped him across his face, hard.

"Shut up."

Willie took the lead rope of the mules carrying Henry. He was sick with fear and tears streamed down his black, dusty cheeks. Daryl held tightly to the two mules. Sam brought up the rear with the rest of the animals. In less than thirty minutes they were on the dirt road leading west towards the O'Reillys. Ten minutes later they rode into the yard. Dorrie and Elmer stood on the porch, staring at the strange caravan.

"My lord, Mister Biggs. What happened to y'all?" asked Dorrie.

Sam quickly summarized the events of the last hour and Dorrie said to her husband, "I tole you sum'body was a shoot'n over in them woods."

"Henry's been beat up bad by that man's brother. I killed him and two of their dogs. That one's hurt, too," Sam said, pointing at Daryl Slater.

"He can go to hell and rot, for all I care, but Henry's got to have help. May I please lay him on your porch, out of the weather?

I'm going to Fort Harwood and get a doctor for him. Willie will keep an eye on Henry and that fellow over there. We won't be a bother to you, Miss Dorrie. Will you please help me with him?"

Dorrie looked at her husband and said, "Pa, git in there and git that bed turned down. Y'all git that man down offa' that thing and git him inside. Mister Biggs, I don't wants to know what's goin' on with y'all. I 'specs him and that'un you kilt is slave ketch'rs, judg'n from his looks and he smells like a skunk. Don't make no never-mind to me. This here man," looking at Henry, "needs hep' right now. That man over there needs some hep', too. But Fort Harwood's too far and besides, that doctor ain't gonna' come up heah, no-ways."

Seeing her comment confused Sam, she added, "All he's gonna' say is for us to fetch Miss Rose. She's 'bout as near to a doctor person as there is 'round these heah parts. Closer, too.

"Elmer. Git one of them mules from that Nigra, knock that stuff on the groun' and git on over to Mister Detwyler's. Tell him we gots us a bad hurt man over heah. Tell him we need Miss Rose." She looked at the man with the bloody towel wrapped around his hand. She saw the splintered bones sticking through the blood-soaked towel. "Wait, tell him two. Tell him we need some medicines, too."

Exhausted, physically and emotionally, Sam sat on the porch and leaned his head against the porch post. His body complained as he stood to speak to Elmer.

"Sir, please tell Mister Detwyler money's no object. Whatever he wants, it's his."

Dorrie looked up to Sam and said, "He ain't like that. Like I dun tole you, he's a good Christian man. All he keers about is if y'all would hep' sum'body if they ever needs it. Pass kindness along, I always say. That's all he wants."

She called out to her husband, "Ask Mister Detwyler if Isaac can come over fer a spell, too."

Daryl Slater toppled from his mule.

Sam shouted at Willie, "Get his mule over into the shade. Leave that son of a bitch laying where he's at. Oh, pardon me, Ma'am, I apologize for my swearing, I do. I'm a bit upset. But that's a poor excuse for me swearing. I'm sorry."

"No need to ask a pardon; that's a poor excuse for a man. Now, tell your boy to pull him in the shade."

"Willie, as soon as I know Henry's going to be alright, me and you'll go back and get what we can out of the camp. Maybe get something to eat, if we can. Just do the best you can for now. Okay?"

"I sho ain't hungry, Massa Sam," replied the slave. If black could turn pale, Willie's dark skin had been lighter for the last few hours.

Sam entered the front room and watched Dorrie gently washing Henry's face.

"This feller's gonna' be alright. He's bumped up pretty good, that's fer sure. He dun stopped bleeding. Least fer now. He's gonna' need a lot of rest. I'll see he gits good care."

Sam dreaded that he had to tell Dorrie he would have to leave soon—matters that could not wait had to be taken care of.

"Ma'am, as soon as your husband gets back with that girl, I've got to leave. There's a body up in those woods I've got to load up, two dogs, too. I'm going to take that dead man and his brother over there, straight to that Griffen fellow's front porch and dump them at his door. The dogs, too."

He pointed at Daryl, "That man out there in the dirt told me himself Griffen's behind this mess."

Sarcastically, he added, "Its only right his boss gets something for his money."

Seeing concern on the elderly woman's face, he said, "I am so sorry that you and your husband are caught up in all this. I'll make it up to you somehow. I am going to give you this money. You and Mister O'Reilly use it for anything you and Henry need. If you need more, when I get back, I'll settle up with you."

Sam and Dorrie faced toward the sound of a carriage as it pulled up in front of the cabin.

Chapter Nine

Elmer slid from the back of his sweat lathered mule and grabbed the reins of the carriage. Inside sat an elderly, heavyset man, dressed in a white summer suit and next to him a petite young lady, a sunbonnet shadowing much of her face. From behind, another horse thundered toward the O'Reillys' cabin.

"Here comes Isaac, Emmett. He'll be here in a minute," said Elmer, as the man in the carriage slowly uncurled his frame, and placed his foot onto the step of the carriage. Elmer watched as his friend carefully guided his left leg through the various positions needed to step to solid ground. The young lady walked around from the other side and held her hand out to him. In her hand she held his elaborately carved walking cane.

The man found solid purchase and she handed the cane to him.

"Here, Uncle Em," whispered the young woman.

Limping, he walked over to the stranger before him. Extending his hand, he said, "Sir, my name is Emmett Detwyler. I'm sorry to hear of your troubles. This is Rose. She's as close as you're gonna' git to a doctor 'round these parts. But she's real good, had a fair amount of training, too. She'll be able to help your man."

He faced the young lady and added, "Go with Miss Dorrie and see what you can do."

With a polite, "Yes Sir," she left.

Sam was struck with the singular beauty of the woman. Dark shadows of trees and bright streaks of sunlight filtering through the pines in the yard, framed her beauty. So much was he affected by her, he found himself staring and realized she was uncomfortable with his attention.

Blushing, he said, "Thank you, Ma'am" and quietly stepped aside.

"Mister Detwyler," he added, "Sir, I'm indebted to you for your kindness. Please allow me to introduce myself. My name is Sam

Biggs. My hired man in there is Henry Atwell. We've run into a considerable amount of unpleasantness and I fear there have been bad
results from it."

Emmett and Sam shook hands.

"My pleasure, Sir. Begging your pardon, we'll discuss things
in a few minutes, but for now, let's go see how your friend is doing,"
said the recently arrived man.

The rider entered the O'Reilly's yard and Emmett said, "That
fellow is the O'Reillys' son, Isaac." He motioned the man over and
said, "Isaac, meet Mister Biggs."

Sam extended his hand to a man about his own age.

"Isaac's my right hand man. Been with me for years. I asked
him to come along, post haste, in the event that you and your people
shall need further assistance of any kind."

The small room quickly became crowded. Henry was sleeping, but not well. Spasms of pain surged through his damaged chest,
causing him to wince.

Rose stepped toward another room and motioned for Dorrie to
join her.

Returning to the room, Dorrie spread her arms, herding the
occupants toward the door. "Y'all need to git on outta' heah, let Miss
Rose start hep'n this man. I'll be out wid some coffee or sumt'n
stronger, if that's what y'all want, in a minute."

The men gathered on the porch while a brief but complete account of the two day's events was related by Sam. Aware of the late-
ness of the day, he spoke of his concern about the body in the woods.
He also told them of his intentions regarding Hesper Griffen.

Detwyler offered to send Isaac back to his plantation and send
some of the field hands to Sam's camp to recover the bodies and anything of value at the camp site.

"If you and your man need a place for tonight, I'll take care of
it. You're welcome to one of my bedrooms and your man there, can
stay with some of my Nigras."

"I'll see to that slaver, too," he said, pointing at Daryl Slater.
"Elmer told me you brought him with you. He's hurt pretty bad. Your
doing?"

"Yes Sir. Wanted to kill him, but didn't."

Emmett was impressed by the straight-talking stranger.

After Isaac asked for directions to the camp, his boss instructed him to put the body in one of the root cellars at his mansion

to slow the deterioration of the sun-heated body. Isaac mounted his horse to get the slaves headed toward the campsite.

"Isaac, grab those two dogs, too. Mister Biggs wants them," he shouted.

"Where you want me to put them?"

"Throw 'em in with that dead boy, they won't mind none. When Mister Biggs and I go up to the house, we'll throw that wounded fellow over there in another one of the root cellars. Tell one of the Nigras to clean everything out of two of 'em and throw some straw in 'em," added Mister Detwyler.

With the generous offer of the unexpected kindness, Sam guiltily acknowledged he had misled the O'Reillys earlier about his intentions and felt obligated to resolve the situation promptly. One lie needs another lie to cover it, he reminded himself. Dorrie came out as quickly as he hoped she would.

Sam stood and said, "I've something to say to the O'Reillys. This will eventually involve each of you, so I want to clear it up now. Miss Dorrie, Mister Elmer, I was not straightforward with the two of you earlier. I apologize for my actions and hope you will feel no ill toward me. I was not entirely truthful when I told you I was a businessman on my way to Fort Harwood. Although I soon hope to have a lot of business there, no mean and hurtful deceit was intended by my actions today." He nervously rolled the brim of his hat in his large hands.

"Please allow me to explain. I'm from Petersburg. My companions and myself are traveling through this area to gather information about that land across the road. I have recently acquired all of it from the previous owner, a Mister Harold Ledbetter."

Emmett Detwyler looked surprised. "That man's still alive? Damn, how old is he?"

"No Sir," responded Sam, "he died a short while ago. Heard consumption got him." Emmett Detwyler showed no further interest.

"He described the property to me in some detail, not much really, so I was—am, on a fact finding trip to verify the description he did provide to me. I was merely trying not to let my own personal plans be known at this time. Wrongfully, I felt by announcing who I am and my purpose for being here, people would view me as a meddling stranger and not talk freely with me."

And turning toward the O"Reillys, "I was wrong. Now, I realize that I should have informed you of who I am and what I am doing here. Miss O'Reilly, Dorrie, if I may, you and Elmer, Sir, have been the friendliest of all my future neighbors I have met.

"Mister Detwyler," he continued, "I have much enjoyed meeting you. Your kindnesses to me have equaled those shown me by the O'Reillys, and I am indebted to all of you. The last two days have been extreme. We have been called slave stealers and highwaymen. We have been stalked by two men with intentions of stealing my man Willie. One of my best friends lies in there suffering and he might die.

"I've had to kill one man in self-defense and now I have to confront a man who appears to be my neighbor and my biggest enemy, at that. And I've never even met the man.

"It is my desire for you to know, in spite of the last two days, I am going to work that land over there. Dorrie, you have been so kind to us. Please accept my apology." His feelings were true and heartfelt.

Dorrie flipped her hand, suggesting the matter should be forgotten. "When'd you say anything about going to Fort Harwood?"

Emmett stepped forward, looked at Sam and said, "Don't worry, friend. We've lived here all of our lives, practically. We've all had run-ins with certain people around here. Most are nice people— and some not so nice. I beg of you, don't act in haste. And likewise, please do not judge us by the actions of some of our neighbors; we're not all like Griffen. We shall not judge you by your wish to keep your matters private.

"You have stated that your intentions are to confront Griffen." Emmett's face tightened, his jaws clenched, and Sam saw a fleeting eye contact between Emmett, Dorrie and Elmer.

"May I offer advice and of course, further assistance if you require it? Griffen is not a man to be taken lightly. He is evil and will stop at nothing to further his depraved goals."

Dorrie and Elmer nodded in agreement.

"There are two types of neighbors you will find here, Sir. Those who live in fear of that man and those who are waiting for him to get his due. If you approach him in haste, I feel your plan will be dangerous. There's not much of any kind of law in these parts and Griffen thinks he's the law. I implore you to slow down. Take time to think. He's not likely to go anywhere. You are upset now and rightly so. Rest a bit and let's talk about it after you've rested."

Rose walked out onto the porch and motioned to Sam. "Mister Biggs, could you step inside, please? Your man would like to speak to you."

Sam jumped to his feet and stepped past Rose. His heart fluttered like a school boy's as he glanced at her. Lord, get a grip, he thought, his face flushed. He removed his hat and said, "Ma'am."

"How're you doing, Henry?"

Henry was awake and appeared in less pain. Grimacing, he said, "I'll be alright. I feel better but this fine lady has explained I mustn't expect to leave for a few days. Sir, I need my wife. She'll be worried sick if we don't get back soon."

Tiring from the medicines, Henry fell asleep after being told of the soon arrival of his wife and children.

Sam turned to leave the room and Rose touched his arm. Electricity shot through his very being. He turned to her, thinking, my whole life is a jumble, now this. I must be acting like a school boy to her.

"Miss Rose, I am indebted to you for caring for Henry. Please do everything you can to help him. He's been through a lot in the last few days. He looks so much better already. God Bless you, Ma'am."

Preparing to take his leave, the beautiful creature again lightly touched his arm.

"Begging your pardon, Sir, he needs some medicines from the doctor in Fort Harwood. He is in too much pain to rest like he needs to. Will you ask my Unc' . . . I mean Mister Detwyler to send one of his people to fetch some more Laudanum and other things to ease his pain?"

Sam tried to speak but unable, he merely nodded.

She continued, "He's got broken ribs and his collarbone's snapped in two. I fear his lung has a puncture through it. He's coughed up a small amount of blood. He can heal from that but he needs to rest and lie still so his body can fight off any fever that might get started. There wasn't much of that laudanum left from the big house and he's going to need more of it real soon. Sir, will you speak to Mister Detwyler about it?"

Sam looked into her eyes and saw her concern for the hurt man reflecting from them. Her care for the welfare of the hurt man impressed him greatly. Impulsively, he took her hands in his, but thinking it improper he quickly released them. "Miss Rose, thank you for everything you're doing and yes, I'll see to it right now."

He stepped onto the porch and told everyone of Henry's progress. He relayed to Mister Detwyler Rose's request for someone to be sent to Fort Harwood for the needed medicines.

The elderly man readily agreed, and scribbling a note, gave it to Elmer. He instructed Elmer to get his most trusted slave and send him to Fort Harwood.

"Mister Biggs, what else can I do for you?"

Sam knew what he planned to do was not without risk; in fact, he knew he was placing himself in a dangerous situation. By law, he had killed a man and seriously wounded another. Although in self defense, not everyone would be inclined to see it that way. He had to let the man standing before him help. He had never asked for help from another soul in his life, but he'd never been in a predicament like this before.

"Mister Detwyler, I'd like to accept your offer of assistance. A day of reckoning is set for Griffen. I am not asking for charity. I have enough money to see this through and I shall pay any expenses that may arise. I have funds in Petersburg which will be forwarded to me upon request."

"Let's talk, but first we need to get past this Mister Detwyler and Mister Biggs. I'm Emmett and I would be pleased for you to use that name from now on."

"Yes Sir. It'd be an honor. Call me Sam, please."

"Done," agreed Emmett.

"Mr. Det . . . Emmett, I'm taking that man's body and those two dead dogs to Griffen's mansion and I'm going to dump them on his porch. It's not going to be a pretty sight, but I've got to face him head-on. That son of a bitch's got to be brought to his knees, and I intend to do just that. When I do, it's going to get real tense, real quick.

"That piece of shit laying over there by the mules," referring to Daryl Slater, "is going to give an entirely different version of me killing his brother when he sees Griffen. Soon as I'm off of Griffen's property, he's going to start lying to save his own neck.

"Will you get one of your most trusted friends to help me record the truth before I leave? And, if you will, I would like for you to witness what that boy's going to say, too.

"Willie and I will be there in front of him, but neither of us will interrupt him or try to influence his version of things. It will be enough that he sees us."

Sam was becoming newly agitated. He felt a growing urgency. "Griffen may have a lot of influence with the local law and if he does, he's going to accuse me of murder, based on lies that trash is going to tell him—if he even lives. As quickly as the truth is recorded and witnessed by you, if you are willing to witness it, I'm going to need it delivered to the courthouse in Fort Harwood. Will you help me with this, also?"

Emmett answered Sam as he hoped he would. "Give me a minute to catch Elmer and the man he's sending into Fort Harwood. I know somebody I trust. I'll get him up here."

Emmett returned soon and again Sam asked for help.

"Emmett, I need a few men that are not the kind to look for a fight and not the kind to back down if they get into one—men you trust, and have them escort me and that trash up to Griffen's. It's a lot to be asked by a stranger, but I need the help.

"I can't take Willie with me, he can't handle anymore. I'm going to have my hands full with all those mules and the trash they'll be hauling. That Griffen fellow will drop me dead before I get to the end of the road in front of his house if I don't have some people with me."

"That he will, Sam," said Emmett.

"After I drop off that garbage, I would appreciate it if they would continue with me up to Westland Crossroads. All my people are waiting there at our camp and there's no way I can get them back here without some help." Sam's mind was churning, trying to foresee problems that may lie ahead.

"Please tell your friends they will be paid well for what I'm asking them to do. Let 'em know I'm going to need 'em for about two days. It might take three; depending if Griffen tries to get the law up in Weldon on me. I'll have to address it if he does."

Emmett assured Sam everything he needed would be ready for him by early morning of the next day. Willie could stay with Joe and May, two of his slaves who'd grown too old to work the fields anymore.

"Now Sam, you've been pretty adamant about what you are gonna' do. You need to listen to me now. You'd never know how crazy Hesper Griffen is by judging his plantation and his crops. He's been successful at it. I'll give him that. But don't let that fool you. He has spells, always had 'em, and he does strange things. Especially when he's drinking. Crazy things. Things regular folks wouldn't never do their whole lives."

Emmett tapped his head and said, "What I'm saying is, his is jumbled up."

"I'm not sure I follow you, Emmett'" replied Sam.

"It's hard to describe. It's like his brain don't work right. He doesn't have normal feelings like most folks. He could shoot a man dead while he's eating with him and if that fellow fell over dead with his head bleeding in his soup, Griffen would keep on eating. Of course, I never heard him doing no such thing, but it wouldn't surprise me one goddamn bit if he has. He ain't normal—he's evil. That's what I'm saying."

That shook Sam, but not his resolve.

"If you go up there and do what you say you're gonna' do, you best not take your eyes off him. Not for a second. He will kill you.

"Now, come on over to the house and let's get you and your boy cleaned up. We'll drop Willie off at Joe and May's. He'll like them. If you are up to it, let's load up that bastard over there," pointing at Daryl, "and throw him in the root cellar over at my place. Then, we'll get you calmed down with a bit of whiskey, so you can think things through a bit.

"One other thing, when my man gets back with those things Rose needs, make sure you get a bottle of that laudanum and keep it with you when you head to Griffen's place. If you're still dead set on going through with your plans, ten minutes or so before you head down that boulevard he's so proud of, give that three-fingered son of a bitch a good dose of that stuff. He won't run his mouth for a long time after you leave.

"For reasons I can't and will not go into, I'm gonna' distance myself from this affair—visibly, for sure. But I assure you, you'll have my full support as far as I can provide it. Let's just say for now, Hesper Griffen and I have a history. We've avoided each other for years. Old wars, old memories, you know. Me and him are getting up in years; too old to die at each other's hands."

"Emmett, your affairs are none of my business. If I am putting you in an uncomfortable position, please accept my apologies and I'll seek a new resolution."

"Oh no, Sam, don't worry about that. I despise that son of a bitch, but it's best if I watch from a distance for now. You didn't hear me say it, but I want to see that bastard dead and rotting."

Chapter Ten

Emmett's mansion impressed Sam. Clearly, his new friend was a man of considerable wealth, yet his home was not furnished in the manner of those individuals who needed to prove to others how successful they had become, with a showy display of custom-made this and French-imported that. But everything in the house had a practical purpose and was of the best quality money could buy.

He began to relax as the ugliness of the day faded. He was appreciative of the elderly man's candor and impressed he might be putting himself in harm's way for a stranger. He understood the dislike Emmett felt for Griffen; he wanted him dead and rotting, too.

He longed for a stiff drink, knowing the calming effect which would come with it. Emmett assured Sam everything they'd discussed was on schedule. Emmett pointed to a couch and told him to sit down and put his feet upon the footstool.

Knowing the sight he must be, muddied and bloodied, he resisted. He did not wish to soil the grand couch. Emmett insisted the exhausted and dirty man sit and more to ease Sam's concerns than his own, threw a blanket onto the couch.

"Well then, sit on that. What do you want to drink before we get you cleaned up?"

"Bourbon and branch water will be fine," the tired man answered.

Emmett laughed at the unusual phrase. He poured three fingers of bourbon into two glasses. Returning, he found Sam asleep and on the near side of snoring. Emmett sat the drink on a side table, stretched Sam into a prone position and covered him with a blanket.

Too quickly, Emmett shook him awake. Instantly, Sam's eyes flashed open, fearing new dangers at hand. He surveyed the room and saw the man Emmett had sent for to record Daryl Slater's statement, sitting across from him. Emmett apologized for awakening him, but reminded him there was much to do and not much time to do it, especially if Sam was still intent on his previously announced plans. Sam assured him he was.

The three—Sam, his host and the new man, Jonathan Ward, a friend of the court as Emmett called him, proceeded with the task at hand. Mister Ward's businesslike demeanor exuded a singular purpose about himself. He was a quiet man, only acknowledging Sam's presence and his wishes. They stopped by Joe's and May's shack. There Willie joined the group. Sam shook Joe's hand and thanked him and May for caring for Willie.

The root cellar door was unlocked and pulled open. Daryl Slater cowered in the cool dark room, whimpering in pain. The sweet smell of fresh straw hid the smell of the fear emanating from the sole occupant. Seething in anger, Sam grabbed at the man.

Concerned, Emmett caught Sam's shoulder. "Sam, hold on. You said you were not gonna' influence that boy's statement. Knotting his noggin might look a bit like force, don't you think? Come over here a minute, I need to speak to you."

He turned to Jonathan Ward. "May I have a moment with Mister Biggs, Sir?

"Sam. Calm down. Go slow. Ward's gonna' record everything said in there. He ain't got a horse in this race. He'll put it down the way he sees it, good or bad. That's his job. Now, if you can, get him aside and tell him why you want this all recorded.

"Stretch it out, so I can slip in there and dose old Three Finger with this here laudanum. Stuff's gonna' take a few minutes to kick in. That'll help the bastard's story come out right on the true side. When he's 'bout shit-faced, I'm gonna' slip thirty, forty dollars into his pocket. And we got to get some money into his brother's pockets, too.

"You ready?" Emmett asked. "We'll work it out every word he says will back Griffen into a corner. With your statement posted at the courthouse, and with Hesper being implicated in this whole mess, I reckon he'll think twice before he comes after you."

With each mention of Hesper's name, Emmett's agitation grew. His face hardened as he stabbed the air with his ever-present cane in the direction of Hesper Griffen's plantation. Sam saw the burn of hatred in his new friend's eyes.

"Like I said, I'll tell him to show me some identification. He'll say he can't get in his pockets with his hand all tore up like it is. So,

I'll look for it. When I find that money on him, I'll make a comment about it, loud enough for a few of the others and Mister Ward to hear. Oh, by the way, Isaac has already got all the men ready to leave at first light. They'll be here early.

"While you were sleeping, Elmer come over and said your hired man is sleeping like a baby, and for you not to worry. Said Rose doctored him up good with that medicine from Fort Harwood. Dorrie's helping Rose take care of him just like she would if he was her Isaac. I told him to tell Rose to stay there as long as he needs her. He'll be fine. Now let's get on with that boy's statement."

Digging into his pocket, Emmett said, "Take this bottle of laudanum, put it in your pocket. Be careful with it. Don't overuse it. If a little bit don't shut him up, give him about the same amount every two hours or so. Just don't kill him with it."

Jonathan Ward recorded the statement and everything Emmett said would happen, did happen. Ward took no notice of the glazed look in Daryl's eyes. Daryl agreed to each thing he was asked and did not appear impressed or puzzled about the pocket full of money, even though he'd never seen that much money in one place at the same time, and never in his own pockets.

Emmett and Sam walked back to the house and Ward left for the Fort Harwood courthouse.

Watching Emmett, Sam thought, That is one cagey old man. What in the world could have ever happened between him and that Griffen fellow for him to pitch in the way he has?

After all the pressing affairs had been seen to, Sam was finally able to take a much needed bath. A Negro house servant named Jonah escorted Sam to a bedroom. On the bed lay fresh, clean clothing. He reasoned they were Isaac's clothing; the two of them being about the same size. Feeling refreshed from the hot bath and the clean clothing, he descended the stairs and found Emmett pouring a fresh drink for him. The two discussed the events of the day and fleshed out Sam's plans. Emmett told Sam he'd already planted money on the dead man's body and cautioned Sam to never be alone with the dead man.

"No need for suspicions."

The whiskey he poured finished Sam's day. Drowsily, he climbed the stairs to his room.

He dreamed of dark-gray clouds of black-powder exploding from his revolver. He dreamed of snakes swimming toward him as he stood waist deep in water. He dreamed of the exotic Rose washing dirt and grime from his face and hands. He dreamed she looked at him and smiled.

The vision of Rose faded with knocking at the door.

A servant had been sent to fetch him for breakfast. He was greeted warmly by Emmett and encouraged to eat a hearty breakfast of eggs, bacon, sausage, and flapjacks—things he'd not enjoyed for a long time.

"You've got a long, hard day ahead of you, better eat up," Emmett said. Sam was surprisingly hungry and willingly did as he was told. They both used the time to learn more about each other.

Sam asked about Emmett's family. Was he married? Did he have children? And he asked other things. But he did not ask the one question he wanted to . . . Who was the exotic creature caring for Henry?

Emmett had never married. He hinted there had been a woman or two in his life, but added none of them took. "All that stuff was a long time ago." The past hung like a wet shirt on Sam's new friend.

Rested and refreshed, Sam offered more information about himself and his plans for the land across from the O'Reillys.

Seeing much of himself in Sam, Emmett was impressed with the younger man's determination to see the day's ugly business through.

He nodded towards Sam, and said to Isaac, as he came inside to tell Emmett everything was ready to go, "Griffen's got himself a problem, I think."

A friendship was developing between Sam and Emmett. The two walked out the back of the kitchen and several men mounted on horses, awaited them. Introduced to each man, Sam thanked them profusely.

Sam dreaded having to once more go over all the events which had brought them together, but they not only deserved to know what they were getting involved in, they should be aware of possible dangers which might lay ahead. He was careful not to mislead them with half-truths, nor did he purposefully omit anything that had happened.

He answered all their questions and to a man, not one reined his horse and left.

Emmett, addressing the men before him said, "I've known all of you most of your lives. Each and every one of you has had problems with Griffen. You all know I have. Today's problems have been a long time coming. It appears our new neighbor here, has walked right into the middle of it.

"Griffen's gone too far this time. He's had his people fighting us for years, and who knows what else he's been up to. Now he's hired slave chasers to steal for him. And it's cost a life. He's got to be stopped."

He continued, "This man come here wanting to start his life fresh with that land over yonder. Look what it's cost him, already." His cane began whipping the air, and that followed by tap, tap, tap, as he stabbed at the ground. Emmett's face flushed with anger. The men watched him intently.

"To a man, we've buried our heads in the sand like those big birds, the ones in Africa . . . or wherever the hell they come from, hoping he'd go away." His face grew redder, the jabbing intensified.

"We owe it to ourselves as much as to our new neighbor to see it all stops now. I felt it was my duty to tell Mister Biggs he should leave all this up to the law. He said he would, but you know what he asked me? Where are they? And I had to tell him there ain't no law 'round these parts what's gonna' stop Griffen.

"Problem is, Griffen is the law . . . thinks he is. We've got to stay within the boundaries of the law, the little there is, as best we can, but I reckon that's gonna' depend on Griffen."

He pointed at Sam. "That man's got to do what he's got to do. All I hope you men do, is see it doesn't get out of hand. I'll not go with you. Only more bad will come out of me going. My getting involved, at this point, would only give the old bastard more of a reason to start pushing back hard. Best I stay out of it for now.

"Follow his lead. He's a good man. Now, get back here safely and then we'll go on to the next step. This won't be over by a long shot but we can make it work."

Emmett sent two of the men to the root cellar to see if they could find identification on the body of Red Slater.

"Look through his clothes."

He knew he could trust the two; he'd known them all their lives and had no fear of them pocketing anything they might find. Exiting the cellar, they walked over to Emmett.

"Emmett, we didn't find no papers or nothing like that on him, but look at this roll of cash he had on him. What you want us to do with it?"

"Give me the money and I'll put it away in case we need to show it for proof. You men decide which one of you will record this and who will sign it as a witness. We can't take no chance of being accused of any wrongdoing."

Sam took his lead from Emmett and asked, "Where did you find that?"

"In his trousers," answered the man holding the cash. The others watched and listened intently. Witnesses, thought Sam.

Isaac harnessed all the pack mules and horses required and had seen to the unpleasant job of loading the bodies of one man and two dogs. A sweetish odor, similar to that of a vase of wet, decaying flowers, permeated the air and haste was made to cover them. In the coming day's heat the odor would become something different—something unbearable.

All the men were armed and most carried a pistol or a musket—most carried both. A rider was posted on each side of the wounded Daryl Slater.

Sam rode to the front next to Isaac and said, "Let's get it over with, friends."

In addition to the two of them, there were another six serving as escorts. The group had in tow two mules, the horses, and a wagon loaded with gear for the trip. On one of the mules, slouched the drugged and swaying Daryl Slater. The body of his brother, Red, with the two dead dogs securely tied to his body, lay across the second mule. The oddly shaped mound was covered with a heavy tarp. Little conversation was shared between the men; each keenly aware of the seriousness of the coming events and the treachery of Hesper Griffen.

Heading north, they rode toward Griffen's plantation. The ride would take nearly an hour to reach the entrance of his mansion. Sam wished to ride straight through, thereby shortening the men's involvement. He had little doubt any of them would abandon the group but there was no need to make the trip worse for them than it was. Bad was bad enough. Although he was destined to confront Hesper

Griffen, with or without their help, Sam was thankful to have them with him.

Whispered comments from the men suggested they knew the time to confront the arrogant tyrant had been avoided far too long.

Sam led the men through the intersection of the road fronting his land. There, he showed them the boundary spike of his land. He pointed toward the large oak trees, and explained the previous day's events had occurred in them.

Sam saw determination on the men's faces and he understood. If he had listened closely, he might have heard their collective thought; It's been a lot easier to deal with this mess until all this happened. But it's not going to go away, not now—that's for sure. Here it is, right at our front doors. Shit, let's get on with it.

They crossed the bridge spanning Swift Creek. Joe and May were fishing along the bank of the creek. Darting in and out of the woods was a towheaded white boy, sunburned to almost the same color of the Negro boy he was chasing. They were involved in a loud and boisterous game, in which shouting and rock throwing seemed to be the number one and number two rules.

The elderly black couple were heard from a distance, shouting, "Hush up, you'ns skeer'n dem fish away, an I done tole yo iffen' you ain't gonna' be quiet, I's gonna' sen' yo back to yo mammy in de fils. Now hush up."

The comment was directed at the Negro boy, who obeyed, and the towheaded youngster fell silent, also. The two boys stared intently at the riders. The old couple lay down their fishing poles, struggled up the side of the road and watched the men approaching.

Isaac spoke to the towheaded lad, "Son, get your things together and go on back to the house. You stay put until I get back.

"Sam, this is my son, Billie. Say hello to Mister Biggs, Son."

The boy spoke in a whisper, and Sam smiled and waved a "hello" to the boy.

Isaac continued, "Uncle Joe, you and May get on back to your cabin. Where's the boy who stayed with you last night?" referring to Willie.

"Suh, he done acks me if he could work in de fils with dem udders ah pull'n corn. Said he was a mite skeer'd 'round all de white folks he be's a see'n up at de big house. Dat's alright, ain't it Suh?"

Isaac answered, "Yes, Joe, that's fine. You and May get back to your cabin, too. You hear?"

Neither the slaves nor the boy answered, but hurriedly gathered their things, their eyes drawn to a worn boot with a blood stained heel sticking from under a dirty canvas.

***

Sam pointed to the rock overhang, informing his new friends that was where his first encounter with the Griffen peace-keepers had occurred.

"Those two fellows I mentioned before, Buck and LeRoy, you know them?" he asked Isaac.

"Know of 'em. Griffen keeps 'em on to run people off his land, and no telling for what else," Isaac responded.

Sam pulled ahead and faced the group. He motioned for them to gather around. Using the bend of the road to shelter them from view of anyone who might be posted as a lookout, he said to the men, "We're close to the lane down to Griffen's. Everybody got their guns ready?"

Looking back at Daryl, Sam said, "I'm going to give him another dose of this stuff. It won't help us none if he gets up there and starts yelling his head off. Griffen will know we're on our way, anyway, but there's no sense in letting this fool add to the commotion."

He slid off of his mare and walked back to the moaning man. The man's hand was swollen and badly infected. Sam could see he was in great pain but his hatred for the man was so complete, so intense, he was tempted to forego the laudanum and smack the festering hand with the butt of his revolver, but remembered the reason in keeping the man quiet.

Daryl stared at the dark glass bottle. He knew it contained the much wanted medicine he had been praying for.

"You want more of this, don't you?" asked Sam, his eyes burning through the man.

Daryl nodded in anticipation. His eyes were red, his face swollen from the recent fall from the mule in the O'Reilly' yard.

He gave the man the usual dosage of the laudanum and added to it for good measure. Daryl's moaning soon ceased.

He asked the men on each side of Daryl to keep the man between them. It would do little good for him to fall off his mule in front of Griffen. He wanted Griffen to see Daryl Slater dismount in another way.

The entry leading back to Griffen's mansion, each side lined with overhanging limbs of massive oaks, and the carefully maintained lawn, spoke of the wealth of the owner. Slaves held their scythes and rakes by their sides and watched the caravan pass.

"Isaac, let's get as close to the porch as we can. The rest of you men divide into two columns. Bring the mules with the bodies of the dogs and that dead man up close to the front, and Daryl close behind. I have no doubt Griffen will be on his porch and he'll have men with him."

At the end of the drive stood a huge mansion. Six large columns rose from the porch floor to the porch ceiling thirty feet above. Window shutters, painted glossy black, were opened, visually adding to the expanse of the house. The entry doors, too, were painted black. One of the doors opened and through it, stepped a man wearing a white summer suit. Sam immediately recognized the white mass of hair and the malevolent, cold eyes of the man before him. He had a head full of tussled white hair. He was followed by four men carrying muskets. Their dress and demeanor indicated they had been hastily summoned from the fields.

"Don't hide your guns. Keep them in your hands, ready and where they can see them. Hammer 'em back on full cock. You fellows on the right, keep your eyes on Griffen and the men on the right side of the porch. You on the left, watch out the same way. I'll do all the talking. Nothing good can result for any of you if he drags you into a war of words. It'll just give him ammunition to use against you in the future.

"I'm going to do something that may surprise you, but I got to do it. I got to make a point with that son of a bitch and there's no other way. Are you all ready? Anybody wants out, now's the time. Nobody'll think less of you. Anybody? Well, okay. Let's pay our respects to Hesper Griffen."

Might turn into a blood bath, Sam thought, and then he prayed, If it does, let it be theirs, not our's.

Nearing the end of the circled drive, Sam walked Queenie onto the well-manicured lawn; his horse trampling flowers and bushes. The flowers scattered, adding a mottled array of color to the green, freshly cut lawn.

Sam and his neighbors neared the mansion's steps. Griffen stepped forward and challenged the men on his lawn. Two men stepped to each side of Griffen—four men with guns—five counting the gun tucked into Griffen's belt. His eyes burned into Sam's.

"Just who the hell do you think you are, Mister? Tearing up my lawn? You got some kinda' problem?"

Griffen's gaze jumped from one man to the next. He locked them hard upon each. "Morning, Ben. What's this all about? John, what's going on here? You never come to visit and now when you do, you got guns in your hands." He smirked at the men.

"Hey, Isaac, where's that old crippled son of a bitch boss of yours? Why didn't he bring his shot-up old ass up here with you fellows?"

Seething, the men remained quiet.

"My name is Samuel Biggs. That's Mister Samuel Biggs, to you. But I suspect you already know who I am."

Hesper Griffen continued to stare at the man before him and did not answer. He folded his arms in defiance, and glared at Sam.

"Hesper, you've caused me considerable problems in the last couple of days," he said, his voice filled with sarcasm matching Griffen's, "and me a perfect stranger, at that."

Hesper Griffen raised his hand to stop Sam from continuing.

Sam thought, Here we go. Thinks he's in control. That shit's got to stop now.

He rose in his saddle, pointing his finger rigidly at the man, and shouted, "Shut up and listen, asshole."

It worked. Griffen, surprised by the ferociousness of Sam's order, half-stepped backwards. The sharp command startling Sam's friends, as well.

He continued, "Like I said before you rudely tried to interrupt me, you've caused me a lot of problems in the last few days. Now I've got some problems for you."

He motioned forward two men, and their mules, one loaded with the dead bodies and one with a swaying man with a dazed look upon his face. He chose his words carefully for his men to hear, but even more, they were chosen for the benefit of the four armed men on the porch. "Fellows, I've got bad feelings about that man on the porch, the one standing close to Griffen."

He stared hard, his eyes burning into each man beside Griffen.

"Watch his eyes. He's a mite jumpy and about ready to pull the trigger. If he looks you dead in the eyes, he's ready. Don't give him a chance. Blow his goddamn head off."

The air filled with tension.

The men with Griffen were nervous. Hired to oversee the slaves, the drunkards, white-trash and ne'r-do-wells, were out of their element, the roll of bodyguard foreign to them. Their eyes diverted, Sam could see they wanted off and away from the porch.

He waved the mule with the canvas covered bodies forward. He pulled a sharp long knife from his boot, and while cutting the rope holding the body of Red Slater and the two dogs, he glared at Griffen.

The canvas fell away. The body of the dead man tumbled to the ground. Griffen gasped in surprise when he saw two bloody and mangled dogs lying on top of the dead man. The grayish-blue tongue of one of the dogs lay like a rag upon the dead man's face. The other dog, missing half of its head, began to attract flies.

"There's one of your problems," Sam smirked.

A light breeze pushed the stink of the bodies toward the men on the porch, adding to their growing anxiety.

Sam's eyes remained locked onto Griffen while he motioned for the next mule. Carrying Daryl, the mule was brought forward. Sam kicked hard, shoving Daryl Slater off of the mule and onto the heap lying at his feet. Instinctively, Daryl's infected and swollen hand shot forward in an effort to slow his fall. His scream frightened the pack mules, the horses and the men.

A startled look flashed across the elderly man's face as he recognized Daryl. He turned to face Sam—his jaws clinched hard.

"I see you remember old Daryl, don't you? He's problem number two." said Sam, his voice tinged with sarcasm.

"Mister," said Griffen. "I don't know who the hell you are or what you're talking about, but you just made the biggest mistake of your life. You other men, I know each and every one of you. You know me. You dumb-ass hicks started growing your own balls, now that you got this man talking for you? Do you really think I'm gonna' put up with this shit?"

Griffen motioned for his rag tag bodyguards to step forward. Alarm flashed across his face—only one man still stood behind him—his gun aimed at the porch flooring.

Sam rode his mare closer to Griffen. Queenie strained to climb the steps at Griffen's feet. He held her back. This was the wrong time and the wrong place to lose his animal to a broken leg. With the hammer of his big revolver on full cock, he leaned forward and glared at the man.

"Your name has come up every time I've met a new person. Those folks said a lot of things about you but not once did anybody say anything nice. Look, your own men have decided they don't like you very much."

Griffen glared at Sam.

"You put those boys lying at your feet on me. Why? So you could add one more slave to your bunch? You got that one killed and Old Three Finger Daryl's likely to die—he's already got the black-rot spreading up his arm. My hired man is so beat up he might not make it, either. If you don't have religion, you ought to try to find some and start praying, 'cause if he dies, you die."

Hesper opened his mouth, ready to spew denials of the accusations hurled at him.

"I've already told you to shut up. You don't look like a stupid man, so don't start acting like one. Just listen. In case you think you are going to come after me or my friends, let me tell you a few things. That piece of shit that's still breathing told me you hired him and his brother to steal my Negro. Old Daryl there, has already given a statement saying you told the two of them to kill all of us if we got in their way." He paused, watching Griffen's reaction.

"You sure as hell got a mean streak in you, don't you?" asked Sam. "That asshole's statement is already recorded in Fort Harwood by Mister Jonathan Ward. You know who I'm talking about, don't you?"

He continued, "When I asked him where he got a pocket full of money," pointing at Daryl, "who do you think he said gave it to him? And we found about the same amount on his brother.

"You know what he told Mister Ward about the money? He said his brother told him you sure were one crazy old fart to give them all that money to kill me and my man, because they were going to get paid plenty for that runaway darky, and most likely they'd have to kill us to get him, anyways."

Again, Sam expected Griffen to deny everything but the seething man remained silent.

"Once that asshole started spilling his guts to Mister Ward, well . . . Hell, Hesper, I got tired of listening to him. He said they had been killing and stealing for you for years. Is that true, Hesper? I can call you Hesper, can't I, Hesper?"

Griffen's forehead was beaded with sweat; not the kind that

comes from fear, but the kind caused by rage. His eyes, filled with hate and menace, darted from Sam, to his neighbors, and to the bodies at his feet, and back at Sam.

Sam was madder than he'd ever been in his entire life and sarcasm peppered his comments.

"You got a lot of problems. You've set yourself up as the law of this whole area for a long time. I think it might be wise for you to change your attitude about things, somehow." He pointed south and added, "I'm ready to start working my land over there.

"Oh, yeah, asshole. One more problem. I'm your new neighbor. That's right, and I'm kind of upset right now. I'd appreciate it if you would start being more neighborly.

"You're probably trying to figure out how you're going to weasel out of this mess, ain't you? Personally, I don't see how you are going to cover it up, what with Daryl's statement over in the court-house waiting to be read. Why don't you just sit here on the porch and think things over for a while." He pulled the reins of his mare, preparing to leave.

"Tell you what. I'm heading into Weldon. You want me to send the Sheriff out here to see you? No? I kind of wish you would. What would you say to him? 'See here, Sheriff, them fellows are all lying about me. They just don't like me?' Or do you have him in your pockets already?

"There might be a chance Daryl's arm could rot off and him up and die on you before anybody gets out here—or you could shoot the worthless piece of shit. Then that'd just leave you, the way I see it. But you need to remember, these men heard what that asshole said about you, too. Witnesses, Hesper. Witnesses.

"Well, hell. There you go. Another problem, ain't it?" He laughed at the man, gently nudged at the reins of his mare and led his friends to the road.

***

A quiet, reserved group, each man deep in thought, each ashamed of their past inactions, rode away from the plantation and turned north. No one spoke. They were dealing with the turmoil in their minds, reflecting on their lives and how Griffen had been in-volved in them.

Sam knew they were feeling less than manly about their past inactions, but he was in no position to judge them.

When he was far enough away, his adrenaline fueled anger

eased. He motioned for the men to stop.

"I want you all to know that was one of the hardest things I've ever done in my whole life. I was damn near scared to death and I don't mind saying it." He chose his words carefully and for their benefit.

"I don't think I've ever been so angry in my whole life. I wanted to kill him. I suppose I would have had to confront that old bastard by myself if you fellows hadn't stood up to help me, but I'd probably be dead now. So thank you. I'm proud to know each of you and even happier you all are my neighbors and my friends."

The men had been badly shaken, but Sam had given them back some of their lost pride.

"That's one very unpleasant son of a bitch back there, ain't he?" All the men nodded their agreement.

"Well, he's through in these parts. Hung himself as far as I'm concerned. There's no way he can try to intimidate or retaliate against one of us without getting his neck tied to a tree. But don't forget, he made a bunch of threats against all of us, so keep your guards up.

"My job is partly finished. My people and their families are waiting for me up at Westland Crossroads. I would like to ask you to help me get them back to my land. I am already in your debt and I know it's a lot to ask.

"If you will do this for me, I promise you; when we get back, we will seek out the proper law from Fort Harwood, Weldon, wherever, Raleigh maybe, to help us set everything right. Once again, anybody who needs to leave for the sake of their families, please feel free to leave now.

"No matter what you decide, I'll be here for you."

He laid the reins against Queenie's neck and she stepped ahead. "Now, I've got to go and get my people."

Isaac rode alongside Sam, the rest falling in behind. Years of tension shed from the men—each feeling better about themselves after Sam's praise salved their long-bruised egos.

***

Passing through Westland Crossroads, the men rode toward the campsite and within a few minutes they arrived. Sam was concerned about Sara's reaction when she did not see Henry. As he suspected, she ran to him, peppering him with questions about her missing husband.

"Sara, Henry's alright. He's been hurt but he's being seen to right now by a nurse. He's got a broken rib and collarbone. He's going to be fine."

Digesting the news, Sara slowly calmed and soon said "He's been hurt bad before. He'll be alright though, for sure? Right, Mister Biggs?"

"He's going to be fine."

George approached to inquire of Willie, "Massa Sam, do Willie be alright?"

"Willie's with Henry. He's fine, George. He did a good job for us, too." And quietly he asked, "How's your back?"

The campers' watched the strangers accompanying their boss. They knew something momentous had occurred. He introduced the new men to his people, explaining there had been troubles in the past few days, and how they were helping them to their new home.

"That's the kind of neighbors we got. They have families just like you. They are farmers like us. They've done me a great service, therefore, they have done the same for you. Let's treat them with the respect they deserve."

He spoke of the beauty and bounty of their new home and of further kindnesses shown to himself, Henry and Willie.

Walter had killed a deer, obviously for sport, something Sam frowned upon, but he was glad this time. At least there would be ample food for everyone. George was assigned the duty to start breaking down the camp, leaving up only the bare essentials for one more night.

Sam made the rounds, greeting everyone warmly. Smiling, he asked, "Can you handle one more day?"

Chapter Eleven

An early start was required to arrive at their new home as early as possible. Concerns about the next leg of the trip were on the minds of everyone, but the presence of the new men held their worries at bay. Doubts about their fresh start in life, were now replaced with confidence as loaded wagons, filled with the previous night's camp lined up, and waited to leave.

Nearing the Westland Crossroads, the Dentons stood in front of their tavern. They and other strangers waved friendly greetings at the passing caravan. Rumors had spread about the new people and the reception they received did wonders to lighten their hearts.

Sam, being cautious, asked some of the men to follow behind. He was not concerned Hesper Griffen would retaliate against the group, but lately, it seemed the man could show up anywhere, anytime. It was best to be wary.

Nothing out of the ordinary occurred on the ride south. Slaves working in the fields stared at the travelers passing by—something they did not see every day.

He was anxious for his people to see the proof of what he'd told them lay ahead—and excited for them to see and touch something substantial, something tangible. He pointed at the iron rod that he had stomped back into the ground and watched their reactions, secretly enjoying their enthusiasm. The group having started the morning's ride apprehensively, had now become anxious to continue. This can be their promised land, too, he thought. And he sincerely hoped it would be just that.

Nearing the scene in which so much violence had occurred; he held the group back. He sent George and the other slaves into the camp to clean up the blood which had congealed and begun to smell. With the gruesome task accomplished, he led everyone forward. All eyes viewed the carnage; absorbing the proof that something dreadful—something violent had happened here.

They were instructed to set up one last camp and ordered to remain alert. With a sparkle in his eyes, Sam told them not to over-build the camp.

"We are going to start our real homes tomorrow. You wouldn't believe it by looking at it, but that creek's called Swift Creek, so I've decided I'm going to name our new home Swift Creek."

Sure that everyone was settled in, Sam left with the neighbors and took Sara along with them to see her husband.

He and his new neighbors gathered at the gate to the O'Reillys' cabin. Again, he thanked them and told them arrangements were being made to settle his obligations with them. To a man, they all declined his offer; such was their respect for the man so recently arrived in their midst. They departed for their own homes.

Sara and Isaac rode into the O'Reillys' yard. Dorrie and Elmer stepped aside; there would be plenty of time for introductions after Sara had visited with her husband. After checking on Henry, Sam told them he was riding with Isaac to pay his respects to Mister Detwyler. He was pleased Henry was doing well.

Henry asked about Willie.

"He'll be here in a bit. I'll bring him back with me. He's been asking about you. Wanted to know how his best friend is doing."

Henry smiled. "Yeah, I kinda' like that little drunk myself," and started laughing. His laughter was short-lived; another surge of pain shot through his chest. Sam and Isaac said their good-byes.

As Sam prepared to leave, Rose entered the room, carrying a tray of hot soup for Henry. Seeing Sam, she lowered her eyes as she said, "Mister Atwell's not feeling as well as he says he does, and that bottle of laudanum's not as full as it was when you left, either. I keep telling him he's got to lie still but that medicine makes him forget a lot of things and pain's one of them."

Sam's face flushed. He could barely speak in her presence, but managed a whispery "Thank you, Ma'am." Leaving, he collided with the opened door, and embarrassed, hurried from the room. Rose turned away, hiding a curious smile as it trickled across her face.

Why does he get so flustered around me? She felt her face flush and a rush of warmth flowing through her provided her with an answer.

Dorrie and Elmer agreed Sara should spend the night with her husband. Sara was his best medicine.

Sam and Isaac departed for the Detwyler plantation. They rode to the rear of the mansion and Willie burst through Joe and May's cabin door, pounding Sam with questions. Gathering his senses, he grabbed the mare's reins while Sam slid off.

Emmett invited both of the men into his parlor and poured each a drink. Settled into comfortable chairs, the two began the narrative of the last two day's events.

"Emmett, I'll tell you one thing. I agree with you, that Griffen's one crazy son of a bitch. That man's dangerous," offered Sam

Emmett nodded, his expression saying, "If you only knew." Once again, Sam noticed Emmett's jaw tightening and the far away look in his eyes.

"Sounds to me like you stuck that son of a bitch's head down a toilet hole and rubbed his face in his own shit. Take my advice and grow yourself extra eyes and ears," the elderly man said sternly

Darkness nearing, Sam rode back to camp, Willie following closely behind. He was impressed with the erected and orderly camp. Sam gathered the men hired for specific skills and knowledge, and informed them they were expected to attend a meeting first thing in the morning.

Their breakfasts finished, the men began arriving. Everyone fell silent as Sam entered the tent. "It's time to get down to business, folks," he announced.

George's job was to keep the coffee hot and coming. The men seemed happy and contented. A sense of community and purpose had begun to evolve.

"Fellows, I'm going to keep it short for now. We've spent a lot of time together already. Long trip, wasn't it? Are your families as happy to have it over with as you look like you are?"

Under their feet lay proof of what they had been told awaited them. Around them and to the far limits of their view, lay their future. Overnight, frowns on long, drawn faces had been replaced with smiles and shining eyes. Sam sat his coffee atop a barrel and held up his hand for silence.

"Listen. We know each other pretty well from our trip. We did good, didn't we?" Once again, the men congratulated one another; offering smiles and backslaps.

"What do you folks think of our new home?" They agreed it was everything he had described to them.

"Well, take a good look around this morning. Everything you see is going to start changing immediately.

"Matt? Where's Matt?" Matt Davis stood up from his chair in the back. Sam waved him forward. "James, you come up here, too." The two men stood next to him.

"You all know Matt is our farm overseer and James is in charge of our timber harvesting. We've got a lot of houses to build and we'll need a lot of lumber. While Henry is laid up, Matt has to do Henry's job, too, so you all pitch in and help him whenever you can.

"Yesterday afternoon, each of you had a chance to check out the site of our future home. I'm sure you have ideas about what you like. Come to me with them. If you're as tired of living in a tent and sleeping on the ground as I am, the good news is we're going to start building our houses today.

"Now listen. It's too early to start making solid decisions about what goes where and who's going to build over here or who's going to build over there. That'll come. For now, we need an orderly plan.

"I wish we'd bought a few more rolls of canvas while we were in Weldon but I reckon we'll need a bunch more stuff in the next few days. All of you, not just Matt and James, start putting lists together of things we need. We'll go over them and see what we can do to get them here.

"Next thing," Sam added, "right now, we're at our weakest moment. I have no doubt some of you, at some point considered turning back. Hell, another mile of that goddamn swamp and I might've gone with you. But we stuck it out. We made it. We're here.

"We're hardly no more than a group of people looking for something—knowing what we want but not quite knowing how to get it. But we're going to get there. Might not be pretty at first, but before you know it, you'll be proud of what we've done and who we've become."

Dismissed, they left to sharpen their axes. Joe Privet and Bob Dayton were told to remain behind.

"Joe, you and Bob are excluded from that portion of the work. I need the two of you to scout for good places for our crops and we need to start winter gardens, today if we can. I figure if we start right now, we can get in a few decent ones. We are going to need as much as you can grow.

"I'll tell George to get the Negroes together to start clearing the land you decide on. You two find it and George will get 'em going. Keep an eye on them, though. Bob, help Joe for now—there's not going to be very much blacksmithing work for now, but there'll be plenty of that on down the road."

His instructions were basic; he realized that—but he knew the men brought their own knowledge with them and as a group they could get things done. Things might start slowly, but they would work out after the men found their stride and what they were good at.

He told Joe to find Matt and send him over to him.

"Boss, you want me?" Matt asked.

"I'm going back to Weldon. Getting started is great but I've got to make sure money matters are all in place. You're in charge. Keep an eye on everything. I'll be back in two or three days. Then I've got to leave for Fort Harwood. I'll be in and out a lot. You know what we need. See to it that things get going."

"What about that Griffen fellow"? asked Matt. "You want some of the men to ride along with you?"

"No. There's no need for that. Griffen's plate's full of problems right now."

At first light, the new day already cool and becoming colder, Queenie was saddled and brought to Sam. Her breath billowing in the cool air, she snorted and pranced, awaiting her master. Grabbing the pommel, he put his foot into the stirrup and mounted, throwing his leg over the saddle.

At Westland Crossroads, he stopped for breakfast at the Denton's tavern. Pleased to see him, the owners warmly welcomed him. A whirlwind of violence had spun through the area a few days before and Sam needed to check the pulse of the folks closer to Griffen's place.

Webb had not overly bragged about his wife's cooking. She did serve a fine breakfast. Sam complimented Vi's cooking and told her Webb had bragged greatly about her. The woman looked at her husband with a knowing smile, which told Sam he'd improved the coming night for one Webb Denton.

He waited patiently for reactions to the past few days. He knew rumors had spread like a wild fire—no way they wouldn't. His opinion of these two people was greatly reinforced by their unwillingness to pry into his affairs. He thanked them for their warm welcome and told them he'd be back through in a couple of days.

Associates in Petersburg had recommended he hire a Mister Adair Graystone to handle his financial affairs. The man had been notified by post from his friends that Sam Biggs, a man of considerable wealth, was preparing to visit him and Adair anxiously awaited the arrival of his good fortune. Sam's camp-weary appearance and road-worn clothing would have spoken well of no man, but the letters praised Sam abundantly.

Entering Graystone's office, he presented his own letters of introduction and references. He found Graystone honest, forthcoming and knowledgeable about the needs required to run an enterprise the size Sam told him he had in mind.

Graystone told Sam of his own recent move to Weldon from the northern state of Vermont. "Beautiful state, Mister Biggs. I love that part of our country and I reckon it'll always be home to me, but the Missus requires a more agreeable climate. We've been here eight years, now."

Tired of the confines and harshness of camp life, he sought out the town's nicest hotel and treated himself to the best of the rooms available. The Weldon was the newest of the town's two hotels and it was lavishly furnished. He ordered a hot bath to be prepared for him. The suite he rented included a nicely appointed bedroom, and a sitting room suitable for entertaining friends or conducting business.

He glimpsed himself in the door-mounted mirror in his room, the first mirror of any size he had been near for a while. He was astonished by his appearance. Where did I get these worn-out rags? he asked, thinking of how he must look to others. Downstairs, he was directed to the haberdashery three doors down from the hotel.

A trip to the barber reversed the wild, unruly, tangle of hair he'd grown unaware of during the trip. Shaving off a three day's eruption of stubble and a trim of his thick, unruly mustache, restored the air of confidence common to all handsome and well-dressed men.

He had barely entered his room when he heard two men struggling up the stairs with the hotel's communal galvanized bathing tub. Many buckets of hot water later he soaked in the steaming tub.

Clean, refreshed and feeling handsome in his new clothing, his hair combed, his new boots shining, he ventured onto the street. He was anxious to see if the behemoth steam-powered sawmill was still being bragged about by the barker and there it sat—still drawing a crowd. The barker had not eased with his loud enthusiasm for "the wondrous machine that can do the work of twenty men."

Sam thought the man looked haggard—defeated.

He did not try to catch the barker's eyes. He knew the man was anxiously searching the constantly changing crowd and finally upon spying Sam, his eyes locked onto him.

"That's him. That's him. My meal ticket's walking straight at me," the salesman's eyes shouted. He abruptly broke conversation in mid-sentence, turned his back on those in front of him, and hurried to shake sweaty hands with Sam.

"Mister Biggs, it's good to see you," the little man said.

"Be at my suite at the Weldon, room three fourteen, three o'clock and let's talk," he said and with that, he left for his room. Might sound rude, barking orders like that, but I've got a lot to get done. The end results won't change much for the man.

At three o'clock a knock resounded at the door to Sam's ex-travagantly furnished room. On the table serving as a desk, sat bottles of various refreshments, compliments of the house, and a tin bucket filled with ice from the cellar, deep within the bowels of the hotel.

"Please forgive me, but I've forgotten your name, Sir. Would you mind telling me again?"

Sam had not forgotten the man's name, but he knew such a statement would jolt the barker's confidence of a "for-sure" sale, thereby giving himself room to negotiate. Always good at reading people, Sam could see the man thinking . . . Does that mean he might've forgotten the prices we talked about?

"Oh, that's quite alright Mister Biggs, you're a busy man. I understand." The first beads of a nervous sweat appeared along his hairline. "No problem. I'm not too good at names myself. It's Ralph, Ralph Chamberlain, of the Boston Chamberlains" he said—hoping to see name recognition, but he saw none, and clumsily extended his hand a second time.

Taking the man's jacket, Sam directed him to the table and asked if he would like a drink. A moderately strong whiskey on ice was handed to the barker.

"Now, this is something you don't see around here every-day—ice, except in winter and then too damn much of it. Nothing like the winters back in Massachusetts, though. Thank you, Mister Biggs."

Sam engaged the man in small talk, inquiring about his family, the Boston Chamberlains. "Are you married? Do you have children? How old are they?"

Idle talk nicked at the man's nerves, wearing them thin. Frayed and jangled, he anxiously waited to find out if his prayers were about to be answered.

"I see you didn't sell your sawmill. You said you had customers waiting in line to take it off your hands."

"Well, you know how it is, Mister Biggs. When you get down to it, most of the time when a man says he'll get back to you, it's his way of saying good-bye."

Just when he thought Ralph near collapse from worry and doubt, Sam said, "Well, Ralph, I came back to see you. Let's talk about that thing down there."

Desperate to be rid of the steam-powered machine sitting in the street, Ralph nearly spilled his drink when he shot his hand into his vest to retrieve an envelope filled with figures.

"Sir, ah, Mister Biggs, I just happen to have those figures you and I talked about some days back. Would you like to go over them again?" Sam nodded and Ralph started repeating the figures hard and fast. He had not changed the figures so Sam decided he would no longer torture the man with his act of indecisiveness.

"Mister Chamberlain, are those all the expenses I am to expect? No hidden charges to spring on me when you deliver it to my place, right?"

"Well, there's delivery charges."

"What delivery charges?" asked Sam—delivery charges had never been discussed.

Ralph's face paled. "Oh, no Sir. You got to pay a delivery charge. Everybody knows that." Sam had purposefully not tried to get the man to back off the selling price. He was already prepared to get the extremely expensive machine, the same one with an extremely large commission built in, delivered for free.

"Well then, tell me, Mister Chamberlain," his voice edgy, "why didn't I know about a delivery charge?"

Ralph Chamberlain slumped, his sale disappearing.

Sam rose, walked to the door, and placed his hand on the knob. "Too bad. We were so close."

Chamberlain placed his drink upon the table; his hand shaking badly. Crestfallen, he stood to leave.

"Think it over, Ralph. If there's some way to do business together, we might give it another try. But I believe if I were you, I'd always discuss all the costs up front. Little things can wreck a deal."

Sam headed downstairs for a much anticipated steak dinner, his appetite aggressive after weeks of bean soup and salt-cured pork.

Chapter Twelve

The next morning, saddled and groomed, Queenie was brought to Sam. He climbed into the saddle and the mare trotted toward the piers. Upon arriving, Sam entered the freight office to discuss business arrangements with the owner, Mister Brantley. Assured his business would be welcomed and rates acceptable to both parties, Sam rose, shook the man's hand and returned to the hotel.

He knew that Chamberlain was sick with worry, desperate to be rid of the machine and that he would return to the hotel with a contract and it would be according to Sam's terms.

At two o'clock, Ralph Chamberlain, contract in hand, knocked on Sam's door.

His business nearly completed, he stopped at Adair Graystone's office near the Hotel. He needed Graystone to find and hire workmen. He needed men like those who came with him from Petersburg. Those were the type of men it would take to build his mansion. And who would know of such men better than Adair?

He needed slaves, too. A lot of slaves.

A strange institution—slavery, he thought, but it had existed for hundreds of years. Sam felt a tinge of wrongness, but he put it aside; he wasn't the one who had started it. History was full of slaves—even the Good Book approved of slavery. He'd never read about such an approval, and couldn't recall a particular scripture about it, but why would preachers lie about something like that? He certainly needed more than the few he had—so what's a man to do?

Even with the country's highest authority, the government in Washington, providing support for owning slaves, conversations regarding slavery needed to be dealt with carefully. Times were changing. The very word "slave" could start an argument in some parts of the country, but it seemed to Sam the quarrels were always the loudest up North.

Comments such as, "If them crazy nigger lovers up there in New York State really feel that way, why don't they come on down here and buy 'em all from us? Just hand all us sinners the money we got tied up in 'em, and take 'em back with them. Let 'em go free. That always stops 'em cold, don't it?"—the rebuttal typical of slave-owners. Besides, the Africans were everywhere. One saw nearly as many Negroes on the streets of Weldon as they did white folk. Yet, there was no denying it; attitudes regarding slavery had changed considerably in the last few years. Hate it or accept it—it exists and it always will exist, thought Sam.

"Find me slaves," Sam said to Adair.

Adair Graystone had his own opinions of slavery, but he did not dare voice his differing views of slavery to Sam. Found money can make a man bite down on his tongue and ignore his principles, or kiss his commission good-bye.

***

Ample daylight remained for Sam to ride over to the O'Reillys' cabin, his mind filled with thoughts of Rose. What is it about her that vexes me so? He visualized her exotic dark skin, tanned just dark enough to produce a clean healthy look. He could see her hair, the color of walnuts; dark brown, almost black, hanging below her shoulders and her heart shaped face, her full lips. And, her sultry brown eyes.

He tied the mare to the porch railing, but thinking better of it, untied it and wrapped the reins around a nearby tree. He had caused enough problems for these good people and did not want Queenie to be blamed for pulling their shack down. Dorrie walked out to greet him.

"Mister Sam, you're back. Elmer, git your old butt on out here; say Hey to Mister Biggs."

Sam reached into his jacket and handed a string-tie bag of Old Virginia Cherry Flavored Pipe Tobacco to Dorrie.

"I know how much you like your smoking tobacco, Miss Dorrie. Truth be known, I like the way it smells. Light some up so we both can enjoy it."

Her eyes glowed with delight. As Elmer greeted him, Sam retrieved a brick of rum-flavored chewing tobacco and held it out to him.

"Thought you might enjoy a good plug or two of tobacco.

Here, give this a try," he said, diverting his eyes from the brown stains in Elmer's white beard.

"Oh, y'all didn't have to do that," answered the elderly man, "but thank you kindly. Now, git on in heah and see fer yo'self how good your man's comin' long."

Henry was dozing when the three walked in. Sara sat darning her husband's torn shirt, trousers and socks.

"How's Henry doing?" Sam asked.

"Old fool's just about wore me out. He keeps on talking about gitt'n back to the camp. He ain't no more ready than a broke leg milk cow. Been coughing up blood, too. Not much, though, and that's about stopped again. You'll tell 'em to stay put, won't you, Mister Biggs?"

"I know he's not ready. Maybe he should rest a few more days, but that's up to the O'Reillys—it's their place. Don't wake him up. I wanted to see how you were doing, too." He snuck furtive glances through the doorways and nonchalantly asked, "Where's Miss Rose? She here?"

Dorrie overheard him and came into the room. "Miss Rose dun left me in charge of Mister Henry. She was 'bout all tarred out. Said she be back in a coupla' days. Mr. Henry'll be fine as long as he stays in bed. I 'spect he'll be sick of us and be a want'n to git on home with his wife, anyway."

Searching for a way to beg his leave, he said, "Well, I've got to get on down to Fort Harwood. I'll stop by Emmett's. See how he's doing. Sara, you keep him still. Tell him I said a few more days will be fine, if it's alright with Dorrie and Elmer. We got started on some cabins and Matt was told to make sure your's and Henry's was the first one done. All the folks at the camp want you and him back. George has about got everybody run off with his cooking."

Sara smiled, her face glowing from the praise.

He left for the Detwyler's mansion, hoping to see Rose. But Isaac met him at the entry to the long, oak shaded drive. He informed Sam that Emmett and Rose had gone into Fort Harwood to take care of the coming winter's food supplies and arrange for the delivery of the massive amounts of materials it would require to run the plantation; food, clothing, shoes, medicines of all kinds, and the myriads of farm related items. After telling Sam he, too, was on his way with the farm wagon, Sam asked if he could tie Queenie's reins to the wagon and ride on the spring equipped wagon seat with him.

"I sure would consider it a kindness."

"Getting saddle sores on your ass, huh?" grinned Isaac.

Sam blushed, admitting his rear felt none too comfortable and figured the cushion on the bench seat would feel like a baby's blanket to his sore bottom. "Got a blister where it's not polite to talk about," he answered.

Blistered butt and all, Sam looked forward to the ride to Fort Harwood and the blanket covered bench proved to be a marked improvement over the shifting and chafing saddle.

The two friends rode toward town. Sam peppered Isaac with questions about Fort Harwood, the seat of Carlton County. Most of the conversation was nothing more than small talk—talk in the way of things he really wanted to ask.

He told Isaac of his recent purchase of the steam-powered sawmill.

Isaac was enthralled at the possibilities of such a machine. He could not picture such a machine, but was impressed with the prospect of having saw cut lumber in every imagined size and length.

"You got any idea how much lumber is up there on that place of yours? You figured out how much lumber it's gonna' take just to build your home, the outbuildings, and the quarters for the slaves? Reckon you'll be getting a bunch more Nigras, too. Won't you?"

"Adair, you know that Graystone fellow up in Weldon? He's working on finding some for me."

"He told you that?" asked Isaac, his face incredulous.

"Yeah. This morning, when I stopped by his office. Why?" asked Sam.

"Nothing. It's just sometimes people'll say what they know you want to hear."

"Isaac, what are you talking about? Just say it."

"Well, Sam. Him and Emmett went at it about owning slaves and Adair ain't none too well thought of in Weldon for his stand on slavery. I don't rightly think he'll look real hard for any slaves for you." He saw irritation in Sam's eyes.

"Now Sam, I ain't saying he's putting you on or nothing, but your best bet's gonna' be at the slave auction in Fredericksburg. That's where Emmett ended up having to get the rest of the ones we needed."

Why, that lying bastard. What else do I need to know about dear friend Adair? Sam asked himself.

But he couldn't wait for Graystone or even Fredericksburg. For now, he needed manpower and he had an idea. He'd deal with Graystone when the opportunity arose.

"Isaac, what do you and Emmett do with your Negroes when the harvest is done?"

"They're always kept busy even if it's work we got to think up. Emmett sees to that. Keeps 'em digging drainage ditches, clearing fields for more crops, mucking the barns. You name it, Emmett put's 'em at it. He says there ain't nothing as worthless as a winter-fat darky, that's what Emmett calls 'em."

Sam laughed at the image.

"Let me run something by you. Maybe you can tell me what you think. If Emmett would hire out his slaves or those he could spare, I'm sure he and I could reach a fair deal. I would benefit by having help to start cutting and sawing the trees. Emmett could cut back on his winter expenses. And none of 'em are going be winter-fat Negroes, either. Everybody wins, you see? What do you think, Isaac, should I approach him about this?"

Isaac didn't answer. He couldn't speak for his boss.

Embarrassed, Sam apologized for unknowingly compromising Isaac. "I'm not trying to get you in the middle of nothing. All I want is your opinion. I reckon your opinion means more to me than most folk's."

The praise from Sam loosened Isaac's tongue. "Well, I think you would be crazy if you don't approach Emmett with the idea. It sounds like a good deal to me. Some winters they do get a bit fat."

Sam had other questions—questions about Rose. He tried to sound casual, indifferent. "Did you say Miss Rose was in town with Emmett?"

"You're a mite taken with that little lady, ain't you?" grinned Isaac.

"Well, to tell you the truth, she sure is something, ain't she? I can't keep my mind off of her. Who is she? Where'd she come from? Tell me about her, okay?"

Isaac thought of the irony—his mother'd told him Rose had watched the road for Sam as much as she'd watched over Henry.

"Well, Sam, about all I know is one day she ain't here and the next day she is." Sam waited for him to continue but Isaac remained mute, he had said all he was going to say on the subject.

"Ma sent Pa over to bring me some of that tobacco you gave

her. She sure was happy with what you gave her and Pa. It's good stuff. Wanna try it?"

"No. Go ahead. Light up. It smells good."

"Pa offered me some of that chewing tobacco, but I can't jaw that stuff," he volunteered.

Ahead, the dome of the new courthouse rose high, gleaming in the sunlight. "Looks like a full moon, the way the sun hits it, don't it?" asked Sam.

Isaac reined the team up and Sam climbed from the wagon. He knocked the dust off his jacket and trousers, hoping to at least make himself presentable. It helped, but not much. He unhitched his horse from the wagon and re-tied it to the iron hitching rail in front of the courthouse. He thanked his friend for the ride and Isaac left on errands.

Sam had two reasons to stop by the courthouse. One was to file title to his new home, Swift Creek Plantation. That was a simple matter; all of the former records of ownership held by the court matched the information Sam provided and he had verification to prove his claim and his identity. Sam's second reason was to visit the Sheriff of Fort Harwood, Sheriff Bucyrus Vance.

Sheriff Vance was as disgruntled with his given name as Sam was with Elwyn. "Call me Buck. No. Really, I insist," he said, greeting Sam.

The obligatory summary of Sam's recent move to the Ringwood area was relayed to the Sheriff, and with the Sheriff's obligatory welcoming of the stranger finished, they approached the reason for the impromptu meeting.

"I thought it would be wise to stop in and talk to you about some recent unpleasantness up my way."

"Well, I kinda' been expecting you. Ward told me about his trip to Emmett's. A bit of excitement, I heard. If it's any consolation to you, Griffen's been a pain in my ass for as long as I've been Sheriffing these here parts, and that's nigh on fifteen years or so."

Sam grew anxious to head into the town proper, but soon found Sheriff Buck enjoyed company.

"All I'm saying is, all the trouble we ever have around these parts, always seems to somehow be related to that old fart or one of his lowlife kin what lives south of town here. And he has practically set up his own empire up yonder where you live.

"Him and Emmett. Now, there's a pair. Ain't no love lost 'tween those two, I'll tell you that. Don't know what it's all about. Don't much give a shit, neither, long as them two stay clear of one another. But you live in a town like this as long as I have, and toting a badge all that time, you hear stuff. If Griffen's half as mean and done half the things people say he's done, ain't no doubt about it, he's the devil's own." He stood and grabbed the coffee pot and two chipped-enamel tin cups.

"Up to now, that old devil's always been careful not to be around the trouble he stirs up. Pays others to do his dirty work. From what John told me, that old fool's done and got his pecker caught in the proverbial wringer this time. Did you really face him down at his own place like Emmett tole me you did? Oh yeah, Emmett stopped by with Miss Rose for a spell this morning, too. I don't know much about you, but it sounds like you've made yourself some good friends around these parts. But there ain't no doubt about it, you made one hell of a big enemy while you were at it. Tell me your version of what happened."

Before he could oblige the sheriff, Buck started again.

"Kinda' spotty, things what you hear. Women, what else? Well, anyway, I'll not tell any tales out of school. I suspect Emmett'll some day bring it up; maybe, maybe not. You want some coffee?"

"I sure do. I got a ton of dust to wash down my throat and I'm so dry I can't hardly talk," Sam said, realizing he might not have to.

"What's your version of what happened up your way?"

Sam relayed everything he felt was important to the man, including how he and Emmett had agreed to send for Jonathan Ward.

"That's been a long time a coming. One thing I'm sure of, that man ain't gonna' come in here complaining about you. Not since you out-smarted that old bastard; getting everything on record the way you did. Damn. Sam, that was pure genius. But it's gonna' gnaw on him."

Buck started laughing as if he'd been waiting for years to get something on Hesper Griffen.

"Rumor around these parts is that when Griffen was in his early twenties, he got hauled down to Raleigh to one of those doctoring places what helps people with sick heads—you know, messed up thinkers. There'd been a heap of trouble with him running wild all over that land up yonder and if memory serves me right, something about him killing a little darky girl. Folk said his mama and daddy were more scared of him than they were of Satan himself. They're gone on now. His father died a spell back and his ma didn't last long after that. Don't hear nothing about it no more. Time I met him; I sure did think they ought to have kept him locked up. Scary man, that Griffen is. He's crazy as hell."

"How's about joining me for lunch? You pick the place," Sam said.

Buck pulled out his watch. "I was about to meet Emmett and Miss Rose at "Momma's Place." That's a little eating place in town, the only one, I might add, and she puts on a pretty good spread. Why don't you go with me?"

Buck found he enjoyed the company of the man, although he thought Sam was not one to say much.

"Food just like your mama used to cook."

That didn't sound appealing and his stomach roiled, but at last he knew where Rose was.

Emmett's carriage was tied to the hitching rail. Sam's heart pounded as he walked through the door.

Emmett stood, motioning for Buck and Sam to join them. Rose could hardly make eye contact with either of the two men as they sat across from her and Emmett. Emmett and Buck joined in conversation, a conversation Sam only heard bits and pieces of. He was distracted by other more interesting things and was trying not to blush—the price he paid to be near her.

Even though at times he appeared brazen and hard, he felt his heart roll in his chest when he sneaked a peek at the beautiful woman sitting across from him. He felt dizzy—she was looking at him.

Sam, forced to join in conversation with Emmett and Buck, found it hard to pay attention to what they were saying. The harder he tried, the more self-conscious he became. The lunch lasted almost an hour; Sam felt it had taken the better part of three days.

"Buck, if you don't mind, I would like to stop by your office, say three or four o'clock, to discuss one other thing before we head back home. I have a few matters to take care of before I leave and might as well see to those while I'm up here in town," said Emmett.

Buck and Emmett walked toward the door.

"Sam. Would you mind sitting with Rose for a bit? You two order some pie. Put it on my bill." Both Sam and Rose declined more of Momma's food. It was not only excellent, but plentiful.

Emmett suggested, "Then, Rose, why don't you and Sam go over to the dry goods store. Pick out some things you need. You don't mind, do you, Sam?"

Sam's heart missed a beat. My God, what am I going to talk with her about? I can't hardly say my own name in front of her. Heart's racing like a quarter horse. Can she see the sweat in my hair line? Oh man . . . Oh man.

He struggled to his feet, his legs about to fold.

"If you would allow me to escort you, Miss Rose, I would be honored." Realizing he could say a complete sentence to the young lady without passing out, his confidence was bolstered.

They walked toward the dry goods store.

Emmett watched the two stroll away, and said to Sheriff Vance. "Buck, I'll be damned. Watching that man was agonizing, weren't it?"

"He's a mess, ain't he?" Buck started laughing.

Realizing this to be the best opportunity he could hope for, Sam politely asked Rose if she would mind calling him Sam.

"I will, Sir, if you'll call me Rose."

Sam stuck his hand out. "Okay, that's a deal, Miss Rose. I, er, ah, ah, mean, Rose." Embarrassed, he thought, Oh my God, that's a deal? And What the hell's with the handshake?

Looking for common ground about which to talk, he asked Rose about Henry's recovery. That proved to be the key to opening the doors between them. She told Sam Henry was doing fine and had improved greatly as soon as Sara arrived.

"Miss Atwell's such a nice person. Henry acts like she hung the moon for him. It makes me feel good to see two people as much in love as those two. Henry can probably go back to your camp in three, four days. I think he'll be fine. But he can't do any hard work, though. Not just yet. I do believe Sara would make you fire him and hire her in his place before she'd let him hurt himself any more. He's going to need light work for at least another month. He sure speaks highly of you, Sam."

The two browsed through the dry goods store. Rose pointed at items she knew were needed on the plantation and the clerk pulled and tallied them. The stockpile grew as she gathered things only a woman knew would be needed.

Emmett had placed a massive order in advance of his trip into

Fort Harwood. All the goods were ready and waiting for Isaac to arrive with the wagon. Sam was impressed with the huge amounts of goods stocked in the mercantile. While Rose browsed about the store, he introduced himself to the owner and established an account similar to one he'd started in Weldon.

Rose asked if he would escort her to Charlotte's Women's Apparel Shop a few doors down. A loose board on the sidewalk caught Rose's shoe. She stumbled and Sam grabbed her by the arm, guiding her back to safety and failing to release her arm; she made no effort to have him do so.

She was welcomed into the store by the proprietor, an old friend, and Rose and the owner left to browse at the latest fashions. Feeling out of place, Sam sat rolling the brim of his hat. Rose asked to look at a stylish hat he also thought particularly attractive. Blue, he liked blue. Rose looked at it and put it down, only to return in a few minutes to inspect it again.

He laughed at her third inspection. "Didn't change much, did it? You really like it, don't you?"

"It is pretty, but I don't think I should buy it. I already have too many hats I never wear." Eventually Rose, lightly touching Sam's elbow, suggested they go back to the dry goods store and wait for Emmett and Isaac.

Isaac rounded the corner with the wagon and skillfully backed it up to the dock.

"You think Emmett's got enough provisions this time, Isaac?" Rose laughed, looking at the overloaded wagon.

"I reckon he has, but if he ain't, he'll just send me back, Miss Rose."

Emmett rode up in his carriage. He waved to everybody and entered the store to settle his account with the owner. Exiting the store and seeing Isaac, he gave him an additional list of errands to take care of in Fort Harwood before he headed home. Emmett walked over to Sam and thanked him for keeping company with Rose.

"My pleasure."

"Sam," said Emmett, "I'd like to speak to you for a minute, if you have time."

"Of course. What is it, Emmett?"

"I think it would be good if you would join me at Buck's. We need to discuss the plans for our meeting with the rest of our neighbors regarding our problem up to the north."

Sam assured him he would be there.

Emmett assisted Rose into his carriage.

One last person remained to be visited before his three-thirty meeting with Emmett and Buck. Sam was met by the same clerk as he entered Charlotte's Women's Apparel shop.

"Well, hello again, Mister Biggs, how may I help you?"

He pointed at the blue sun hat. "Well, Ma'am. Miss Rose sure took a liking to that hat. I'd like to buy it for her."

The lady removed the hat and wrapped it in soft linen paper and asked Sam if he would like the box gift wrapped. He thought that a novel idea and chose a pale blue ribbon.

"Ma'am, I would like to put a note in the box. Do you have any of that fancy writing paper like folks use at Christmas? You know—something soft and pretty?"

"How's this, Mister Biggs?"

She busied herself with the wrapping. I'd give him this hat for free if he would let me read that note, she thought, handing him the beautifully wrapped box.

He looked at the box and said, "No Ma'am, this won't do. Do you have a tow sack that I could put it in? I got a long ride ahead of me and that road's a mite dusty."

***

Three-thirty. Emmett and Rose waited for Sam on the veranda of the courthouse.

"Rose dear, Sam and I are gonna' meet with Buck. Man talk. It might bore you. Do you want to go over to the library and read for a while? We won't be long. I'll come and get you when we're done."

He and Sam entered Buck's office. They needed to explain their reason for the afternoon's appointment—the meeting at Emmett's, to discuss plans for the need of law in the northern part of the county.

The first words out of Emmett's mouth set the tone for the next half hour.

"What the hell's going on, Buck? The county treats us like we're throwaway bastard children. They take our tax money and give us promises as receipts."

Buck remained quiet. He'd had the same conversation with Emmett many times before—too many to count. "Emmett, you and I have had this same conversation at least a dozen times. It's out of my hands. You know that."

"Buck, we got problems." said Emmett. "Somebody's gonna' get kilt, if something ain't done about it. Talk to them again. Tell 'em they got three choices. They can step up like men and do the right thing and send your people up there, or shit their pants when Raleigh comes over here wanting to know why we've applied for a separate county—one just for us—or watch us take the law into our own hands. You know what that's called, right? Vigilantes."

He stared, his eyes cold and hard, into Buck's. He wanted the point driven home. "I'm telling you, Buck, it's gonna' be one of the three."

"Emmett, what do you expect outta' me? Those goddamn crooks don't give a shit about you and your neighbors. Things ain't going to change. But, if you get the county, I'll be your sheriff."

"Next month, we're going to have a meeting up our way. I think it'd help if you come. At least show us your support, Buck," suggested Emmett.

Buck watched the men's faces—expecting anger, but saw only resignation.

"We'd be obliged if you'd do that,"

Emmett suggested the county elected leaders be asked to come to the meeting, also. Perhaps between Buck, the officials, and the northern citizenry of Carlton County a solution could be reached.

"If they come—fine. If they don't—that's alright, too," said Emmett. "But Buck, I'll tell you one thing for sure. Griffen has finally gone totally fucking crazy and he's gonna' go after anybody he thinks is his enemy."

Buck leaned forward, his forearms on the table, his attention focused on Emmett.

"And there-in lies the problem. He's got to where he thinks everybody up there is his enemy and he ain't far wrong, either. But he's so far gone he don't know it's all his own doing." He paused, his next statement needed to be worded carefully.

"As much as I respect you, Buck, and your office, don't be surprised all to hell and back when folks up there won't leave their houses without their guns loaded, cocked and spoiling for a fight. That's what things are coming to."

Buck turned to Sam. "Are you in agreement with Emmett?"

"Yes, Buck, I am. Totally. When I think back to what's happened to me and my people in just the last few weeks alone, I can't understand why that bastard's still alive. Somebody shoulda' killed him a long time ago. That's what you do to a mad dog, right? Put it down. It's hard for me to imagine what all those folks up there have been putting up with for years." He paused, careful to not make veiled threats.

"It upsets me, and I'm the newcomer. There was not one law person for me to turn to for help. Would you have helped, Buck? I had to go to Emmett and my neighbors and drag them into my troubles. Seems to me they deserve more law up that way than they got, which is none." He stood as if to leave.

Turning to face the Sheriff, he asked, "Did you ever hear if you don't try to solve the problem, you become the problem?"

"Well, you didn't come to me did you, Mr. Biggs?" said Sheriff Vance, angry that he'd been challenged. "And who the hell do you think you are, talking to me like that?"

Sam ignored the comment and continued, "It bothers me to no end that I've had to kill a man and then had to cover my own ass in order not to be charged with murder. Yeah, Buck, I'm kinda' mad right now, but I'm not stupid enough to stand here and say something out of line."

Cautiously, he added, "I want it on record that I've got a bad feeling about that man. If he comes after me and mine . . . and that includes my neighbors, I'll do whatever it takes to stop him. You can read whatever you want into that answer, but I'll make no first move on him. We need you and the county to help us. If you all won't, it looks to me we've got no choice but to help ourselves."

Sam looked at Buck. His outburst bothered him. Sam saw that. "Sheriff, I can't hardly live like I've had to and I intend to stay here. I've made good friends here, so try to help us out at the meeting, please." He turned without a goodbye and left the room.

Asking for help was his way of apologizing.

Buck stood to walk Emmett out. He assured his old friend he would do his best. They watched as Sam rode away.

Buck looked at Emmett and said, "You think you can keep an eye on him for a few days? That man's wound tighter than a clock spring."

"I'll try."

Chapter Thirteen

Henry's sons, David and Allen, with Willie close behind, ran to meet Sam as he rode into camp. Both the boys wanted to know if their father and mother would be along soon; while Willie, anxious about his good friend, yammered away about Henry.

In the mayhem, James Motley, enthusiastically asked his boss, "Mister Biggs, you seen all this land, yet?"

"Well, no. Not all of it. We tried to get through most of it, but did it on the run, so to speak. All I know is there's a lot of timber and some prime areas to set up our sawmill when it gets here."

Motley appeared confused, so Sam explained the recent purchase of the steam-powered sawmill to him. James told Sam he'd had some experience with a machine like the one he described.

"You and I should scout for a good location to set it up when it gets here," said Sam. "Bob, too."

"Willie, go find Mr. Dayton. Tell him to come here for bit." Soon, Bob appeared and he overheard the last of the conversation. The news of the sawmill purchase was repeated.

"We are going to start building our homes here and spread out as we need to. We've got a lot of water, enough land cleared by nature, and look at all those oaks. They'll keep us cool in the summer heat, sheltered in the winter. None of the oaks or pines in here are to be cut down. I want to keep it the way it is. Clean out the scrub trees and underbrush, though.

"Up that way," he said, pointing east, "less than a half mile, Reedy Creek comes in from the north, and adds to our water supply. Mister Detwyler said as long as he's lived here, those two creeks have never run dry. Makes sense we stay put in this area, but we'll check out some other areas, too."

"When y'all rode through here the other week, did y'all go up on that big mountain up yonder?" asked Bob.

Sam told him they had seen it from a distance on their first trip through, but it would've taken too long to ride to the top to check the view and besides, the pack mules were about worn out. "Maybe we ought to ride up and check the view from the heights. Might see a better place for the sawmill. Who knows? Now's the time to make sure we've chosen the best location."

***

Nearing exhaustion, he lay upon his cot. Intending to only rest, he fell asleep. The last thought he had was of men stacking rough-sawn lumber to dry.

"Massa is yo 'wake yet, Suh?" asked George peeking through the door flap. "It's nere 'bout sun up."

The morning's sun began to filter into his canvas-covered cabin. Considering the size of the wash basin, he washed carefully and told Willie to get him a fresh supply of hot water so he could shave. He laid out fresh clothes for the day, knowing within an hour's ride they would be as dusty as those he'd discarded, but at least he could forestall the resulting body odor. He wanted to fully bathe, but it would have to wait until he returned. He considered a quick bath in the creek, but the nip of cold air suggested it would be unwise.

With the rising sun came a beautiful, cool morning. The three men mounted and rode west.

James and Bob vied for Sam's attention. James excitedly called out the names of the different trees, explaining what each was commonly used for, while Bob described the machinery which would be the most important to purchase for harvesting the timber.

Sam was impressed with their enthusiasm. He knew without these men his endeavor into the timber business would be foolhardy, at best. So as they continued to talk, he listened, absorbing it all.

Eventually, they crossed over the trail he, Henry and Willie had ridden along the first day; the trail leading from east to west. This time he and the two men rode up the steep grade of the hill.

Halfway up the hill a gouge ripped deep into the earth, led out from a distant stand of trees.

"Somebody's stealing your trees," said Bob, matter of factu-ally.

Sam nodded. Dark shadows fell across his face.

Climbing the steep grade, Queenie searched for solid footing.

Emerging through the tree-line they rode into a clearing exposing the highest point of the hill. Their mounts, breathing heavily, were foamed with sweat.

Tying their horses to trees, each man silently scanned the distant horizon; the faraway places where the sky touched the earth. This was the highest point of land on his property and the view was magnificent; the blue and gray-green line of the horizon fifty miles distant in all directions.

"I've seen some sights in my life; things I'll never forget, but I'll tell you something, I've never seen anything like this," said Sam. Turning full circle he studied the area. He looked at the position of the early morning sun and checked his pocket watch.

"It is a sight, ain't it?" said James.

"Close to ten. That means that way is due north," Sam said correctly, pointing north. "What do you think?" asking neither man in particular, expecting an answer from both.

"Yes Sir. That's north," they responded.

"Then that's Weldon over there. Look. See that dark area? Downtown. Just to the west is Westland Crossroads where you camped those nights. What do you think?"

Both of the men were reluctant to agree or disagree. They lacked Sam's sense of direction. Sam picked up a thin, straight branch, and skinning off the leaves clinging to it, he used it as a pointer.

"That dark line, the one heading south from Westland Crossroads; follow it down that way," he said, pointing south, dragging the pointer across the horizon.

"That's the road we took down to Ringwood. Yonder's Brinkleyville. Remember me showing you that boundary stake? That's where it's at."

Bob's excitement grew. "Mister Biggs that means almost everything around here is ours; I mean yours, don't it?"

"Yeah, you're right. It's all ours."

Sam pointed the stick back toward the north again and toward the large mansion, slave quarters, and outbuildings belonging to Griffen. They were small dark specks and hard to see from the distance.

"That's Griffen's place down there," he said, pointing at a large, white mansion.

They mounted, preparing to leave. A movement far below at

the edge of the woods caught Sam's eye. Four riders sat astride their horses, making no effort to hide themselves. It was obvious to Sam, he and his friends were the objects of their attention. James saw the men at the same time as Sam. He reached into his saddle bag and pulled out a telescope. Sam asked for it and was given the field-glass. He focused the lens onto the four men.

"Speak of the son of a bitch. Don't make any sudden moves. That's Griffen and three of his people. They're armed. Bob, lead off to the right and head toward those trees. We'll watch 'em from there. Get your guns out and ready."

While handing the telescope back to James, a plume of blue-gray smoke billowed into the air over the distant riders' heads. A second passed before a small branch of one of the pines near Bob's head snapped with a sound that only a bullet could make, and hitting close enough to know the men below had intended for the shot to be lethal.

A thunderous boom raced up the hill. All three of the men jumped from their horses, grabbing their guns as they did. Boulders and trees served as shelter against further attack from Griffen and his men.

"Pour everything you got down on those assholes. Take a shot at us, will you?" said Sam. Their guns roared. The ground around the men below churned with dust. A musket spun off and away from one of the men. A horse stumbled, front legs buckling before it regained its footing. The men sawed at the horses' mouths with hard yanked reins and sinking spurs into the animals' flanks, they dashed into the trees.

"Jesus Christ, what's their fucking problem?" Bob asked, pouring powder down the barrel of his gun.

"That's your introduction to Hesper Griffen. I'm starting to get a little tired of that man. Look, for now, don't say anything about this to the rest of the folk. I'm afraid there's going to be more of it on down the road. He's showing off for his men."

So much for the hoped-for peace and quiet. That was gone. Griffen was saber-rattling, a part of saving face. Sam knew his enemy was well on the way to regaining his lost nerve. Things would begin to escalate now.

His concerns were for the safety of the men with him, but he could hardly afford to show fear. He stood straight and confident, staring in the direction of the drifting gun smoke. He felt four distant pairs of eyes watching him from the cover of trees. Defying the men below, he pointed the stick toward the west and continued talking to his men.

"Arcola's that way. It's a pus-hole of a town. It's got a ratty little tavern, but it serves up a good glass of ale and a mighty strong root beer. Ask Willie," he said, chuckling at the strange comment. Bob and James looked at each other, confused.

He pointed back in the direction they had used to climb to the summit. A column of smoke drifted upward. "Sara's cook fire."

The men rode east along the top of the hill. Soon they dismounted and tied all three pairs of reins together and walked to the edge of a boulder strewn cliff.

"That's Reedy Creek, the same one that joins up with Swift Creek above our place.

"That looks like it could be a good place to set up our mill, doesn't it?" Sam asked. "What do you think?"

They discussed it, but each knew the decision had been made.

"Let's head back," said Sam.

Riding down to the camp, they chose a different route and carefully watched their backs. Soon they rode upon a very large tree, recently felled by saw and axe.

"Mister Biggs, Sam. You know what kinda' of tree that is?" asked James.

"A walnut?"

"Yes Sir, and it's got to be one of the biggest I've ever seen. That one tree alone is worth a small fortune. The whole country's gone crazy for anything made out of walnut."

Sam's eyes grew dark. The same dark shadow as before, fell across his face.

"You reckon those trees are worth dying for? Burn it."

***

The mammoth steam-powered sawmill arrived two weeks after Sam purchased it. Ralph Chamberlain, sat regally upon a strong and well-bred horse purchased with commission money. Following him, a long procession of unusually large mules, pulled an extremely large wagon. And behind it, two wagons, filled with workers, brought up the rear. The big wagon had been altered to carry its heavy burden, the massive steam sawmill. Each person in camp stared at the black machine. They were in awe of something so large it required eight mules to pull it.

The wagon had been extended and equipped with four separate axles. All of this being controlled by a rag tag group of men serving as Chamberlain's teamsters.

"Good Morning, Mister Biggs," said Ralph Chamberlain. "Where do you want this godda . . . , this thing, Sir?"

Knowing they had agreed on this day for delivery, Sam told the man the foundation was not ready and he wasn't sure when it would be. That caused considerable anxiety for Ralph Chamberlain.

"Well . . . ah but, ah . . . Mister Biggs, we agreed on today." With his temper getting the better of him, anger colored his face. "I gotta' get that infernal wagon and those damn mules back to Weldon. You do know, Sir, I had to buy them at my own expense, don't you? Had to go all the way to Tarboro for 'em, I did."

Ralph felt his new wealth entitled him to an apology from Sam. Sam ignored the man and walked toward the machine.

"Mister Brantley, the dock owner, said he'll give me what I got in 'em. Something about pulling barges with 'em. I don't much give a fried dog turd what he wants those mules for. They ain't been nothing but a heap of trouble."

His face grew redder, his left eye began to twitch.

"I ain't sure God ever made an animal as mean as those things. Goddamn mules from hell, they are; chased us about as much as we chased them. At least I'll get some of my money back, but I might kill one or two of 'em just to get even with 'em.

"Look here, all I want is to get that goddamn contraption off that goddamn wagon and get back to the goddamn world." He paused to catch his breath, ready to swoon from the heat. The new Ralph Chamberlain amused Sam.

"How the hell can you all stand it out here?" Sam listened to the man, thinking, That's one excitable fellow. If he keeps working himself up, he's liable to jump off that horse and shoot all eight of those mules and might take a shot at me—just for the pleasure of it.

"Ralph, it is Ralph, right? Get down off that horse, that's a splendid animal, by the way. Good blood. Come on friend; let's get out of the sun for a bit."

Calling for George and Willie, he told them to get Chamberlain's teamsters, an odd mixture of mean looking men, something to drink; cool water or tea, but nothing with liquor in it.

Sam led Chamberlain into his tent and offered him a drink.

Late morning or not, he knew from his trip to Weldon the man would accept it and poured him a double shot of whisky.

"Ralph, please accept my apology. I know I'm at fault for the delay. Let's work it out so you will spend no more of your profits. Just give me a few minutes to confer with my men, to see if they still feel as I do about the place in which we wish to set it up. I'll let them know you want to get the wagon over to the site so you can unload it."

Seeing a calm flow through the irritated man, either from the understanding he would suffer no further monetary losses; or from the sudden jolt of alcohol shocking his nervous system, Sam continued, "Here, take this bottle and jug of water, fix yourself another drink if you wish. Make it a strong one this time. We'll work it out, don't worry. I'll be back in a few minutes."

Stepping through the tent flap, he turned to add something, but Chamberlain's head was tilted back, as he drained the glass, while reaching for the bottle on the table.

He found James and Bob inspecting the sawmill. They had a thousand questions to ask about it.

"Walk with me. What do you think of those mules and that big wagon?"

"Well," answered James, "Sam, I gotta' tell you, those are some of the biggest logging mules I've ever seen, and I've worked a bunch of 'em in my time. They're in good shape, but you know those logging mules got a mean streak in 'em. I ain't never seen a logging mule yet that won't try to kick your head clean off if you get close to 'em. What you got in mind?"

"What if I could get us those mules for the right price, can we use them in the logging camp? And if I get them, can you handle them?

Turning to Bob, "Would that wagon be of any use to us? You think it'd be strong enough to haul trees out of the woods to the mill?"

"That wagon hauled that sawmill down here from Weldon . . . who knows from where before that. It'll haul anything we can get on it, I'd say," Bob replied.

"James. You think we should get them if we can?" he asked, pointing at the mules.

"Judging from the size of those trees we saw, if you can get 'em, you oughta'. Ain't no plow mules ever gonna' pull those logs out of the woods. But, I want to say one more time; they're mean. No Sir, I don't much like 'em, but we got to have 'em. Most likely we're gonna' need more of 'em, too." He added, "But you can't ever let them think they got an advantage. They'll come at you."

Goddamn, thought Sam. "You sure you can keep those mules in that corral once you build it up some more?"

Bob and James agreed it was barely strong enough for the gentle mules corralled now and they were dwarfed in size compared to the logging mules.

"If you're gonna' buy those loggers, we'll see to it. Might have to hobble 'em a few days, but yes Sir, we'll get it right. But somebody's got to make sure everybody stays clear of 'em."

Sam lifted the tent flap and entered. Ralph had taken him up on his encouragement to fix himself another drink. The man had poured himself a number of extra drinks and that pleased Sam. A man in a good mood's a man who can be traded with. Ralph stood and wobbled to one side when Sam walked in. Sam asked if he needed anything else.

"No Sir, not yet," slurred Ralph, eyeing the nearly emptied whiskey bottle.

Holy smokes, Sam thought. Man's got a stopping problem.

Problem or not, he intended to use the man's weakness to his advantage.

"What are you going to do with those mules and all that gear once you're done unloading that sawmill?"

He picked up the bottle and held it out to Ralph. "Can I freshen your drink?"

"Much obliged," replied Ralph. "Brantley over at the piers said he wants 'em."

"Maybe I can take the mules and those wagons off your hands if you're through with them after today. I might be able to find some use for them around here. You said you got three hundred dollars of your commission invested into this delivery, right?"

Sam could see the man's drunken mind sorting through drunken thoughts.

"Hey, wait a minute," said Ralph. "I don't remember telling you that." Sam quickly poured him another drink.

"Mr. Biggs, I paid that man in Tarboro three hundred and fifty dollars, U.S. American, for those critters and them wagons. Sir, I'm no damn fool. Three hundred and fifty dollars' what I paid for them mules and stuff and that's what I gonna' get for 'em if I gotta' drive 'em all the way back to Weldon. No Sir. Three Hundred's what I said," confusion clouding his drunken mind.

"Too rich for my blood, Ralph. Go on. Pull the wagons down to the next creek over and do whatever it is you got to do to get them unloaded. I understand. No problem. Enjoy your drink and I'll go tell your men you'll be right along."

Turning to leave, he spun full circle. "You know Ralph, that don't make much sense to me. You've got to spend the rest of the day unloading that sawmill—and at a considerable expense, I would think. Then you've got to work those mules and those teamsters for at least two more days, just to get 'em back to Weldon. That's got to cost you what, a hundred dollars a day?"

Not allowing the drunken man time to think, he pulled out his wallet and removed two hundred dollars in paper notes.

"Now, if that's what you want to do, keep on spending your commission money, fine. Don't matter none to me. Let's get on with the unloading. But if you take this for fair trade, you and your men can ride on out of here now. Two Hundred for everything. Do the math, Ralph. You'll save money by selling your rigs and mules to me and you won't have put up with those mules farting in your face ever again."

Ralph stared at his glass. "Mr. Biggs, anybody ever tell you you got a way of cutting to the quick of a thing? Put it the way you just did, I reckon I would be throwing good money after bad. Why don't you get us one more drink to close the deal. I'll write you out a receipt. Put some whiskey in mine this time?"

***

Mules, wagons and drunks. Sam was tired, totally exhausted, and yet so much to think about. He was not complaining, he'd never been happier in his life. He often worried himself out of sleep at night but soon fell back asleep, after realizing that it would all be worth it someday. Thoughts of his future life with Rose soothed him. He had decided that's what he wanted; what she would want, too, and the thought lulled him to sleep.

Work was piling up. He needed Henry to take over his position soon. The recent delivery of the sawmill represented yet more work. One of the largest concerns of all was to find out how Emmett would respond to his inquiry about using his slaves over the winter.

Willie was told to saddle Queenie and bring her to him. Loading the recent gift for Rose, he headed to Emmett's plantation with hopes of seeing both Emmett and Rose.

Upon entering the grand entry, Sam was approached by a finely dressed house servant, an elderly black man whose singular job appeared to be to grab hats and coats and disappear with them. The servant pointed toward the wrapped gift and asked if he might take it, as well. Sam declined, telling him he would keep it near him.

"As you wish, Sir," the servant replied formally, and left with the articles of apparel.

Emmett invited him to lunch. Sam tried to beg off, feeling it might appear he had planned such an invitation. He offered the reason for the visit, stating that he wished to conduct business with him. But Emmett insisted he stay for lunch regardless, and informed him Rose would be delighted to see him again.

"She spoke highly of you on our way back home last week, Sam. Said you were a Gentleman, she did. So you must join us. We all got to eat. Business can wait."

Emmett returned to the grand entry, after informing the kitchen staff to set another place for lunch. Sam and Emmett stood and watched as Rose descended the curved staircase.

Sam's knees began to buckle.

Emmett watched the two of them out of the corner of his eyes. "Rose. Dear. Please come down and welcome Mister Biggs. He's joining us for lunch." He saw a glimmer—a sparkle, maybe, in her eyes when she looked at Sam.

Sam wasn't sure of what he saw in her face. He was busy worrying about the beads of sweat budding on his forehead. Trying to be nonchalant, he removed a white, folded handkerchief from his vest pocket, gently touching those areas in which he was sure small ponds of misery were collecting and said to the vision approaching him, "Good morning, Miss Rose, it sure is hot out there," and again thought, Oh no. Not again. And here it is, about ready to snow.

She extended her dainty hand and bid him welcome. "Mister Biggs, it's so nice of you to come and visit us. Would you like Jonah to put that away for you?" she asked, pointing at the wrapped box.

He answered, "Oh, no. Miss Rose, this is for you," and handed the box to her. "I hope you like it, Miss Rose." She took the box and asked if she should open it. Sam and Emmett encouraged her to do so. Rose lifted the cover and removed the card Sam had included and read, "A rose by any other name, is still a rose."

"Shakespeare," said Sam.

He had chosen the words with great care; sure they would impress her with their hidden meaning. He had no idea what they meant, but had heard them so many times he was convinced it meant something pleasant. Instead he saw a puzzled look in her eyes, and he was sure he saw her face flush.

Emmett watched the two as they performed the awkward dance of guessing how the one might feel about the other.

Rose lowered her eyes and said, "Thank you, Sam, ah . . . Mister Biggs, it's lovely."

Sam fidgeted with his hands. He had no idea what to do with them. He began wishing for the return of his hat, so he could, if nothing else, roll the brim up into a unrecognizable mess. He considered sitting on his hands but, no, that wouldn't do. At last, he locked his fingers together and held his hands before him.

Emmett welcomed the sensitive moment into his too-long solemn home. He broke the silence of the awkward moment, saying, "Well, come on you two; let's eat."

Enjoying their lunch, Emmett asked Sam what it was he wished to discuss. Thinking Rose may not be interested in men's business affairs, Sam said he did not wish to bore her with everyday details so Emmett suggested the two go into the library. Rose asked if she could retire to the sunroom in the back portion of the mansion.

Coffee and brandy were brought to each man by yet another member of the house staff. A Carolina Gold cigar was offered to Sam by his host. He wished to decline, but thought it would be in poor taste and after lighting the cigar he found it pleasant.

He explained to his host that he had spoken to Isaac about hiring his slaves to work on his place during the cold, slow months quickly arriving. Emmett acknowledged Isaac had approached him with the idea.

Sam knew Isaac worked for Emmett but he could not speak for him. He explained the proposal was a spur of the moment idea at the time.

"But I do think it would be a good deal for us both," he added.

"Sam, don't worry about it. It does indeed sound like a good deal. You need workers, I'll get monetary relief." The men discussed

Sam's needs and Emmett's reimbursement for the slave's services. Reasonable and fair, both. Sam told him that he would welcome the slaves whenever Emmett could let them come.

Chapter Fourteen

"You remember we are meeting here on the fifteenth to discuss our problem to the north, right?" asked Emmett. "Everybody'll
be here. There's talk about hiring a deputy of our own if Fort Harwood won't listen to us. I spoke to Buck last week, again. He said all
the county folk, as well as Mayor Jarvis would be here, but he said for
us not to read too much into it."

"I'll be here," answered Sam. "One more poker in the fire
right now just might do me in. But, yes, I'll make it. Henry's starting
to help a bit more each day. Emmett, you'd think I was trying to steal
that man away from his wife, the way she goes on. But he needs to
work as much as I need him. He's getting stronger every day."

They stood, ending their conversation. Sam coughed nervously into a closed fist.

"Emmett, would you mind if I visit with Miss Rose for a
while?"

"Son, if she don't mind none, I don't reckon it'll bother me
much, neither."

He walked to the doorway and called for Jonah.

"Go tell Miss Rose there's a young man calling on her."

Jonah disappeared into the large house. He returned momentarily, and motioned for Sam to follow.

"Suh, Miss Rose be in de sunroom. Cum' dis way." Jonah
opened the doors leading into the room.

Sam's eyes adjusted slowly to the darkness of the dimly lit
room. The sunlight struggling through the thickly leafed shade trees,
fought a losing battle. Eyes adjusted, his first thought of the room was
of the immense wealth required to design and furnish a room such as
this.

He had viewed only a small portion of the lavish room before
he saw movement to his right. His eyes riveted upon Rose, her beauty
accentuated by beams of fading sunlight streaming behind her in or-

anges, yellows and pinks. Motes of dust floated behind her shadowed
face, adding to the otherworldly effect.

A leaded and stained-glass window, placed high to add
needed light to the room, magnified the fading sun as it fell toward
the far horizon. She stood next to large vases of floral arrangements.
His heart pounded. He was amazed such a beautiful creature would
consider spending time with him.

"Isn't this the prettiest room you've ever seen?" she whispered. "I love to sit out here for hours on end," her voice catching at
his approach.

She'd changed from the dress she had worn at lunch to one
which was a perfect match for the hat he had given her.

He'd thought of no other person since they had parted at Fort
Harwood. Taken aback by her beauty, he wanted—needed her to keep
talking so he would not have to search for words lost to him now.

"Rose, you are absolutely beautiful."

Her face flushed. He could see she too, struggled, searching
for the right words. The revelation calmed him, quietening his racing
heart.

Finding her voice, she said, "It's the most beautiful hat I've
ever owned. But why did you spend your money on it? Uncle Em
would have bought it for me. He spoils me like a child, you know?"

"Yes, I do, and that's precisely why I wanted to buy it for you.
God . . . ," he gasped, "you're radiant."

 He stepped toward her, taking her hands into his—an act as
natural as breathing. Raising both to his thumping heart, he placed her
open palms against his chest.

Captivated by the new sensation, she moaned barely loud
enough for Sam to hear. Feeling his heart's labored beating—curious
and enthralled, she held her hands there as he circled her small body
with his massive arms, and pulled her close to him. She lifted her face
and her lips met his.

The kiss was not the ravaging kiss of two souls seeking desperately to consume the other before they disappeared from the new
world they each wanted so much to enter. No, it was a gentle, soft and
tender kiss; so soft it begged for more; so tender, it would not frighten
the other away. A kiss screaming of their desire for each other.

With longing, passionate thoughts racing through his mind, he
released her from his arms. He did not want to release her—but he
knew he had to let her flee, if that was what she needed. She gasped

for breath, not because of the fierceness of his hold—she had forgotten to breath. She fell away ever so slightly, and he whispered her name, "Rose."

It was Rose who suggested they ride out into the plantation. He was as anxious as she to be away from the mansion, from Emmett, and the curious slaves. Alone with each other.

"Sam, give me a moment, I'll be right back," she said.

He watched her walk through the French doors and heard her summons, "Jonah, go to the stable and have my carriage and Lady Lucy brought up to the house. Tell Toby to take our guest's horse back and see that it is well attended to."

They embraced anew, each fearing the other would break if they allowed the full strength of their emotions to escape. Sam fought the desire to pull her tighter, closer to him.

Rose placed her open palms onto Sam's face, exploring it, assuring herself he was really there—really holding her—and neither of them able to speak to the other.

Their minds so full of overwhelming passion; words could not be formed—words that could convey their feelings. They kissed again—their passion increasing.

Nearly undetectable, a knock sounded at the door. Jonah spoke softly, "Miss Rose, dat dare carriage of your'n is out dare in de front, and I dun tole Annie," referring to the heavyset house servant in charge of the household duties, "to git sum'a dat dare wine what's in de cell'r for yo. If dat be's all rite wid yo."

Walking toward the front entry, Rose held out her arm, stopping Sam, and asked him to wait for her. She stepped into the library and spoke to Emmett.

"Uncle Em, Mister Biggs and I are going to take a ride along the river, do you mind?"

"Of course not, dear. You two have a nice ride."

Sam was deeply touched when Rose bent and kissed the forehead of her beloved Uncle Em.

The two walked away, and behind them, Emmett smiled.

Toby held Lady Lucy's bridle in his hand. The small white mare snorted and tossed her head while pawing the ground, excited at seeing her owner. Rose reached into the picnic basket, in which a very astute Jonah had placed apples. She removed an apple and held it out to the little mare. The mare quickly snatched the apple, seemingly expecting it. Sam spoke approvingly of her choice of animal.

"Oh, Uncle Emmett picked her out and gave Lady Lucy and the carriage to me. I don't know much about horses, I'm afraid, but isn't she wonderful?" She stood next to the mare and combed the flowing mane with opened fingers. Sam stepped close to Rose and the animal shoved her head between the two, separating them.

"If I didn't know better, I'd say she's jealous of me."

"I guess I might've spoiled her a little," Rose laughed.

She handed the reins to Sam. "She's little but she likes to run with me."

"Where to, me lady?"

How quickly he had grown comfortable with her, now that the most wanted, and most feared of all intimate moments had passed. The kiss. A simple act—simple, but huge in implications. He had a burning desire to touch her, to hold her.

Pointing toward a distant tree line, she said, "Let's ride to those oaks. It's the most beautiful spot in the whole world. Well, it used to be. It needs to be cleaned up now." They rode through the slave quarters. Sam was impressed by the number of slaves, mostly women and little children, waving and shouting greetings at Rose. She appeared delighted to see the women and children, and they—her. She returned their waves and called out to many by name.

The men folk were finishing the late fall work before they could rest. Sam guiltily wondered if they knew how short their winter's rest would be.

From ahead, Isaac approached. He tipped his hat to Rose and Sam. "Good afternoon, Miss Rose, Sam."

They greeted him and asked how he was doing.

"Fine, just fine. While I was up at the big house Emmett told me you and he have worked out terms for a bunch of the Nigras. I'm glad. Should be some relief for both Emmett and me. Don't let me hold the two of you up. You two watch out for those storm clouds. If they let loose, they'll wash the ugly off a billy goat, they will."

He lifted the reins, preparing to leave and added. "I'll be up to your place tomorrow. Emmett wants to make sure the Nigras understand what's going on and just what it is they're 'spose to do. Miss Rose, Sam," he said, and touching the brim of his hat, he slapped the reins on the horse's rump.

Nearing the trees, the two searched for and found each others' hands. The fields bore proof of a heavy crop, just as Sam recalled Dorrie had said. Rose pointed to a narrow wagon road and he guided the horse and carriage onto it. The oaks were immense, their crayon colored leaves rustled in the late fall breeze, high above an area that in another time had been well maintained. A creek bordering the property, flowed sluggishly along, much like the wrongfully named Swift Creek.

The place had an abandoned feel to it, but sometime in the past, it must have been a favorite for Emmett and Rose—their friends, too. And Emmett's folk before him. They continued toward an area set apart from the rest of the park. A thick tangle of undergrowth worked hard to hide the dominant features within a black wrought-iron fence—badly eroded tombstones.

A tall four-sided monolith of white marble, elaborately chiseled and decorated, stood at the head of a family-sized tomb of the same white marble. Ivy vines crowded out names and dates as it climbed the sides. Etched into the slabs were the names, Edward Emmett Detwyler, and just below that, Mary Steton Detwyler. Those names followed by the necessary words which reflected happiness and sorrow—Born and Died. And scripted below—Your loving children, Emmett and Abigail.

Rose was deep in thought, the markers saddened her. Sam put his arm around her tiny waist.

"Uncle Em and his sister loved this place. But look at it now," she apologized, her eyes brimming, ready to overflow. "It's so overgrown, but Uncle Em said he was going to send a bunch of our Negroes out here to clean it up." She blinked her eyes, dispersing building tears. Sam watched as Rose continued to look at the two lower names. He dared not interrupt her. Some things are private, he thought. But a sister? Why never a mention of an Abigail?

Rose pointed to a hitching rail secured on deeply set cypress posts and Lady Lucy walked up to the railing without rein from Sam.

Sam stepped down, and extended his arm to Rose. He held her aloft, smiling at her. He lowered her slowly, the weight of her body pressing against his chest as she slid down him. He kissed her as her lips fell to his.

From the basket she removed another apple for Lady Lucy. "Here girl, you did a good job. Now be good and I'll see if I can find another one for you when we're ready to leave."

Rose put her arms around the horse's neck and murmured lovingly to it. Sam watched as the horse watched her. Lady Lucy stared at the basket when Rose promised her another treat.

"It's kind of a ritual. I've spoiled her, you think?" she asked. "Lady and I come up here a lot, don't we, girl. Me for the serenity—Lady for the apples."

"Can I come up here with you and Lady from now on?" Sam teased.

Rose laughed at the man she was beginning to adore, "I suppose you'll want an apple?"

They spread a blanket upon a shaded area cleared of briars and weeds. He removed his jacket and folded it into a pillow. His heart skipped when the pocket Colt slipped from the sewn-in holster and landed between he and Rose. He suspected she'd heard rumors of his *him* many quarrels, his many fights, but he did not wish to confirm them with the presence of the revolver.

He grabbed the revolver, quickly slipping it under the corner of the blanket, thankful that Rose had been distracted wiping dust from two crystal glasses. He'd barely settled against the tree before she handed him the bottle of wine and asked him to open it.

Jonah had forgotten the cork screw, so Sam pushed and pulled at the cork. Desperate to remove it, he considered using his teeth—he'd removed many that way but thought better of using the unsavory method now.

The cork popped out with one final push of his aching thumb.

"How's that?" He smiled and reached for the glasses.

He leaned against the trunk of the oak. Rose held his wineglass as he positioned the jacket-pillow behind his head, then she leaned back into him. Holding her in his arms he gently teased her temples with his lips. He was intoxicated by her smell and the way her body molded into his. They began talking of insignificant things, their voices whispery. They shared intimate thoughts of their lives and their dreams.

Fearing the darkening skies and the building rumble of distant thunder, Rose gathered the picnic basket and blanket and loaded them into the carriage. True to her word, she gave Lady Lucy another apple. Sam walked up behind her. He put his hand upon her shoulder and turned her toward him. Cupping her face, he kissed her. Sam drew her close, holding her, neither saying anything, and then he lifted her into the carriage.

On the way back to Emmett's mansion, he told her of his plans for Swift Creek, admitting they sounded grandiose, but assured her he could do those things and that he would do them.

Lovers are inclined, when they are at ease with each other, to discuss mundane things and their heart's desires. Rose removed her gloves and after taking his hand into hers she leaned her head onto his shoulder. They both were quiet for the remainder of the ride home. No need to talk, their happiness came from being near each other. Arriving at the mansion, he placed a hand under each arm and lifted her above him and out of the carriage.

Jonah smiled at Rose, the smile a father would smile at his child, and tried to suppress a grin.

"Shoo. Jonah, now go on, go on" she said to him, waving him away. But he continued to grin, knowingly. Sam longed to hold her again, but they were being watched from the mansion by Emmett, and the slaves who could not contain their curiosity.

"Rose," he asked, "Madam, with your kind permission, may I call upon you again?"

Coyly, she answered, "Yes, you may, but don't keep me waiting, Mister Samuel Biggs, or I just might come calling on you. You don't want that scandal, do you?"

"Well, I sure don't have a problem with it," he replied, his eyes teasing her.

Emmett knew the two were in love, although neither had spoken to him of their feelings. He remembered a love, a love of a long time ago, and thought, in time they will come to me. They will tell me of their feelings. I'll have my chance to wish them happiness.

***

The following morning, Sam was awakened by George handing him his first cup of coffee.

"Well, Massa, all dem folks be a cum'n dis morn'n from dat udder man's place to stot cut'n down dem trees. Dat's right, ain't it, Suh?"

"Yes, it is, George. Go get Henry and Mister Motley for me."

He pushed aside the door flap and added, "Tell Willie to get us some coffee over here."

Henry arrived shortly, Motley close behind and next, Willie, with the coffee.

"Well, fellows, it's about time to start with Emmett's people.

We know what's needed. No need to go over all that again. So tell me Henry, where did you and James decide to start cutting trees?" Listening to the men talk, a sense of something momentous, a sense of adventure filled his mind.

His seed of a long ago thought had sprouted, sending its roots into the ground. He could see his future—their future.

The slaves Emmett hired out to Sam proved to be good men, good workers. Sam inquired about them and was reassured by Henry all was fine.

James Motley proved to be the timber man Sam had been advised to hire. The man went at his work with a renewed lease on life. They agreed pine was needed foremost. Winter and cold were rushing fast toward Swift Creek and much building needed to be done. Although the extra income was enticing, harvesting of the hardwoods have to wait.

***

Bob Dayton, through trial and error, had coerced the huge sawmill onto the strong mortar and brick foundation. It had been a difficult project and the logger mules proved to be a valuable asset.

But Bob had neglected to inform Sam his reading and writing skills were somewhat limited—totally limited, actually; so Sam asked Henry to send either of his sons, David or Allan, to the sawmill to read the instructions to Bob. The boys took turns reading to the man and on pay days, the youngsters jingled loose coins in their pockets.

The four young men hired by Sam for work requiring strong backs were the labor force Bob requested. They were good men, young and strong, full of piss and vinegar and young enough to know being paid on a regular basis was a wonderful way to exist.

Weekends, when not found working, would find them in Weldon, Arcola, Fort Harwood or some unknown town, but they would be back the following Monday morning, ready for work; always broke and always the worse for the wear.

Henry ordered them to stay out of trouble and not to bring trouble back with them. They'd all heard stories about Sam and they did not doubt what they'd heard. He was the kind of trouble they didn't need.

"Town's one thing, out here's another," Henry warned them.

At Arcola, they were surprised to see James Motley, but only the one time. James and the tavern owner sat alone, seemingly sharing old stories. None of them paid any attention to James or the tavern keeper. They might have been drinking, but not much, if any at all. They themselves, had been drinking heavily and their concerns were limited to how much money was left in their pockets, how much whiskey remained in the bottles and if there was enough time left to use it all up—the money and the whiskey.

They never said anything to anyone about the chance sighting of James Motley, but after sobering up, thought it odd their first impression of Motley had been that he was a pious man, one not given to partaking of hard liquor. But, none had seen him drinking. And what if he had? It was none of their affair. They were not about to put their noses where they didn't belong. They'd been warned not to do that.

***

Joe had been busy clearing close-in parcels of land for the much needed winter gardens. James saw to the removal of all the trees that cluttered the intended garden plots. Together, they cleared over ten acres of prime land. Sam was greatly impressed with the work the men had accomplished. Seeing such a large piece of land cleared of tangled undergrowth, he envisioned the way Swift Creek Plantation could be someday.

He was pleased with Bob's progress with the sawmill and glad he had decided to set it up north on the banks of Reedy Creek. He'd based his decision on the excessive noise it made and on the amount of heavy black smoke he remembered from his one ride on a steam train. Whenever he had time, he rode to the mill-site and checked on Bob's progress.

He was impressed that a man who could neither read nor write could put the machine in place and get it ready to run. It was only so much black iron and steel to him; too many parts, and too many instructions.

Although Bob was not educated in reading and writing, he was a quick learner and he had a mechanic's way with understanding things. Listening to the two Atwell boys, he readily grasped the meaning of the instructions read to him. Often, he asked the boys to re-read things to him.

Embarrassed to have children reading to him, each time he would say, "Just checking."

He was confident the large black machine was ready for its test run. An amazing amount of dried wood was required to build a fire to superheat the hundreds of gallons of water the boiler held.

The fire in the box began to increase, and so did the soft noise created by air being sucked into the gaping maw of the firebox.

The noise sounded like logger mules breathing and exhaling each breath, and all in unison. The surprisingly loud whoosh . . . whoosh . . . whoosh, of the behemoth grew. The growing noise alarmed Bob. He feared he had erred in the extreme. The very air around him pulsated as the mouth of the firebox devoured all the air it could gulp.

Bob assumed the fire would reach a saturation point at which it would be sated, but as the noise grew, his confidence plummeted.

Pulsating, the roaring firebox vibrated the air, luring the curious inhabitants from the camp. Women and children alike, cautiously entered the lair of the huffing beast. The dragon spewed billowing black clouds of smoke high into the air and began to rain red-hot embers.

Faces became smudged from ink-black sootied tears, yet curious eyes remained opened as wide as saucers, never averting from the source of the noise. Not wishing to be blown to hell and back, and fearing to be any closer to the Fire and Brimstone machine, they retreated a safe distance from the roaring black monster.

Sam, too, rose with a start from his desk and rode to the clearing. He rode pass women and children who stood watching, their mouths agape, pointing fingers at the storm brewing before them. He'd expected noise when the sawmill was fired, but still, he was alarmed at the intensity. The noise reminded him of the train ride to Baltimore; but this was louder—much louder and it rumbled like thunder across the fields and deep into the woods.

Bewildered workers gazed toward the source of the roar, an unknown fear growing in their chests.

Big birds, small birds, buzzards and insects wanted nothing to do with the building storm. Deer and the forest's small animals fled. The immense clouds of dense black smoke began to cover everything with soot. Cries of pain resounded as red-hot cinders found bare skin. Hired hands and slaves came running toward the sawmill, drawn by curiosity, while fearing the worst.

Those who had heard of Armageddon were sure the end of the world was upon them. Seeing Hell on earth, they fled, some on foot, others on their mounts. Entering the protective edge of the woods, they paused for one last look at the fire-breathing, smoke-belching, spark-spitting black monstrosity.

Finally, the boiler reached the point where it could no longer contain the mounting steam pressure.

Bob yelled to the boys, "Y'all need to read that book to me a little faster. You hear me?" hoping for some overlooked instruction that would deter the inevitable explosion.

The boys did as they were told, anxiously offering their interpretations to Mister Dayton, no longer caring if they offended their elder.

"It says here, when the needle gits on the red part of the gauge and hits three hundred and fifteen pounds, you need to pull the chain of the combination pop-off valve and whistle, and it says in big red letters, DO NOT DELAY!" shouted David.

Bob looked at the gauge and yelled at the boy.

"What's it at now, son?"

"You oughta' pull it, Mister Dayton," shouted David, jumping from the platform.

Allen was already out of hearing range and rapidly adding to it.

Bob grabbed the chain and pulled. The pressure reached its maximum. The pop-off valve opened simultaneously with the whistle. The instantaneous release of pressurized steam exploded with a deafening roar, and gave birth to bedlam.

The air churning rumble mingled with the ear piercing scream of the whistle, and blended with the thumping and roaring of the firebox.

Sam alone stood his ground. He wanted to run, but reasoned flight would not instill confidence in his people. He locked his heels to the ground. Bob hit the floor in front of the firebox, and held tightly to the chain.

Fortunately, he knew the water reservoir needed to always be filled, recalling little Allen's instructions, "While there is a fire in the box, never allow the water tanks to run dry." There was still one hell of a fire in the firebox. He yelled at the four young men in his charge to stay close to the roaring machine, water in hand, while the fire died down.

Everybody had seen enough for one day and steady hands were needed to continue with the mechanics. There were plenty of hands around, but none were steady. As the fire died low, the noise abated. Sam walked over to Bob and placed his hand on the man's shoulder.

"Nice job, Bob. Try less fire next time." He faced the men slowly returning from the safety of the forest, and to provide proof that he had not been frightened himself, said, "What are you all standing around for? Go find those mules."

Chapter Fifteen

The day of the meeting arrived. Sam needed Henry to accompany him to the meeting. He suspected the possibility of inquiries or accusations into the death of Red Slater and the wounding of his brother Daryl, a wound which eventually ended with the amputation of the man's arm below the elbow.

How nice it would have been if Griffen had only heeded the warnings directed at him. None of this would've been necessary, he thought, but he could hardly imagine the bastard would sit back and not force the issue again.

However, Griffen had been as quiet as a church mouse—perhaps a good sign for the group, but Sam doubted it. He still wondered why Griffen called Emmett an old crippled son of a bitch. He also remembered Emmett's odd comment about how only bad would result if he went along on the ride to Griffen's.

For a while, Hesper ceased his acts of terror, the exception being the recently fired shots at Sam and his friends while they scouted his property from the heights of the Devil's Hump—the name he had given the anomaly. He knew men like Griffen stopped only long enough to rethink their positions and never quit out of fear.

The old man might have feared nothing but he had to know his dominance was being seriously challenged. He'd been embarrassed by the rough treatment Sam heaped upon him, and in front of his own men. Anybody would have been embarrassed by such rough treatment. Sam expected revenge and had been only mildly surprised by the attack up on the hump.

If he put himself into Griffen's shoes, he would have sought retaliation himself. He believed Griffen would make his move, and soon. The old man could not sit around, licking his bruised ego much longer. He wondered if any of Hesper's men would be at the meeting, spying and snooping for their boss.

Arriving at Emmett's, he looked for Rose. However, she and

Jonah were in Fort Harwood picking up yet more supplies—supplies not really needed, but a convenient way for Emmett to keep her away from the possibility of an ugly meeting. Mixed feelings of wanting to see her and his desire to shelter her from ugly things tore at him.

Sam and Henry were surprised at the large group who gathered. Many were the neighbors who had helped them, and others—strangers to them both, came along, also.

As a matter of formality, Sheriff Vance and the Mayor arrived together and not far behind came the Carlton County officials. Mayor Jarvis was a slight man and needed a three day old stubble of graying whiskers removed from his face. His hands shook, the kind of shaking that required whiskey to calm.

"How the hell did he ever get to be Mayor?" Sam asked Emmett.

"Bought and paid for," answered Emmett. "Keep your eyes on him and those men what come up here with him. Watch them watch him. Folks say he's been getting money from Griffen for years just so he'll leave this part of the county alone and he spreads it around to the county boys so they'll do just that. He's not here for our benefit. No. He's watching his men. There's no loyalty among thieves. No trust, neither."

Buck sought out Emmett and Sam and sat with them. He didn't care what the Mayor or the officials thought. He, long ago, had won the election to his post based upon his honesty—the losing opponent, hand picked by the Mayor. And afterward, the Mayor offered him money to look the other way on certain occasions. So Buck threw him in jail. The Mayor shouted curses at Sheriff Buck and threatened to fire him. Buck retaliated and the town folk rallied around him. Two days later the Mayor was released from the smelly cell. Afterwards their relationship remained distant, but cordial.

The Mayor and the county officials stayed clear of Buck. They had tried to unseat him from his post but the people of Fort Harwood believed they had elected a good man. They thought him an honest man, and prayed he was the town's savior.

Buck called everyone to order and a discussion of the many problems throughout the area began. Jonathan Ward removed his pad from his vest pocket and proceeded to record the minutes of the meeting.

Heated discussions included those of crops needlessly destroyed; livestock butchered for the smallest cuts of meat—or out of meanness, and gangs of men camping in forests, refusing to leave. In fact, unwanted and brazen trespassers had warned landowners to get off of their own land.

Guns fired into the late night were common.

Arcola appeared under siege from boisterous and hell-raising highwaymen, its streets awash with gamblers, drunkards, slave catchers and vagabonds of all kinds. Traffic on the roads had fallen off. Businesses suffered greatly. The area's slaves lived in fear and all of this at the behest of one man who thrived on turmoil and fear—Hesper Griffen.

Emmett had been asked to speak for the group. Sam thought Emmett to be the logical spokesperson since he was the area's longest resident, but was not surprised by his refusal.

"No. Not me. I'm getting a little long in the tooth to take on more responsibility."

Isaac, too, was a reluctant spokesman but the second choice of his neighbors. He was known to be an honest man and one given to stating facts and avoiding rumors. If a thing was black, he said it was black. If a thing was white, white it was. He was acutely aware of all the problems his neighbors endured over the years. And they liked him because Emmett Detwyler liked him.

The discussions centered around Griffen. Emmett appeared withdrawn, but he listened carefully to every word; he took it all in.

Everyone who desired to speak, was encouraged to relay to the county leaders their personal confrontations with Griffen and his henchmen. Everybody had a story to relate, yet some appeared cautious, even reluctant—perhaps fearing reprisals.

None of the men who had been with Sam withheld their comments. They'd seen the malignant hate in Griffen. And they saw something in Sam they did not see in themselves. Here, if he would have it, was their champion, their lawman.

"For as long as I can remember, and I've been here a long time, all the way back to Sheriff O'Malley's days, we've been asking for somebody to be sent up here to help us. Instead, we've been ignored," said Isaac, gaining the floor.

All the men rose to show their support for him. The county leaders closed rank, fearing an attack. They snuck furtive glances at the Mayor; seeking advice.

"Sheriff Buck is only one man. We know he can't come up here every time we need help. This meeting is no disrespect of you, Buck. We know what's going on."

He pointed a finger at the county leaders, and said, "It's you bastards. Things are going to change. Why is that so hard for you to understand?' His eyes burned into them.

"Think about it. We've already paid for it. You've taxed the hell out of us. Any one of these men will provide the land for a jail and living quarters to be built on. Just tell us where you want it. Emmett'll take you straight to a piece, right now. Right, Emmett? Ben will. John? You too, right?"

Seeing boredom and indifference on the faces of the elected county leaders, Isaac's temper flared. He pointed accusingly, at them.

"Did you men come to listen to our complaints or are you figuring to keep on pocketing our tax money, like the thieves you are?"

With such an accusation hurled at them, the officials rose, prepared to protest. Likewise, so did all the others present. Wisely, the officials regained their seats after Isaac raised both hands, calling for calm.

"Funny, ain't it, considering we've paid all of our taxes just like the rest of the county? But they didn't have to come begging to you, did they? The way we see it, you'll either do something about it or you won't. After all these years, that's what it's boiled down to. The rest of the county gets all the help it needs. And we don't get shit. That seem right to you?

"So now, you've got a problem. Starting last month, we decided we're not paying no more taxes. We're saving the money but the county's not getting a dime of it. Soon enough, Raleigh's gonna' send somebody up here to find out what's going on. And when they do, heads are gonna' roll down main street."

Murmurs erupted from the county men. Their sarcastic smirks said they hardly feared interference from outside sources.

"There's been rumors some of you fine upstanding sonsabitches—you Mayor, and your lackeys here," he said, stabbing at them with his finger, "might be getting extra money finding its way into your pockets, now and then. Griffen handing money out to you? And our tax money? You pocketing that, too? Sure as hell ain't spending it up here. But you are going to provide law up this way. Plain and simple."

The neighbors stood and roared their approval of Isaac's demands.

"Strong talk, ain't it? Pisses you off, right? So what? You gonna' deny it? Go ahead. Those fellows in Raleigh might be surprised county money ain't never been spent the way it shoulda' been. Now that'd make for an interesting meeting, wouldn't it? Want me to set one up?" In turn he looked eye to eye, at each of the officials.

"Listen up. Once again, Mister Ward's services are much appreciated. We asked him to come along; you wouldn't have. Minutes of this meeting are being kept—after all, it is our meeting, and Mister Ward has agreed to supply us with a copy. Right, Mister Ward?"

The man of few words nodded, and continued to scribble onto his pad.

"It's a shame, ain't it, that we had to ask him to do this. Says a lot about you thieving bastards, don't it?

"But you are gonna' do what we tell you to do." He slammed the table top with his fist. The officials jumped and quickly spun to check the crowd, expecting to be rushed.

"You people want to weasel out of what we're owed, go on, try. A copy of Mr. Ward's notes will be sent to those men in Raleigh, if something don't get done quick. If you fix the problem like you're supposed to, that would be good and we'll forgive you your trespasses.

"So here's what I've been asked to tell you all. Begging your pardon, Buck, if the county won't help us, we're about ready to take over for ourselves, and we'll do whatever we have to do. Call us vigilantes if you want. Hell. We're almost there, anyway."

Stepping from the porch, he simply said, "That's about all I got to say."

The officials from Fort Harwood climbed into their fine carriages to leave. With Jonathan Ward far off in the distance, Isaac nudged Sam and asked him to join him for a few more words with the county men.

"Hey, hold up there," he yelled. They waited, huddling together, and watched Sam and Isaac approach.

Still fuming, menace in his eyes, Isaac said, "Sheriff's already told us we're getting mighty close to becoming vigilantes up here. Maybe you sonsabitches ought to think about that some. If you turn us into vigilantes; guess who we're coming after first."

With an exaggerated smile upon his face, he said, "Oh, by the way, Mister Ward didn't hear that, now did he?" Isaac winked at them, smiled, smacked the horse's rump, turned and walked away.

"Damn," said Sam, "I think you just started a war," as he patted Isaac on his back. He'd seen something new in Isaac and he liked it. He thanked Isaac for speaking on behalf of all the men.

"War was started a long time ago, but I mighta' heated it up some," Isaac responded.

Sam turned to Emmett and said, "Emmett, what do you think'll happen?"

Not realizing how prophetic his words would be, Emmett said, "Not a goddamn thing. They can't see how deep in shit they got themselves. Money's keeping 'em blind. We are gonna' end up finding our own Lawman. You want the job?"

"Hell no. Might want to offer it to Isaac, though."

Emmett laughed. "Fiery little bastard, ain't he?"

Chapter Sixteen

Emmett dozed in his favorite stuffed chair. Over the years it had earned, and finally lay claim to its spot in the room. It sat at the edge of the light and the warmth forced outward into the room by the fire in the oversized fireplace. The rest of the furniture in the room still looked new, but none of it was new—just never used.

The chair wore its age like Emmett, frayed around the edges, and colors fading. It did double duty each and every night, comforting and nursing a tired and worn old man in a vain attempt to restore his body. Each and every night it fought a battle to keep the man's demons at bay. The chair won most nights. On the nights it lost to Emmett's demons, he drank heavily.

Jonah set an after dinner brandy on the lamp stand. The brandy's rich amber color, diffused by the light of the orange flames of the fireplace passing through the crystal prisms attached to the shade of the lamp, splattered dancing colors upon the surfaces of the room.

This was the best part of the day for Emmett. Time to count his blessings and not think of past sorrows. Time to review events and decisions of the day. Time to tear them apart and study them.

Tonight, he felt especially old and tired. Well, hell, he thought, I am an old shit. Tired. Always tired, it seems.

Some of those nights, the brandy floated him to that drowsy place in which only pleasant thoughts existed—next door to a place where sorrows resided. But not dead and gone, the sorrows fought hard to force themselves out of the deep and dark recesses, demanding to be dealt with again.

And always, the highlights of his day were the moments he shared with Rose. They talked of the day's events, enjoyed their meals together and retired to Emmett's sitting room.

Rose loved to sit with her beloved Em, enjoying his company. Emmett would light his pipe and read, sometimes aloud to Rose.

Beautiful, beautiful Rose—his sole reason for living now, and seemingly the only joy remaining in his life. Pushing sixty; he had everything he'd ever wanted. But Rose . . . What's to become of Rose? he worried each day. What will become of her when I'm gone?

She clung to her Uncle as if he'd hung the stars and created the Heavens himself. She glowed when she was near him. She wore her happiness on her sleeve, caring little if others saw her delight in his presence. He, in turn, felt like a newborn's father. Seeing the child each morning he wondered how such a beautiful creature could exist in such an ugly world.

He'd vowed to her when he'd brought her to her new home, scared, confused and heartbroken; "As long as I'm alive, you'll never have reason to be afraid again. You'll be safe with me. You'll see."

Now his darling Rose had found Sam. She basked in the presence of two men. Emmett was happy for her. Sam will protect her—he's a good man. Emmett had watched from afar. He understood a lot.

His eyes filled with the gritty sands of sleep. Rose entered the room to cover him with his favorite blanket to ward off the night's chill quickly overtaking the room. She bent over to kiss his age-spotted forehead.

"Uncle Em, you need not even try to go to sleep down here," she reminded him. "You know better than that. Jonah's going to be in here in ten minutes to get you off to bed. Don't make me come back down here, " she scolded him and kissed him good-night.

"I love you," she whispered.

She left his side, leaving the room. Emmett, not asleep or wishing to interfere with his nightly portion of adulation from her, remained quiet, eyes closed.

"Rose, sweetheart, tell Jonah to turn down my bed. I'll go on up. What do you say you and I ride over to Sam's in the morning?"

***

The ground was covered in hoar frost. The early morning dew had frozen, turning the grass white and spiky and noisy to walk upon. Rose and Emmett stepped out of the rear of the mansion and onto the large porch. Emmett placed his hand upon Rose's arm.

"Rose, wait up. Ain't that Buck? Wonder what brings him up here?" he asked, pointing toward the rider. Rose did not answer him. Already, he was slowly stepping down the steps to greet the sheriff.

"What brings you up here this fine day, Buck?"

The sheriff answered, "Well, I thought I'd bring the latest news up to you. Those sons of bitches in Fort Harwood have made a decision, of sorts." Looking over to the porch he saw Rose watching the two men.

"Pardon me, Miss Rose. How are you this morning?" he inquired, touching the brim of his hat. Rose greeted him warmly and told Emmett she would wait inside while the two conducted their business.

Buck waited for Rose to go back into the warmth of the house. "Emmett, those men have decided since you all were so adamant about your expectations for law and order up this way, and mostly I think, considering the fact they really don't want Raleigh poking around up here, they said they were willing to see what they could do to help you folks out some—their words—not mine." Buck stopped long enough to think of some new way to convey his feelings about Carlton County's finest.

"Most worthless bunch of shitheads in North Carolina," is what he ended up with.

Seeing Buck heading toward the hotter side of mad, Emmett invited the man to dismount.

"Get down off that horse. Get on up here and let's get out of this cold. We'll go to the library. You want coffee? I could use a little more, myself."

He held the reins of the Sheriff's horse and yelled toward the barn, "Toby, get your slow ass on over here and get Sheriff Buck's horse. Get it watered and give it some oats, too. Where the hell is my carriage, anyway?"

Just as Emmett finished shouting, Toby led the horse and carriage through the double doors of the barn and answered his master, "Yas suh, I's a cumin'."

The two entered the house. Each sat in finely crafted chairs, stained dark and covered in ox blood maroon leather. Between the two, stood a beautifully handmade and intricately carved desk.

Buck admired the chairs and desk and thought they probably cost more than he would make in a full year of sheriffing, and there they sat, hardly ever used.

Jonah, forever vigilant, brought steaming fresh coffee and a tray of Annie's morning sweets to the men as they sat down.

"What's got you so worked up this morning, Buck?"

Sipping his hot black coffee, Bucked stared hungrily at the ⌐
biscuits, preserves, butter and morning sweets. Obviously, he would
not be offended if he was invited to partake of the steaming breakfast
treats.

"Oh, where are my manners? I'm sorry, Buck; help yourself to
whatever you want. Rose and I have had our breakfast. Tell me.
What's going on?"

Buck took a bite of a buttered and strawberry preserves slath-
ered biscuit.

"Well, those assholes started acting like they probably oughta'
throw you folks a bone, just to shut you up. But they got to remembering that John, Mister Ward, was doing a lot of note taking up
here."

He grabbed another biscuit, broke it open and spooned honey
on it.

"Anyway, one of those rock-heads went to see Mister Ward
and told him they wanted his notes. Told Ward he had no choice
about the matter neither, being he was a public servant of the county
and all. Ward told him to go to hell." Buck laughed hard, spitting
crumbs as he did.

"Well, what did those good friends of ours come up with?"
asked Emmett, his impatience growing.

"They found a man in Zebulon who either wants to get out of
Zebulon, or has to, one or the other. Name of Leggett, Jessie Leggett.
Used to live near Fort Harwood, from what I been told and he moved
down to Zebulon a few years back. I knew him in passing, but that
was about all.

"They grabbed Bill Daltry, my Deputy and told him he was
gonna' have to work up here until they could find another man to
work with that Leggett fellow, but Billie's got family so he up and
quit. Hell of a mess, now.

"That new man seems alright to me, but I don't know much
about him. Heard tell years back he was a axe-man for old man
Evan's timber crew. He might not be much of a heavy thinker, if you
catch my drift. I think he's looking for light duty and I sure hope to
hell that's what he gets up here. That'd be nice, Emmett."

"Skip all that, Buck. What are they gonna' do?"

"Well, Emmett, they said for you all to get that cabin and the
jailhouse ready and they'd send that new fellow on up here when everything's done."

Emmett bolted to his feet and looked at Buck.

"No, hold on there. Wait just a goddamn minute. Where's the money for all this?"

Buck shrugged his shoulders and replied, "You gotta' ask them about that."

Emmett pounded the desk hard, hard enough to make Buck jump.

"Like hell I will. We said we'd donate the land, but ain't nobody said nothing about us reaching in our pockets to pay for a cabin and a jail. That ain't gonna' happen."

Buck held up his hand to keep Emmett from exploding into a fit of rage.

"Don't forget the labor," he laughed. "I reminded them about what was said at the meeting. Well anyway, they agreed, get this, since you all were taxpayers, maybe they could use some of the money in the county larder and get a carpenter from out of town to build it."

Buck poured coffee into his saucer and blew upon it.

"I just looked at them and said, 'You reckon?'"

"Next, they told me to ask Sam if he'd donate the lumber to build everything with. You believe that shit, Emmett?"

"You got to be kidding. First give 'em the land, then they want the labor for free and now you're telling me they want the materials free, too?" Emmett whipped the air with his ever present cane.

"Now Emmett, hold up. I told them if they wanted to ask Sam to donate his lumber free, they had to come up here and ask him themselves, cause I sure as hell wasn't gonna' do. But they ain't got the balls."

His face reddened as he turned toward the door, hoping Rose had not heard his comment.

"Well, what then?" asked Emmett, impatience spreading across his face.

"After listening to their bullshit, I told 'em if they wanted me to, I'd come on up here and talk to you, but I said I'd probably have to tell you maybe you ought to go on and send somebody down to Raleigh and get their bosses up here to straighten out this mess. I knew you'd be mad as hell about what they said. Looks like I was right."

Emmett sat in disbelief. Buck continued, "Mayor Jarvis said for me to tell you all to start back paying your taxes and then they'd get started. So what's your answer?"

"Fuck 'em."

"Okay."

Buck grabbed another biscuit.

"Then I told 'em they oughta' get a list of materials ready, anyway. Sooner or later they got to do it, no matter what happens up here. So if you're gonna' see Sam, give him this list.

"And just between me and you, tell him to bid it high. He's already got the job—they don't want Raleigh nosing around . . . that is, if you folks still want to go through with everything."

Emmett took the list and put it in his vest pocket. He informed Buck that he and Rose were heading over to Sam's when he rode up. "This might put a smile on that man's face. You won't believe how much lumber he's got cut and stored already. It'll be his first paying job, if he takes it. He might not, though. I reckon he can use the money. But if nothing else, he might get a laugh out of it."

Buck's horse was brought from the stable. Buck asked, "Emmett, what you want me to tell those fellows?"

"Don't tell 'em nothing. I don't know what's gonna' happen."

"Can I take a biscuit with me?"

***

Emmett reined the horse and carriage over to the railing in front of Sam's cabin. Sam stepped through the door, holding a sheath of papers and a pencil in his hands.

"Keeping account's not my strong point," he said. He was pleased to see Emmett and especially, Rose. He asked them to come in and join him for coffee or tea as he stepped forward and extended his hand to Rose. He helped her from the carriage.

To observers, they may have appeared to remain too long in each other's arms.

Refusing help, Emmett carefully climbed from the carriage. Willie held the reins, ready to lead the horse and carriage to a makeshift stable.

"Hello, Willie, how you been?"

Willie was delighted that Massa Detwyler had spoken to him. He puffed his chest out and stood taller, aware the other slaves were watching.

"Jus fine, Suh, jus fine," he answered, his teeth shining brilliantly white behind dark lips.

"Sam, how you been, Son? Haven't seen you for a spell. Making all that money, right?"

"Yeah, wagon loads. Come on in. Let's get out of this cold. November and no snow on the ground."

"Snow or no snow, it's colder'n hell, ain't it?" said Emmett. Sam led the two inside and pulled two more of his straight-back cane-bottom chairs close to the stick and mud fireplace built into the back wall.

"Well, it's not much, but it's all I got right now. At least it's clean and warm. I'm outside most every day, and it does feel good coming in from the cold."

Sam was not apologizing for his living quarters or even concerned if they met other's approval. He knew Emmett's own folk had started their place in much the same manner.

Rose wouldn't judge him for how he had to live for now. They'd discussed their future. She knew the cabin was temporary—she knew he would be permanent. If any emotions showed in her eyes, they were of pride and adulation.

The logs had been stripped of their bark to keep the bugs and insects from calling it home, also. Stacked neatly and as straight as possible, the log walls had been chinked with sand and clay, mixed with field straw.

The stick and mud fireplace was added before the arrival of the first cold night. It had not been added as an afterthought—they had merely run out of time with so many other cabins to get ready before the first snow fell. It drafted well and heated the interior in spite of the canvas roof and windows.

Some of the earliest rough-sawn pine planks were made into tight fitting shutters and doors.

Already, there were over a dozen similar log and canvas cabins erected, and more nearing completion; all built with rough-cut and dried planks from the new sawmill. From afar came the rumble of noise; hammering, sawing and yelling—men working together and producing a lot. One could see a new cabin or barn rising in all directions.

Alone and near the creek, workmen were erecting the foundation of a much larger building. These men were highly skilled tradesmen and they had built many large and fine houses in the past. This particularly large house, Sam and Rose's future home, faced toward Swift Creek.

And it was big—that in keeping with a master's personal

dwelling.

Emmett was taken aback by how much was being accomplished. "Darndest sight I ever seen," he said to Sam.

A well crafted church, plain and simple, not burdened at every odd corner and roof edge with gingerbread trims, neared completion. The planking from the sawmill had a pleasing, clean look after being whitewashed. It had been built on a gentle rise east of what was beginning to look like a small town springing up out of the wilderness.

Sam was not a religious man, nor was he one to be sucked in by a preacher's promises. But the people who came with him needed a place to worship their own private God, so he'd built it for them.

They'd have to decide how to share the church since practically each family came with a different religion, even though they all professed to worship the same God. That, in itself, presents one of the many contradictions of religion, Sam thought

A one room school house neared completion and it would be ready at the start of the New Year. They would need a teacher soon. Ads had been posted near and far for a schoolmarm, but no one had inquired yet.

Little thought had been given to the inevitable separation of the white children and the slave children. For now, their favorite game was somehow related to seeing who could get the most mud on their clothes and in their hair.

The air was nippy and the children could see their breath vaporize as it was exhaled, yet they seemed to hardly notice the cold.

"We thought we'd take a short ride this morning, exercise Lady Lucy a bit, but "Her Majesty" was too smart for Toby to catch. Rose offered her an apple, but she's too smart to be bribed. Smart critter, that one. She ended up with the whole mess of apples . . . and a warm place to eat them," Emmett laughed.

"I suggested we ride out and see how things are coming along over here. So, here we are, Son."

Sam assured Emmett he was doing fine and everything was proceeding as planned. "Not as fast as I'd hoped, though. And it cost a lot more than I thought it would." he grimaced.

Emmett told Sam it was a fine thing he was doing, making sure his people were being put into permanent houses before he was.

"Never crossed my mind to do anything but," Sam shrugged. "Most of them have never had a house nearly as good as these, and we'll improve them next year. Without them happy, nothing's going to get done around here."

Emmett had called him Son twice since his arrival, an odd fact not lost on Sam.

A nearly inaudible whump . . . whump . . . whump rumbled from the heavily forested area to the northeast—something felt more than heard. Sam and the others at Swift Creek had grown accustomed to the feathery vibrations in the air.

The sawmill had been running for over a month. The furnace required a constant supply of wood and water and had to maintain a constant steam pressure, even overnight. The work days were long and lasted until all of the day's logs had been sawn and stacked.

The mechanics of the ungainly machine had been difficult to master. The mill had run cautiously for the first week; and at a loss of considerable money, but, no loss of life or limb.

Sam was pleased at how well the machine functioned. Already, they had not only been able to produce enough planking and structural materials to start building the necessary housing and other buildings, but a great deal of lumber had been stacked to dry in the sawmill yard. Sam had reached the point, sooner than he expected, in which he could start selling the surplus lumber.

Any day now, he and Henry would head out to locate lumber markets. He'd take James Motley along for advice. Always cautious, his search for the markets would be more of a fact finding mission than a contract search.

Two short blasts blew from the sawmill.

"There's the noon whistle. Still scares the animals, but the rest of us are used to it. You will stay for lunch, won't you?"

His guests looked forward to Sara's cooking. George was instructed to throw more wood on the fire and inform Sara there were two more guests for lunch.

"Willie, go tell Henry to come up to my cabin. Tell him we have guests."

Henry arrived shortly and he and Emmett greeted each other. He removed his sweat-stained, smoke-streaked hat and greeted Rose.

Sam had confided in Henry; eager to share his good fortune, but swore him to secrecy about his proposal to Rose. Henry had many times proven he was not one to take Sam's wishes lightly. Trust was never a concern between these two friends.

Sam asked Henry to be his best man when he and Rose did get around to marriage. He was proud of Sam's friendship. He asked if he could tell Sara and Sam had smiled, agreeing it would be alright if she would keep the secret, and of course, Henry vouched for his wife. But the next morning she playfully pinched Sam's cheek. Henry was embarrassed but Sam didn't mind.

Emmett told Sam and Henry about Buck's visit. Carlton County was still trying to avoid its responsibility to its northern citizens.

Let's wait and see, seemed to be the attitude of the men.

No one really expected much; therefore, not much time was used to discuss it further. But Emmett was anxious to surprise Sam with his first paying lumber order and announcing he would like to propose a toast for Sam's latest business venture, he handed him the lumber list for the new living quarters and jail.

"Sam, I would like to congratulate you on your first lumber sale." Rose and Henry joined Emmett and heaped praises upon him. Rose's eyes glistened with pride.

Emmett said, "Take it from me, Son, bid it high."

"Well, boss man, if we're finally gonna' start making some money around these parts, I reckon I'll get on back to work and get some more of those trees drug up to the mill." Henry shared good-byes with everyone and left the three alone.

They enjoyed Sara's meal—the woman could cook.

"Rose," asked Emmett, "are you about ready to get going?"

Sam answered for Rose, "Emmett, if it's alright with you, I would like Rose to stay a bit, that is if you don't mind, Rose?" Rose wanted to stay. Emmett stood and agreed to Sam's request.

"Just get her home before dark, alright?"

Willie raced ahead and returned with the horse and carriage for Mister Detwyler. Emmett smiled at the two and prepared to leave. Sam walked to the carriage with him. He told the elderly man there had been rumors of Griffen sneaking about.

Emmett's face grew taunt, as he said. "Sam, don't you take that son of a bitch lightly. As much as you think he might be worried about law problems—he ain't. He's gonna' try to kill you, but when he's ready. Don't ever take your eyes off him again. He'll shoot you in the back." Pausing, he added, "He'll kill Rose, too."

Sam was shocked by the strange statement. It was something new, something never said before, and it confused him.

"You really, really, need to trust me on this one. All that's left in him is dead. His soul's gone. Down deep, all he is, is a killer." Emmett held his eyes on Sam's for a long moment and then slapped the reins across the back of the horse and headed home.

Alone, with no one to share their time except each other, they embraced. Their embrace, soft and tender—each holding the other, was enough. The soft heartbeat of body against body and the whispery tickle of gentle breaths against each others face confirmed promises made. A whole life of passion awaited them. Their passion was exciting, adventurous, and certainly enjoyable, but for now they wanted to hold each other and whisper.

He discussed his plans to leave soon to research the lumber market. He and Henry would be leaving in a day or so. That settled, they focused on other needs, other desires.

Afterwards, they discussed their new home. Rose had much input about her likes and dislikes regarding the Swift Creek Mansion. Sam listened intently to her, but he knew he could be happy in the very log and canvas cabin he was in now, if she was there with him. He knew she was used to a finer home and that eventually she would have whatever her heart desired.

He and Rose had discussed the different mansions in the immediate area; those of neighbors and friends, and he reminded her he'd had a close look at Griffen's mansion, too. The mere mention of Hesper Griffen's name wrenched a shadow across her face. He felt her tremble, and that bothered him. The happiness and joy they were sharing—destroyed by the mention of the name.

Sam's concern was growing. If he and Rose were to share a life, they would have to share everything in that life; things pleasant and things not so pleasant. Rose and Emmett's reaction at the mere mention of Griffen's name was something that would take time to understand, but they would have to be the ones to open the doors to the dark secrets the two of them shared. He'd help; he'd do anything to protect her from harm. How many times had he asked himself if he had been the one that started all this strange uncertainty? How many times had he answered with the fact that whatever it was between Emmett and Griffen, it had been there long before he rode into Carlton County? Whatever it was, it had to be resolved.

Breaking into his thoughts, Rose asked what he wanted most in the new house. All he insisted upon was one of the large rooms on the first floor be left for him to do with as he pleased.

"You know, a place to have a smoke and a drink, now and again. Maybe my desk against that wall," he said as he pointed at the rough sketches the two of them had been drawing and redrawing. "Maybe a bed over in that corner so I won't have to chase you all over this big house." He grabbed her, playfully.

And playfully, she laughed. "You wouldn't have to chase me."

Sam insisted there be a widow's walk built into the roof line, like those built onto the large mansions along the Atlantic shores. They were all the rage. The ocean, with its outer banks was a very long way to the east, but he had always liked the looks of the walk. Those same unique designs were becoming popular with most of the larger homes being built further inland, far away from the ocean.

They had decided yet one other important thing. They were going to tell Emmett of their intention to marry. They decided to wait for the next day. Rose asked Sam to lunch and afterwards he could ask Emmett for her hand, properly. In doing so, he would show his respect to her cherished Uncle Em.

He asked Rose if she thought Emmett would be agreeable to his request and she answered he would not only be agreeable but happy for the two of them.

Their plan to speak to Emmett agreed upon, Sam reluctantly acknowledged he would have to be the one to open the door to their dark secret. He felt a sense of foreboding. He had seen the melancholy Rose nearly drowned under at the mere mention of Griffen's name, the opposite of Emmett's angry reactions. Someway, somehow, Griffen has to be connected to this family. He kept coming back to that one conviction. But how?

He could see and feel the joy radiating from her whenever she was in a safe place, a place where she knew she was sheltered from the evil of the man. He had to broach the subject. He could not let her, his wife to be, continue to carry the weight of such a problem. His wife would never be allowed to live her life burdened with the opposing weights of her secret misery and his immense love of her. He feared she would break and fold into herself.

He took both of her hands in his and said, "Rose, you can ask anything about me or my life that you want. I'll never lie to you. Not even a small lie. We can't have a life together unless we trust and believe in each other.

"No secrets—never any secrets," he said.

"I'm on my way to forty years old. I've done a lot of things in my life, some good, some bad. But Rose, I've never done anything to purposefully hurt any other living soul. I'd give anything I own to take back some of the things I've been forced to do lately, but I'm not going to give you up."

She realized Sam had made a decision—one that would affect the rest of her life. She also knew long-withheld secrets would have to be divulged. She did not want to go there, but knew she had to.

"I suppose some people will judge me a sinner, having spent most of my life gambling. But I never stole from anybody. I never drank that much, nor did I chase women. I'm no saint, but I'm no devil, either. There's blood on my hands, but I didn't want it there. I'd do it again, in a heartbeat, if I had to do it to save the life of someone close to me. I'll do it quicker than that, if someone tries to harm you." He was looking for a way to broach the dark, dark subject with Rose.

He felt her tense. He did not know how deep the root of her and Emmett's shared secret reached, but he suspected they were entwined in some way with Griffen. Venturing toward unopened doors, he needed to reassure her of his ever deepening love for her and his total respect for Emmett.

"I've always been alone. I've never wanted to share my life with any other soul. Not out of selfishness; I just never met anyone like you—but then I found you. I'll never make my life work, or any of this around us work, unless you are here to help me." He was nearing panic, fearing the demand he had to make would break her spirit.

"I'm going to ask you something that may hurt you, but maybe, it'll show you how much I love you. It's a chance I have to take."

Rose's eyes were downcast, her face drained of color.

"Go on, ask me what you need to know. And yes, there are things . . . ," her voice fading. She folded her trembling hands and placed them in her lap. Sam reached for her hands, wishing to calm and reassure her.

"Rose, I can't help but feel that you and Emmett share a secret. I wish I could tell you that your secret is of no importance to me, or us, but you know it is. Whenever the name of Hesper Griffen is mentioned around either of you, it's like a sadness takes hold. What's going on, Rose? Tell me. I can help. You and I can handle it."

Sam paused. He looked at her, giving her time to answer. Rose continued to stare at their clutched hands. Sam's heart thumped heavily in his chest as a tear—his tear—fell upon her hand.

He lifted her face to his and said, "Look at me. Look. My God, Rose, what's this all about? I'll take care of it. I swear that to you."

Her face turned pale. Dark circles had spread under her eyes. She knew how much Sam despised Hesper Griffen. She was frightened that what she had to tell him would tear them apart.

She lifted her face, her eyes pooling with tears, and said, "Sam . . . Hesper Griffen is my father." With that, she collapsed into his arms and sobbed. She was spent, emotionally wrecked and physically drained from forestalling the eventuality of telling Sam things he needed to know.

Rose's comment was unexpected.

How can that be? It sent his mind reeling with confusion, overpowering all logic. Yet he acknowledged it had to be true. No one could make up such a thing.

She was nearing collapse. He led her to the bed and laid her upon it and lay beside her, his arm over her, protecting her.

"Well," he said to her, his arms pulled her close and prayed she felt protected, "we'll just have to deal with it. Sleep."

Frayed and worn, her tired soul no longer willing or able to deal with ruined emotions, she collapsed, and spiraled into a deep sleep.

Sam remained beside her. He was not able to, nor desirous of sleep. After a very long time, he reluctantly stirred her from the much needed sleep. A rest that did not mend her tormented heart, but maybe, just maybe did provide a respite from her pain.

He gently nudged her, "Rose. Rose, darling. Wake up. I've got to get you home."

Her eyes, were red, swollen from grief. She looked like a lost child and he despised himself for forcing so much pain from within her tormented soul. He vowed to himself that she would never shed another tear of sadness in her lifetime.

He kissed her lips softly, and just as softly, her forehead, her teary eyelids, and her temples.

"Rose, he might be your father, but I'm going to be your husband. From now on, you will be the most loved woman in all the world. Emmett and I will both see to that."

"I know," she said. "Sam, I need to go home, alone. Will you have Henry drive me home?"

"Rose, that's not a good idea, not with the way you feel right now. I'll take you home."

"No, Sam, I need to talk to Emmett. He's lived with himself and his past too long. I know everything. I know what he needs. He needs time to prepare himself for you—for both of us. It's time for Uncle Em and I to deal with the past."

Chapter Seventeen

After a very long night and equally long morning, Sam knocked on Emmett's front door. Jonah opened the door and welcomed him in. He was directed into the sitting room and told Emmett would be down momentarily. A lazy fire spread its heat throughout the room. He sat near it, watching the dancing flames, and was soon lost in thought. He heard Emmett's cane hitting the steps as he carefully descended each tread, searching for solid footing. Now, for the first time, he heard the slow dragging shuffle of an old man. Emmett appeared to have aged ten years overnight and he struggled with the weight of the new day. Sam stood. He and Jonah stepped toward him, but determined to be his own man, he waved them away.

"Good morning, Sam. You doing alright this fine day?"

"I'm alright, Emmett. You?"

"Tired. Sore. It's called old age, I think," forcing a broken laugh.

Sam had never seen his friend look so old, so worn. He wanted to comfort him—make him feel better, but that would be wrong of him and he knew it.

Emmett walked to his chair and sank into its comfort. He sat motionless, he too, staring at the fire. Jonah stood behind him, awaiting his master's orders.

Emmett asked Sam if he would like a smoke. Although not a heavy smoker, he wanted one—needed one now. Soon Jonah brought coffee, brandy and cigars.

"Rose said you wanted to see me today," said Emmett, pausing to let Sam confirm the statement.

"Yes Sir, I do."

Emmett looked at him, but remained quiet.

"Sir, I don't know any other way to ask you this, so I'm just going to ask it straight out. May I have Rose's hand in marriage?"

An eternity passed for Sam, but he never diverted his eyes from Emmett's. Color slowly seeped back into his old friend's face. Emmett relaxed and the worry and wear that had erupted on his face overnight, melted away. His lips spread into a smile.

"Son, she's already yours."

Raising his brandy, he toasted Sam. "To you and Rose. Welcome to our family, Son."

***

With things yet to be said, huge and momentous things, Sam sat quietly, his heart thumping. Emmett was finding his way to tell their story, his and Rose's, so he remained quiet and respectful. He knew Emmett was not one to run on with careless conversation. He would say whatever was on his mind, clearly, precisely, in order for once to be enough. It would be complete, it would be true. Emmett set his brandy down, took a sip of his coffee and lit his cigar.

Sam gulped his brandy, and wished for more. He wanted to be calmer—he needed to be calmer than he was.

"Rose and I had a long talk last night. We were up 'till late hours and I agree with her and you both, you can't enter into this marriage without knowing everything you need to know. And Son, there's a lot of history to this place. Really, it's three stories—one about her mother, one about her father, and the other about Rose's life with me.

"Rose is my heart—more than that, she's blood-kin. She's my niece . . . more of a daughter, really. When Rose come home she told me what the two of you discussed yesterday. She said she didn't tell you much more than Griffen being her father."

Sam dared not interrupt Emmett. He knew he was going to hear things even he had not expected.

"And yes Sam, that son of a bitch is her real father. Few people know what I'm gonna' tell you, but you need to hear it for Rose's sake."

Sam's alarm grew. No longer stunned by Rose's disclosure, he was more confused than ever. His mind churned. He recalled Isaac's brief comment about Rose. He knows more than he let on. Strangely, he felt betrayed. Emmett's her uncle? What the hell's going on here? Yes, Rose had called Emmett "Uncle Em" many times. But until now Sam felt it had been merely an expression of her love—her way of showing love to the man who had been so benevolent and so caring of her. So many more questions remained, each needing answers.

Emmett interrupted Sam's baffled thoughts. "Where to start? In order for you to understand, I've got to go back a ways so this will make sense to you. Rose is gonna' be your wife and I am very happy for both of you. She knows Griffen is her father. She knows I am her uncle. And she knows that I've had to concoct an elaborate history to hide her behind. And everything was done for her sake . . . , everything," he paused, gauging Sam's reactions, but Sam's face remained a mask of confusion.

"You'll understand in a bit."

Sam certainly did not understand, not now. He wanted to—and hoped he would. He understood these two people, one he had grown to respect and one he had grown to love, must have gone through hell. Emmett rapped the floor with his cane and Jonah immediately entered the room.

"Go fetch Miss Rose."

"Yas Suh."

Rose entered and walked over to Emmett. She gave him a kiss on his forehead, and then sat next to Sam. Sam took her hands in his.

"Rose, Emmett said yes."

Her eyes sparkling with joy, she stood and rushed to her beloved Uncle.

"Thank you, thank you, thank you, Uncle Em. I love you so much." Sam had risen to show respect for the love the two shared and she rushed back into his arms. She hugged him with all of her might.

"And I love you, too," she whispered in his ear.

Emmett waited for the two to release their embrace and sit next to each other.

"Rose, I'm gonna' tell Sam a story about you and me. You know most of it, the important parts, but there are things I couldn't tell you, not just yet."

He watched her closely, praying she would be strong.

"You were protected and safe—that's all I needed, and all you needed, then. But now it's time for you to know the rest. I have to tell you everything, or you'll never be able to get on with your life."

***

Facing Sam, he said, "Me and Sissy—Sissy's my sister, were born right here in this house, upstairs in that bedroom right over us," as he pointed above. "Her birth name was Abigail. Me and Dad called her Sissy. She was Rose's mother.

"This was a quiet, out of the way place back then. Still is." He shook his head thinking of the solitude of their younger days.

"Dad's sister and her husband, Aunt Ella May and Uncle Robert were about the only folks what ever visited us. Me and Sissy got our schooling here at home. Fort Harwood was too far away but Sissy did get sent to Raleigh for something Mom and Dad called a "Finishing School."

"When she was gone off to that school, I was bored to death what with nobody else around. That's how I come to meet Griffen. I know'd he was odd the first time I ever seen him. You know, messed up, up here," he said, pointing to his head. "Like his marble bag didn't have no marbles in it. Hard to put a name on it. He was, well, different. Cruel. Mean."

Sam saw hatred in his friend's eyes. Emmett's jaw clinched.

"He know'd a lot of stuff and I kinda' thought I wanted to be like him, but me wanting to be like him got my sorry ass throw'd into Rocky Mount's boys' school. I'd started acting more and more like him. I reckon I kinda' got outta' hand.

"Now Sam, you might be asking yourself right about now, what's all this got to do with Rose? Mostly, what I'm doing is, I'm trying to show the two of you how a person like Hesper Griffen could ruin somebody's life—how much sway he held over people.

"By the time I come home from that boys' school, Hesper'd started getting stranger and stranger.

"Folks said his daddy told him he was gonna' send him off to the same school I'd been throw'd into 'cause of the way he was acting and the next day his pa found his best stud stallion dead, shot in the head. Everybody said it was Hesper what done it, and I still think it was him.

"And there's the story about a little darky girl what got herself kilt back off in them woods 'tween Arcola and his ma and pa's place. There weren't no doubt that somebody crazy had to have kilt her—what with her tore up all to hell and back the way she was, and not a stitch of her clothing around nowheres.

"Everybody in Arcola suspected Hesper done it; him being a raging terror and all, but he didn't give a rat's ass what nobody thought.

"When I got home from that boys' school, I didn't want nothing to do with him ever again.

"But then, Sissy come home."

Chapter Eighteen

"When she come home from that finishing school place, she come home different. She was changed. She'd always been a tomboy, but when she got back she seemed withdrawn, distant somehow. It didn't take long; maybe a couple days before she warmed up to me and it didn't take no genius to see she was already tired of being home. Couldn't blame her. Weren't a damn thing for her or me to do around here."

Emmett's expressions changed drastically, depending on who he was talking about. Sam had seen the stressed and tightening muscles on his face whenever he spoke of Hesper. Now he saw the calm, almost whimsical expressions as he talked about his sister, Abigail.

Emmett feared for Rose, his face strained with concern.

He prayed she would not be saddened by him dredging up memories from long ago.

"Rose, sweetheart, I asked your mama what good she thought that school did for her. She told me she never really wanted to go to the school as much as she wanted to find out some of what the rest of the world was like. 'Tween here and Raleigh was the only world she'd ever seen, so in a way, that was her world then.

"I wanted to know what the people in Raleigh were like, too. So she told me they weren't no different than folks anywhere. She had a broader view than I did, 'cause she'd been places I hadn't. She said it was her opinion the world was filled with two kinds of people and all of 'em just sitting on top of a split rail fence. On one side was a field of fresh cut hay and life on that side was soft and smelled good, and on the other side was a cow pasture with packed down dirt and fresh cow patties and it didn't smell so good. But nobody could sit on top of the fence their whole lives. At some point they had to choose which side to get off on; either step down on a grass welcome mat or step down in a turd." Emmett chuckled, recalling how he had laughed over her colorful choice of words.

"I reckon that's still true, don't you? Sam."

Sam smiled and nodded.

"It weren't long before Sissy and I started taking rides out into the countryside again. And it weren't long before Hesper Griffen's name come up—it had to.

"I didn't have nothing nice to say about him. But with no other fellows around these here parts, she seemed interested in him and I sure as hell didn't like that one bit.

"She wanted to be off and gone all the time. She took to riding every which way up and down all the roads out there," he said, with a flourish of his hand.

"One day she come back earlier than usual. When she found me and got my attention she pulled me off to the side to tell me about her ride up on the north road.

"You ain't got to get your brain in a sweat to figure out who she met, do you? Yep, Hesper—Hesper Son of a Bitch Griffen.

"She asked me a bunch of stuff about him, like, was he a big man? what he looked like? did he drink much" and why he acted strange?

"Now Sam, I'm gonna' tell you, I weren't quite sure how to handle that situation. All I know'd was that I didn't want him worming himself into her life, so I told her flat out to stay away from him. Hah . . . like that would work.

"I tried to reason with her; told her he weren't no good. And told her if she messed with him, she was gonna' get hurt. That's what I said to her. Might as well been talking to that chair you're sitting in.

"She looked at me with them big doe eyes of her's and said, 'Okay.' Just one little word from her and I didn't believe a word of it."

The grimace on Emmett's face eased after he unfurled his aching legs.

"The thing you got to remember, is that son of a bitch was the onliest man around these here parts what was near 'bout her age, or close to it."

Emmett stared out the window, gathering his thoughts. "Seemed to me she coulda' set her sights some higher, though. I pretty much figured she was planning more accidental meetings with the oversized ox. Out of my hands, but I told her she was sitting on a split rail fence of her own making and she was about ready to step down into cow flop.

"About that time, Dad died. It was hard on all of us, but Sissy took it real bad. We all had to make some hard decisions. What to do . . . how to hold this place together, but Sissy weren't too good at making decisions—for sure, not good decisions."

Again, Emmett struggled to his feet and paced. His hip and legs hurt as he tried to walk off the pain. He bent from side to side stretching muscles grown too old and too tight to flex. He grimaced as he stretched. His energy seemed to plummet.

"It's only two in the afternoon, plenty of time to finish the story. You young folks take a break. I'm gonna' lay down for a spell. We can finish up in a while."

He stepped onto the lower tread, lighting a cigar as he did. He slowly climbed the stairs as he headed for a waiting bottle of Laudanum.

Sam and Rose strolled to the privacy of a small park by the creek.

He held her tightly in his arms—hoping to comfort her. The last two days had crushed her. He saw proof in her drawn face and dark eyes.

"Are you alright?" he asked, feeling her body relax as he put his arms around her and pulled her close.

"I'm fine. It's you I'm worried about. Are you okay?" Rose inquired. "Uncle Em's reliving some hard memories. Probably more than I'll ever know. I wish I could make him understand that he wasn't responsible for my mother. Nobody's responsible for anybody in the long run, don't you think, Sam?"

Sam bent and kissed her long and lovingly. He said, "Maybe, but I want to be responsible for you. It would give my life meaning." She laid her face against his chest. She loved him dearly.

Back in the large room, Jonah served steaming coffee. Emmett came down from his nap, looking rested. A false bravado masking his tired face, he cheerfully asked if they were ready for the balance of the story. Sam suspected Emmett might have fallen victim to the lure of the bottled opiate he himself had warned Sam to be so cautious with. Even so, he knew it was not his position to judge the man.

Emmett sat in his chair, obviously in less pain, and continued.

"Where was I? Oh yeah. Our Mother, Rose's Grandmother, didn't last long after Dad died. I wanted to run off from this place.

Too sad to go, too sad to stay. Me and Sissy was numb, just plain numb. Neither of us could feel much of nothing no more. All of our lives, me and her had been part of a family, and now we was all what was left of that family.

"I tried to be strong for her but I didn't know how or what to do. And then, after a while she come back; come back even stronger. Maybe more determined not to die off like everybody else, except me, and we started being a family again. It was like she had decided since life was unsure and dying so final, she was gonna' do some crowding into hers. We did alright for a long time. Her's got too crowded, though.

"We managed to get along with just the two of us taking care of this place. One thing that Sissy insisted on was total say with the house servants, and I was glad to give it up, 'cept for Jonah. Having Jonah around somehow made me feel closer to my father and he pretty much kept me acting like a master's 'spose to.

"Her keeping the house running good gave her more purpose than she'd had for a long time.

"Times weren't that hard for us after we settled in and started running the place like we was supposed to and I'd begun to think that Griffen was gonna' be a thing of the past.

"But looking back, it seemed destined that son of a bitch would come waltzing back into our lives, and sure as hell, he did. Sissy'd started taking her rides—meeting him.

"Of course, I know'd what she was up to when she went on her rides, but I couldn't do much about it. Sometimes she'd come in earlier than I expected, sometimes a lot later than I thought was right. Then sometimes she'd come home, her eyes red from crying and soon enough she'd be up in her room laughing. Next time, here she comes laughing and, yeah—then, I'd hear her crying. She had enough reasons to be a mite messed up—stuff I didn't know nothing about 'till later on."

Again Emmett paused, an anger building in him like Sam had never seen.

"Hesper Griffen ruined that girl. I shoulda' kilt him when I had a chance. Had enough reasons to kill him—had more reasons than I know'd I had. Almost did it, too. Got it all planned out and loaded myself up with guns to shoot him dead and got ready to ride up there and shoot the bastard full of holes. God would have blessed me if I'd done it, but my plans got changed when Sissy come home beat all to hell and back. Big fat lip, black eyes, busted nose, straw and twigs sticking outta' her hair. I fetched Jonah and told him to get running for Doc and Sheriff O'Malley—O'Malley was the sheriff then. Doc's been gone for a long time. I was real mad, what with Sissy a hurting like she was. But hell, Sam, there weren't nothing to be gained by shooting him when he was drunk—bastard wouldn't have suffered enough for me.

"If it hadn't been for Doc getting out here fast, I don't reckon none of us woulda' survived that night. Doc fixed her up with nerve medicine and she finally fell asleep. But she wouldn't even talk to Sheriff O'Malley. Afraid it'd get back to him, I suppose.

"What started off as one of the worst days Sissy and I ever had, calmed down enough so me and her could try to get things worked out again. Not necessarily back to normal. Lately, normal had been kinda' bad.

"We talked mostly about Hesper, who else? She went all the way from saying how much she hated his sorry ass, to asking me if I thought she oughta' forgive him.

"After a coupla' days she packed up a bunch of her clothes and grabbed Poppy, her Nigra girl, and took off back to Griffen's place again."

He sipped his coffee and dug through his vest for another cigar.

"I didn't see her for nigh on a year after that. But then one day, Jonah come out to the fields and told me I needed to come to the front yard 'cause Sissy'd just pulled up.

"I didn't know exactly how I felt about that. I rounded the corner and sitting in the carriage, there she was. Her hands folded, and her trying to look at me straight on, but she couldn't do it. My heart missed a beat when I seen how near she was to folding in on herself.

"I'd prayed she'd moved on with her life, if that was what it took for her to be shed of Hesper—even if it meant she'd moved far off somewheres and I'd never get another chance to see her again. But that ain't what happened.

"As clear as if it were yesterday, I remember her trying to sound all happy and brave and I was at a loss for words. She asked me if I was going to give the new bride a kiss.

"I walked over to the side of the carriage and reached up to her with my hands and before one foot hit the ground, she was hanging on me, crying like a baby, 'cept a whole lot harder.

"After her telling me she was married sunk in, I took her by the shoulders and looked at them tear soaked, red eyes of her's and I asked her if she'd married that sorry-ass bastard and what the hell was she thinking. Then she really busted loose crying.

"I was going to take her into the house but she started walking slower and slower and sat down on one of the porch chairs. She wanted—needed, really—to be in a place where she could keep an eye on the road. I understood then that she'd run off and didn't tell nobody where she was going and I know'd she'd done it out of desperation.

"I asked her when and she looked at me like she had no idea what I was asking her, so I asked her as clear as I could how long ago did she marry him.

"She told me six months or so and that Hesper told her he'd sent one of his Nigra boys down here to invite me to come to their wedding. She looked puzzled and asked me if I didn't know about the wedding and I had to tell her the truth—which was no. Hell, Sam, I didn't even know where she was all that time.

"She went on about how she thought I didn't come because I hated her for all the problems and the way she acted all the time. She asked if I woulda' come if I'd know'd about it?

"I hugged her and assured her of course I woulda' gone; at least that's what I figured she needed to hear. Mighta' been true, but I doubt it. And she busted out with a new flood of tears so I told her all I'd ever wanted was for her to be happy, but it seemed like she worked real hard at making herself miserable.

"While she's crying like a baby, she said she know'd she made a big mistake marrying into that family. Said Hesper's mother and father couldn't stand the sight of her and that Hesper was crazy as a person could get and still be able to breath. She said she didn't just go off for a ride—she had the stable boy harness her carriage and she ran with Poppy as fast as she could.

"She told me she reckoned there was a bunch of trouble on its way, but she didn't have one place left where she could go. Told me I was the only person she could come to and that I was the only person she know'd who was not afraid of him and said he know'd it, too.

Chapter Nineteen

"So there we where, right back where we'd always been. I sent Jonah to find one of the Nigras to hide up the road and watch out for anybody coming this way. I got some of the hired fellows and told 'em to grab their guns and get up here to the house.

"About time when the chickens go to roost, Jonah's boy come's a foot'n it back down the road and told me some fellows in a wagon was heading this way. The one driving the team said he come to fetch his boss's wife, and I told him he'd play hell doing it.

"What that idiot didn't know was Harley Hatfield, my overseer then, had slipped up next to the mules and when that fellow stepped around them mules, Harley clobbered the hell outta' him. Knocked him plum out." Enjoying the memory, Emmett laughed—his first good laugh of the day.

"That other fellow up in the wagon got a gun stuck hard in his ribs by a 'nother of my hands and we tied 'em both up good and throw'd 'em back in the wagon. I smacked them mules' asses and sent 'em runnin'.

"But that wouldn't stop Hesper. He'd be coming, and soon. We both know'd it. So I had to get Sissy outta' here and hide her somewhere. Uncle Robert and Aunt Ellie's place was the only place I could think of and it was a long way off. The further the better, I told Sissy. They lived in Lumberton, down close to South Carolina.

"She started packing stuff to take with her and that's when she told me she was with child. That damn near knocked me down. I asked her if Hesper know'd it and she said he didn't. That was a relief. Daddy's need to know about their babies, but I sure was glad he didn't know about his'un.

"On our way through Fort Harwood, we stopped at Sheriff O'Malley's office and he said he'd send some of his men up here to keep an eye open for Hesper or his men.

"Me and her got down to Uncle Robert's and after I told them what was going on up here, they took her in. They were getting on in years and first thing I thought was they couldn't handle much of a change in their lives, but I was wrong. They took to Sissy and she took to them.

"She was 'bout near scared to death, knowing I had to leave soon, but it didn't take long for her to see she only had two choices to decide on; to stay there hid away, or come back with me and wait for Hesper to come and get her. So she stayed there. First smart thing she'd done in a long time.

"I visited her as often as I could. She needed a bunch of her things and money too, so about every six months or so, I'd go down and take stuff to her.

"Elmer helped me as much as he could; so things worked out pretty good."

He looked at Rose. The drawn expression on his face softened.

"She looks so much like her mother," he said to Sam.

"My first trip back proved she was with child, alright. Big as a watermelon and 'bout ready to pop," he laughed. "She had changed so much, too. She looked healthier and the worry lines on her face was gone and most important of all, she was happy.

"Uncle Robert went into Lumberton and made sure the Doctor know'd about the baby coming. Told him Abigail was a niece of his from down around Atlanta whose husband died so he took her in. I stayed a few days with them and we got a few more plans figured out.

"I asked Uncle Robert if he could figure out a way to get her name changed down there to something besides Griffen—anything to throw Hesper off her trail and that I'd pay all the expenses plus some extra for his troubles. He said she ought to be named Bailey like his name, then there'd be less for people to wonder about. I agreed it was a good idea and he went and done it. When I got back down there the next time, he introduced me to Miss Abigail Bailey.

"That's how come Rose's last name is Bailey . . . and not Griffen"

He tapped the cane on the floor and Jonah instantly appeared in the room.

"Jonah, go get us something a bit stronger than this coffee." Jonah left, knowing that meant whiskies for the men, coffee or tea for Rose.

"Once I know'd Sissy was gonna' be alright, well . . . at least safe and protected, I had to get back up here. Still had this place to keep running."

He held Rose's hand. "I was worried about this little girl coming into this world with no daddy around. I hoped Uncle Robert and Aunt Ellie could be some help to Sissy when it was time for you to be born," he said, giving her a fatherly kiss on the cheek as he held her hand.

"I didn't have to worry none 'bout that. They was plum crazy 'bout you."

Rose smiled lovingly at her Uncle.

"On the way home I stopped at Sheriff O'Malley's and asked if anything happened while I was down there in Lumberton. He said some stuff, things like Griffen riding up in the yard out there, and yelling at the house for me to send Sissy out, and raising hell in general."

Emmett continued. "After a while, things started taking on a normal pace and that kinda' had a way of making me slow down with the constant worrying about Sissy and Hesper's trying to find her. I started thinking Griffen had decided to let it go and quit with his hell raising. I was sure wrong about that.

"I finally got a chance to go back down to visit with Sissy and Uncle Robert and Aunt Ellie. I didn't know this little thing was waiting for me, too," he gently brushed aside a tear falling down Rose's cheek.

"You were two months old when I got there and darn if you weren't about the prettiest thing I'd ever seen—still is, ain't she, Sam?"

Rose smiled at Emmett and blushed.

"She sure is," replied Sam.

"I stayed about a week, that trip. Got to know the Reverend Hicks and his wife Liddy. Good folks, them two. They still write to me and Rose. 'Cause of them two, I got to find out stuff I didn't know about Abigail."

Chapter Twenty

"On that same trip when I first seen Rose they come out after the Sunday go-to-church meeting to visit with Uncle Robert and Aunt Ellie, and of course by then, they had grow'd fond of Sissy and carried on over her and the new baby like Lord A' Mitey. They'd been told enough to know what Sissy was up against and they were sworn to secrecy.

"They sure are good people." He paused, his voice low and soft, "I owe them a lot for all they done for Abigail and Rose. We both do."

His face flushed crimson. It always did when Emmett's rage was building.

Rose recognized the growing rage and stood to leave.

Sam watched Rose stand. He correctly feared there might be things she'd never heard and that she could handle no more.

"Excuse me," she said, "I don't need to hear this. I'll be back soon."

He stood, intending to go to with her, to comfort her.

"No. Sam please stay," she said.

Emmett continued, "After Sunday dinner we all went out on the porch to get some air and I got to watching Sissy and Reverend Hicks and his wife, and all of 'em looking at each other like they got a secret. Sissy got to fidgeting like she didn't want to be nowheres around. I was toting Rose around with me and Miss Hicks come over and took her and went inside the house. So I figured I was about to hear something I might not be wanting to hear.

"Reverend Hicks got me off to the side and asked if I would take a walk with him. When Sissy seen that, she run off back inside the house.

"Me and Reverend Hicks walked to a pond out back where'd I'd set up a bench and a swing, mostly for Sissy to swing the baby on when she got here, and he asked me to sit down and talk with him.

"He told me he always told the folks in his church they could come to him with any problems or things what might be bothering them. But what he told me next cleared up everything I'd ever needed to know about Sissy being the way she was. It ain't pretty—but it's true.

"He said Sissy had a real hard time telling him stuff what needed to be told to somebody.

"Remember how I told you Sissy'd come home happy sometimes; busted up and crying the next? That was the night she come home crying, beat up, bruised and with grass and twigs in her hair. He said Sissy told him she'd been bleeding so bad from . . . ah, you know . . . down there, that she had to keep changing her clothes to hide it from me. She never did come home looking that bad again, but there was other things . . . "

He stood and walked over to the window, contemplating how far he should go with this part of the conversation. He was not a vulgar man and dreaded what he felt he should say. He chose his words carefully.

"Plain and simple, that husband of her's did things to her what no man should never do to a woman, 'less she wants him to. And what he done, no woman's gonna' ever want that done. He told me when they was seeing each other, Hesper'd forced himself on her. They'd both started drinking a lot . . . well, he always did, and I believe she started drinking just to be accepted. She told the Reverend sometimes she drank so much she'd pass out. And Hesper'd take advantage of that. Let other men sleep with her so he could watch.

"And there were other things . . ."

Emmett abruptly stopped talking. Shaking his head, clearing it, he gave himself time to gathered his thoughts. "I thought I was going to come apart when I heard that stuff.

"Sissy told the Reverend that Hesper cried like a young'un about the stuff he'd done to her and the stuff he'd made her do and promised he'd never like it again. Fooled Sissy, though. She believed him 'cause she needed to believe him.

"He'd treat her like a queen one minute and like trash needing to be throw'd out the next. I asked Reverend Hicks how somebody could let themselves be treated that way and take so long to run off from it. He said Sissy told him all she ever wanted was for somebody to love her and figured Griffen deep down know'd what he done was wrong, 'cause he'd cried so hard and begged her to forgive him and not leave him and said he'd never do it again and sure enough, he didn't—'till he forgot his promises and that didn't take long.

"He's a dead man—I remember thinking.

"Sam, Sissy reckoned I mighta' know'd about Hesper forcing himself on her and that other stuff, but I never said nary a word to her about it. Weren't no need to—the past was gone and that's something Rose don't know nothing about. All she know'd, 'till later on, was her mama and the man she was told was her daddy didn't live together cause he died.

"I didn't never think nobody could do them kinda' things to other people. It ain't natural. But I can't see no reason to ever tell Rose anything about it now. But that's between the two of you and that's all I gotta' say about that."

The implications of what he'd been told and what it could do to Rose were immediate and Sam knew she'd never know about it.

Continuing, Emmett said, "What with Sissy and the baby needing stuff, I had to get some money down to her and besides I sure wanted to see that little girl again," he said, looking toward the door Rose left through moments before.

He hoped she would return, and hoped she wouldn't.

"Elmer was helping me with some of my plans and me and him was gonna' meet down close to his house. We was trying to be secret about things, but I kinda' dropped my guard, I reckon.

"I rode on through the cut close to where me and Elmer was 'spose to meet up and out in front of me steps four men. Hell, I know'd it was Griffen 'fore I ever even seen 'em. I weren't worried about him shooting me, not a bit—figured I had something he wanted mighty bad. Sure as hell was wrong about that, too.

"They drug me off that horse and Griffen tore into me. My horse lit outta' there like they done stuck a red-hot pike in its ass. Good thing, too—saved my life, hauling out the way it did. It weren't no more than half a mile to where Elmer was waiting for me and that was the direction my horse run off in.

"Griffen sunk a boot right in my gut. Made me throw up like I'd been drinking coal oil. He asked me where I took his wife after I stole her off from him. Called me a wife-stealer. Weird, off the wall, crazy stuff.

"He told me I had two minutes to tell him where she was. But

I didn't say nothing. He got real mean then. I tried to get up on my feet. When I looked up at that bastard to tell him to go to hell, he's kinda' like falling back, like he's gonna' try to run off. He's looking past me, hard down the road, back in the dark. He had a gun in his hand and pointed it at me. I tried to make a run for it, and got shot in the ass doing it.

"Elmer'd heard the ruckus and come running at the same time Hesper shot me in the ass—tore a chunk outta' my hipbone 'bout the size of a walnut. Elmer shot one of them fellows what was helping Hesper, deader'n a rock. He told me Hesper and them other two fellows lit out through the woods like scairt' rabbits. Four days later, I woke up in my bed with Doc sitting there staring at me.

"Doc told me I had a coupla' busted up ribs and a ear almost tore off. He sewed it back on with catgut, and told me if I moved around much, it'd fall off again. So I didn't and it didn't. See?"

He started laughing as he held his hair back and exposed a ragged, scarred ear.

"Don't worry, I ain't gonna' drop my pants and show you where I got shot in the ass."

Chapter Twenty One

"One day 'bout eleven, twelve years ago, Reverend Hicks, sent me a letter. When I opened it, he told me somebody'd kilt done Abigail and that Rose was staying with him and his wife.

"How would you like to open a letter like that?" he asked Sam and hung his head for a long moment.

"God, I thought I was going to die and after that bit of news, I went back to reading, fearing even worse news, if that was possible, and the rest of the letter scared me pretty bad, too."

Sam's heart ached for Emmett and Rose. It wasn't hard for him to imagine how grief-stricken they must have been. Him losing a sister, her losing a mother.

"The letter said all he know'd was what Rose was able to tell him and the Sheriff down there, and that weren't much. He said I needed to come and get Rose 'cause she was in a bad way, what with every living person she know'd as family gone, 'cept me; Uncle Robert and Aunt Ellie dead and gone and now her mama, so I got down there within two days.

"Rose was near 'bout thirteen years old then and Sam, you ain't never seen such a lost person in your whole life. She clung on me like she was scared to death. And when she weren't hanging on me, I was hanging on her. It was a hell of a mess.

"I was worried about bringing her back here. Seemed like it would have been a death sentence for her, but there weren't no way I could leave her there in Lumberton.

"A lot of things got to running around in my mind. Like how would it look to have a young girl out here with me? What would folks think? What if Griffen got to wondering who she was?

"By the time me and her got back to Fort Harwood, I'd fig-ured a way to hide her in plain sight. Doc told me he was fixing to quit doctoring up folks in a month or so, but said he'd stay on a bit longer if that would help some and she could work as a nurse at his office 'till things settled down for her.

"I told her the people in town needed to get used to her so the nosy ones wouldn't start asking a bunch of questions about her. After I explained to her that I'd come see her every two, three days. That helped some.

"So Doc went over to the Fort Harwood weekly paper and put a notice in it telling folks in town and the rest of the county that he was gonna' stay at doctoring folks for another month, but that was it and they needed to get themselves 'nother doctor.

"She lived with Doc while he was closing up his office. That way I could make out like I was stopping to see Doc and all the time, I was really visiting Rose.

"It took a while for her to tell me and Doc what she seen happen to her mama. We didn't push her none about it. We figured after she learned how to deal with it, she'd tell us. Then one day, she said after coming home from school, she heard her mama yelling and screaming and said it scared her real bad. She said she hid behind the well in the back yard, not knowing what else to do and two men busted outta' the kitchen door and they was dragging her mama with 'em and yelling at her mama to shut up. They tore out of that yard and she ain't never seen her mama again," Emmett said, shaking his head as if he felt the pain within the frightened child.

"Rose told me she seen two men and she described one of 'em real good. Said he was a short fat man and he was with another man that she didn't remember much about. She'd told the sheriff in Lumberton the same thing. I reckon he tried to find somebody down there what looked like she said, but he didn't have enough information to go on.

"He told me when I went back down there, that they hadn't found Abigail's body so I tried looking around but it was just me and I couldn't get nowhere by myself, so I come back here to make sure Rose was alright. About a week later they found Abigail's body floating in a swamp close to Lumberton. Reverend Hicks sent me another letter and told me he was sorry, but they couldn't wait for me to come to her funeral, cause she had to be buried quick. 'Bout two, three weeks later, I went down there and helped get rid of the house. Gave it and everything in it to the Reverend's church for folks what's in need. Got her a nice tombstone made while I was there, too.

"Then things went bad over at Doc's place."

Emmett, greatly agitated, began pacing the floor. Sam and he both remained quiet for a while. Sam thinking of the horrors Rose had gone through—Emmett trying to calm his building rage.

"Now look, Sam. This is important. Doc seemed anxious as hell to see me when I got back in town. First thing he said to me was we had a problem. So I asked him what happened, but before he could tell me, Rose come out and clamped on to me and all the time she was crying and saying she seen the man what kilt her mama. I couldn't see how that had happened 'cause Hesper avoided Fort Harwood as much as he could and did most of his trading over in Arcola or up in Weldon.

"I know'd Rose was not allowed in the front office—ever, and only outside when Doc or somebody was with her. And she weren't never allowed on the office side of the curtain, neither. She could hear folks what come in to see Doc but she weren't supposed to never open the curtain and look in.

"She said she heard a man's voice and it sounded like the man she heard when her mama got kilt. That scared her real bad, so she run out the back door and hid on the far side of the house behind the rosebush at the corner of the fireplace. Then a fat man come out of Doc's office and walked past her and she got a real good look at him. Doc went looking for Rose 'cause she weren't in the house. He found her hiding under the house, back behind the chimney, scared to death, so he took her inside and got her settled down and asked her why she went outside by herself. She told him what she seen.

"My anger was getting ahead of me. I knew he was going to say it was Griffen, who else? So I asked him who was in his office?

"Doc looked down at Rose and then at me and nodded his head like he wanted her out of the room, like he didn't want her to hear him, so I told her to go back in the kitchen and put on some coffee.

"Doc said Shorty Jackson was the only man what come to the office all day. You know that Jackson fellow, Sam—that short fat fellow who owns the tavern over in Arcola. And Hesper ain't short and fat. He's kinda' tall, tall as me, and skinny.

"Now, that damn near knocked me over—her saying she saw Shorty in Lumberton. But I thought 'bout it for awhile. Griffen did do most of his drinking at Shorty's tavern and they were kinda' like friends, so it didn't take much to put the two of them together. Me and Doc decided we needed to keep what Rose told us to ourselves 'till we could get some proof.

"But back to our plan. About a month later, me and him went back to the paper and he told that paper man to run a new notice for his niece. Doc told him she needed a new place to live and that she was getting good at learning nursing and he'd appreciate it if somebody would take her in.

"Just like we planned it, when he finished his part of the talking, I stepped right up in front of the paper man, acting like I'd just got this big idea and asked Doc—mostly so the paper man would hear, why couldn't she come out to my place and help take care of the Nigras and some of them other folks up my way? Told him one or the other of 'em was always getting sick.

"What better way to get the story spread around about how come she was living out at my place, than let the paper man get a hold of it and tell everybody for us?

"Doc said that was a good idea. So when the paper come out, that paper man even run an article about how 'the town folks was sure gonna' miss their nurse after she moved up to the Detwyler's place to help with the folks up in the north part of the county.'

"And soon, it was the right time to pack her up and get her on out here. She ain't never been far outta' my sight since then.

"That's why Rose lives here with me." Emmett sighed; relieved he had finished the story.

But he wasn't through.

"Shorty coulda' been one of the men she seen. She seemed sure she'd seen him before and it was only about a month, maybe two, after her mama got kilt, so the memory part was right, but Sam, Shorty didn't kill Abigail, there ain't no way. Shorty's a coward, Sam, you know that. Not only is he a coward, but he can't put two thoughts together without forgetting the first one.

"And why would he kill her? What coulda' possibly been his reason? Everything keeps going back to Griffen. I've wondered a thousand times if Rose could be wrong. She'd been through hell but she was just a child so I didn't hound her no more about it. I did make sure she never, never went near Arcola or by Hesper Griffen's place. Weldon, neither. I didn't want her to see Hesper. Not just then. That coulda' turned into a real mess, if she did.

"I know," he said, pointing up the road leading toward Griffen's plantation, "he kilt Abigail—sure as there is a God in Heaven. That's why I been telling you over and over not to ever turn your back on him.

"And I'm going to kill him. I've been waiting a long time for Rose to grow up and get a life all her own. I'm up in years and I'm ready to pay the price if I get caught for doing it, and it'd be worth it if that's what it takes to keep her safe.

"Son, I believe you love Rose as much as she loves you. I'm glad you two youngsters want to get hitched. I think you'll be good for each other. But Sam, listen to me, close. He'll kill you, me and her, too, if he gets a chance. His sickness and his hate's gonna' make him do it. Now go to Rose. Hug her and tell her you love her, too. She needs you real bad right now."

Chapter Twenty Two

Sam sat dazed. He watched the French doors, fearing Rose's return, yet desiring it. She had been through enough and he longed to comfort her.

"I wondered why you held back from confronting that bastard. Figured your reasons were just that, your reasons. But damn, Emmett . . . ," he said, his voice trailing away. He shook his head at the magnitude of the story. "I am glad you held off the way you did, but if anybody ever had a reason to kill that bastard, it's you and I got even more reason's of my own, now. Between the two of us, we'll find a way to protect her from her own father."

He looked at Emmett. He saw a weary man before him. "That's an incredible thing to have to say—protect her from her own father." He shook his head. "Sure puts a twist on things, don't it? That bastard shoulda' been locked away years ago. Rose having to live like that. Goddamn.

"Emmett. I promise you this; I'll do what I can to help her handle it. If Rose can't handle it, I'll go up there with you and we'll both kill him; might get me hung too, but at least Rose can have her life back."

Emmett stared at him, he knew how Sam was feeling. He knew what Sam was thinking.

"No Sam, don't even think about it. You are her life now. Don't you see? He's good as dead, he just don't know it, yet."

"What I need to know," said Sam, "is . . . does Griffen know Rose is his daughter, or not? From all you've said it sounds like he doesn't. Do you know?"

"If he know'd it, he woulda' done something already. That's the way he is. But Sissy told me he didn't know she was pregnant— and he didn't know where she went after she left him, at least for the first twelve years." answered Emmett.

"He found her though. Somebody coulda' figured out Sissy

was from the Fort Harwood area and went to Griffen with it. I don't reckon we'll ever know how he found her.

"There was a record of her getting her name changed to Bailey, and her baby, our Rose, was recorded as a Bailey and all that was filed in the Lumberton courthouse, once. That I know for a fact. Did you hear me? I said was. I've got every one of those records. And Griffen ain't never once acted like Rose was ever even born. So my answer is no . . . , " his voice trailed away.

Confused, Sam waited for a further explanation about the strange comment. "Alright, let's keep things the way they are for now. If she ever wants to confront him, it's going to have to be her decision, but what good would come out of it? He wouldn't believe it, anyway. I'll tell her what it could mean for her, but I'll not stop her from doing what she feels she must do," said Sam.

The two men sat, exhausted. Emmett lay his head against his chair and stared at the ceiling, resting his eyes—resting his mind. Sam sat with his hands between his knees, his head hanging, deep in thought.

Finally, with nothing left to be said, Sam stood.

"I'll go speak to Rose. Give me a moment with her, Emmett."

Entering the darkened sunroom, the light of the day fading, as dark foreboding streaks of dimming sunlight passed through the stained-glass window high up in the wall; he stood, watching her lying upon the divan. She'd covered herself as if she were chilled—or hiding. He knew she was not cold, and understood the tears streaming down her cheeks. Entranced by a tear breaking across the bridge of her nose, he watched her, and listened to her catching sobs. He prayed he would not interrupt her gentle breathing and searched for a way to comfort her. Mostly, he watched her. How could she have survived so much?

"Rose, I'm here," he whispered, and softly touched her cheek.

She heard his whisper, and feeling his touch, she struggled to open her swollen eyes, as her frayed mind floated in the hazy and all becalming moment which pulls one toward its gift; the gift of sleep.

"Sam," she said, "Are you through? Are you alright? Is Uncle Em okay?"

"Never mind us, we'll make it. How are you? Don't be sad. It's over. That's a lot the two of you have been through. Go back to sleep, now. I'm sorry I woke you, but I wanted to tell you how much I love you before I left," he whispered, and grabbed another blanket. "Let me cover you better. You look so tired. Go back to sleep."

Rose sat up, cutting him off with a touch of her fingers to his lips. "No Sam, I'm coming with you."

She needed him now. She needed assurance from him that he still loved her—that he still wanted her, in spite of her past, in spite of her father.

"Rose, none of that was your fault," he said, wrapping his arms around her, protectively, lovingly. "You never had any say in any of it. Your father was only a man that slept with your mother. Nothing else. Do you think I could ever love you less for that?"

Her chest heaved. She sobbed. He'd said what she needed to hear.

Her heart rolled in her chest. How she loved the man. She wondered if he was really there—or the only pleasant part of a long, sad dream.

"Rose, let's get married right away. Why wait? Let's get started with our lives."

"Oh Sam. You've been in my mind and my heart every minute since I first saw you. Yes, I'll marry you now. I don't want a big wedding, I never have. Uncle Emmett's getting up in years and he's wearing out. I want him so much to be part of our lives. He's more of a father to me than anyone has ever been. You see that now, don't you?" she pleaded, searching his face. "I'll never ask for much, but this I must do for him. That kind, loving man deserves to be a big part of our wedding day."

He smiled and hugged her tightly. How could he deny her? "Then he will be."

Emmett heard their footsteps and watched silently as they approached. He knew what they were going to say—a Father knows such things.

He handed a glass of bourbon to Sam. Sam quickly drained it, hoping it would bolster his courage. He also held a glass of wine for Rose, but she refused.

Looking at the two, he smiled and said, "I suppose you're moving up your plans a bit, huh?"

A flood of relief poured over Sam. "Rose is going with me. We'll be getting married probably within a week or two. If and when she wants to come home, I'll see to it. She can bunk with Sara and

Henry can bunk with me. It might not seem right to some, but that's the way it's going to be. Anybody got a problem with it—they just got to get over it."

The elderly man, the wise man he was, watched Sam's eyes. He understood there was no need to suggest they re-think their decision. His future son-in law had made a decision, and that was the way it would stay. All he could do, if it came down to it, was tell people they should mind their own business and that they would be wise to keep their comments to themselves.

He stood and walked over to his beloved niece. He encircled her with his massive arms and said, "She was mine for a long time, she's yours now. You take good care of her."

***

The following days were filled with joy. Sam and Rose fit each other like gloves. One could, and often did, finish the other's sentences—and they found humor in it. They spent long hours riding throughout the plantation, away from the curious eyes of Swift Creek.

Sam had seen it all, but he was unwilling to share his beloved Rose with anyone. Of all the beautiful places on the huge plantation, they were both drawn to the Devil's Hump. Alone, in the solitude of the high hill north of Swift Creek, they talked freely about their future, their plans, their dreams, their hopes. Each asked the other about children and both agreed they wanted a house full of children.

Sam chided her, "Rose, that's a big house."

Days spent alone, just the two of them, melded them into one person, one mind, one soul. His love for Rose grew until he ached with his longing to be married to her.

Likewise, Rose teased him that they should elope, but both knew this wedding was for their friends—and Emmett.

***

A life long bachelor, Sam wisely left the wedding arrangements to others. What did he know of such things? Even Henry had to remind him to get a ring for Rose.

"Did you get the ring yet?"

"What ring? Oh God . . . " he responded.

"Sara said to tell you size five and a half.

"You like your suit?"

"Oh shit," moaned Sam. "Go tell Willie to get Queenie ready

for first light. Reckon me and her better go get Rose a ring and me a suit."

Henry laughed, "Just how much do you know about getting married, Sam?" he asked the flustered man.

"Well, nothing . . . but you said you feel like you've been married all your life. That's why I picked you as my best man," he answered, grinning. "You keep up the good work. Now what else do I need to do?"

Henry was proud, honored, to be Sam's best man. He thought of Sam as his best friend.

He confided in Sara. "I've never heard of a boss standing by their employees the way Sam did—good times and bad, and Sara, I'm scared to death of standing up in front of all those people, but I am the Best Man."

Rose hardly knew any more than Sam, but she was determined to muddle through.

Friends invited, the list grew. Sam invited friends from his earlier Petersburg days.

Rose wanted the Reverend Hicks to perform the wedding and Sam readily agreed—one less thing for him to think about. Being of the nonreligious nature that he was, the Mayor of Weldon would have been sufficient for him. But yes, Reverend Hicks was the right choice, the only choice, really.

The Reverend and his wife, Liddy, arrived days before the wedding and when Rose and Emmett greeted them, a flood of emotions rushed through the four.

Rose knew her mother would have been overjoyed that the Hicks had come and their presence made her miss her mother so much.

Chapter Twenty Three

Friends from near and far arrived on the day of the wedding.
As a surprise for Sam and Rose, Emmett hired musicians to add to
the enjoyment of the celebration. Sara, Henry, Emmett and others
planned an entirely different wedding than that which Rose and Sam
expected, but the two were delighted with the attention showered
upon them. All the minute details, from place settings to chairs and
tables were well thought-out and executed.

A growing number of slaves, sent by Emmett, arrived to assist
with everything from serving food to stabling and grooming the
horses as the guests arrived.

Emmett's intention was to spoil Rose while she was still his
and not yet Sam's.

The gazebo Sam built for Rose stood at the end of a carpeted
aisle. Flowers entwined in the lattice, added to its beauty. Fidgeting
nervously, Sam stood in the Gazebo, Henry at his side. In the back-
ground stood the nearly finished mansion.

From afar, a skilled musician strummed a hauntingly beautiful
song which slowly evolved into the wedding march. Sam was instructed by Reverend Hicks to face down the aisle separating the two
sections of guests. Following his lead, the guests did likewise. A mur-
mur arose from the crowd. At the far end, Emmett stepped onto the
flower-covered aisle leading to the gazebo and on his arm was Rose, a
vision of a white and radiant angel.

Overwhelmed, Sam felt his heart race. How can a woman that
beautiful possibly be willing to marry a rogue like me? he wondered.

Rose held tightly to her Uncle Emmett's arm as if he might
desert her with his much needed support. Her satiny hair fell upon her
lace covered shoulders and cascaded down the front and back. A
white bodice fit tightly, accentuating her tiny waist and ample breasts.
Her layered diaphanous skirt billowed, a light breeze ruffling each
descending layer trimmed in matching white lace. Around her neck

hung a strand of pearls, a gift from her dear Uncle. The necklace began with tiny seed pearls and each adjoining pearl grew in size until large pearls circled a sparkling diamond pendant. A white, translucent veil covered her smiling, but pale face.

Emmett's face radiated his happiness. The crowd too, smiled warmly, some wiped tears away, and watched as she approached Sam.

Two precious and beautifully dressed little girls, preceded Rose, each tossing flowers, a sprinkle of petals here, a clutched handful there, into the crowd on each side of the aisle. Although only a few of the petals made it to their intended destination, the murmured oohs and aahs were heartfelt and sweet. A teenager, the oldest of the three held Rose's train off the carpeted pathway.

Rose, visibly shaken, never took her eyes from Sam. With locked arms, Emmett guided her to the steps of the gazebo. Henry stepped forward, taking her arm in his and led her to Sam.

Sam and Rose faced the Reverend Hicks.

"Your name, Sir?"

"My name is Samuel Elwyn Biggs," Sam replied.

"Samuel Elwyn Biggs. Do you love this woman?"

"Yes, I do, with all my heart. God is my witness."

"And your name?" he asked Rose.

"My name is Rose Detwyler Bailey," she whispered.

"Rose Detwyler Bailey. Do you love this man?"

"Yes, I love him with all my heart, and God is my witness," again, whispering.

"Take your betroths' hand and the two of you face your guests for them to witness this union."

He scanned the quests, searching for Emmett. "Who gives this woman to this man so they may be wed?"

Emmett arose, grinning, and faced the guests. "That'd be me, Emmett Detwyler."

Rose looked at Emmett, her eyes glistening with tears, and mouthed the words, "My Father."

Understanding her, his eyes misted with tears, also.

And to Sam, Reverend Hicks asked. "Mister Samuel Biggs, what are your intentions toward this woman in front of you?"

"To have her as my wife, if she will wed me."

"Miss Rose Detwyler Bailey, what are your intentions toward this man in front of you?"

"To have him as my husband, if he will wed me." she replied.

Sam was instructed to take Rose's hands. Five minutes later the two were man and wife. The Reverend faced the newlyweds toward the guests, and said, "Each of you present is a witness to this union. Is there anyone among you that does not wish for these two to be wed? If so," he grinned, "you need to be on your way."

The guests roared their approval and laughing loudly, showed their agreement.

"Well, I reckon nobody's gonna' complain none. So I present Mister and Missus Samuel Elwyn Biggs to you" He faced them toward their guests.

Taking Sam's hand, he placed Rose's in it, and said, "Well, Sam would you like to kiss your bride?" and removed Rose's veil.

"Yes Sir. I believe I would like that."

Again, the guests roared their approval, confirming it with cheering and whistling.

The newlyweds stepped from the gazebo and were immediately surrounded. A few of the women gently dabbed the corners of their eyes, preventing the teary destruction of rouge and make-up.

"Let's eat," shouted Emmett.

George and Willie, both dressed in the fine clothing Sara acquired with Sam's permission, were sent among the guests to announce the beginning of the celebration dinner.

Sara hovered everywhere, wanting to be sure the wedding would go as planned, secretly enjoying the responsibility. She assigned others to oversee much of the cooking, George in control of much of it. Long tables were heaped with food.

Sara and George planned a feast for the slaves and following Sam's orders, they were to have the same foods as the wedding guests.

The mouthwatering smell of pork barbeque, basted with vinegar and flakes of hot red pepper, slowly cooking all day over pits filled with smoking hickory and mounds of red-hot coals, permeated the air.

Dozens of chickens had been smoked over the same pits. Brunswick stew, a strange concoction of chicken, ham, different kinds of beans, tomatoes, okra, and who knew what else, received hungry looks. Coleslaw by the tubs and cornbread by the basketfuls loaded the tables almost to collapse. A feast was spread before them.

The neighboring wives brought cakes and desserts of every

kind and secretly watched to see how the labors in their own kitchens were judged. Husbands brought considerable amounts of spirited beverages.

Children ran amok through the crowd, playing games adults could no longer understand nor barely remember. The louder the children became, the louder the guests became. Young adults, arms entwined with their beloved, strolled the beautiful grounds, paying attention only to those on their arms. The sagging oak branches provided shade for everyone.

Much teasing was directed at Sam, all in good humor. Back slapping, followed by lowered voices, indicated some of the men had drank enough to think they could speak of things which lay in store. Once told, more backslapping and boisterous laughing followed.

Sara stood at the head of the serving line, not only to welcome each person, but to continue supervising the proceedings. She received accolades from the guests, praises she rightly deserved.

Subservient, but wily, George knew how to take advantage of his station and Willie—everyone liked Willie because of his childish, easy nature, were at the head of the tables with Sara. Their outfits of white knee pants, white shirts with ruffled collars and cuffs, pleased and amused the guests.

Willie was mesmerized by his new clothes, the bright red sash wrapped around his waist, and especially the glossy black shoes he wore. He made exaggerated efforts to show-off the shiny black shoes, inching them out into the view of the guests.

George rapped Willie's head with his knuckles.

"Willie, if yo doan quit yo dans'n and prans'n lac a damn lut'l peacock, I's gonna' knock yo black ass clean outta' dem purty black shoes."

The meal devoured; men sat rubbing their stuffed bellies. Sated, some napped, others drank hard liquor, and became louder by the minute. The occasional ribald joke did not sit well with Emmett and many of the other men. Emmett watched those guests closely and was not hesitant to tell anyone over-imbibing of hard liquor, he'd take it as a personal affront to himself and the newlyweds if they continued. Emmett was not one to repeat himself if needed. Instead, he approached the man's wife to suggest she keep an eye on her husband.

Invariably, the drunken husband and his embarrassed wife left shortly thereafter, their children crying and staring as their playmates ate hand-cranked ice cream.

Women sought shelter from the heat of the day under tents and relayed the latest tidbits of gossip. Muffled giggling, and the occasional loud throaty laugh, cut short by a quickly placed hand over the mouth of the offender, rolled out toward the crowd. A secret joke—perhaps a bit of wedding night advice, being shared by the inner sanctum of women; things meant for their ears only.

They watched Sam and Rose, wondering when he would free his bride so she could join them; each hoping to share wonderful little secrets of wifely advice and amusing stories with Rose.

Sam and Rose, while completing the rounds, thanked each of their guests for coming.

Soon, Sam was urged to release his bride and join the men to discuss manly affairs, as men are wont to do. The men, Sam's new friends, old friends and neighbors, carefully ribbed and teased him about his upcoming wedding night, offering advice which often bordered on risqué. But each man cautiously weighed comments made to Sam.

Who among them had not heard he possessed an explosive temper? Some had seen the dark side of their new friend while others had heard exaggerated stories of the man's temper and wisely thought it best to offer no comments other than well wishes.

The wedding party continued into the early night. Emmett invited guests to spend the night at his mansion. Others left in groups, desiring not to be alone on the dark roads.

Hesper Griffen seldom overlooked an opportunity to terrorize his neighbors.

Sam and Rose watched the last of their guests leave and entered their log and canvas cabin. Both were exhausted, but it was a warm, comforting exhaustion. No passionate kissing or anxious fondling was needed. Instead, undressed, they crawled into bed. Sam blew out the lanterns and lay back. The room was barely bright enough to see as they stared at each other without talking. Finally Sam said "Miss Biggs, I love you," and playfully rolled over, pretending to fall asleep.

Rose stared at him, her mouth agape. She hit his arm with her tiny fist, "Hey, you."

His face aglow with mischief, he reached for her, and whispered, "Come here, Miss Biggs."

Chapter Twenty Four

Their lives settled quickly into the routines of marriage. Sam found marriage agreeable and Rose, happier than ever, glowed. She missed her Uncle Emmett and spent many hours with him. With each trip to visit him, she returned with more and more of her personal items and slowly started turning the small log and canvas cabin into their home.

She was under no illusion the big house would be completed soon, nor had Sam led her to believe it would be. They knew another year would be required to finish it to where they could move in. Fortunately, the two thrived on the closeness the cabin required.

But the cabin became increasingly cramped with each of Rose's visits to Emmett's. Even though they craved closeness, there came a time when they realized Rose had far too many keepsakes.

Sam needed more skilled craftsmen to expedite the completion of their new home and again, Adair Graystone located such skilled carpenters and tradesmen from as far away as Tarboro. The workmen came expensively, but weighing the benefits against the extra cost, Sam gladly accepted the men and progress was immediate.

"How you doing on that other thing. The slaves? Found any?" Sam asked Adair.

Graystone's eyes shifted to the ground. "They're hard to find right now. I'm still looking."

Sam waited until the man faced him. He stared at him and walked away. He thought Adair seemed apprehensive.

Thaddeus Samuel Biggs arrived a year after his parent's wedding. The newborn was a foreign thing to Sam. He was frightened by the smallness of the baby, but only until he held his son for the first time. A bond between father and child formed immediately. The newborn's eyes, slowly beginning to focus, riveted upon his father's blurry face whenever Sam spoke. The father's eyes locked onto his son's blue eyes and the two stared, each engrossed with the other. The mother teared at the sight of father and son. Sam's trance was broken by her plea, "Sam, can I hold him?"

With the arrival of the baby, more room was needed. And again, Adair Graystone was told to find yet more craftsmen—many more. The building soon began to look like a mansion, but before it could be occupied, Rose began awakening each morning feeling ill. Samantha Bailey Biggs arrived at the cramped cabin and once again Rose begged her husband to let her hold the child.

"No," he teased her. "You've had her for nine months."

***

Sam stood on the uppermost step of the stairs leading up to the large veranda. He held his morning coffee in one hand and Tad's tiny hand in the other. He released the boy's hand and let him crawl backwards, down the steps—something Tad now insisted upon since discovering the up and down purpose of steps. Upon the thick green lawn, Tad ran amok, chasing the family's dog, and playfully hitting it unmercifully, whenever the dog allowed itself to be caught.

Sam laughed, thinking of the timid turkey gobbler Tad had cornered. It fluffed its feathers, spread its wings wide and puffed out its breast, revealing glossy black chest feathers accenting a red beard hanging from its throat. It fanned its tail feathers in a wide arc—proud of its war stance. Tad stopped crowding the creature, which moments before had been one fourth its present size, and turned to flee.

His eyes opened wide with fright. Thus far, Tad had voiced no concerns or questioned the bird's ability to explode in size. A resounding peck on his head from the strange creature looming over him, resolved the issue.

The toddler, badly frightened, darted past his father and sped up the steps. Afterwards, he scanned carefully in all directions before leaving the safety of his father.

"Time for breakfast, huh, buddy?" asked the adoring father. Together, they joined the ladies of the house; Rose and often Samantha, in the dining room. After Isabella Lynn was born, Beulah was mindful to bring the baby down for her father to hold and cuddle, after the breakfast was over and before he was off to work.

***

From the porch, Sam could see the white crushed shell drive

which meandered from the main road, around the side of the house, and circled back toward the front porch. He'd been asked many times why he'd broken with tradition by having an entry approach from the rear, and why, for that matter, had he faced the mansion backwards, the front hidden from the view of curious and staring travelers? All the other mansions were designed around the focal point of a lane leading straight to the Master's Grand Manor and always through a canopy of large oak trees, which formed a leafy frame for the mansion.

He never tired of being asked the question. He'd built the mansion for himself and his family—for their enjoyment.

He sought approval from no one but Rose. He had no desire to impress his neighbors, nor anything to gain by doing so. He had been impressed with the large oaks in the beautiful grove and promised himself never to remove one oak from the paradise. Not only did the drive meander back and forth, dodging his beloved oaks, but all of the side roads servicing the big house were laid-out similarly, maximizing the beauty of the park-like estate.

He'd planned a smaller dwelling for himself, something suitable for a bachelor, but with Rose his plans changed. She'd never asked for the changes, but as Sam's love grew for Rose, so did his plans for the mansion. Now he wanted his darling wife to have a big home.

Swift Creek Mansion faced north toward the creek for which it had been named. The main house was situated on the twenty-three acres of the sandy soiled, oak shaded grove. The house towered above the trees. The white crushed-shell circular drive formed a large turn-around in the front lawn. In the encircled area, Rose planted flowers and shrubberies to magnify the gazebo in which she and Sam had exchanged vows. They enjoyed being alone in the beautifully trellised building, but those moments were limited to spring and fall; too hot in the summer, too cold in the winter.

Spring was the most beautiful season in which to enjoy their garden. The vibrant colors of the flowers Rose planted were everywhere, emitting wonderful fragrances. But spring brought with it those damned Roanoke Swamp size gnats, mosquitoes and three-corner flies. Their arrival invariably overwhelmed the beauty and the fragrances of the flowers and limited Sam and Rose's enjoyment of the shade and comfort of the gazebo.

Fall drug with it the cold weather which drove away the damnable pests, but killed off the colorful and heavenly scented flowers, replacing them with dried husks the color of death—dark browns, blood reds, and fading yellows.

While others enjoyed long lazy rides in their white carriages, joyfully exclaiming their delight upon with the fall foliage, Sam was often depressed by the dark and dreary colors. Still, if only able to view the wedding gazebo from afar, both Sam and Rose, husband and wife, held the retreat close to their hearts.

The front lawn sloped gently toward the slow moving creek. By the creek, at the far left corner of the front yard, Sam had killed Red Slater. He had been reluctant to include the long ago camp-site as a part of his front yard, but reasoned greed and stupidity alone had caused Red's death. After sorting it out in his mind and putting it to rest, he often found himself absentmindedly strolling over the very spot where Red had lain in death. Now, some years later, the violence of that day no longer plagued him.

He never told Rose about the Red Slater corner. She would have avoided the corner and never worked her miracles with her planting, if she had known.

Sam and Tad fished there—Sam fished; the boy threw rocks and twigs and tried to float warships made of lily fronds. All the slave children and those of the hired men were allowed to fish and play wherever they wanted. Indeed, they had run of the entire plantation, their parents' permission given.

Sam never dwelt on his lack of a childhood or what he recalled of those strange years. Much of his happiness was derived from watching the romping, wonderful children. Boundaries did not exist to limit the children, black and white, from their playing.

The sides of the lawn, its undeclared boundaries far apart, were planted in an exotic array of bushes, trees and flowering vines.

Fountains strategically placed for their beauty, served a secondary purpose of a continuous and plentiful water supply.

Recalling how impressed he had been with the black iron statues of the little slave boys edging so many entryways back in Petersburg; their clothes painted on in whites, blacks and reds, he had four installed to hold the reins of visitors' horses. The statues were a source of amusement to some of the plantation Negroes, a source of fear for others.

Sam thought it clever how the parents of the disobedient child scolded their rebellious charges with, "Yo keep on be'n bad lacs yo is, de Massa gonna' ketch chew an turn yo into one ah dem dare iron niggers lac dem he's got stuck in de groun' up dare in front ah he's house. He gonna' put yo in a hole and see if he can grow he'self some good young'uns. Den what chew gonna' do?"

Small pools of water, encased in decorative white bricks, covered with plaster, overflowed with water lilies and floating clumps of flowers. Gold fish and frogs hid in desperation to stay beyond Tad's reaching arms.

A covered well provided all the houses' fresh water needs. Water used for drinking and bathing was filtered through endless vats of sand and charcoal; the filtered water, stored away in the cool cellars under the big house. A large cistern collected rainwater from the rain gutters of the expansive roof for housekeeping purposes, and it, too, well hidden by heavy foliage.

Rose had also planted her flowers and shrubs around the summer kitchen in the back yard.

With the yard-workers singing and yelling greetings to one another, and the constant exuberance of the playing children, there was seldom a quiet moment. But all the noises were happy noises—a celebration of life.

Chapter Twenty Five

The mansion Sam and Rose designed and built for themselves and their hoped-for children, had not changed much in design but considerably in proportion. Across the front of the house, six equally spaced columns ran from the porch flooring to the porch ceiling, twenty-four feet above. They were of the popular Georgian design with fluted ribs running from top to bottom. Decorative "capitals" trimmed the tops and solid bases supported each column. Windows dominated the front wall of the house, providing abundant light for the interior.

Across the rear of the house ran a full length lower porch. It, too, had equally spaced, smaller versions of the front columns with the same capitals and same bases. The ceiling of the back porch was twelve feet from the planked flooring. Above, another full length porch, it too, with matching columns, served as a good vantage from which to view the plantation.

At both ends of the house stood two chimneys, each reaching high above the gabled roofs. A total of eight fireplaces kept the interior warm during the coldest of months.

Sam's widow's walk, built into the high roof line, added to the beauty of the house, but it was seldom used. Twice, he coerced Rose into joining him in the widow's walk.. Once, to gaze upon the lush carpet of green spring had painted upon Swift Creek, and then to show her the expansive and colorful fall foliage. And alone, he would show their guests the distant horizons of Swift Creek Plantation from his widow's walk.

The mansion was painted white with dark green trim. Whitewashed siding, long the only available method to beautify and protect to a lesser degree the exterior planking, was used on all the out buildings, including the cabins of the hired hands and the slave quarters. However, the mansion itself was painted with real paint, not the chalk and lime based whitewash which washed from the exterior walls with each new rain.

Sam's taste ran toward oak and mahogany paneling, and most of it stained a rich dark color. His combination office-library was lined with book shelves and stained with the same dark finish.

Rose, bewildered by her husband's tendency to stain everything dark, won her argument to have the balance of the interior finished with plastered walls, which she decorated to her taste, with exception of the foyer and the grand entry. Neither could get the other to agree with their wished for decorations, so a compromise was reached for decorating the two rooms serving as the focal point upon entry into the mansion.

Rose pressed her point of how tired she was of everything being so dark, so they agreed on marble wherever it could be used to separate the foyer from the grand entry

Sam's elaborately hand-carved black walnut French-doors finally arrived. Rose's delight in the doors, complete with the stained-glass windows she herself had painstakingly designed, and which Sam had managed to keep a secret, made the expense more palatable. In addition, installed on each side, were matching stained-glass panels which magnified the beauty of the doors and heavy brass hardware focused visitors' attention to Rose's stained-glass masterpieces.

Upon entering the foyer, guests stepped upon pure white marble squares. Marble columns, matching the purity of the floor tiles, supported the twelve foot high ceiling of the foyer. Elaborately molded ceiling crowns complimented the marble floors and columns. Stepping through the foyer into the grand entry, and onto Sam's prized oak floors, two curved stairways, one on each side of the large room led up to the second floor. Dark oak railings, affixed to pure white banisters, drew attention to the dark maroon carpet running up the stairs and onto landings at the bottom and the top.

The wall at the rear of the grand entry was finished in matching, darkly stained oak trimmed with blocked panels. Carved trims accented doors, ceilings and the blocked and recessed panels. Two oak doors concealed in the paneled walls, when opened, revealed a deep dining room beyond. Under the stairs spiraling upwards, French doors on the left led into a formal living room and on the right, into a sitting room where Sam and Rose and the children enjoyed much of their days.

The balance of the downstairs was equipped with a large

kitchen and sleeping quarters, one for George, one for Beulah. George was to be available for the family at all hours. Beulah likewise, was ever present for the children. A sewing room for Rose was placed away from the constant noise of the kitchen, affording her peace and quiet.

The upstairs consisted of six bedrooms. Sam and Rose's bedroom overlooked the lush green lawn and the slow moving creek. Tad and Samantha shared a bedroom in order to be closer to their parents and invariably they found their way into their parent's bed by morning.

The interior was elaborately furnished in expensive furniture—not for himself, but for his Rose. Suppliers in Weldon, Fort Harwood, Rocky Mount and Raleigh collected substantial amounts of Swift Creek's money. The occasional custom piece was ordered from England and France. Thick carpets and heavy curtains adorned the floors and windows of every room. The master bedroom was fit for royalty and Rose was Sam's Queen.

It was in the master bedroom that Isabella Lynn was born.

Land to the west, and close-in to the mansion, contained the simple frame houses built for the hired men and their families. The same massive oaks sheltered the families from the intense burning rays of the sun, providing a modicum of relief from the hot summer nights and served as a wind-break for the frigid cold of winter gales.

A well maintained road between the rows of slave cabins on each side, afforded a sense of community and belonging for the growing number of its inhabitants. Centrally located wells were dug to serve the families' needs. Further along the roadway, stood more cabins in various stages of construction, proving the steady growth of Swift Creek Plantation.

As Swift Creek grew, so did the need for more and more slaves. Adair, it seemed to Sam, remained adverse to finding the slaves he needed but always, shortly after being rebuked by Sam, their numbers increased.

Butcher shops, stables, pens and all manner of buildings were erected. The requirements for daily rations of freshly butchered hogs and slaughtered beef were staggering. Large barns were erected at convenient places and heavily stocked with tobacco, corn, hay, and cotton.

The original whitewashed church long ago had become too

small. A new, larger house of worship was built in its stead. The people had spoken, mostly to Rose, so the new church was built in such a manner as to compliment the good taste of the folk of Swift Creek.

The former church was small, compact. The new church, large and built for growth. The first, although nicely trimmed, was plain and simple while its replacement was elaborately trimmed to please the eyes. Its belfry held a very large, very loud bell; rung for the congregation and other neighbors to hear.

Here, too, boys clamored to be chosen to tug at the bell ropes; enjoying the up and down ride. To them, the earsplitting clanging of the bell was merely the annoying cost of the fun filled ride.

The slaves had their own church. Theirs was much larger than the white folk's church. It had to be, there were so many more of them, and seldom did one soul miss the church attendance or its many social events.

Services at the white folks' church were well attended. Rose attended each Sunday with Tad, Samantha and Beulah in tow. Rose cuddled Isabella Lynn throughout the services. Sam, occasionally shamed into attendance by Rose, twitched and squirmed in his seat, anxious to be elsewhere the entire time. He had no desire to sit and be told what or who he should believe in, so eventually he refused to accompany his family to the Sunday meetings.

Exceptions to his refusal were weddings and funerals. Young couples from both Swift Creek and the adjoining plantations were wed in the church. Sam enjoyed the serenity of the weddings and with each argued anew with Rose that weddings should not be compared to the Sunday sermons. Weddings were always about long and happy lives; the sermons were hardly ever about anything but Hell and how to stay out of it.

The small sawmill established east of the mansion could no longer be considered merely a hopeful experiment. The first steam-powered machine, still ripping planks and beams and belching hot ashes and black smoke, was now one of three.

Chapter Twenty Six

Much had been accomplished in the past few short years. Swift Creek Plantation proved itself a viable and prospering plantation. It grew into a community filled with ambitious and good people.

Sam's desire to provide for his wife and children always occupied his mind, while old problems, county problems, remained ignored.

He recalled Emmett, long ago, told him not to expect much from the corrupt county. And not much had changed. It took rumors of Raleigh sending someone to see why tax receipts from the county had not been received, before Carlton county campaigned with old but cleverly reworded promises, each freshly buffed, varnished and polished, and then presented as something new.

Knowing they had been greedy fools, the county men sought to cast blame upon others. Urgently, they needed a jail and living quarters built somewhere north of Fort Harwood, in order to thwart Raleigh's inquiry into their dubious past, and the possibility of hemp ropes throttling their necks.

Again, they approached Sam and his neighbors—offering their worn-out promises of a new jail as bait for withheld taxes. Sam and his neighbors had learned from the county's past inaction and lies. They scorned their efforts and laughed at their further attempts to deceive them.

And they continued to withhold taxes.

The dirty, dying crossroad town of Arcola, saw an opportunity for growth and donated a long abandoned plot of land at the southwest corner of the intersection for the urgently needed new Deputy Sheriff's office.

Sam, Emmett and their neighbors laughed, remembering how the county had complained about the distance between Fort Harwood and Arcola.

"Too far away to keep an eye on things," the county countered, refusing the offer.

They laughed even harder about how quickly the long ride shortened after being told a free lot and free labor now awaited them in Arcola.

Still stinging from being charged for the lumber to build the new jail, they begrudgingly notified Sam to ship the lumber to the new site.

Always direct and now indifferent, Sam replied, "Not until you pay me." Curt and to the point. Not understated, nor overstated and not caring if he was offensive—merely his way of doing business.

Being bested by Sam, someone they considered an enemy, they complained to Sheriff Buck, seeking his intervention.

"What the hell do you expect me to do? You sent the list for him to bid. He bid it. You accepted it. He milled it and stored it. Pay the man."

Ten minutes later, Jebediah Lancaster, the newest of the county officials, slowly opened the door, peeked around the jamb, and asked, "Sheriff Vance, you in there? I got Mister Biggs' voucher for you." He shoved the voucher into the room before entering.

Buck left for Sam's the following morning. Upon his arrival, Sam and Rose welcomed him into the recently completed mansion. He relayed the past day's events to Sam while handing him the voucher.

Sam found it amusing.

"That lumber's been set aside since they accepted my bid, Buck, and that was a long time ago. Ain't no way for it to get any drier. So they're really gonna' build that jail, huh?"

"Looks like it," responded Buck.

Sam asked Buck to ride along with him out into the plantation. A friendship had developed between the two men and now their conversations were hardly ever of a business nature, only that of two friends—each enjoying the company of the other. Both avoided the small talk of law matters, neither caring anymore about Carlton County. Each knew better than to discuss long ago broken promises.

"Henry, get the big wagon loaded with the lumber for the new jail. Hitch it up to a team of the logging mules." Henry left to do as he was told.

Sam said to Buck, "While he's getting that done, let's go check on Joe and see how he's coming along with the clearing."

He had been unable to check the progress of the land being cleared by the field hands, but he was confident Joe was doing just that, progressing. He correctly assumed Joe would push himself and those under him to get more acres under seed than he expected.

A lot was riding on the success of the coming year for Joe and his family. He thought highly of his boss, and hoped the faith which had been placed in him would be substantiated by his efforts. He wanted to exceed Sam's wishes with enough cleared and plowed land to put in ever-increasing amounts of tobacco, corn, and cotton.

He'd been a farmer all of his life and knew Mister Biggs, although wealthy, was spending excessively to get the plantation to start paying its own way. Sam's money and how he spent it was none of his business, but he needed to put down roots for himself and his family. And if he didn't put forth a full effort he always felt guilty, knowing he could have done better.

Virginia was overcrowded and this part of North Carolina would fill up fast, too, he reasoned, so he sought to make his mark now and Sam proved to be the man to throw his lot in with. He knew the crops were necessary to help refill the coffers or at least lessen the constant drain. What better way to secure his future at Swift Creek than invest himself deeply into it? His desire to help make the plantation self-sustaining was showing progress.

Sam and Buck rode up to the sweat-soaked and smoke-streaked man.

"Joe, how'd you do all this?" Sam asked, his eyes reflecting astonishment at what Joe had accomplished in so little time. Beyond them lay acre upon acre of the rich, loamy soil, ready for the spring plowing. Much of the land had been dragged to pull out tree roots, briars and brambles, and then heavily disked with weighted tillers to chop up the soil, leaving rich fertile fields.

Even Sam, with his limited knowledge of farming, knew the freshly turned soil was ideal for bountiful crops. Around them, scattered fires burned off worthless piles of underbrush and unwanted trees.

"So what do you think? We've been at it hard." Relief and pride surged through Joe when he saw the admiration on his boss's face.

"Sheriff Vance," said Joe, acknowledging the lawman's presence.

"How are all those fellows working out for you?" inquired Sam. "Looks like they're putting in some mighty hard days for you, Joe."

"They're good men, for the most part. They work hard. Earn their pay. That yellow haired fellow over yonder, name of Delbert Haney . . . I'm gonna' let him go after work today. He's got a habit of showing up and leaving when he wants to," said Joe. "I can't afford none of the rest getting ideas off him."

"Who is he? Where'd he come from? He's not one of Graystone's people, is he?"

"No Sir, he ain't. He's from over near Arcola. I hired 'em on about a week and a half ago when we was dragging them big trees out of that field over yonder. Said he could work logger mules, so I tried him out. He can chain a tree, a big one, it don't matter how big, quicker than any two fellows I ever seen. Click his tongue and them mules'll drag it out like they's playing with it. Won't do it for none of us. Rather chase our asses. Goddamn mules. Everybody here's scared to death of them things. Hell, Mister Sam, I stay clear of them mules myself. But Haney's like an old hand with 'em. And they do jump when he says jump, too." He stared at Delbert.

"But when we got them trees pulled off and outta' the way, he started slacking off, acting like he was the chief mule-driver and his only job was mule work. Won't do nothing 'cept work them mules. He's strong enough to swing an axe or pull a saw. It won't kill him. So if he don't change his ways before the day's over, he's gone."

As Sam looked at the man, Delbert Haney slid behind others and sneaked furtive peeks at him and Buck. Sam's gut told him to cut the man loose. "Fire him now. Don't wait. Pay him and run him off."

Anxiety creased Joe's face.

"Mister Sam, I didn't mean to do nothing against your ways, but I needed that man real bad that day. Was I wrong doing that, Sir?"

Sam placed his hand on Joe's shoulder, and said, "You didn't do nothing wrong. Don't worry about it. If you need to do it again, hire another man just like you did him, but the first time you got a doubt about him, don't drag out the firing; it'll only get harder." He pointed at the man, making sure the blond haired man saw him do it.

"Fire him. Don't let nobody get under your skin. They'll try to hold on and none of us need that, understand? You've done one hell of a job up here. Keep it up."

Relief rushed through Joe. "Thank you, Sir."

"You ever seen that man?" Buck asked Sam.

"No. Can't say as I have. Why?"

"Well, I know him. And he knows me. Tried to let on like he don't, but he does. Throw'd him in jail for drinking and fighting back in Fort Harwood six months ago. Fancies himself a scrapper, ready to fight at the drop of a hat. I've been looking for him. He got bailed out but never came back to court to pay his fine. First I've seen of him since he got bailed out."

Haney shuffled toward a larger group of men nearby, trying to hide from the eyes watching him.

"I suspect he ran to Griffen and Griffen hid him out. No doubt about it, I got him now, though. Son of a bitch threatened to whip my ass, too. Hell, all them drunks do that. They're all alike. One pint of that dog piss whiskey they drink turns 'em into chest thump'n giants. Every one of 'em threatens to pound on my ass when I throw 'em in jail and apologize like young'uns when I set 'em free. And by the way, guess who bailed him out?"

He could see the disgust in Sam's eyes.

"Yep. You got it. Griffen."

"Goddamn it, Buck. How's it I can't go one day without that son of a bitch's name coming up?"

"Well, Griffen's been around here a whole lot longer'n you, there's that. Plus his full time job's stirring up the slop jar. And then there's the fact that he don't like you none too much, so I reckon you'll be hearing from that man a bunch a times."

"Joe, where does that fellow go off to after work?" Buck asked.

"Well Sheriff, judging from the way he smells and looks when he gits to work, I guess he must drink every night till he passes out and then sleeps it off somewhere near that tavern up yonder in Arcola."

"Sam, I gotta' go back to Fort Harwood to get the papers on that asshole," said Buck. "I can't get back here till tomorrow morning and them county boys want me to be there with the load of lumber."

Sam was irritated that his honesty was being challenged.

"Hey. Whoa. Hold up. Don't look at me like that," responded Buck. "It ain't to count your load—I got to do it to make sure them

Arcola folks don't miscount it. If you can hold off till morning, I'll ride along with you.

"It's about time I let them folk up there know who the law is, anyway. Don't want them to get to thinking they can show my deputies new ways to do Sheriffing. Can't have that, can we?"

The day was already on the backside. Sam doubted he'd have time to get to Arcola and back, so they agreed on an early start the following morning.

"Unhitch the mules, Henry. It's getting too late."

With the morning, Sam and Henry climbed onto the wagon, ready to deliver the lumber. Behind the lead wagon, followed another wagon filled with slaves to unload the heavy lumber. The mules made easy work of pulling the wagon. They arrived at the donated building lot in Arcola mid-morning.

Buck followed with a horse in tow for his soon-to-be prisoner. He held back behind the wagons, hoping the activity they generated would provide a diversion when Delbert Haney showed up.

Sam told Henry to pull up in front of the white-washed dry goods store and both climbed from the wagon.

It still remained the only building in the crossroads town not covered with fading and heat cracked planking. At least one store owner in the town made an effort to keep the place from looking like something it already was—just another dying town. Sam opened the door and stepped into the sparsely furnished store.

"Morning, Lonnie," he said to the owner. "Where's everybody at?" He looked around the room and out through the one window.

"Why, it's you, Mister Biggs. How are you? Ain't seen you in a long time." Sam answered the query about his health, assuring him he was fine and inquired of Lonnie's health and that of his wife.

"So it's true, the jailhouse I mean? They're really gonna' build one up here, huh?"

"Yeah, Lonnie, I reckon you folks are about ready to get one. I got the lumber all ready to unload, but don't know where to drop it. I was told somebody was going to meet me here."

"Well then, I reckon somebody oughta' be along soon," replied Lonnie. "But ain't nobody around except them fellows over yonder at the tavern. Shorty's the man pushing for the jail. Him and them other drunks oughta' be up and about by now. Won't you fetch your man and join me and the Missus for some coffee? She just made a fresh pot."

Sam stepped out onto the porch and beckoned Henry to join him. Jumping from the wagon, Henry told a slave to hold the team.

"Mattie, this here's Mister Biggs. He's the fellow what invited us to him and his bride's wedding. Sam, this here's my wife, Mattie. I'm sorry we couldn't come down to your place. Nobody for us to count on to run the store while we was gone. No disrespect intended. The wife got real mad at me, but, ah, you understand, right? Heer'd tell it was a humdinger of a wedding, though. Your wife's that nurse from Fort Harwood what lived out at Mister Detwyler's, ain't she? How's your bride doing, Mister Biggs?"

"Call me Sam." Sam responded

He introduced Henry to the store owners and told the man his wife was doing fine. He thanked him for asking and added he was not offended—he understood.

Lonnie offered to have one of the boys playing in the street run to the tavern to see if anybody was up and about. Sam thanked him and reaching into the candy jar, he took a few pieces of the rock candy. He handed Lonnie a five-cent piece and asked him if the nickel would cover it. Lonnie scooped up a few more pieces and gave those to Sam.

"Thank you Sam, but that's too much." Sam thought it clever that Lonnie gave him extra candy and held onto the change. A bird in hand . . . he thought and smiled.

The store keeper walked to the front door and yelled, "Charlie Ray. Come here." A towheaded, freckled face boy of about nine tucked his hands into his dust covered bib overalls and ran through the doorway.

"Yas Suh, Mister Johnson, here I is."

"Go on over to the tavern and tell Mr. Jackson the lumber's here and this man wants to know where to drop it. You come straight back here and tell me what he said, you hear me?" The boy nodded and turned to leave. Sam held out his hand and gave the lad a piece of the rock candy. Politely, he took the candy and smiling a gap-toothed grin, thanked the stranger. Sam gave Henry the rest of the candies and told him to distribute them among the slaves. After Henry left, he asked Lonnie to hand him two more pieces—he wanted to surprise the towheaded youngster again when he returned.

Back from his mission, Charlie Ray entered the store. As he spoke to Mister Johnson, he watched Sam.

"Mister Johnson, Mister Shorty done tole me to tell yo̶u̶ ̶.̶.̶.̶ he'd be here in 'bout half hour and fo' me to tell dis here man to hold on to his britches."

Lonnie stared nervously at the floor and said, "How's 'bout another cup of coffee for you and your man? Mattie, fetch the pot, will you, Dear?"

Sam pulled his pocket watch from his vest and looked at it a bit longer than necessary. He glanced at the dust covered creature slowly edging toward the door, dragging out his departure, hoping.

"Come here son, take this," said Sam. He ruffled the boy's straw-colored hair and gave him the two pieces of candy.

"Wow." exclaimed the boy. "Thanks, Mister."

Sam, Henry and the two store keepers sat enjoying fresh coffee and small talk. Sam learned the Johnsons were hoping, praying even, that maybe—just maybe, the new jail would signify to the outside world Arcola was growing, or that it could grow, if given half a chance. But it was easy to detect deep down they felt little would come of it.

Thirty minutes passed and still no Shorty.

Sam stood and thanked Lonnie and Mattie for their hospitality and invited them to visit he and his bride. His leave taking stretched an additional five minutes—five more minutes in which Shorty still did not appear.

Henry did as he was told and led the mules over to the edge of the building lot and next to the dilapidated planked sidewalk.

"Dump it in the street," said Sam. "If that man don't care enough to show us where he wants it, damn if I do, either."

The wagon was nearly emptied when a squat fat man came huffing out of the tavern, pulling at his suspenders. He shouted for them to stop.

"Not there, you goddamn stupid niggers. Pick that shit up and git it back on that goddamn wagon, right now. Y'all hear me?"

Sam stepped from the far side of the mules. Hearing Shorty giving orders to his men, he recognized the mouthy little man as the ill-bred and obscene tavern keeper from his last visit through Arcola. Shorty stumbled, trying to stop his considerable bulk from narrowing the distance between him and the man he instantly recognized as Sam Biggs.

"Oh, it's you, Mister Biggs, Sir. Ah . . . I thought them niggers was taking a short cut. You know how they are if nobody's watching 'em. Right? That's fine, right there, yes sir. Right there's just fine."

Sam's cold hard stare froze the man in place. "You don't want it there? Move it when I'm gone. Don't mess with my people."

Sheriff Buck rode up, hand in his lap. A fool would have known a gun was within inches of his gloved hand.

"Shorty, how're you?" Buck asked the perspiring fat man, while Shorty's eyes jumped from Sam to Buck.

Clearing his throat, the tavern owner answered, "I'm doing alright, Sheriff. You?" The expression on the man's face was plain to read. He wished he'd never come out of the tavern, but weighing circumstances, concluded the lawman's presence a good thing, since once again he'd managed to offend Sam Biggs. He reasoned the mean son of a bitch by the wagon would not jump on his ass with the Sheriff nearby, but he wasn't sure he could count on that.

Sheriff Vance looked down at Shorty. "Now, Shorty, you and me go back a spell, don't we?" Shorty looked up at the man on the horse. He saw a man with a serious demeanor on his face and he promptly decided co-operation was the order of the day.

"Yes Sir, Sheriff, reckon we do," he nodded.

"You got a man in there name of Delbert Haney?"

"Yes Sir, I reckon he is."

Buck glared at the man. "Either he is or he ain't. Which is it?"

"Yes Sir, he's in there"

"Drunk?"

"Yes Sir, he is. Sobered up some, though."

"Anybody in there with him? What about guns?"

"Yes Sir. Old man Griffen's in there with a couple of his men. They all got guns. Haney, too."

Buck looked at Sam and Shorty. He told both of them to get on the far side of the wagon and to get the Negroes and Henry down and out of the way.

"Sam, I know you and Shorty are not real fond of one another, but I don't want to have to come out here and pull you off of him, understand?"

Chapter Twenty Seven

Buck walked the horse and the mule to the only hitching rail still standing in any direction. He slid from his horse, grabbing the big revolver out of the holster strapped to the pommel, as he landed. He threw the reins over the old and decaying rail. The end post collapsed into a swirl of dust, no longer able to hold the weight of the rotted rail and an added pair of reins.

"Sonsabitches want a new jailhouse but can't even replace the goddamn hitch rails. This shit-hole oughta' work out real good," he muttered sarcastically.

He handed the reins to Shorty, saying, "You're the new hitch rail. Take these animals over there and hold on to 'em."

Buck's sharp command warned Shorty he should not argue; just hold the horses like he was told, and hold them until Buck wanted them back.

Buck stepped onto the planked porch, slapping his dust covered clothing with his hat. Reaching to open the door to the tavern, it jerked inward, out of his reach. A drunk and wobbly Delbert Haney stepped out holding an almost emptied bottle of whiskey. His bloodshot eyes widened as he saw the Sheriff standing before him. Knowing he held his last drink for a while, he tilted the bottle up and drained it.

"Sheriff Buck, what chew doing here?" he asked the lawman, slurring his words.

"Well, Delbert, you got to come back with me to Fort Harwood. Why'd you run on me, you idiot?"

Full of whiskey, Delbert suddenly became brave.

"Sheriff, I reckon I ain't gonna' go wid chew right now, but how's 'bout I come in later and spend the night, if that's alright wid chew?" He lowered his hand towards a pistol stuck behind his belt.

"Hold up, Delbert." Buck's hand flashed forward and he grabbed the gun by the barrel and hammered Delbert's forehead with the butt. "I ain't got time for this shit. You're already drunk, now you gonna' go get stupid on me? Get up. Let's go," ordered Buck.

Delbert staggered, struggling to stand erect. Swaying to and fro, he said to the Sheriff, "Look here, Sheriff. I just got fired yester-day—and now this. You need to quit bother'n me 'fore I whoop up on your ass real good."

Buck looked at Sam and sighed, "See what I mean?"

Buck stepped forward, and grabbing a handful of the drunken man's greasy hair, yanked him closer to him. Haney stumbled, losing his footing as Buck slapped chains on his wrists.

"Hey Sheriff, if I got's to fight chew, let me fight chew fair," said the perplexed, drunken man. He tugged at the clasps on his wrists.

"Now what'd chew go and do that for?" Delbert asked. Buck grabbed a rope from the pack mule's saddle.

"Haney, you're more goddamn trouble than a pair of trousers full of chiggers at a church social. Now, you can ride or you can walk—don't matter much to me. Or you can get your ass drug clean back to Fort Harwood with this here rope. Either way, you're going."

Seeing the futility of arguing with Sheriff Vance, Delbert said to Shorty, "Tell Griffen I ain't gonna' be out there today, but don't tell him why."

"Tell him yourself, fool, he's standing right behind you," snapped Shorty, pointing behind Delbert Haney.

Hesper stepped through the doorway and glared at Sheriff Vance and harder yet, at Sam. Stepping closer to Delbert, he kicked him in the seat of his pants.

"Vance, you don't give a shit who you ride with, do you?" said Griffen, thumbing at Sam.

Sam stepped toward Griffen. Buck held out his hand, stopping him. "Griffen," said Buck, using the old man's last name, showing him the same disdain he'd been shown, "don't get involved in this. It ain't none of your business, understand?"

The old man ignored Sheriff Buck and continued toward Sam. His hatred for the man who had embarrassed him, and in front of his own men, was so apparent it could be felt in the air.

"You still kissing up to Emmett Detwyler? Old crippled-ass bastard got you to marry that girl, did he? What'd he have to give you to marry that skinny, butt ugly little thing?"

His rage instantaneous, Sam exploded. He leapt toward the

sneering man.   Grabbing Griffen by his coat lapels, he spun him around, and slammed him against the ragged planking of the tavern. His mind filled with rage—blackness prevailed. One thought flashed like an explosion through his mind; kill the son of a bitch. Kill him. His fist balled hard. He pulled it back behind his head with every intention of beating the man senseless.

Buck grabbed Sam's granite hard fist—clinched and ready to smash into Griffen's face.

Shrugging his shoulders, Buck said to Griffen, "Well, sure as hell reckon it's your business now."

Sam's anger raged. He pushed to get past Buck.

"Sam, that ain't the way. Maybe it is, but at least don't bust his head open till I'm outta' here." Buck shook his head, feeling contempt for Griffen and with a knowing chuckle he released Sam's hand.   Sam grabbed Griffen's lapels and slammed him against the broken boards. Something snapped loudly. Shoulder blade or plank? The noise awakened Sam's senses and pulled his soul back from the dark killing place.

Griffen winced, yet he would not give up his sneer.

"You still cutting up little Negro girls so you can sniff their clothes and play with 'em, you sick son of a bitch?" asked Sam.

Griffen stood erect, his face flushed, and his sarcasm and sneer were replaced with a mixture of expressions, ranging from surprise, hatred, a tightening of his jaw muscles and then back to a sneer—but now a forced and shaken sneer.

Buck watched Griffen's reaction at being slammed by Sam against the wall, and saw Hesper glance at him. He was standing in the presence of pure evil; a diabolical, cold blooded and quite insane person.

"Griffen," warned Buck, "I already told you to stay out of this. You keep it up, I'll tie you and Haney face-to-face and plant your asses on that mule's back. As drunk as you two are, neither one of you'll sober up for a week. You say one word, you even grunt in pain, you and him's gonna' end up playing kissy face all the way back to Fort Harwood. But if you're as smart as you got yourself believing you are, you'll wipe that smirk off your wrinkled old face and go on home."

Hesper stood erect, stepping away from Sam. He tugged at his lapels, straightening them. He tried to show no emotion but a grimace of pain shot across his face. He walked eastward past the tavern and at

the far corner called out to his slave boy, a youngster no older than
Charlie Ray, "Bring me that fucking horse right now. Quick, or I'll
tear your goddamn head clean off and kick it clear 'cross the street."

Sobering up, Delbert walked over to the horses waiting to take
him and Buck back to Fort Harwood.

"If you're about through, I'll ride with you back to your
place," Buck said to Sam.

The wagon emptied, everyone mounted and they headed toward Swift Creek.

"Two times I been in this town and two times I've had to fight
my way out," Sam said to Buck.

Sam and Henry said their goodbyes to the Sheriff and entered
the road to their homes. They agreed no good would be served by dis-
cussing with others the day's events. Sam was greatly agitated at
Griffen for the things he had said but it confirmed the old man had
never figured out who Rose was. He felt obligated to tell Rose of the
conversation and just as obligated to say nothing. What good would
come of it?

She ran to greet him as he rode to the corral. Sam kept his concerns to himself.

***

Weeks passed. It had snowed once or twice, but not hard.
Peace seemed to be returning to Swift Creek. Dark and foreboding
clouds formed far off in the horizon. They spoke of the coming of a
dark winter and of dark things men can do.

A good and happy life was rising out of the troubled past.
Emmett and Rose maintained their closeness, each loving the other.
Sam found great solace in the elderly man's presence.

Emmett's heart was filled with joy as he saw Sam's tenderness
with Rose. He could see Sam adored, worshipped his Rose and the
children—his grandchildren.

Happiness was what he needed and he radiated happiness
whenever he spent time with them. He'd missed out on so much when
Rose was born. She was like a daughter to him and he yearned for a
chance to make up for so much he'd not been there for. Sometimes he
felt guilty that he had supplanted Rose's father—that was what it had
amounted to; but he was practically the same as her father and he
loved her more than his own life.

Emmett and Sam often rode together in Emmett's carriage to
inspect the fields, to visit the supervisors and to share small talk. They

enjoyed each other's company, Sam needing advice and direction from the accomplished farmer; Emmett needing to talk to Sam—away from Rose.

Emmett pulled back on the reins and locked the foot brake. "Sam," he said, "me and you got to talk about something, out here, away from Rose. There's some stuff that's got to be taken care of, just in case, you know, like if I up and die. I've been meaning to bring it up but couldn't find the right time. Probably never will be a right time, so I'll just get on with it. Son, I'm getting up there in years and I can't leave you and Rose having to worry about some things that could come up."

Sam could tell this was one of those conversations where he should listen—a one sided conversation, so all he said was, "Emmett?"

"Remember me telling you about Big Ed O'Malley, right? The Sheriff back there during all them bad times, with Sissy getting kilt and all, down there in Lumberton and me getting my ass shot all to hell? Big Ed could see how Griffen weren't never gonna' give up his obsession about Sissy running off on him, so he done something I never thought he'd do, and he weren't 'spose to do it, neither. That man put his whole life out on a limb for me and Rose. He went way outside the law. He come up one day and tells me he's got something for me and that I needed to hide it away so nobody'd never see it, at least, not 'till I had to use it, if I ever did."

Sam was curious, yet he remained silent.

"Remember I told you I had some things about Abigail and Rose that maybe I shouldn't of had?"

Sam nodded.

"O'Malley told me the way he seen it, the only way anybody could get tracked down was with the records folks got to keep about their births, proof that they paid their taxes, wedding certificates, liens, death papers, you know, stuff like that. And the only place that kinda' thing was kept was in courthouses. The way Griffen got on to how Sissy was living down there in Lumberton ain't real clear, like I told you, but somebody musta put two and two together and gone to him with it. Ed thinks what he done mighta' kept Hesper from ever knowing about Rose.

"He told me they went down to Lumberton, he wouldn't say who else went with him, and they stole all them papers about Sissy getting her name changed to Bailey. I'd told him about her doing that so she could hide her and the baby from that son of a bitch she'd married. Well anyway, Ed took the name-change papers. It's in this here package." He said, handing Sam a large roll of bound papers. "O'Malley took the birth certificate for Rose and he gave me that, too.

"Look." He said, removing a form from the top. "Rose Detwyler Bailey.

"Ed told me he grabbed up a whole mess of extra stuff to throw off anybody looking to see what all was missing. 'Confuse 'em,' he said. But when O'Malley got through, it's like her and Rose never even existed down there. Thanks to Ed, I got it all. He said he was thinking about burning that courthouse to the ground for good measure. Damn, now that's something, ain't it?"

Sam nodded. It seemed both extreme and funny, but he remained quiet.

"Just think how miserable Rose's life woulda' been if Griffen ever found out who she is. I owe—we both owe Ed a whole lot for what he done. Now, one last thing, Sam. I'm on the back side of old, about worn out and I know it. But I ain't worried none about that dying shit. Everybody's gonna' do it. Getting tired, anyway. But I am worried about you and Rose and my little babies when all ten of 'em finish getting here." He laughed as if he thought ten was a wonderful number.

Sam saw the humor in what Big Ed had done, but he couldn't laugh. He was astonished.

"The deed to my place is in here, too. I want you to keep it going. It's a good place and there's a bunch of folks who can help you run it. Like Isaac. You wouldn't ever hardly have to go over there, except to check how things are once in a while. And there's the Nigras. That place is the only home they got."

Emmett looked at Sam, questioning him with his eyes and again Sam nodded.

"Anyway, back to Ed. After busting into that courthouse in Lumberton, he come back up here to Fort Harwood and busted into that one, too. Said it was fun. Fun . . ." and again he burst into laughter.

"He looked for anything that might say Rose on it. All he found was the marriage certificate for Sissy and Hesper. He didn't take that, weren't no need to; everybody know'd them two had been married."

Emmett, still laughing, said, "So there weren't no need to burn that one to the ground, neither. If anybody ever looked through them records before O'Malley took 'em, you can bet they woulda' gone straight off to Griffen with what they found and got paid plenty for it, too. I don't reckon that happened, but we'll never know, one way or the other. Ed said he done what he felt had to be done—right or wrong."

Sam told Emmett he was grateful to him and wished Ed was still around so he could thank him, too. "Emmett, don't worry about your place or the slaves; they'll never be scattered off your plantation."

Emmett nodded, his way of thanking Sam.

"Let's go see the first three of your ten grandchildren," said Sam.

Chapter Twenty Eight

James Motley, stood in front of the recently finished mansion. It was a beautiful building—the talk of the neighbors, and he had once been proud of his contribution to it. But now, he dreaded going inside Swift Creek mansion.

How he wished he'd not been so greedy.

He climbed the steps, stopping in front of the hand-carved and darkly-stained French doors. He stood looking at the multi-colored stained-glass windows, wishing he could see through them into the foyer. Things felt different—like he'd been summoned to the big house—not invited. With a sweaty hand, he hesitantly lifted the heavy brass door knocker and let it fall against the sounding plate. The loud hammering noise raced down the hall and faded into the far recesses of the huge mansion and off into oblivion.

Oblivion? Is that where I'm heading? he wondered. True, he and his wife had been invited here many times as guests of Sam and Rose. Sam had considered them friends.

"My God, what have I done? What have I done?" he cried.

How many times had he been in Sam's office so he, Henry and Sam, could discuss business? But Sam's note had been curt and to the point. No . . . My friend James, or Please stop by my office, just—Be at my office at one this afternoon. Don't sound like an invitation this time, James thought. And as summoned, here he stood, right on time.

George answered the door, and motioned for James to step into the foyer.

James, seeking any response, any hint, or any sign which might help him understand Sam's abrupt letter, asked, "George, how are you doing this fine day?" Seeking big answers from small talk.

George added to James's bewilderment by answering only, "Fine, Suh. Please cum dis heah way."

"Not much help, George. Thanks a lot," James mumbled.

The hard heels of George's shining black boots echoed off the floors, walls and ceiling.

James thought it odd that he, in contrast, made a conscience effort to tread lightly, while he followed George across the highly polished oak floor.

George opened the doors to Sam's beautifully appointed library-office. With a barely discernible nod, Sam motioned for James Motley, Swift Creek's Lumber Manager, to enter.

James watched his boss, hoping for any sign or reaction from the man that might explain why he had been summoned. But he knew they were on to him but he prayed they were only at the snooping around stage. "Please let there be time to undo what I've done," he prayed.

"Motley, sit down," said Sam and James did as ordered. Time to start kissing ass, he thought. Being called by his last name did not bode well for the head of Sam's growing lumber empire.

"James, how much lumber have you and that crooked deputy friend of your's stolen from me?" Sam's face was red, his jaws clinched.

He'd known about James's theft for over a week, closer to two. He and Henry had followed the two of them, James and Arcola's new Deputy Sheriff, Jessie Leggett.

They had watched the thieves cut and haul off one of the most valuable trees on the plantation; a black walnut worth a king's ransom.

The loss of the trees was not what bothered Sam, he had more of them than he could count—he'd misjudged the man.

Why did he do it? Sam had asked himself a thousand times. The answer each time—greed. He certainly knows their value. Maybe he's been making contacts behind my back. There's stupidity, too. Stupid of him to ruin his life. That's a fact, thought Sam.

"George, close that door and don't come back 'till I call for you, understand?"

"Yo sho can count on dat," mumbled George, departing for a far away place in the big mansion.

"James," said Sam, leaning toward the man, "we're not going to talk about how you've cheated me. Talking about the past five years wouldn't mean a thing, not anymore. I'm not going to remind you how good you had it here on Swift Creek, you know that already. You know it's gone, too, don't you?

"Henry, tell him how he ended up in this mess."

Henry knew his boss was angry and that his anger would hinder him from thinking clearly. In his mind, he could visualize Sam flying off the handle into a rage and killing James. Hardly likely, but he'd seen some sights with the man. It would of scared the hell out of him, but it wouldn't have surprised him.

"James, you know where you fucked up? Did you think I wouldn't notice how many days you left work early, or didn't even show up? Remember how you'd tell me stories about how sick your wife or one of your young'uns was? I was surprised to see your wife up and about the other day. Actually smiling, she was. Thought she mighta' died, the way you carried on about her," he said sarcastically.

"Did you forget I'm responsible to Sam for everything that goes on around this place? Now, when that man over there," pointing at Sam, "comes down to the mill to talk to you and you ain't there, not just one time, not two times, but more'n that, what do you think I'm gonna' say to him when he asks where you're at?" He paused and waited for an answer, which didn't come.

"Well James, I told him you'd been acting kinda' strange and he told me to find out why. And that's what I did. Now here's where it took a while to put everything together. For one thing, you couldn't even look me in the eyes. Stuttered like a damn fool, you did. Hands shaking like a leaf. What'd you think, I wasn't gonna' be able to pick up on how all the workers were getting moved all over this place like chess pieces? So I followed you. You never even looked over your shoulders once to see if you were being followed. You are one stupid son of a bitch."

Henry's temper began to expose itself; a seldom seen sight. He rose and stood over James Motley.

Sam held up his hand to warn him he was now about to go too far. "Henry, hold up. Don't hit him. Let's get down to why he's here and not in Fort Harwood with Buck—chained to the wall. That's what you been wondering, ain't it James, why you're here and not in jail, right?"

"Yes Sir, I do kinda' wonder why you ain't got the sheriff out here," he answered.

"Well, Carlton County ain't known for doing much up this way. The way Henry and I got it figured is, you and Leggett got some help. First off, you're in a mess right now, and I mean a jail-time kind of mess. I don't think you've got the mind for stealing. You sure got the heart for it, but you ain't got the know-how. So that leaves your Arcola deputy friend. Henry and I saw the two of you together and we know you and him teamed up.

"James, here's the way it's going be. Oh, by the way, you got any idea that you're going to get outta' this mess without paying full price for your misdeeds, you need to see this." Sam stood up and said, "We don't need Buck."

He opened the door leading into the adjoining room. "Say hello to Mister Motley, fellows." Two men, each holding large hand guns, and those lowered at James's eyes, spoke almost in unison, "Mister Motley."

"Here's the deal," Sam said, as he chuckled to himself. "James, I really do mean it, it's a take it or go to jail kind of deal. You give up your friends, help me set 'em up; I'll let you go home to your wife and kids. You won't be staying on here, but you can stay out of jail. It's up to you. I want all of your friends and you are going to give 'em up to me. No might, no maybe. That's the way this deal works."

He bit the end off a Carolina Gold and offered a cigar to Henry.

"So. Who's behind it, James? Don't make no sense to me that Leggett's the man behind it. I talked to him too many times to believe that. That idiot can't even put his socks on without looking at draw-ings hanging on the wall first. I doubt he can even read. Who calls the shots? Who controls the money? Who divvies it up?" Every-thing—everything always leads to that single question, Sam thought, Who controls the money?

James, knowing he had no other choice, answered Sam's ques-tion. "Hesper Griffen; he's the man you're looking for."

Sam's face did not betray him. He wasn't surprised; he knew who was behind it.

"Alright, James, we got us a start. Tell me how you got your-self in this mess. How you and Leggett got things done; everything you know about your little enterprise. And for your sake, you better know it all. You do that and don't lie to me, and I'll help you out." Sam was trading with his own employee. He needed firm, solid facts and a little mule trading sometimes got you a better mule to ride.

Sam wanted it all. From the men that loaded the axes into the wagons, clear up to Griffen himself.

There-in lay the rub. Nobody had ever been able to catch Griffen at his treachery. Griffen had been stealing off Sam's land long before Sam owned it and now, years later, he was at it again.

Why's he doing it? He doesn't need more money. It takes a lot of nerve to steal a man's property right out from under his nose. So if he doesn't want the money, what does he get out of it? Harassment? Revenge?

"Mister Biggs, we only took three trees off your land. I swear that's all. The way it works is, Griffen would tell Leggett to get his friends from Fort Harwood ready for another load. Leggett would come to me and tell me to pick out one of the best trees—a straight one, no limbs down low. Then, I had to send my people, I mean your people, to work as far away as possible. Those Fort Harwood fellows would come up the long way around so they could get them mules and them big wagons up here without nobody from here seeing 'em. You got too many friends 'tween here and Fort Harwood to use the old road like they used to.

"All of 'em waits at Shorty's tavern to get started. Shorty went with us some; two times I know of. Heard he's gonna' come along next time. They load them logs up and head out past Griffen's place to the docks up yonder on the river above Weldon. Altogether, if Jessie's got it working right, they can get one wagon loaded and delivered to Weldon in a day. They work hard and fast to get them trees down and loaded quick.

"That was mostly the hardest part. After everybody got paid, me and Jessie'd get two hundred dollars each. Griffen, well, I reckon he got all the rest and according to Leggett that old man got a buncha' money for them walnut trees. But I ain't never seen him, not even once. Leggett did all the talking to Griffen. And he handled all the money from the man that was buying them trees. That's about all I know. What I got to do to get outta' this mess, Mister Sam?"

Ignoring the question, Sam asked, "When are you fools going after another load?"

"Leggett told me to be ready one week from yesterday. Six more days."

"Well, I want to know everything that goes on. Don't even try to make a run for it. Those two fellows in there, they're your new best friends. Now go," said Sam. James was handed over to the two men and they were told to take him home and keep an eye on him.

"Sam, you aiming to go to Buck about this mess?" asked Henry.

"I don't know. I've got some concerns about that. I want to leave him out of it, if we can. It might complicate things if we involve him. Buck's changed a lot in the last coupla' years. I'm not saying he's not dependable or nothing like that. It's just that his heart don't seem to be in it no more; kinda' like he's beat down by life in general. If we go to him now, he's got to let those county fellows know what's going on. That's his job. Way I see it, he can't tell them nothing he don't know nothing about, right? Maybe we ought to leave him out of it this time. But I reckon we oughta talk to Emmett about it first," he added.

He stood and walked around the desk.

"How long do you think it'd take to get back to Griffen if the county boys get wind of this mess? How is it Griffen always stays one step ahead of the law? Who's feeding everything that goes on around here to him? Who is it in Fort Harwood that must owe something to Griffen? No, for now, I think me, you and Emmett'll handle this. We'll set this thing up." He stared at the top of his desk, thinking.

"That Deputy's going down for this and so is Griffen and his kinfolk. Leggett's scared of his own shadow. But he's most likely more afraid of Griffen, so we can't be none too careful. Those inbreds from Fort Harwood won't run from a fight, neither, so we got to watch out for them, too. They might be stupid, but we got to figure they're dangerous. Griffen's the one that's going to be hard to trap. Slicker than greased pig shit, that man is. He always kills off problems he runs up against, and now his problem's going to be me and you. And I intend to break him of that killing problem he's got.

"We got less than one week to get things worked out. We're going to need help. And right now, outside of you, Isaac and Emmett, I don't much know who else we can trust. We got to give that some hard thought. With this surprise from James, I'm not ready to trust nobody, except you three. And if you don't need this Henry, tell me. No hard feelings. But, I am going to get it done, one way or the other."

"What about our neighbors, Sam? Some of 'em will help us."

"I know they will, but I got to think on that, too. Things have calmed down for most of those folks. No thanks to that Arcola deputy's station. That son of a bitch wouldn't arrest a man if he saw him stick a knife in his own wife. He'd swear he didn't see a goddamn thing. Give him a bottle and a woman and he won't leave that jailhouse 'till one or the other's used up."

"You know I'm in. I'll start lining up the boys I know . . . hope we can trust. I sure don't want to start thinking we got any more crooks on this place 'cause of one bad one. What you want me to do?" Henry replied.

"Let's have a drink." He called for George. "I need to calm down a bit. How about you, Henry?" The two men, one a boss, one a hired man, yet both the best of friends, began making plans.

***

George's hard heels clapped against the oak floors as he hurried to the front doors. Close behind was Beulah, almost running to get to the door, herself. When George told the house help to move, they moved fast.

"Good day, Miss Rose. Heah, let me git dem dare boxes. Beulah, you git obber heah an fetch dat dare baby."

Although very overweight, Beulah, moved quickly, and taking Isabella Lynn into her massive arms, started cooing to the tiny sleeping child.

Rose was holding her son tightly by one of his small wrists and held Samantha in her arm. The boy tugged hard, pulling away from his mother. When he saw George he wrestled himself free of her grip, squealing, "Unca George, here, here" and held his arms up, begging to be picked up by the smiling white-haired Negro. Samantha squirmed and once free, toddled down the hall looking for her father.

"Is Mister Biggs here, Beulah?" Rose asked.

"Yes'm, he be in dare," she said, pointing toward the library.

"Take Isabella to her father, you know how he is about that child. Let him see her and then put her down for her nap." Beulah nodded and headed towards the library..

"George," said Rose, "You take Tad to see his father, too. Don't let him fuss over that boy too long. You're hungry, right Tad?" she asked the boy as he dug his fingers into George's frizzled white beard. "When Mister Biggs lets him go, take him to the kitchen and get him something decent to eat. No more sweets. His Grandfather's been sneaking sweets to him all day."

The six of them headed for the library. Rose acknowledged Henry with a smile. "Time to stop for a minute. The little ones want to see their Daddy."

Sam's face glowed as he held Samantha, while peeking at the sleeping baby, Isabella, and winking at Tad.

"Henry, let's pick up tomorrow morning where we left off. I need to spend some time with my wife and children." Sam greeted his wife with a hug.

"Uncle Em said to remind you we're supposed to be there tomorrow for dinner. I told him we'd come. Okay?

"He looks tired, Sam. He's in a lot of pain, now' a-days. I'm worried about him. He's using way too much of that Laudanum.

Sam needed to talk to Emmett. He'd always respected Emmett's advice and he needed it now, more than ever.

Releasing his wife, he extended his arms for Tad. George rubbed at his stinging cheeks; relieved to be free of the child.

Sam sat alone in his office after Tad and his sisters were put to bed for their afternoon nap. Samantha was sleeping soundly up in the children's shared bedroom. Tad fought sleep, becoming crankier by the minute and suddenly he quit his fight to stay awake.

Sam's mind churned. Is there room for forgiveness? James might be sorry for what he's done, but he still needs to pay for it. He's got to be an example to the others.

Chapter Twenty Nine

Henry entered the foyer of the big house without waiting for George to come and open the heavy doors. Circumstances were such Sam would hardly be upset if he let himself in. Motley followed him, his head bent, his eyes studying the floor. Hearing the front doors opening, Sam stepped into the hall.

"It's you. Come in, come in. Got Motley with you, I see." Henry grabbed James's arm, and pushed him through the door into the office.

"Sorry Sam, busting in like this. Just don't want nobody to see this sacka' shit. Some of the folks already been asking a bunch of questions about him," explained Henry, as he guided James past Sam and sat him next to his desk.

"Don't worry about it," Sam said. "Got something to tell us? Well . . . do you, Motley?"

"Yes Sir. I reckon I do. Those things you told me to find out about . . . well, I did like you told me. You still gonna' let me go when all this is done, ain't you?" he asked, without lifting his head. Sam merely stared at the man; and did not provide the hoped for answer.

"What you got, Motley?"

James fidgeted and picked at the clumps of balled yarn on his worn shirt sleeve. "Deputy Leggett told me that Griffen man wants us to haul another load of them trees outta' here next Friday. But I done and told you that. He's gonna' go on down to Fort Harwood and get them kinfolks of Mister Griffen's ready."

James told them they were going to stay in the same area where they'd stolen the last walnut tree. "It's kinda' outta' the way. Not much traffic. Ain't never nobody around there."

Feeling nothing but contempt for him, Sam asked, "You got all my people ready to clear out of there next Friday?"

The term my people, once used by Motley, no longer could be—he had forfeited that privilege.

"Yes Sir. They've already been told they'll be moved to cut trees somewheres else."

"Leggett suspicious?"

"No Sir. Not yet he ain't. Man's thinking more about money than being careful. It'll go the way it always does," said Motley, squirming in his chair.

"You setting us up, Motley? 'Cause if you are, you and your family will never get off this place alive, understand?" The intensity of the veiled threat frightened James and startled Henry.

Motley turned ghostly pale.

"No Sir. I ain't lying to you. All I want is to get this behind me and be clear of this place, like you said I could if I worked with you, and I done everything just like you tole me to do. You still gonna' let me leave without Sheriff Vance grabbing me, ain't you, Mister Biggs? Right?"

Sam, ignored the whining man.

"Henry, take him home and get back as quick as you can; we got plans to make."

Returning soon after, Henry asked. "What's on your mind, Sam? How you want to handle this?"

"Let's ride over to Emmett's. I've been thinking about it. We need Isaac to help us. He knows every foot of land out there. He's hunted it for years. It'd be real smart of us to have him along, if he'll go with us. If he don't want to go, I'll leave it at that, but I got to talk to Emmett first, clear it with him. I don't want to get any more of our people involved in this mess than we have to. But Isaac, yeah, he'd be a big help. Let's go see what he has to say."

Sam and Henry sorted through the men they believed they could trust. One man gone bad, didn't mean all the men in Swift Creek were crooks. In addition to Isaac, the two men hired to watch Motley volunteered for the extended service. They were in it for the money, and extra pay would hardly be ignored. For them, there was not a right side or wrong side, only money. With James Motley becoming a thief, doubts about the rest of the plantation's men had been planted. Henry didn't want to let Motley's failure cause him to doubt the others, but it did.

The plantation's blacksmith had always been steadfast, straightforward and honest in everything he did. Sam had no reason to distrust the man but Henry had spent more time with the man than Sam, so he deferred to him. He asked him if Bob had ever given him any reason to doubt his loyalty to Swift Creek. Would he stand up and fight alongside the two of them? Henry assured Sam he trusted Bob—he'd never had any doubts about the man and yes, they should talk to him. Henry approached the man and Bob willingly agreed to help. That left Joe and Matt. Some of the men would be asked to stay near the plantation and serve as guards and Sam wanted Matt to be one of them. The slaves would be less afraid if someone of authority stayed within their sight.

The number grew to nine good men, each with reasons of their own to fight. Loyalty or money. They would fight like hell if it came down to it. Each of these men had worked hard to help establish Swift Creek and each would fight to save it. Doubts ended for Sam and Henry; they trusted these men.

Isaac's reasons to help Sam would be twofold; he was Sam's friend and if Emmett wanted him to help Sam, he wouldn't hesitate.

The men who would accompany Sam had enjoyed a good life at Swift Creek Plantation. He'd seen to that. They were not wealthy, but they were better off than most of the families on adjoining places. They'd never been looked down on or treated as inferiors by him. They knew that wasn't in the man.

The promises he'd made to them, even those sounding too grandiose, had come true, just like he'd said they would.

"He needs me, simple as that," they agreed and cleaned their guns.

Emmett snoozed in the wing-back wicker chair on the front porch, his white hair mussed by a morning breeze. In his hand he held a glass of iced tea, tilted, and ready to spill over. He heard the riders and roused from the grainy edge of sleep.

"Sam, Henry, get on up here," greeted the elderly man. "Caught up with your work? Must be nice. Ready to go fishing," he laughed. But Sam and Henry appeared solemn to him.

"Everything alright? Rose okay? Izzy alright?" he asked, using Isabella Lynn's nickname. "Tad, Samantha, they okay?" Emmett motioned them to chairs as Sam assured him those he'd asked about were fine.

"We got a problem over at my place. Kinda' sprung up right under our noses. If it wasn't for Henry catching on to it, it mighta' got out of hand. Looks like our friend up to the north's back in the lumber business again. Been stealing the hardwoods. So far just the walnuts.

Henry caught my man Motley helping that new Deputy Leggett fellow from over yonder at Arcola get those trees cut down and off my
place. Seems like that deputy approached Motley with promises of big
money and got him to help set it up where he and his people could
come in and get those trees down and outta' there in a hurry. Leggett's been at it for a long time, but he's hedged his bet—getting Motley involved. Those people who help him are the same ones who were
stealing trees back when I first arrived here. Leggett told Motley everything to do with it; including that Griffen's behind it."

"What do you need, Sam?" Emmett asked, his face solemn.
"Need men? Guns? What can I do?"

Sam replied. "No Emmett, all I need is for you to let Isaac go
with us—if he will. He knows every inch of that whole area—every
tree, every gully. I'm going to bring the whole bunch of 'em in. Alive,
if they'll let me—dead, if they don't. I know you're going to want me
to go to Buck with this. Truth is, I'm not ready to go see Buck, not
just yet, anyway. Nobody's going to stand in my way, no law people,
and Buck will try. So no, I'll bring 'em in. I got all the men I need,
except Isaac."

Emmett answered with, "Well, if Isaac wants to go with you,
tell him I said okay, but I'm gonna' go with you, too."

Determination had replaced the anger on Emmett's face. And
like Emmett saw the fierce resolve in Sam's eyes, Sam saw the same
staring back at him.

"This ain't your fight, Em."

"How the hell can you say that, Sam?" Emmett's anger flar-
ing.

An argument would have been useless.

"Alright, Emmett. Get ready."

Isaac agreed to accompany them, especially after being assured that Emmett was not only alright with it, but was joining them,
as well. His friendship with one of the men and devotion to the other
spoke volumes about the man. The three discussed strategies and
agreed to assemble the following Friday morning.

"Tell Emmett early next Friday. Six A.M., okay?" Sam told
Isaac.

***

Friday morning, twelve men gathered. Twelve, counting Motley—the finger pointer. Three of the Negroes were brought from the
field to tend the pack animals and extra gear.

Each man, with the exception of Motley, had their guns loaded and ready. Motley knew he was going along for the ride, no matter how much he begged to be left behind. He felt the contempt of the others toward him. Badly frightened, he remained silent.

Sam told the men everything that had been going on and what to expect. Then he told them to shoot to kill if fired upon.

Bob Dayton, the blacksmith was saddened by Motley's actions. He felt betrayed and rode away from further contact with the man he'd once considered a friend.

"We're dealing with some old boys out of Fort Harwood who won't think twice about shooting and running," Sam stated. "Be careful. Don't give them a chance to do either. That deputy leading them will be as desperate as they are to get out of there—more so, what with him being the law and all; he knows he'd get strung up quicker than the rest. Hell, fellows, we're going be right at the edge of the law, ourselves. Anybody got a problem with that?" No one answered, no one left.

"From the minute we get there until we got those bastards tied up and loaded in the wagons, don't take your eyes or your guns off of 'em. Let's go."

The caravan headed toward Arcola. Henry rode in the rear. An hour later, each picked out the best bushes, trees, boulders and underbrush to conceal themselves behind.

Isaac had hunted the area many times before and knew the best approaches to get in close, undetected by the thieves.

The mounts and extra horses were left far back and held by the slaves. Motley was returned to the slaves and horses. He wouldn't run. He was too close to earning his freedom.

The heavily armed men improved their camouflage, using leaves and clumps of grass. Silently, they awaited the arrival of Deputy Sheriff Jessie Leggett and Griffen's kin.

From the distance, and rumbling toward them, came the creaking and moaning of heavy wagons. The drivers yelled and cursed at the big mules. They'd been drinking, and that increased the likelihood of violence.

Behind the wagons, men on foot carried axes and long crosscut saws, laughing at each other as if they were headed to a favorite fishing hole.

"Those fellows with the axes and saws got to be Hesper's kinfolk," Sam whispered to Henry. Behind them, rode two more men.

Sam recognized them both. Shorty Jackson, Arcola's bartender and owner of the local tavern, followed by the gangly deputy, Jessie Leggett. They rode straight to the tree Motley said they would.

"Get them wagons outta' the way and drop that big son of a bitch quick," Leggett shouted at the thieves. "Quicker y'all get it done, the quicker we can get the hell outta' here with the old fart's tree, and the quicker we get our money. Start cutting." The men moved the wagons, grabbed axes and saws and set about their assigned duties.

Low on the trunk, hard swung axes chopped out a wedge of wood. On the far side, two men pulled furiously at the long saw. The missing wedge would fell the tree close to the wagons.

Sam watched closely, waiting for the exact moment to charge in. He held his left hand aloft and dropped it; that being the agreed-to signal. Instantly the thieves were surrounded. Within seconds, the axes dropped, and the long saw hung in mid-cut, ringing discordant musical notes.

Three of the axe-men dived into the cover of the underbrush. Sounds of their desperate flight to freedom resounded back from the thick trees.

"Fellows, we got to get on with this. We might have trouble heading this way soon if they get back to Arcola," said Sam

"Leave 'em where they are, boys. Don't do it," he shouted, as some of the thieves stepped toward their weapons.

"Reckon you'll hit the dirt deader than a rock before you touch those guns. But go on; give it a try if you want 'em that bad."

And to the shaken Deputy Sheriff, he said, "Leggett, you'll pardon me if I don't call you Deputy, won't you? Throw your gun over in front of me. You point it at me, well, you know—just don't do it, Okay?" The Deputy's hand shook badly. Sam watched closely to make sure the man did not accidentally pull the trigger.

"Hey Shorty, how you doing? Not enough money in the liquor business for you, huh?" Sam asked the fat tavern owner. The man, perpetually red in the face from his excessive drinking, heavy smoking and the undisputable fact that he had the equivalent of another Shorty tucked behind his belt, turned pale but he managed a sickly smile

"Well, you know how it is, Mister Biggs, I wish it'd been a little better."

"I'll bet that's the truth, don't you, Henry?" Sam laughed.

He shouted to his men, each with a gun aimed at the man in front of him, "We need to speed it up a bit. So don't take any chances with these assholes. If they think they got to run, let 'em. Just don't let 'em get too far before you drop 'em."

Long ago, Sam had learned how frightened people became when they thought you didn't give a damn whether they lived or died. All of them had heard stories about the crazy son of a bitch from Petersburg who had no problem shooting folks he didn't like—folks he had no reason to shoot. Sam had heard all the same stories. Even Shorty had bragged how he had faced down Sam Biggs during the much talked about encounter at his tavern months earlier. If not enough to prove how ignorant he was, Shorty'd bragged about how he'd made Sam personally re-stack the jailhouse lumber where it really belonged, neatly on the sidewalk.

"That's right. All by his lonesome. I wouldn't even let his niggers help him," he lied, proudly tugging his suspenders with his thumbs.

Sam shouted, "Listen up. One at a time, I'm going to tell you to drop your trousers and shove your hands around back and grab your fat asses. Ain't going to be a pretty sight, but you're going do it, no two ways about it. Never saw a man yet who could run with his trousers bunched up at his ankles. Put your hands behind your back. When you get your hands tied, the fellow behind you's going to pull your trousers back up and put 'em in your hands. Now hear me good, this is kinda' important. Hold on to them real tight. You drop those britches . . . well, see, I ain't going to know if it's an accident or not, so I got to figure you're about to kick 'em off and run, and I don't believe I'll let you do that."

He looked at his men in order to emphasize the don't run rule.

"Men, we don't have time to chase none of these hicks just 'cause they went and got stupid. They run, shoot 'em down like rabbits." Seeing sufficient alarm in the captives, he said. "You first, drop your pants."

Armed men followed men with hands stuck down the back of their trousers and led them to the waiting mules and wagons.

Sam sent the slaves to gather everything that had been left behind. He might as well confiscate it for his own. He was due that and then some.

They arrived at his out-buildings in the late afternoon and the Arcola and Fort Harwood part-time lumberjacks—full time thieves, were thrown into one of the barns. Field hands were sent to empty more barns so the prisoners could be separated.

Motley, in fear for his life, and knowing Leggett, Shorty and the others knew he had turned on them, once again, pleaded to be let go.

Sam took him aside and said, "Alright Motley, I do believe those boys will kill you, so go on home. Don't run on me. You're close to being done, but we ain't through, yet. Another day or so, you're free, so don't do it. Go on and wait for me."

The tack barn was locked tightly and Sam asked Bob, Joe, and the two hired guards to watch over the prisoners. Soon, reports of emptied barns filtered back and the thieves began to be separated.

Griffen would have found out by now about his men's failed attempt. It was inevitable. No doubt he would have been drunk when told of yet another interruption of his tyranny and alcohol would re-new his rage.

Sam could not afford to think the man too drunk to retaliate. His concerns for Rose and the children grew. The shouting and com-motion from the barns would surely frighten her.

"Emmett, would you mind watching over Rose and the chil-dren? She'll be a whole lot less worried if you're there. Tell her I'll be there as quick as I can. I can't come just yet. Too many things I got to sort out. I'll send somebody for you when things settle down back here."

Glad to be near Rose and his grandchildren, Emmett agreed.

Hesper's kin, Shorty and Deputy Leggett; finally separated, sat pondering their fate.

The occasional shotgun blast roared through the night and with each shot the thieves grew more and more apprehensive.

Sam and Henry stood beside the barns. And loud enough to be heard by the occupants, Sam said, "Shorty ain't worth the trouble it'd take to pack a pound of powder up his ass and drop a ball on it. What do you think?"

"Well, Leggett's the key," answered Henry, loud enough for Leggett to hear him. "From what Motley says, he's the one who deals with Griffen. But it sounds like they do their business in Shorty's bar, so I agree with what you say about Shorty. Where there's whiskey, there's gonna' be loud talking and lots of it, too. Shorty'll know more than he'll say he does. You can bet on it. All of 'em's gonna' lie to save their asses. And somewhere in all those lies is gonna' be all the truth."

"It's getting dark,' said Sam. "Griffen might be on the way. Hard to tell. Might be too drunk to move. Best we put some of our men out in the woods to keep an eye open for him. Tell 'em to come running if they see anybody they don't know."

At two o'clock, the night exploded with a rumbling blast. Henry fired both barrels of his shotgun simultaneously into the air as he and Sam exited the woods near the tack barn in which Jessie Leggett had spent the longest night of his life.

Nearing the small building, Sam called out to the guard standing by the far corner, "It's me and Henry, point your gun somewhere else. We're coming in." Sam motioned for the man to unlock the heavily planked door. Before entering, Henry broke the gun open and blew grey tobacco smoke into the breach. He then held his cigar near the breach of the shotgun, hoping to disguise the source of the heavy smoke drifting from the killing holes of the shotgun. Leggett can think what he may, Sam thought.

He pulled the door open and his lantern spread its light into the darkened room. Henry held the barrels down into the light shining on a man cowering in the corner. The light from the lantern cast a yellow glare on Sam's and Henry's faces. Leggett's eyes locked onto the curling smoke drifting upwards from the barrels. He spider-backed away from the two men.

They stepped into the small room. The smell of the saddles and leather harnesses of the work animals had always smelled pleasant to Sam but now the smell of sweat and urine ruined the odor of the leather.

"Sure made a mess out of that son of a bitch, didn't it?" said Sam. Leggett's eyes remained locked onto the smoking barrels. "Get up, you stupid bastard. Let's go," said Sam, kicking the man in his shin.

"Wait . . . where we going? What you gonna' do?" Leggett asked, and foolishly added, "I'm the Deputy for this area. You can't . . ."

Sam slammed the gun-stock into the man's gut and said, "Can't what?" Coughing and gagging, Leggett stumbled backward and waited as the two men stepped toward him. His eyes darted from one to the other and at the two barrels inches from his face.

"Leggett, you're about to meet your maker. Coupla' your buddies already been greeted," answered Sam. "And I think the good Lord's pissed about right now."

He and Henry grabbed the man's arms and pulled him through the doorway.

Chapter Thirty

Tearing strips from a soiled flour sack, Henry tied one over
the darting eyes of the deputy and bound his arms behind his back
with another. The loss of his sight frightened the man. Sam and Henry
each grabbed an elbow and guided him into the woods. He was desperately afraid and Sam wanted to flood his senses with more of the
same fear.

They guided him into a tree, which the two of them stepped
around. Keeping their own shoes dry, the thief's boots filled with water as he stepped into puddles and ditches. Briars, brambles and low
hanging limbs, tore at his partially exposed face as they led him
through the jumbled growth alongside a wagon path heading deep
into the woods.

"Where y'all taking me? What y'all gonna' do?" asked the
man, trembling uncontrollably. "Y'all can't do this. Not to me, I'm
the Deputy Sheriff. Y'all know that."

Sam grabbed the man's shoulder, spun him around, and spray-
ing spittle onto the Deputy's beard stubbled face, said, "I got your
badge, you dumb shit. If a badge is what makes you the law, well, I
reckon it's me now. But don't worry about it. When we're done with
you, I'll throw it in the hole with you. Pin it on you, if that's what you
want."

Hearing the clatter of a ramrod sliding up and down the barrels
of the spent shotgun, packing down fresh loads of powder, buck and
ball, the deputy's legs folded. He collapsed to the ground, his body
racked with sobbing. Henry pulled at the man's arm, attempting to get
him back on his feet. Failing, he released the man's arm and let him
sag into a fetal position.

"Ain't no use, he won't stand up like a man." Leggett, hearing
Henry's willingness to leave him where he lay, prayed they might
change their minds.

Instead he heard, "Then shoot him here; we'll drag him over

to the hole. Can't be that hard."

Sam's theatrics produced the anguish he sought from the frightened man.

"Please, Mister Biggs, Mister Henry. Don't do this. You can't kill a man over something like a tree. What kinda' people are you? What I got to do to fix it with you? Name it. I'll do anything. Please, don't shoot me down like a dog. That just ain't right, Sir."

Henry looked at the disgraced man and smiling, said, "Sam, let's send somebody to fetch Sheriff Buck. This idiot's his deputy, it's his problem. Let him take care of his own mess. We kill him; he's just gonna' be another dead body for us to get rid of. We got plenty enough outta' Shorty for the Sheriff to hang this one, too. Besides, I'm getting awful tired of all his yowling, ain't you?"

He kicked the man at his feet and said, "Will you please shut your damn mouth before I put my boot in it?"

Leggett struggled to muffle his wracking sobs, nearly choking himself.

The silence from above seemed an eternity to him.

Relieved the fiery Sam Biggs had not discarded Henry's suggestion out of hand, he said, "Mister Biggs, let me outta' this mess. I know some stuff y'all might want to hear. Bad stuff. Stuff Sheriff Buck might want to hear."

Sam placed one knee on the ground, and balancing himself with the other, bent close to the man. Stepping away he fanned at the air. "Whew. Damn man, you done mess yourself?" He stared at the man sitting on the ground. He walked a short distance away. "Like what?" he asked.

"What you think, Henry? We going to believe anything from a man who just shit his pants?"

"Well, I reckon there ain't no harm in letting him talk. But let's stand upwind. We still got options. But then again, it might be best for everybody if this asshole just disappears. Downside's, if we take him in, Buck's gonna' start looking into what's happened up here. Maybe we oughta' just kill him and be done with it. Throw him in that hole over yonder—or let 'em lay where he is. Nobody'll know but us. Them wild hogs most likely'll dig 'em up and eat 'em anyway. Ain't no accounting for a hog's taste, is there?"

With his captors appearing to be undecided about what to do with him, Leggett felt his future shaky, again.

"What you got to tell us, and why do you think we'd want to

hear it?" asked Sam. Leggett pushed himself up into a sitting position. The odor convinced Sam and Henry he was desperate to save his life.

"What do you think's going to happen to you if I agree with Henry and we haul your ass over to Sheriff Buck's, especially since you've disgraced your office, and him, in the process?" He looked up at Henry and said, "Henry, take that rag off his head. I want to see his eyes. You can tell a lot by looking at a man's eyes." He stood looking down at Leggett, "Who put you up to this?"

Leggett lowered his eyes, afraid to look at the man in front of him, afraid not to. Defeated, he answered, "Hesper Griffen."

Sam said, "Look, I'm going to break it down real simple for you. As stupid as you are, you're going to understand what I want out of you. Number one. I want that son of a bitch gone from these here parts. Number two. Dead and gone. You think those fellows you hired to help rob me sat out here with me and Henry and we all played mumblety-peg and drank tea? They gave me a lot more than you're offering me. That's all you got to say to me? Well, what do you think Henry?"

"Shoot him," shrugged Henry.

Leggett choked. "If I give you enough to put him away, will you go to the Sheriff and tell him it was me who done it; you know, if I give you enough to lock him up for good?"

"Start talking. I'll decide," answered Sam.

"Sir, I'm scared. Real scared," he whimpered.

Sam waited, his impatience increasing.

"Griffen, Hesper Griffen, he's the man what lives up above your place. He pays us to steal them trees. He's been at it for years. And he pays off those county boys down in Fort Harwood to stay clear of here."

"Who in Fort Harwood?" Sam asked, already knowing the answer.

Leggett looked from Sam to Henry, shaking his head from side to side, "If I tell y'all that, you got to promise me I ain't never got to go back to Fort Harwood—never. Deal?"

"If you don't start talking you won't have to worry about going anywhere. Now talk," said Sam, his patience worn thin.

"Just take a look at who's been at his job the longest. Mayor Jarvis's been around forever, ain't he? He's always got his hands out to Griffen. That be enough for now?" asked the frightened deputy.

"Well, it ain't enough for you to expect any special treatment out of me," said Sam. He stood, and taking his lead, Henry stood also.

"Come on, let's go" Sam said to the man.

Realizing he was still in trouble, Leggett begged, "Wait . . . wait, there's sumpt'n else."

Sam shook his head. "Okay, one more chance. Last chance, too. What is it?"

Sam was not at all prepared for Leggett's answer.

"Hesper and Shorty kilt a woman, a white woman down yonder in Lumberton about fifteen , sixteen years ago. Shorty said Hesper done the killing and got away with it, too."

Sam's mind exploded with the implications of what the man said. He calmed himself as best as he could.

In the corner of his mind, stood Emmett and Rose—crowding him—staring at him, pleading with him to share the answer to his next question.

"Who was the woman? Why'd they kill her?" Sam asked, knowing the answers to the questions. Leggett, seeing Sam's reaction, knew he had a ladder up from the bowels of hell.

"Shorty said Griffen told him she was his wife. Said he done finally found her down there in Lumberton and they went and kilt her. Man didn't blink an eye neither, when he tole me. How's that for just plain crazy?" his face twitching behind a nervous and forced grin.

"Don't know if you know this," he said, "but Griffen married the sister of that Detwyler fellow. Now that was before my time, but Shorty told me all about it. He said she was 'bout as crazy as Griffen. Except she was crazy wild, not sick in the head crazy, like Griffen is. After a couple years of his drinking, and beating on her, she run off from him. Griffen went stark raving mad and got drunker than a mash eating hog. Stayed drunk almost from then on. Started talking crazy about how that Detwyler fellow done stole his wife away from him and how he was gonna' kill both of 'em dead."

Sensing an interest in the old murder, he added, "That was some real strange talk, too. Shorty said Griffen called that Detwyler man a wife-stealer and said she was a harlot. Everybody knew Mister Detwyler and that woman was brother and sister. Griffen knew it too—'cept he didn't know it, understand what I mean? Nary one soul never said a word to him about how he was mixed up about it, neither. Griffen woulda' kilt anybody what argued with him about . . . hell, about anything.

"Old man Detwyler had the law on him a mess of times. Onliest thing what come outta' it was it gave Griffen another reason to want to kill him. He told me Griffen tried to kill him, too. Shot him in the ass, he did. Said Detwyler damn near died from getting shot by him. Did you know that?"

Leggett saved his last nugget of information and if it didn't improve his lot with the men in front of him, nothing would.

"There's something else, too. Griffen wanted somebody to kill you and your wife, Mister Sam. Didn't know that, did you? Guess who it was he told to shoot y'all. Me. Yeah, me. Griffen said ain't nobody gonna' talk to him the way you done and get away with it. Mister Biggs, I'm here to tell you there ain't no way I was ready to do something like that. But I sure as hell didn't tell him that.

"Near 'bout a week later, Shorty come by and he told me that Griffen was mad at me 'cause I didn't do nothing, and said he'd been told to find me and kill me. That was about a year after you and Miss Rose got hitched. Shorty and I were both scared to death; him scared of me and me scared of him, so me and Shorty shook hands and swore off killing one another. That wasn't much, but it was all we could do.

"Then one day, Griffen tole us to forget shooting y'all. But I sure as hell ain't never forgot about it. Shorty neither. Shorty knows all this shit. He'll tell you I ain't lying none.

"Like I was saying, Griffen told Shorty he'd looked and looked for that wife of his for years. I heard a lot of stories about that man, I shore did. The sheriff over in Weldon told me how Griffen got accused of killing a little nigger girl and about how he rubbed her blood on his hands and smeared it on his face. Told me he kilt some of his own niggers, too, for trying to run off on him. Said he shot some of the runners in the back of their heads—right in front of their wives and children, after they got brung back by the slavers. Don't know how much's true or not, but I 'spect most of it.

"But the one thing he talked about all the time, though, was Detwyler and that wife of his and how he was gonna' cut her up 'cause she done run off on him.

"Somebody told him she might be living down yonder in Lumberton. Shorty said him and Griffen went on down to where she was 'spose to be living and they found her and kilt her. But he swears he didn't have nothing to do with killing that woman.

"They throw'd her body in a swamp outside Lumberton a ways. Shorty's mostly talk, but he did say he helped Griffen load her up and drag her out in the swamp. But here's something really messed up. After they throw'd her in the swamp; she just floated and floated and wouldn't sink down none. Then Shorty said that crazy son of a bitch told him to wade out there to where she's floating around and stick a bunch of holes in her with his knife. He said he done like he was told to 'cause what with her already dead and all, he didn't think she'd mind much—asshole. Said she still wouldn't sink none, though; so Griffen told him to get some rocks and tree limbs and stuff and pile 'em up on her. Said he done that, too, scared not to. He told me he started puking his guts out and Griffen got all mad at him about it, so they left. I know you're gonna' think I'm making this shit up, but I swear to God above and all that's Holy, that's what Shorty done told me."

Sam knew the man was telling the truth.

Leggett stopped talking, his eyes grew wide. The revelation hit him like a bolt of lightning. "That's really what you want to hear about, ain't it? Ain't got nothing a'tall to do with them trees, do it?"

"Griffen, that's all you want. Goddamn it," he said. "Why couldn't you have come to me three months ago? Fuck them trees. I woulda' handed Griffen over to you like a pig tied up and stuffed in a tow sack with a apple shoved in his mouth, if I'd know'd all this shit was gonna' happen."

Back under lock and key he sat mumbling, "Griffen, all those years you crazy son of a bitch, threatening to kill me for the smallest of things, making me feel like a turd-eating dog when I was around you . . . making me play the fool in front of your drinking buddies. Well now, I got your withered up little balls in my hands and I'm gonna' do some hammer work on 'em. You better believe it, too, you sick bastard. Shit. Them goddamn trees don't mean a fucking thing to Sam Biggs."

Tricked, he felt tricked—and used. But after feeling the cold breath of death on his face, he now felt alive. Everything he'd told Sam about the trees and who'd put him up to it was like a breeze barely strong enough to blow out a candle—he'd handed a tornado to Sam Biggs.

Sam asked through the closed door, "What's Shorty going to say when I ask him about this stuff? His answer's going to match up with yours?"

No longer trembling and sniffling, Leggett said, "Yes Sir. He ain't no fool. He's got to be thinking he's in a whole lot worse trouble than me. He knows some things, just like I do, and I reckon he's gotta' do whatever it takes for him to get outta' this mess alive, same as me. But everything I done tole you is the Gospel Truth, according to Matthew, Mark, Luke and John, so help me, God"

"Henry, get him over to the settlement and tell the Negros to throw him in the creek with a cake of lye soap. Get him some clean clothes. He's going for a ride."

***

Soon after, sandwiched between Sam and Henry, Leggett was escorted to Emmett's plantation. Emmett looked worn and pale from the activity of the previous day. A short night's rest had done little to restore his energy.

He ordered Leggett to repeat his story to Emmett. Sam watched a new weariness overwhelm his dear old friend. The vivid descriptions continued and they were difficult for Emmett to listen to.

Leggett added, "Him and Shorty were getting pretty drunk up there at the tavern when Hesper told me about how he . . . you know . . . shot you in the ass . . . sorry, your backside. He carried on like it was the funniest thing he'd ever done in his whole life. Then he put his face in mine and said if I didn't believe him about shooting you, he'd show me where the bones of one of them fellows what was with him that night when he done it, was laying in the woods up close to his house. Said he had to kill him 'cause he was gonna' go to the Sheriff in Weldon on him; you know, turn him in. He said that man wanted money to stay quiet and that people what betrays him, ends up dead. So Griffen gave him a mess of lead instead."

Emmett rolled his open hand, telling the man to continue.

"Then he looked at me real hard; I mean he looked clean inside my head and said, 'You understand what I'm telling you, right?' Well Sir, I closed my eyes and I seen me looking like a pile of bones laying in the leaves, so I answered him with the truth, 'Yes Sir.'

"Hell, everybody 'cept Griffen talked about you, Mister Detwyler', like you was some sort of founding father 'round 'bout these parts. About all I'd ever heard about you was how you tried to charge people who wanted to cross your land. Griffen said he thought it was a pretty good idea and said you was too stupid . . . sorry, but that's what he said, to know a good thing when you had it, so you went and ruint' it."

It had been difficult for Sam to bring the news to Emmett. His friend's health was failing. He knew it—he could tell. He'd lost weight and struggled more and more with his bullet damaged hip. The damage to the bone had long ago healed over, but he had bad days.

Sam knew if anybody deserved to know what he had just been told; it sure as hell was Emmett. If anybody had a right to settle accounts with Griffen, it was Emmett.

"There's something else. When he finds out what happened, us getting caught and all, he'll come looking for us. He's liable to try to kill us and y'all, too."

A knowing look passed between Sam and Emmett. Leggett's announcement had not surprised either of them. Instead each saw an opportunity.

"If he's heading this way, maybe after all these years we can be done with that sorry-ass bastard," said Sam.

Sam told Emmett his intention was to leave him out of the new trouble. After all, this last round with Griffen and the Arcola assholes had only involved him, making it something personal—one man stealing from another. But with Leggett's accusation of Hesper murdering Abigail, and him bragging about it, well, hell, he knew Emmett was entitled to know about it. In fact, he had to know about it. Holding that shattering bit of information back from the man would have been like cheating him out of something of extreme value; his right to decide for himself if he was willing to let Griffen live or die. Sam had already decided Hesper Griffen was a walking dead man—nobody was going to harm his wife.

Emmett's reaction was of renewed anger, one of anxiously planning revenge. He was sick to his stomach with Leggett's news.

All the violence, now being relived, was resurrecting old memories, dredging them up from the bottom of a lake full of memories— being stirred and rising anew. All of them rushing back, hard and strong, swirling like a tornado, slamming Emmett in the gut. He welcomed them with renewed hatred.

"We got plans to make, Sam," said Emmett. Griffen was as good as dead.

"Tell him the rest," said Sam.

Emmett's face sagged, his shoulders slumped. He looked worn and weary.

Leggett obeyed. "Mister Detwyler, Griffen told me to kill Mister Sam and Miss Rose, too. I told him they had babies and he said kill them, too."

Emmett's face turned deathly white. His voice failed him. Finally, he turned to Sam, "Is Shorty up at your place?" his inquiry cold and hard.

"Yeah. Got him separated from all the others."

"Will you take this piece of shit back and bring Shorty up here?"

Leggett's heart skipped, his hopes dissolving.

"I will, but what do you want him for? He's going to say the same thing Leggett's said, word for word."

"Sam, think about who I told you Rose said she seen at her mama's house. She seen two men, but the one she described is Shorty. She ain't never changed her story, not one bit. But, Sam, I know'd it weren't Shorty what done the killing. You know'd it, too. Am I right? And now we know the other man was Griffen."

Sam agreed with Emmett, but he feared his friend was heading down a dark road.

"Bring him up here. Me and you already agree we got to go after Griffen. Buck and his bunch ain't gonna' help. And Griffen ain't gonna' walk away from this mess."

"Say it, Emmett. What're you thinking?" Sam asked resignedly.

"Rose was only thirteen years old when she told Doc who she seen. She'd been through hell. That child'd seen some bad things. And I never doubted she'd saw Shorty, but Sam, if we're going to go get Griffen, let's do it right. Let's be positive she saw Shorty and still says it's him. And I want him to be the man that tells her who kilt her mama."

"Emmett, do you know what you're asking of her?"

His mind churned. "Yes," his voice faltering, "Sam we gotta' do it."

"I can't do it, Emmett. She's been through enough."

"Look. She knows Hesper Griffen is her father, right? She knows somebody kilt her mama, right? She knows Shorty was there— she seen him. But she didn't see Shorty do the killing, did she? And she never said she seen the other man do the killing, either." He stared at Sam, determined to press his point.

"No, but . . ."

"Wait," said Emmett. "Let me finish. If Shorty was there, like she says he was, Shorty sure as hell knows who done the killing. So let Shorty be the one that tells her who kilt her mama. Let him say the name. Let him tell her to her face it was Griffen. It'll make killing him right."

"Emmett, that changes things, don't it? If we got Shorty and Leggett, and they both know who killed Abigail, we could take all of 'em to Raleigh. Let Raleigh try him and hang him. They're witnesses, Emmett."

"Maybe. But you know that man. You really think we could get him to Raleigh? I don't."

Sam's heart ached for his wife.

Finally, he turned to Henry, "You and Isaac take him back," pointing at Leggett, "and throw him in the barn. Grab Shorty. Don't say nothing to him. Let him stew. Meet me and Emmett at the rear of my place. Don't go in the house with him. Wait outside by the summer kitchen."

He and Emmett left for Swift Creek. Each knew soon Rose would hear of Hesper Griffen's death and prayed that she could accept his death if she knew he was the one who killed her mother. And they prayed his death would erase the man's very existence from her mind.

Leggett's revelations changed things. Emmett began rethinking his insistence for Buck to be told about their latest problem with Griffen. No way would one man stand between him and Griffen. That is not going to happen, he thought. All bets are off. To hell with those teat suckers in Fort Harwood. Fuck 'em. What are they going to do? Find a way to protect Griffen again while hanging both the deputy and that other fellow, Shorty?

Send for Buck or not? Either way Griffen was about to die.

Chapter Thirty One

Henry pulled the barn door open. "Get off your goddamn asses and get out here. Hurry up."

Leggett, locked in his barn, put his ear to the door.

"You fellows made a big mistake throwing in with these two fools," said Henry, pointing at the barns that held Leggett and Shorty. "Me and Mister Biggs have been told a lot a stuff about each of you. Got yourselves some real gut-spillers with them two. I reckon we know just about everything you ever done in your whole miserable lives and now we know what you look like. So you need to remember that—remember it good.

"Mr. Biggs decided we ain't gonna' kill you for stealing his trees, not this time. He still wants to shoot every fucking one of you, and he's got the right—you were on his land, but Mister Detwyler's keeping him up at his house for as long as he can—trying to talk him outta' coming down here. Maybe you oughta' lay low. Now get on outta' here quick. Someday you might want to thank Mister Detwyler for talking him out of it, too."

The men from Fort Harwood cleared the steps in their hurry to recover their mounts back in Arcola; not a very smart place to run to, not with Griffen waiting in Shorty Jackson's tavern. In their hurry, they tore new pathways through the undergrowth below the trees and along the meandering lanes and service roads.

Henry inserted the key into the crude lock and pulled the door open.

"Shorty, out." he demanded.

Shorty thanked his version of a Heavenly Father, seeing an opportunity to flee toward Arcola and back to his dirty, dark and smelly tavern. He spun around to run but a hand shot forward, grabbing his collar.

"No . . . no, not you, you dumb shit, you're staying. Shorty, if ever there was a good example of the righteousness of hanging, it's you," said Henry, laughing at the befuddled look on the man's face.

Shorty's face was chalky white. "What's that son of a bitch done and told y'all? Whatever he said, he's a goddamn shit-eating liar. He's lying, he is. You hear me? If his lips are moving, he's lying. Y'all can count on that."

"Shorty, damn, you are good. That's exactly what Leggett said you'd say. Got anything you want to tell Mister Biggs, or do you want to make peace with your God for killing that woman down there in Lumberton?" he asked, as he pulled at the startled, hyperventilating man and slammed the barn door shut.

"Oh, by the way, did Griffen tell you that woman you killed was his wife?"

Shorty instantly bolted back to the closing door ."Hey . . . wait up . . . no, no. Oh hell no. That's bullshit. Plain and simple. I ain't never kilt nobody. That old bastard never told me to kill no woman. What'd you just say? She was his wife? Oh, man, fuck me. Hey, I don't give a damn what that deputy done told you. Hesper Griffen woulda' tore my head off and shit down my neck if I'd kilt her. All he talked about all the way down there was how he was gonna' cut her heart out and stomp on it."

Henry told the scared man, "If you tell that story to Sheriff Buck when he gets here, things might go a hell of a lot easier for you than for your buddy Griffen. Old Griffen's gonna' go see his maker soon, and I ain't talking about the Good Lord. Devil had to have made that son of a bitch, so you need to decide, and real soon—talk or don't talk."

Nearing panic, Shorty pleaded, "Git Sheriff Buck on out here. I'll talk. I'll tell him everything he needs to know and stuff he don't know he needs to know. But you got to know something yourself. I ain't kilt no goddamn woman. I didn't and that there's the truth. Here. Listen. Tell you what. Put me in that barn with that ignorant bastard and stand next to the door. You'll hear the truth then, I'll betcha that, or I'll beat the shit outta' him. Son of a bitch's so far up Griffen's asshole, he got to stick his head out to talk to him."

"Mister Biggs wants you up at the big house. Let's go."

***

The three men stood by the rear of the mansion, waiting for Sam and Emmett.

The door opened, Sam stepped out and beckoned them inside.

"Wait in here till I call for you."

Returning to the dining room where Emmett stood, he called for George. "Where's Miss Rose?"

"She be upstairs in de bedroom a rest'n some."

"Go wake her up. Tell her I need her."

"Henry, you and Isaac bring Shorty in here," said Sam, solemnly.

Rose entered the room, looking from her husband to Emmett.

"Sam?" she asked. "What's wrong?" concern creasing her face. And as she did, Henry and Isaac entered the dining room with a short fat man sandwiched between them.

"Sam, what's going on?" she asked again, looking at the gathering men. Suddenly, she stiffened in alarm. Her eyes darted from her husband to the fat man, then to Emmett and back again to the man between Henry and Isaac. She backed away from the man that she'd seen in her dreams a thousand times.

"Rose, do you know this man?" Sam asked his wife, his nerves frayed from what he was asking of her. He could see she was badly frightened; as he stepped towards her, she stepped backward, again.

Confusion marred Shorty's face.

Rose stepped behind the safety of her husband and continued to stare at the man. Her face paled. She spun toward the china cabinet and rushing to it, grabbed the revolver Sam kept hidden on top of the plate-rail to protect his family. She faced Shorty, struggling with the weight of the heavy revolver, while tugging at the hammer with both thumbs.

Sam heard the loud click when it locked into full cock. Quickly, he pushed the heavy barrel away from the men standing beside the massive oak dining table, fearing Henry and Isaac were in harm's way.

Shorty, still confused, collapsed to the floor and began a desperate crawl underneath the oak table.

A hole appeared in the oak floor. The huge revolver kicked her tiny hands upward. The percussion blasted through the room, shaking crystals from the dining room chandelier while the remaining prisms chimed myriads of tinkling notes in sharp contrast to the echoing explosion of the Colt. The residue of burned gunpowder stung the eyes of everyone while wispy tendrils of smoke drifted from a splintered hole in the dark oak floor.

Panicked, she cried, "Sam, Sam. It's him. It's him. He killed my mother." She tugged at the hammer, determined to shoot the monster hiding beneath the table.

Immediately, Shorty understood what was happening. He began shouting, "No . . . no . . . It wasn't me. It wasn't me. Griffen . . . he kilt that woman. It wasn't me."

Sam looked at Emmett. Emmett's eyes ached with grief for Rose.

Shorty had just signed Hesper's death certificate.

"Tell her again who you just said," demanded Emmett.

"It was him. Griffen. He done it, Miss Biggs. I seen him do it," answered Shorty.

"Get that son of a bitch out of here," Sam said to Henry. "Throw him back in the barn and put more guards on 'em. You and Isaac start getting things together. We'll be leaving in a few minutes."

Shorty struggled to his feet. He looked at the woman standing in front of him. He knew who she was—who she had to be. He'd never been involved with any other murder so she had to have been at the house when Griffen killed his wife.

"Miss Biggs, please, it wasn't me, I swear to you. I was there, I admit it, but there wasn't no stopping that man. I begged him not to do it. But listen . . . listen . . ." his voice fading, while he was pulled towards the back door.

"Hold up, fellows. Let him talk," said Sam

"Thank you, Mister Biggs, thank you, thank you," said Shorty, cowering behind Henry. "Griffen told me and that Deputy Leggett to come down here and kill you and your husband and anybody else we could find, but I begged him not to do it and I got him to stop. That's got to be worth something, don't it, Ma'am? . . . Miss Biggs?"

Sam heard Rose's soft whisper, "My own father was going to . . ." He caught her as she sagged to the floor. He lifted her and carried her upstairs to the bedroom and laid her upon the bed. Everyone was told to leave the room. Soon, her eyes opened but Sam saw only confusion and the heartbreaking sadness in them. He bent toward her and placed an opened palm on each side of her face.

Feeling the hands which had caressed her all these years, she pleaded, "Sam, what's going on?" He expected the question and dreaded it. Distressed, he knew he'd broken his promise to protect her.

"Rose, sweetheart, I'm so sorry. Me and Emmett just found out a short while ago that we had solid proof Hesper killed your mother. But we had to be sure, beyond a doubt, that the man down there would give him up. The only person who was there when it happened was you, but he didn't know you were there until you said it just now."

"No, Sam," she responded, shaking her head. "It was that man down stairs," refusing to acknowledge the father she'd never known was a killer.

"Rose. Think. Did you see him do it?" referring to Shorty, he asked her softly. "Did you see him kill your Mother?"

The terror of the long ago day washed over her.

"No," she whispered. "I don't understand. Are you sure he said Hesper Griffen? Did he mean my father? But Sam, how can a man kill his own daughter?" She begged her husband for an answer.

She felt revulsion for the man responsible for the tainted blood coursing through her veins.

"It wasn't because you were his daughter, Rose. Your mother saw to it that he'd never know about you. He wants to kill you because you because Emmett loves you. He wants to kill me because I love you. He'll come after our children, too, Rose. He's like a ball of twine—he's rolled tight but beginning to unwind."

His anger building, he no longer heard his wife's pleas for him to stay with her—to protect her, like he'd promised. He was ashamed of his broken promises, but knew nothing would change his mind.

He had to be strong. He needed to comfort her, but for the first time ever, she would have to wait for him to beg her forgiveness, and he would beg that of her.

Standing to leave, she clutched at him. "Where are you going? Don't go."

"Emmett and I are going after him. Fort Harwood won't do anything. We don't even know if Buck's coming or not. We'll ask, but . . . " He didn't want to think about it anymore.

"Rose, I've got to tell you as quick as I can what's going to happen. We're going after Griffen. If he comes along we'll take him to Raleigh. If not, . . . " his voice trailed away.

"We caught that new deputy Leggett from over in Arcola and that man down there along with some of Griffen's men stealing from us. Motley was helping them.."

She looked surprised when hearing of James's involvement.

"That Leggett fellow, told us a lot of stuff me and Emmett already suspected. He said Shorty'd bragged about how he and Griffen killed your Mother. I believe him. Shorty didn't kill her, but he's as guilty as Griffen is. He watched Griffen kill her. There's no other way. He's out of control. He threatened you and our children. It's over.

"I'm going to tell Beulah to bring the children in here to sleep with you. George and one of our neighbors will be outside in the hallway. I'll have men outside the house, too."

Tears continued to stream down her face. When the children—still asleep—were brought to her, she demanded they be laid close to her.

He kissed his children, and hugged his wife. She tugged at his arm. Preferring to stay, he pulled away from her and left to join the rest of the men.

They knew what they were about to do would turn them into vigilantes; knew their actions would make them as lawless as Griffen and his men, but their options were fading. Buck was in Fort Harwood, and they were here alone—like always. Buck could come, maybe he should come, they reasoned, but the law and Buck were both on probation with Emmett and Sam.

It was their war, his and Emmett's—the others helping out of a sense of right and wrong. There should be no need for them to be punished for doing something Carlton County had refused to do.

So again, he and Emmett discussed the issue and decided to send for Buck. There was no room for mistakes. Buck had to be told.

"Alright, let's tell Buck, let him know what's going on. Let him decide for himself what to do. He'll either come or he won't. And that's what we'll be left with."

Emmett provided a running account to Elmer and sent him to Buck. Elmer listened carefully, not needing to write any of it down; things of such magnitude were unlikely to be forgotten or understated, and he headed to Fort Harwood. The balance of the night was spent preparing for killing.

A hard day had arrived and daylight was burning.

Getting Griffen on theft charges would be nice, but in the long run it would mean little. The head of the snake had to be cut off. Griffen was insane. Not only did his actions prove it, his closest allies vouched for it.

Plans needed to be made and they had to be good, solid plans. The common goal was understood, the basics of war tried and true— arm yourself to the max and be willing to kill those willing to kill you. Guards were assigned duties and each informed of the chance of an ambush from Griffen.

Stealth and speed were paramount. The deadly chase had begun. Fearing easy detection in numbers, Sam pared the group down to himself, Henry, Isaac and Emmett.

The guard of the two prisoners, Leggett and Shorty, was increased. George was given the specific duty of telling Sheriff Buck, if he came, that the four of them had left for Griffen and were heading to Arcola.

They rode in silence. The road from Ringwood to Arcola was the only direct route. A possible ambush from Griffen, if it came, could come from the thick woods on either side of the road. Guns were held straight ahead, half cocked.

The shuffling noises of foraging field mice, the angry chatter of squirrels darting about in the tall oaks, were magnified by the growing tension.

Ahead lay the barely discernable outline of the dying crossroads town.

To the east, the remnants of the gray-blue clouds of a recent light summer shower, just enough of a shower to settle the dust slowly drifted away.

Nearing Arcola, Sam saw the whitewashed store front of the mercantile belonging to his friends, the Johnsons. The sidewalks were bare of people and horses. No shoppers, no children chasing one another. Nothing. Still too early for the few residents to venture into the street.

The storm had been a short-lived one, but it had blessed Arcola with a dust-settling rain.

The gray, fine dust on the road was crusted paper thin. The hooves of the four horses broke the crusty skin, scattering the paper-thin flakes. No other living thing, with the exception of a crippled dog, dragging its damaged leg, had ventured out since the storm. Strewn flakes proved the dog curious of the absence of any life. It rambled from door to door; sniffing, searching and leaving an unsteady trail of paw prints.

The men rode into the center of the intersection and continued four abreast. The door to the jail was closed and there was no sign of recent occupancy. The stable doors were slightly ajar; opened enough for someone to step through and unload their guns into them. The flutter of a loose curtain behind a broken window gave pause to the men.

A movement in the window of the mercantile, caught Sam's eyes. Lonnie Johnson raised his hand to catch Sam's attention, and beckoned him with his fingers. Sam acknowledged the store owner, nodding to let him know he'd been seen.

Aware possible danger awaited them, Sam whispered for Henry and Isaac to ride past the whitewashed store and turn into the alley running to the rear of the mercantile. He told them to dismount after they had ridden out of view of any person possibly watching from the tavern or stable across the street.

Things seemed surreal, the air thick with danger. Time seemed to alternately speed up and slow down.

Gut instincts; better go with 'em, Sam reminded himself, thinking of the many times they had saved him in the past. The tavern felt wrong to him. The stable, old and in varying stages of collapse, felt just as wrong. It could hide a small army of enemies.

"Emmett, pull your horse up to the rail and keep him between you and that tavern. Grab your guns and powder and head for that store, the dry goods. I'll watch the tavern and stable. Isaac and Henry's got us covered from the sides. I know that fellow in the store there. Name's Lonnie Johnson. You'll know him when you see him. He's a good man. I'll be right behind you. Okay, let's go."

The men dismounted and drug off their guns and ammunition. Watching the street and buildings across from them, they backed through the door.

"Lonnie, thanks," said Sam, his eyes riveted to the buildings across the street.

"You know Emmett, don't you?"

"It's a pleasure to see you again, Mister Detwyler. My wife, Mattie. Sam, what the hell's going on?" Lonnie asked, urgently. Sam held up his hand to let the man know he had to check on Henry and Isaac.

"Sorry Lonnie, I'll tell you in a minute. You got a back door?" Lonnie nodded and led Sam through the storage room at the rear of the small store, and to the heavily locked rear door. Lonnie's hands

shook while he unlocked the crude locks. Sam stepped through, carefully looking for any living thing other than Henry or Isaac. The two
men saw him and both hugged the rear wall as they slid along it. Sam
waved them into the storage room and asked if they'd seen anyone
lurking nearby. Both reported they had seen nothing out of the ordinary.

"Place is quieter than a graveyard," replied Henry.

"Saw a dog dragging a busted up foot, that's all," added Isaac.

"Let's get this door locked," said Sam.

"Who's over at the tavern, Lonnie?" Sam asked.

"I don't know, now. A while ago, Griffen was in there and two
other fellows were with him. Then three fellows come running up
from down your way, their clothes all torn to hell and back, bleeding
like they done run up on a bobcat in a briar patch. Them fellows went
in that bar and about five minutes later a gun went off. One of them
other fellows or Griffen, maybe, I don't know which one, shot one of
them new fellows. The other two busted outta' them doors like their
britches was on fire. That other'ns still in there, but I think he's dead
as a corncob. His buddies ain't come back to check on him, neither.

"About a half hour ago, Griffen and them other two fellows
what was with him, got their horses outta' the stable and rode off that
way," he added, pointing east.

"Emmett, how's about you and Isaac stay in here with Lonnie
and Mattie?" asked Sam. "Me and Henry'll slip out back and go
round the side and see who's dead or dying over there in that tavern.

"Lonnie, lock that back door good when we leave. Keep those
guns stuck out the window and crack the front door. You all see
somebody that looks like they might be wanting to hurt me and
Henry, shoot the hell out of them."

Mattie, on cue, headed for the safety behind the counter. Emmett inched open the rear door and nodded at Sam. "Go," he said.

Sam and Henry carefully edged their way around the side of
the building. Finding a mule hitched to an empty wagon, they pulled
the harness off and led the mule out to the edge of the street. Stooping
to keep their heads below the mule's back, Sam slapped its rump. The
startled animal jumped and trotted across the street. With Sam and
Henry desperately hanging on, they barely managed to get the mule
stopped at the far side of the tavern.

Both stepped up onto the planked sidewalk and slowly, carefully, inched toward the door of the tavern. Hunkered low, Henry on

his knees, Sam standing above him, they held their guns ahead of them.

"Anybody in there? You got ten seconds to answer," shouted Sam. Ten seconds passed much too quickly for both men. They shoved the guns forward and fired deep into the dark interior. The explosions from Sam's heavily powdered big bore and Henry's double-barreled shotgun roared through the building. The percussion from the guns shook accumulated dust from the exterior siding and blew the window curtain through a broken pane. The blasts still ringing in their ears, they dropped their weapons and grabbing their belt guns, dashed inside. The dash inside was followed by total silence, with the exception of a yelping dog fleeing down the alley next to the tavern.

Emmett and Isaac stiffened with anticipation, fearing there would be more shooting, but no further explosions came from the inside of the tavern.

"Sam. Henry. You all right? Say something, damn it," barked Emmett. Sam and Henry stepped out of the darkened tavern.

"Well, Griffen and those two friends of his have already set about fixing up his problem. One of those fellows we let go is laying in there shot through the head. He sure ain't going to steal no more trees off me. Ain't going to say nothing against Griffen, neither."

Lonnie and Mattie slowly emerged from the safety of their store. Lonnie stuck his head into the tavern, and to Mattie, he said, "Griffen kilt that man, I told you he did."

***

The hard thumping hooves of a fast moving horse gained their attention. All six faced down the Ringwood road. Approaching was a big man on a big horse, his jacket blowing in the wind; his gun stock resting on his thigh and the barrel raised into the air. Instinct required the armed men, standing in front of the tavern door, to train their weapons upon the approaching stranger.

"Put down them goddamn guns, you idiots. Pardon me, Miss Mattie. Just what the hell do you fools think you're doing?" Sheriff Buck yelled at the small army in front of him.

Emmett and Sam were neither surprised nor pleased when Buck rode up, but Buck addressing them more as a Sheriff than a friend, did not sit well with either of them. The scowls on their faces indicated they had no use for a law-abiding attitude being shoved at them, not now, not this late in the game.

"What the hell brings you up in these parts, Buck?" Emmett sarcastically asked the Sheriff. Then added, "We got a problem up here, so we didn't exactly expect no lawman to show up."

Buck felt the burn in his friend's voice, but held his temper. "Emmett, is that fair of you? I can't come up here unless I'm told there's a problem and you waiting until you're ready to fix it yourself before you send Elmer, don't seem right to me. Seem right to you, Emmett?" He challenged Emmett for an answer which did not come.

"Sam, Elmer said you locked my deputy up in your barn. That right?"

"Sure as hell is. On your way back, stop and get him if you want him. Make sure you got Elmer with you when you get there. Sheriff or no Sheriff, I don't think those boys watching him's going to hand him over to you unless somebody speaks up for you. Get that asshole Shorty, too, while you're at it. I kinda' told those fellows that I'd speak to you about how they've been helping us out. They been telling us some mighty interesting things, Buck."

He glared at Buck. "Stuff you already ought to know if you'd been doing your job. Frankly, I don't give a shit, sorry, Miss Mattie, what you do to 'em. Tie 'em upside down on a tree trunk and let the dogs piss on 'em till they drown. Sorry, Miss Mattie. Go fetch 'em. Listen to them or not. I don't care." He spat his words angrily. "Me and Emmett's going on with our plans."

Buck looked hard at Sam. "And what kinda' plan you got, Sam? You four just gonna' ride up on Griffen and them others and kill 'em? Shoot 'em dead? That your plan?"

"That's the general idea."

"Emmett, that your plan, too? You just going to ride him down and kill him? You two the judge and the jury, now? You gonna' be the executioners? You think Griffen's gonna' stand there and get himself kilt? Reckon there might be a small chance he might put a hole through your thick skulls?"

Emmett challenged Buck with, "Unless you're here to do it for us, you're goddamn right that's what we got in mind. Don't start shoving your fancy law talk down our throats. A little late for that, ain't it, Buck?"

In all of the years Lonnie and Mattie had lived in Arcola, struggling to survive, never had they seen a firestorm like the one brewing before them.

Mattie was desperately afraid things would escalate, so Lonnie, after getting his own nerves under control, pointed at Shorty Jackson's Tavern. "Sheriff, there's a dead man laying in there on the floor. Griffen or one of his men done kilt him dead. I don't know which one and me and the Missus don't care. We're gonna' get some clothes together and get on down to Fort Harwood 'till things settle down round here." He put his arm protectively around his frightened wife.

"And that's a goddamn shame, ain't it Sheriff?" His anger gathering momentum. "We want to—need to go to Weldon. Mattie's got her a sister what lives there. We ain't got enough money for Fort Harwood but, Sheriff, we'd have to go by Griffen's house to get to her sister's place no matter which road we take to Weldon from here." His eyes filled with defeat and bitterness.

"That's the way it's always been round these parts. That son of a bitch you call your deputy ain't never done his job, and not one fucking soul from Fort Harwood ever come up here to check on him."

Mattie's eyes grew wide, hearing her church going husband using such language.

"Except you, two or three times maybe, in about the same number of years. You ain't got no idea at all what we been going through, do you? Don't know if I can wait to get out of this town and the further away from Carlton County I get, the more happy I'll be. About willing to give it all up and turn my back on this place . . . like you and the County did."

He turned and walked toward the door to his mercantile, trying hard not to look at his wife, trying hard to regain his composure.

"Fellows, let's get going. Griffen and those other two are about an hour ahead of us, already," said Sam, walking away from Buck.

Buck dismounted and stepped toward Sam and Emmett.

"Wait, hold up, Sam. Give me a minute to see if Lonnie will cover that man up with a blanket or something and ask him to stop by the courthouse and tell them what's going on up here.

"If you'll let me, I want to ride with you. I'm tired of trying to be a fucking Sheriff. It's hard to be a good one with both hands tied behind my back." He looked from Sam to Emmett.

He'd made his decision. He reached for his badge and ripped it from his shirt. Pale white skin showed through the tear.

"Fuck it," he said, throwing it into the dirt beneath him.

Sam stooped, picked up the discarded badge and put it in his vest pocket.

Buck watched, expecting a lecture. "That copper piece of shit ain't gonna' hold me back no more. Ain't but one way to end all this—it's time for Griffen to get what he's got coming."

Buck stepped across the street and spoke to a defeated Lonnie. He handed Buck a few ragged blankets and Buck covered the body.

Flies could destroy a body in the heat. Especially with the humidity worsening by the minute.

Buck closed the door and scratched the head of a limping dog, sniffing at the door of the tavern.

Chapter Thirty Two

Including Buck, five men approached the stable. Before them, three pairs of boots had broken through the flaky crust on the planked sidewalk, leading out to the stable, and disappeared through the doors. No footprint of man or horse came back out onto the street.

Logic said the owners of those boots were either still in the stable, pointing their rifles at them, or there was a way out through the back.

Sam sent Henry and Isaac to each side of the run-down stable with orders to check the rear of the building. Quickly, they returned with the news that the rear doors had been forced open and three horses had headed east.

Four men—forced to become vigilantes, and one man with a hole ripped across his breast pocket, followed the tracks.

***

Arcola lay behind them, deserted for now, perhaps never to be occupied again. Some towns—towns with certain types of personalities—certain types of reputations, were a lot like some men. With enough bad things said about them, the easier it was to stay clear of them. Some towns died that way, leaving only the empty husks of collapsing buildings. With each passing season, the crumbling buildings became more and more like ghosts of the their former selves.

Arcola had never had much said about it and the little said was mostly bad. It probably deserved to die. It might self-destruct anyway, after what was destined to happen this day.

***

Buck made an effort to take charge of the manhunt. That was his way, his training, right or wrong. His reception by the others was cool. That surprised him.

Deep in thought, he wondered, What happened to me? Did I grow old, complacent? Did I forfeit my sense of loyalty? Is that how

I kept my job? How about the loyalty I owe these men? They're the ones who were deserted. Out of sight, out of mind? Is that where I went?

He silently vowed to return to Fort Harwood and make things right.

Feelings toward Buck had changed. Lately, Buck had seemed distant, indifferent, to Emmett and Sam. They felt betrayed, like they had before the Arcola jail had been built; and still, they felt deserted and alone.

In fairness, they knew Buck's hands had been tied. Had they asked him, maybe he would have explained, but now they were weary of the whole ordeal. Things should have changed for the better when the deputy had been stationed in Arcola. But even with that, things remained as they had always been.

Sam and Emmett held fast to their plans, not willing to change them merely because Buck had decided to join them. That was not about to happen.

All of them had spent years caught in the middle of Griffen's tyranny. They'd watched him descend from bad to worse, from sick to sicker. They knew there was only one solution remaining.

Sure, they wanted Buck to help them, they needed him. It would add a sense of rightness to their plans. They could use all the help they could get, but they had grown weary of asking. So here they were, heading toward the outside of the law. They'd admit it if it ever came down to it; they weren't ashamed of the way they felt. What other choice had they been left with? To them, it seemed Buck had spent the last few years of his life struggling to sit atop his fence. He now had a hard choice to make—soft hay or fresh turds.

He would have to rethink his own convictions, and be willing to act on the new ideas of the right and wrong of things. He had to weigh his own standards. He had to be his own man

But not these men. They had decided and their decision was carved in stone.

And just because some law seemed specific, maybe it wasn't necessarily the only way to go at a problem. Maybe laws could be bent a little. Maybe laws should be bent—tested to see what it would take to break them. Maybe all laws should be tested to see if they even deserved to be laws. Sam and Emmett were about to test some laws—and break them if necessary.

***

In the distance, Sam saw the intersection of the Lewisburg-Raleigh Road, the road leading off to the right and through the center of his land. Upon arriving at it, Henry pointed to the torn up ground below them. A major decision had been made on this spot.

The freshly pawed soil spoke of the three riders' indecisiveness and echoed those words spoken by Hesper Griffen. "Boys, here's our choices. Go home and sleep it off, or go kill Sam and Emmett. And don't forget them other two idiots, Leggett and Shorty. Might as well kill 'em all and be done with it."

"They went down that way, Sam. They're gonna' go to our place," said Henry, pointing south.

"It sure don't leave much doubt about what that dead man back there told Griffen," said Emmett. "Griffen's got it figured out. He's got to know it all, by now. That trash woulda' told him everything before Griffen killed him. I don't know if he knows Leggett and Shorty spilled their guts about what he done to Abigail, or not, but we best figure he believes they did."

He continued, "He'd be a damn fool to ride into what he believes is an armed camp, but my bet is, at least he'll try to see how close he can get up to us—see if he can find an advantage.

"He don't know we're back here, not yet. They won't be able to see us, not with the sun behind us. If he could, he'd already be off to his place getting some more men together."

"That's what I'd do if I were him. What do you think, Sam," asked Henry.

Sam answered, "Griffen's ride down to spy on us might be an opportunity for us. He's not going to be as heavily armed now as he will be after he finds out what those two fools told us. I doubt those fellows riding with him are the killers he'd regularly hire on if he had a plan. That's a plus for us. My guess is they're field hands and got caught up in this mess," he said, "but, he's got some folks that'll do anything for him when he needs 'em. He pays 'em enough, you can count on that." He sat on Queenie and studied the terrain.

"Instead of trying anything now, he'll most likely check what he's up against and then go fetch his regular killers. Then he'll come at us full strength. And that ain't going be a fair fight. So, I say we take the fight to them and finish it. We can't give him a chance to improve his stand."

He pointed to the edge of the woods. "You all wait here a minute, I'm going to see if I can get a better view up by the curve."

He rode Queenie over to the edge of the road. With the thick trees serving as a screen, he dismounted, and on foot, looked down the Lewisburg-Raleigh Road. Rising thermals turned the road surface into mirages of pools filled with black water. In the distance, the figures of three men and three horses shimmered and danced.

"That's them; a mile down yonder. They ain't in no hurry. Emmett, what do you think?" he asked his elderly friend.

"Let's not crowd 'em. Let 'em ride past that curve down yonder. We can use that bend in the road to our advantage. When they get outta' sight, we'll ride hard to close up on 'em, gain some ground on 'em. Do it one or two times, we can get a hell of a lot closer to 'em. Maybe close enough to surprise 'em."

Emmett looked tired and worn. In his hand, he held a dark pocket-sized bottle of Laudanum. He drained the last of its contents. "Maybe you boys ought to go on ahead. I don't believe you got time to wait on me. I'll come up quick as I can behind you. I ain't hurting too bad today. The heat helps some with the pain. I'll rest a bit. Keep looking hard so you see them before they see you. If they see you, they're gonna' haul ass deep in them woods and it'll be hell trying to find 'em.

"But Sam, if Griffen and them fellows do head left off that road and go down in the woods, they're gonna' be nigh on to your place. You all will have to move fast if they do that. Start in quick chasing 'em. It'd be proof enough for me about what they're up to." His eyes were blackened from the harshness of the past few days.

"Let me rest a bit. I'll cut across the woods and hook up with you closer in."

He continued, "Sam, I'd feel a lot better if you'd let Isaac circle round to get to our boys watching things down at your place and get them fellows moving up towards where Griffen's heading. We'll need all the guns we can get."

Sam agreed and Isaac, given instructions, left for Swift Creek Plantation, using animal trails and old paths that only he knew existed.

As he rode, Sam looked back at his old friend. He feared Emmett had fallen victim to the same drug he'd warn Sam to be careful with.

Sam, Henry and Buck waited for Griffen and his men to ride

around the far curve in the road. Until they did, little else could be planned. Soon, the three ahead of them rode down the shoulder of the road.

Arriving at the curve, Sam, scanned the road. Ahead, he saw the bridge spanning Swift Creek. A well used cattle trail led from each side of the dirt road down into his woods. Griffen and the two riders with him were no longer in sight. They had entered the woods and headed east toward Sam's plantation, less than a mile away.

"It's going to get a bit more interesting now, so stay alert," said Sam. They entered the woods, hunting their enemies. The tracks were easy to follow, the sandy, white soil recorded their passage. Sam tugged at his mare to stop and the men discussed tactics.

The sagging limbs of the oaks, the one feature which had so strongly drawn him to settle along Swift Creek, were now an impediment to them. They grabbed their guns and ammunition and continued on foot. Far ahead they could hear the horses they had been following as they, too, voiced their annoyance with the low hanging limbs.

Griffen and his hired hands, likewise had found progress nearly impossible; they too, hindered by the sagging trees.

"Grab everything you need. Tie them horses up good. Last thing we need is for them to run off on us and head back to the stables before we get a chance to see what's going on down here," said Griffen.

Behind them, Sam, Henry and Buck narrowed the distance between themselves and their prey. Leaving the cover of a large grove, they broke into a clearing. Griffen's horses stood hobbled at the far edge of the clearing, heads down, grazing on the abundant grass. Past the horses lay the banks of Swift Creek. A windfall tree bridged the narrow creek, apparently the route Griffen and his men used to cross.

Remaining stooped and quiet, the hunters listened for noises that would give away Griffen's location. Suddenly, a blast from a rifle exploded from the woods ahead of them, coming from the direction of the settlement

Isaac had ridden his horse hard. Lathered and breathing heavily, it hung its head. He slid from the animal's back. He too, heard the gunfire and watched as the barn's corner trim fragmented into splinters. As dust blew into the air, the guard dashed behind the far corner of the tack barn.

Leggett crashed into something inside the barn in his effort to find anything that might provide shelter, and then all remained quiet within the locked door.

The startled guard shouted to his friend watching over Shorty, "Where'd that shot come from? Who fired it?"

Shorty's guard fled for the safety behind Shorty's barn. He pointed toward the woods and they both saw the wispy remains of black-powder smoke slowly dissipating.

Isaac shouted from the edge of the woods. "Over here. It's me, Isaac. Shoot over yonder at that smoke so them sonsabitches'll stay low."

He saw the guards watching him. "I'm gonna' go over to the right and see if I can get a clear shot down along the edge of the woods."

He stooped and crawled, using the undergrowth edging the woods as cover. From behind an oak, he saw Griffen and his men hiding in the thick of the woods.

They were talking excitedly to one another and Isaac could hear one of the men yelling at the other two.

"You sons of bitches, you run off on me now, I'll shoot you myself. Don't believe me? Try it. Now start shooting," cursed Hesper. The closest man, forty yards distant from Isaac, laid his rifle across a tree limb and lined up the bead at the end of the barrel on one of the guards.

Isaac's gun exploded, kicking hard into his shoulder. He blinked his eyes rapidly to clear the smoke and fine particles of burnt powder from them.

The man heaved to the left. A large piece of soft lead cut through muscle and ribs, and blew apart his heart. The rifle he had seconds before aimed so well at the unsuspecting guard's head fell and now lay beside the wasted body, freshly loaded, and unfired.

Griffen and the other man, seeing Isaac busy pouring a new load of powder down the musket barrel, broke and fled deep into the woods.

They fled in a direction leading them away from the three men hunting them. In seconds, they disappeared.

Sam, Henry and Buck were not close enough to see the men, but close enough to hear them and know all hell was breaking loose in front of them. Unaware Griffen and the second gunman were escaping, silence reigned supreme.

"Isaac, you hear me?" yelled Sam.

"Yeah Sam, over here. Sam don't do nothing. Just stay where you are. One of 'em's dead, but I don't know which one. I can't see the other two. Let's wait it out a bit, see what they plan to do."

"Griffen . . . Griffen . . . you hear me?" Sam shouted. "Throw your guns down and come on out." No answer; he crept closer. Minutes later, with Henry and Buck close behind, he saw the crumpled body of a dead man lying at the base of a tree.

Still he waited; ears tuned for noises.

"I think they're gone, Isaac. See if you can get in closer. We got three guns ready to unload on 'em if a leaf even blows the wrong way."

Minutes passed. "Come on in, Sam. They're gone," shouted Isaac. Sam, Henry, and Buck entered the clearing where Isaac waited. Sam rolled the body over and asked Buck if he knew the man. Buck answered he'd never seen him before.

"I've picked up a trail. Two men. They're heading that way." Henry said, pointing in the direction of Hesper Griffen's plantation.

Isaac returned from calming the guards. Sam nodded and said, "Let's do it."

The four men headed back into the woods and followed the rough and broken trail used by Hesper and his man for their escape.

Tangles of broken limbs, patches of briars and the harsh effects of the previous night's drinking hampered Hesper and his gunman's retreat. Each panting and puffing, sought safety behind trunks of old growth oaks. The two gained only little rest.

They needed to continue north, hopefully, back to the safety of Griffen's plantation.

They crawled a short distance through the underbrush and drank thirstily from the waters of the slow flowing creek. Hearing the rustling of feet against brush, and the occasional whispered voices, they grabbed their weapons and continued their escape.

Unaware Griffen and the remaining man were fleeing straight toward him, Emmett remained cautious. He assumed he was close to Sam and the others.

He was surprised when two dirty and sweaty men stepped out from the trees in front of him; one a stranger with remnants of rotting leaves and debris sticking in his beard, grabbed his horse's bridle. The other man—not a stranger—never had been a stranger, lifted his gun and aimed it at Emmett.

Griffen laughed out loud. He clicked his tongue as if chastising an errant school boy, his head jerked uncontrollably to the right.

"Well, well. I'll be damned. And they say there ain't no God." He looked at the other man. "You know who this stinking pile of horse shit is?" The man shook his head and he didn't much care.

"Tsk . . . tsk . . . tsk," said Griffen, admonishing the man on the horse.

"Emmett. Just the man I was looking for. Well, actually you and that little asshole buddy of yours," he added sarcastically, 'Mister Sam Biggs,—and breaking into a crazed laughter, repeated, 'Big Sam Biggs.'" He looked sideways, hoping his hired man would see how clever he was.

"This here fellow's the famous Emmett Detwyler, that's who he is—or soon to be was," he grinned, pointing at Emmett, and broke into his demented laughter again. His head again jerked oddly to the right and his eye twitched.

Emmett's riding jacket concealed a double-barreled shotgun, his right hand curled around the stock, his finger around the trigger. The roar of the exploding gun made Griffen jump, confusion clouding his mind. The man in front of Emmett's horse released the bridle and fell. His body fell squarely on its ass, his legs straight out. He fell back against the tree he'd hidden behind moments before. His arms splayed out and down, holding the bleeding mass upright. His dead eyes stared at the trampled brush and briars beneath Emmett's horse.

Emmett's mount danced to the right when the gun roared near its head. Surprised, Griffen foolishly grabbed the bridle, and was thrown awkwardly to the ground. He slowly stood and stared at the arrival of his death. He watched Emmett's hands as Emmett pulled the trigger. The flash from the barrel lit the area around them in a rosy hue. The concussion of the blast, combined with the impact of super-heated pellets of soft lead, tore through clothing, flesh, mangled organs, and drove Griffen backwards.

Staggering, he fell to his knees. He looked quizzically at his stomach and placed a palm against a growing red spot. His expression changed from astonishment to one of bewilderment. He fingered at the hole in his belly. Pulling the bloodied hand away, he held it close to his face, and stared at the rivulets of blood inching down his fingers. He rubbed the blood-soaked fingers together and sniffed them. His eyes struggled to focus on Emmett. "Now, why'd you go and do that?"

Emmett dropped the spent shotgun. He dismounted and stepped close to his dying enemy, "Are you happy now, Hesper? All your fucking, miserable life you've been trying your best to get here and now, well . . . here you are. Got yourself killed. And for what?"

Hesper stared at Emmett, his face showing no discernable re-action, his eyes locked tightly onto Emmett's, and again his right eyed twitched. Emmett continued, "You dumb son of a bitch. Yeah . . . " He paused, dealing with his roaring emotions, his face inches away from his life-long enemy, and whispered, "You know you're dying, don't you?"

Hesper moaned, his upper body wavered.

"Hold on. Not yet Hesper," said Emmett. "I'll prop you up with a goddamn stick, I will. So help me God. You're gonna' hear me out before you get greeted by Lucifer himself. Answer me a question. Why did you kill Abigail? Why did you do that? Why couldn't you just let her go and be done with it?" Griffen's face twitched as he forced a scowl and worked hard at answering Emmett's question.

"You took my . . . ," his voice fading as he struggled to keep himself erect.

Emmett continued, "Were you going to say your wife? That I stole your wife? Are you so goddamn crazy you still think I took your wife? Damn it, man, she was my sister. You know that." A slow re-alization, a too late, dying kind of realization, slowly replaced the scowl on Griffen's face.

"How much more killing do you need? Why did you send somebody to try to kill Sam and his wife? Why? Answer me, god-damn it. Are you ready for this, you stupid son of a bitch?" Emmett paused, his emotions overwhelming him. "You don't even know who Sam's wife is, do you?"

Griffen managed a sneer which in itself asked, "And why would I give a fuck?" but his eyes betrayed him. They held a puzzled, inquisitive look in them. "Such a strange question to be asked," they seemed to say. And again, his right eye twitched.

The look of a child too stubborn to act concerned spread across Hesper's face. Finally, he forced a single word, "Who?"

Emmett had waited years to tell him this. He looked deep and hard into the evil eyes before him. He saw enough life remaining to enjoy saying, "She's your daughter, Hesper. Your very own blood. Your's and Abigail's daughter."

On the dying man's face, a mask of disbelief evolved into that of a man trying to weigh possibilities—feasibilities—and quickly followed by one of understanding.

Emmett stared at his old enemy, watching the man come to terms with all he had heard in the last few minutes of his confused and horrid life. Griffen's head sagged. He could stand no more pain, no more memories. Emmett wanted more than ever to see a look of sorrow, remorse, or anything that showed the dying man was totally aware—totally sorry. But it never came. Disgusted with the way Griffen had wasted his life, not only his, but so many others, he ended the conversation with, "Abigail had to leave you, you stupid bastard, so you wouldn't kill your own daughter. She was that afraid of you, but you still tried, didn't you?"

He realized Griffen's death was not enough for him—and that it never would be. He only wanted to leave. He felt nothing for the dying man behind him. No sorrow, no regrets, no relief, nor pleasure in knowing it was finally finished. Strangely, he'd grown weary of the long years of hating the man. Hesper would die and should die on his own. Emmett was not going to give him any more help. He wouldn't even try to remember the spot so the body could be retrieved.

"Rot where you fall, you son of a bitch," he said to the man as he stood.

He turned and stooped to grab the reins of his horse. A thunderous blast exploded behind him. The flap of his jacket blew outward, away from his body. His horse yanked hard and reared. Emmett instinctively slouched, expecting yet another blast. He waited for the coming surge of pain to rush through him. He knew how that would feel. Small pink particles of a very dead Hesper dripped upon his hand. He watched as the same pink splattered across the massive chest of his horse and painted the wide leather chest strap a pale, rosy hue. He watched, thinking how odd it was that everything seemed in slow motion.

Still facing away from the explosion, cringing, expecting yet another shot, he wiped at the mysterious warm wetness on the nape of his neck.

The pain did not come. He spun and saw Hesper's lifeless body folding inward, crumbling into itself, falling forward. Unfired, a Colt fell from Hesper's hand. The dead body that had been Hesper Griffen and the Colt seemed to take forever to hit the blood-splattered white sand.

Emmett saw Buck standing thirty feet away, holding a smoking rifle in his hands. Behind him Sam, Henry and Isaac were lowering their unfired guns.

Buck said to the startled man, "Emmett, never take your eyes off a man you've pissed off that much."

Sam walked over to Buck. He handed the copper badge to Buck and said, "Put this on."

He then approached Emmett and asked, "Emmett, you alright?"

Emmett looked at him and said, "Sam, it's over."

Epilogue

Swift Creek Plantation flourished. Sam and Rose remained inseparable. Their love for each other flourished along with the plantation. He had dared to dream so much and the evolution of his dreams had far exceeded his expectations.

His mind often drifted back to the hellish drudgery of crossing that awful Roanoke Swamp. Strange how he could still smell the rot of the place—how he could feel his clothing sticking to him from the misty vapors rising from the brackish water. So many things in his life had changed, but the sound of three-corner flies buzzing above his head, searching for just one more tasty bite—just a small bite—still made his skin crawl.

All he had hoped for back then was to be able to clear enough land to support himself and his few slaves. He'd hired men to help him. They'd come dragging their dreams with them, as well. He and they had hoped to make something out of the place they had come to. They too, needed to survive along with him and they had. And things had worked out good for them, too. They had grown more as friends than boss and worker. There had been the loss of friendships, but new friendships had replaced those lost.

The slaves were as much responsible for the success of Samuel Elwyn Biggs as the rest. They were treated with kindness, too. Rose's tender heart demanded that.

He had not considered a real family, one of his own, not in those first years. That had seemed too extravagant. His every wakening moment was already consumed with the daily requirements of Swift Creek.

Rose—his beloved Rose, changed everything. She helped him

to see the good in life, the little things, the attainable thing
did slowly evolve.

Ironically and unexpectedly, her father had shown Sam the
many bad things life could throw at you. Weaker men would have
tucked tail and run.

Dear sweet Rose. How had she survived it all? he wondered.
How had she sorted through the sordid confusion that had been Hesper Griffen?

How many men could say they had watched their wife's father
fall dead—the top of his head gone, and feel nothing? Sam could.
He'd lived it. Few could say they had stood above a lifeless body and
felt no more for it than if it was a tree toppled by wind. Sam had stood
there and he had felt nothing, his emotions long since burned to cinders. A character flaw? Maybe, maybe not, considering. Few people
would have been becalmed by such a dreadful sight. Sam was at last,
calm.

Later, his thoughts had tormented him about his indifference
toward the loss of that life. Gradually, the horrors of the death he'd
witnessed, and in which he had been secretly pleased, faded and then
banished—and once banished, refused re-entry.

What a trip, he often pondered. How did any of us survive? So
much harshness, so much death, something bad around every corner.
But oh, so much life, so much life.

Little Tad, with the loose blond curls and angelic face, with
eyes the color of a cloudless Carolina sky, had grown into a larger
version of the little boy he once was.

Sam saw some of himself in his son. Gladly not much, just
enough for a good balance. Tad was not of the same fiber as his father
at that age, nor did he have to be.

Sam had been born into a life of hardness and then raised with
the harshness always delegated to the poor. Seeking a new life, hopefully one less hard, he had stumbled into Griffen. So he'd become
harder, more determined and more unbendable—no other choices,
really. He had been forced to new degrees of hardness so many times
and had to lift himself above it to safer levels each time. Tad would
find his own level. *him*

God had blessed he and Rose with three of life's greatest mys-
teries. Their son Tad, the adorable Samantha, and the loving, always
happy, Isabella Lynn. And in doing so, God had revealed to both of

them the sole reason for their lives—love.

How he fawned over his family.   Three females and two males. Seemed reasonable and so right, the female of the species, so much nicer than the male. Swift Creek suffered from no lack of happiness. Sam and Tad worshipped and pampered the women folk and they adored and clung to the men who fawned over them.

Nearly twenty years all told, had passed since riding through that stinking toilet of a swamp. So much had happened. Good and bad.

Emmett had shared Sam's lack of remorse. A great justice had been done, Emmett reminded Sam. He had confided in Sam, the one and only time the two spoke of that afternoon—that afternoon up there in the woods, that he had wanted to be the man who killed Griffen—by himself—nobody else helping. But then, there was Buck—he just had to come along and part the man's hair from behind, didn't he? He told Sam he'd dreamed about it—about killing Griffen.

He realized afterward, if it had really and truly been his gun that killed the man, with no help from Buck or anybody, it would have been far too hard for him to ever look at his beloved Rose again, knowing what he had done.

It would have changed their relationship, even if she never knew a thing about it. Because it would have changed him. And if she did find out, she would have pitied him for being forced by things out of his control to have to go that far. Her pity alone would have altered the love the two shared. It would have had to. The strangeness of it would have claimed the two of them as two more victims. Griffen would have won, after all. Yes, he had wanted to kill the man, but in the long run, what Buck did, helped his mind settle—helped him distance himself from all the malignant hate.

Sam and Emmett never talked about it again. Maybe they should have, maybe they'd needed to, but both were too afraid. Even healing wounds, wounds finally scabbing over, would bleed again if you kept digging at them. If there was a God that had watched the evils of that man, he must have truly been a righteous God—letting him pay for his sins the way he did. Emmett had found a semblance of peace in that. Sam, too.

Sam had to be the one to tell Rose about the death of the man she knew was her father, and she needed to hear it only from him.

Sam's love and devotion to his wife required him to tell her of the events which had transpired. She was entitled to know and he was obligated to tell her. Each had long ago vowed to the other—no secrets—no secrets, ever. He relayed a purposefully brief and selective, but honest description of the man's death to her. Grief, shock or sorrow for her beloved husband and adored Uncle sent her reeling into solitude.

Rose's haggard face haunted Sam. She could not and would not speak of the man's death—her father's death, ever again. Her mind dwelled upon the unanswered What ifs of her life . . . and the horror and the finality of killing.

Sam minimized Buck's involvement in the affair back in the woods, and then held his silence.

She never said an unkind word to Buck. That was hard on the man. He couldn't look at her and she guiltily avoided him. She did not want to add to his burden.

Then, and only because she was forced into a dreaded conversation, did she say the name Griffen. After Griffen's death, the very survival of his run-down plantation was in question. It was barely held together by the slimmest of good intentions of good hearted people—people concerned for the well-being of the slaves, those scared and lost souls, those people that Griffen left to fend for themselves.

By default, fate, or a simple act resulting from the poor records of Hesper Griffen, Rose was named the heir of the Griffen plantation and all living things upon it. Abigail and Hesper, man and wife, had remained man and wife until their death; if only on paper. Desiring to be shed of any connection to her father, Rose was vehemently opposed to accepting title to the place.

The existence and the mere survival of the plantation had now run the full gamut, from being owned by a man that chose to ignore it; preferring his sordid life over it, to a state of confusion and total disrepair, to now being owned yet again, by someone who didn't want it. But it was only right she accept it. She had to. The slaves, two hundred and seventy-three of them, each frightened and confused, were pleased past terrors would never be visited upon them again. They were overjoyed their new master—to them, a living legend, was the very man who had thrown the dead man and the two dogs on the old master's lawn. Because of him, there was justice in their world, after all.

Rose and Sam encouraged Henry to take over the empty mansion and run it for them. True, it stood in ill-repair. Huge and no longer much to look at, the passing years of neglect had been unkind, but it was still full of promise.

He was torn between leaving one plantation of which he had been such a big part, working alongside his boss and his friend, Sam Biggs, and starting all over again. But opportunities like this would never come along again and Henry knew it. So he accepted the offer. He was a good man and deserved better than to continue in a subservient role. Agreements were drawn up and signed by all involved, giving Henry huge financial benefits with status and prestige thrown in. With Henry's close supervision, the abandoned mansion and plantation once again thrived.

He and Sara restored the long neglected mansion to its former opulence. Rose never set foot into the home of Henry and Sara. But they were not offended. They knew why. The slaves, after years of not understanding the hardness of life, found the peace they had never experienced under the old Massa, whose memory was quickly fading.

Emmett died while resting in his worn and faded chair. His death shook Rose's world to its very core. Her heart was badly bruised, leaving her devastated. One of the two men she loved more than her own life was gone and she was cast back into Hell's catacombs. The heartbreak of losing the man she loved so much, ate away at her desire to live. To her, death had become the paw of some fearsome, dark monster with long killing claws which cut the life from those she loved. She would mend but her heart would be forever scarred.

Again, Rose found herself the reluctant owner of yet another hugely successful plantation. Fortunately, Isaac was there to fill the void left by Emmett's death. Unlike the fear Griffen's slaves struggled with, Emmett's slaves were filled with sadness and deep concerns and rumors spread among them.

Isaac counseled them to stop spreading rumors. He assured them little would change and that he would speak to their new Mistress. He scolded them for doubting that Rose would always take care of them and like children, they were becalmed by the mere mention of her name.

Sam, this time on his own; his Rose struggling to not lose her way with her loss, approached Isaac with much the same terms the two of them had offered Henry, and Isaac accepted.

The business relationship between the three men, Sam, Henry and Isaac, formed the single largest plantation in the entire state of North Carolina. Sam and Rose maintained true ownership, but the lives of Henry, Isaac and their wives were changed forever.

Elmer and Dorrie were promptly moved from the run down shack up on the Ringwood road, into the luxuriant mansion by their loving son and daughter-in-law. Sam and Rose spent many afternoons with these precious people and they prospered together. The men enjoyed each other's company and the women folk needed each other's company just as much.

Happy parts of their past lives were retold and relived. Plans for the future were often discussed and polished as time passed and new needs arose. Some things were never mentioned.

George grew old, yet he struggled to stay near Sam. He was encouraged to go down to the creek and go fishing, but he doubted his old Massa could make do without him, so he remained at the big house.

In a long forgotten coat pocket, Sam found the root beer flavored candies he had bought from the Johnson's mercantile in Arcola many, many years before. Like life, they had lost their luster, but not their magic. Recalling Willie's antics, he gave these to Willie, also. And Willie got drunk, again.

Although his temples had turned gray and his beard salt and pepper, the man-child's mind and heart remained that of a twelve year old. Sam thought of Willie as the only true innocent he knew and held a special place in his heart for the simple-minded man.

James Motley was allowed to leave in peace. He had disgraced himself and his family and they were never seen or mentioned again in Swift Creek.

Leggett and Shorty were cuffed and hauled back to Fort Harwood by Buck when he left the afternoon Griffen died. They did not fair well in jail. Buck was sickened by the haste of the rigged trial; rigged by the face-saving and money-grabbing county leaders.

Their pleas for someone to fetch Sam and Emmett fell upon deaf ears. Buck sent a deputy to see if they would come, but they wouldn't—still bitter. In the end, it would have been too late anyway. Leggett and Shorty were quickly tried at the outer fringe of the law.

Shorty, by his own admission, was with Griffen and admitted he was involved in Abigail's murder just a little bit and he was hung for that little bit.

Jessie Leggett begged for mercy for his errant ways but received none. It was convenient to accuse him of other misdeeds, so other misdeeds were heaped upon him. The former Deputy Sheriff was found deserving of a rope around his neck.

A collective sigh of relief was heard emanating from the guilty consciences of the Carlton County officials but heard only within the group as two men preformed a strange dance at the end of county paid- for hemp ropes.

Dismay and a glimpse into his future ran through Buck's mind and heart as the town folk gathered to watch the morbid spectacle unfolding before them.

Buck worked hard to live up to the promise he'd made to himself two years before when he'd resolved to clean up the dirty town. He tried, he tried hard, but in the end, he couldn't do it. The elected county men countered his every challenge with threats of their own, while spreading money and favors through all of Carlton County.

A crowd of town folk gathered outside the jail and silently watched Buck as he drug his belongings out of the jail and loaded them onto his wagon. He faced the crowd and ripped the copper badge from his chest, the second time in as many years, and tossed it into a recently deposited pile of horse shit and rode out of town. Almost two years to the day since he had been able to accomplish any good at all, and that was shooting Griffen, he rode to Swift Creek Plantation to say his goodbyes. He never wanted to measure his life by such standards again. He was encouraged and then pleaded with to stay. A new county could be formed, he was told. Swift Creek Plantation was now as large as many existing counties, but Buck was defeated, demoralized and determined to leave. Another good man lost. He, like those before, gone and perhaps, never to be heard from again.

Elmer and Dorrie were treated with much respect and love. Elmer died peacefully in his sleep. Dorrie awoke with a dead husband lying next to her, so she could vouch for the ease in which he departed.

Her health deteriorated from that day forward, until in death, she too, slipped away. No one who knew the totality of the devotion which existed between the two, doubted she'd search through Heaven looking for him. The two were buried in the Detwyler family cemetery, near Emmett's grave. Space was left for three others, Rose, Sam and someday, Abigail.

Thaddeus Samuel Biggs, the only son of his doting parents, Sam and Rose Biggs, was enrolled and sent to VMI, the recently established Virginia Military Institute in Lexington, Virginia. Sam wanted so much more for his son—more than was offered on the plantation. He, Rose and the girls could give him love, but he needed so many other things.

The young man needed firmness and direction, both things due him from his father. But Sam, a man larger than life to all others, could not find it in himself to be hard or firm with his son. Without guidance, what good were directions? He knew, and Rose knew the boy needed the structured life offered by the military institute. What they did not know and could have never known was a time was coming—a time of great trouble, an uncivilized time, and in the not so distant future, when Tad's life would depend on the training he received at the famed school.

***

Late afternoons, while the sun was losing its day long battle to keep Sam and Rose's world aglow, Sam enjoyed the view from the wrong facing direction of Swift Creek Mansion. The summer's heat, the warmth of his afternoon brandy and the comfort of the wicker chair often lulled him asleep.

And when it did, he saw himself leaning against the porch column, watching the family he so dearly loved. Rose, Samantha, and Isabella Lynn walked hand in hand, while Tad, throwing rocks into the creek, followed his mother and sisters. He watched as they strolled through the flowering gardens, and along the banks of Swift Creek. How beautiful his Rose was, dressed in the billowing dresses she loved so much. His two little girls dressed similarly—miniature versions of their mother, ran ahead of her, gathering garden flowers, wild flowers and an assortment of pretty and not so pretty weeds.

Twirling umbrellas, Rose used her's to block the late summer heat; Samantha and Isabella Lynn, using theirs as toys. Tad had begun a search for stones and partially hidden by the overgrown weeds by the creek, he stood and waved to his father.

The soothing murmurs of distant sweet voices, the shrill and joyous peals of laughter as they walked hand in hand, faded.

Upon awakening, he often sneaked quick peeks to each side so he could wipe away seed tears before they grew and fell, and exposed his tender heart.

George, his approach slowed by age and aching legs, sought out his master, bringing him a Carolina Gold cigar.

Sam turned to him, needing answers to new questions which had plagued him since returning from his last trip abroad.

"George, tell me. Do you like it here?"

George, having never been asked that question before, answered, "Yas suh, I sho 'nough do."

the End

AS THE CANNONS ROAR

And to be released soon, the second book of a trilogy of the family saga of Samuel Elwyn Biggs, his wife, their children and their descendants.

AS THE CANNONS ROAR
by d. v. murray

AS THE CANNONS ROAR
by d. v. murray

Prologue: The Trinity that is human life: Body. Brain. Soul.

Shimmering like the wind-blown surface of a spring filled with crystal clear water, a brilliantly white and vaguely human form floated above an arched threshold. Spider-web thin tendrils of vapor seemed to connect the mist to the form on the ground. The golden threshold separated the darkest of all things dark and the brightest of all things bright, and awaited the command to depart the wrecked body below it—or the command to stay and give it hope.

A voice beyond man's hearing said, "No. Do not leave yet. Stay near him, protect him."

Smiling, the form had been commanded to stay.

The air, full of static and tension, trembled above the crumpled and bleeding body. Captain Thaddeus Biggs did not feel the tension nor the static. In the west, zigzagging flashes of red and pink ripped across the skies, announcing the approach of a thunderstorm. But he did not see the flashes. A deafening noise, similar to that of a laboring train, barreled down upon the carnage scattered all around, nor did he hear the roar.

Moments before, the ground shook violently. The union

artillery shell, packed with gunpowder and bits and pieces of scrap iron and slag, its singular purpose to destroy everything within its reach, had accomplished its mission.   Large and small pieces of shrapnel, all deadly, found their targets. Men and horses fell to the ground—most dying or dead as they fell.

Clods of dirt and loose soil rained upon his body as it lay at the edge of the crater left by the Yankee shell. Cool rain began to soak the wounded man's light-grey artillery uniform, quickly turning it dark, as the fabric began to streak with mud from the dissolving dirt.

The man lay motionless—deathlike, beside the newly formed crater, its razor-thin edge separating life and death.

Heavy cannon collapsed upon the ground, their carriage and wheels disintegrated into a splintered oblivion. Caissons exploded with ground shaking fury as the powder stored within ignited. Blue-gray tendrils of smoke and wispy steam rose sluggishly from the depths of the newly formed crater and floated away from the raging battle. Raindrops hitting the scattered shrapnel of iron and steel, sizzled into small haloes of steam and were instantly dispersed by a light breeze.

A curtain of red fell across the man's face. A tear began to form in the corner of his left eye, a trickle of blood fell from his right. It broke across the bridge of his nose and dripped into his sweat and rain soaked beard.

And then darkness, only darkness.

Slowly, striations of beautiful bright lights and spasms of flashes began to dance in the darkness behind Captain Biggs' closed eyelids. As quickly as they began, they faded.

The quivering mass inside the young Captain's fractured skull had regained enough of its nearly spent life to know time was wasting, and that time was of the essence.

"If our body dies, we all die," it shouted, realizing the dire straits it and the body were facing. Instinctively, it began sending signals of desperation throughout the body at the edge of the crater—and at the edge of death. Convulsions began to contort the body on the ground.

"Stop fighting me," it screamed, and it lay still. Twitches of a bleeding eyelid and a dirt covered cheek, begging to be noticed, spoke of an unknown degree of life yet remaining within the tattered body.

Like loose leaves of a book, its binding given way to age and the pull of wind, splintered thoughts swirled from the body. The organ at the center of the man's being knew the thoughts were of great importance. Desperate to gather the bits of fleeting knowledge before they sailed out of reach and were lost forever, it greedily grabbed them. Packed together, they created confusing images. They could be sorted later, reasoned the quivering gray orb; perhaps they contained the foundation on which life could be rebuilt.

"Hurry up, hurry up. Get going," it commanded the other organs. Unknown to the motionless soldier, its thinking part struggled desperately to halt the death-march its owner was on.

The throbbing center of the man grew stronger, yet the combined weight of pain and the constant struggle to restore the vital parts sucked hungrily at the limited strength which remained.

"We have to become one—quickly," it shouted. Gambling, it used the last of its strength and sent tingling signals throughout the body to restore itself.

By fractions, the broken body and the swollen brain merged; each taking from the other what it needed to survive.

Eyes flickered, suddenly they opened widely, willed by something other than themselves—a loud command or an unspoken thought from a deep and hidden place, a place with two distinct parts separated by an arched threshold.

"Yes," cried the brain. It now knew it could survive and it would survive. The shimmering form, the protector, once thinking its work on earth was completed, whispered encouragement. "You can do it, you can do it, but you must want to."

The Captain's senses began to slowly organize—not much, but a start. He saw blurry gray clouds floating high above. He had the sense that a crystal mist was falling upon him, seeking to enter every pore of his body. He smelled the acrid smoke of burned gunpowder and the metallic odor of blood. He heard not a sound except the intense roar growing deep inside his head. The last sense to restore itself was that of pain. How very badly he hurt!

He lay still, not knowing if he could move or if he should try.

He didn't know if he wanted to move. Alive or dead made little sense to him. He had not gotten that far yet, but alive *seemed* right. Dark thoughts—more vision than thought—continued to race before his unfocused eyes. He heard booming noises from a hill that he could only see in his mind.. He felt the sticky warm flesh of something—or someone, sliding down his exposed neck. Such visions were strange and confused him.

As the body and brain began to merge, the body grew tired and became complacent. It was the shell, the vessel, the protector of everything and it was failing its job. Thankfully, a growing awareness of guilt began to build, the result of the manipulations of the brain forcing it back to the realities of life or death.

"Don't you dare quit on us," demanded the orb, sending the message coursing through the man.

The body felt the soothing touch of the mist. He heard it say, "You must live. There are those that need you."

And embarrassed to think it had considered giving up, it willed his eyes to dark forms and shadowy movements above him. Frightened, the eyes closed and rolled back, retreating toward a remote, dark and becalmed place. But sensing the importance of the presences, the eyes returned to the shapes hovering above them.

"Captain . . . Captain . . . Can you hear me?" asked the form looming over him.

AS THE CANNONS ROAR
by d. v. murray

Chapter one:

The dream again. Sam Bigg's eyes flashed open, his pupils dilating in the near dark of the early morning, his heart pounding wildly, as beads of sweat trickled down his temples.

How many times had he seen his son dead—his body mangled and twisted among broken caissons, crushed muskets, and the debris of war? How many more of those dreams will haunt me, he wondered, as he fought off sleep, to fight off dreams.

He lay close to his wife, yearning for her touch, for the assurance she was still next to him. He was careful not to touch her and moved away. The room was warm and he feared the warmth of his body against hers would magnify the heat and awaken her. It always did.

She, too, had been sleeping poorly, but he did not want her awake, not just yet.

The dream began fading, but not before horrid faces stared at him, taunted him, and called him a fool. The familiar demons, pointed bony fingers, and asked, "What did you do to your son?"

Rose, lay still, studying her husband's strained and restless face. She knew the dream had returned. She knew it was best if she lay there quietly, and let him work through it, he always did. She understood the decision he'd made a long time ago was now taking its toll.

He was still handsome, handsome in only the way older men can be—hardened and dignified. Deep furrows creased his face, his skin dark and leathery from long days spent in the burning sun. His hair, now gone salt and pepper, and the ever-present mustache were tussled from the previous night's tossing and turning.

Her face flushed, as her body reminded her she was still attracted to him. She knew he would be pleased to be awakened in that special way he liked, but she remained quiet, and continued to watch the dancing, fluttering eyes behind his closed eyelids.

He looked haggard—too worn to exist. His eyes rolled and jumped in a frenzied dance, as they watched scenes only they could see. The dream tore at him.

Feeling the horror of the dream, he refused to open his eyes—he knew she was watching him—he felt the concern in her eyes.

Often he told her of the dreams when he awoke. Only the dream about their son made his eyes twitch so, his face contort, his breath catch.

Long ago, before the dreams of Tad started, she had witnessed the same sleeping, dancing eyes. They reminded her of how poorly her husband had slept after her father died in the woods, a half mile distant of where they now lay. *If only I could help him*, she whispered. Her inability to do so tormented her.

He'd told her of things, things he'd seen—but only enough for her to know he'd been present at the death of her father, and that he'd watched her father, Hesper Griffen, die. She knew he'd lied to her—not in a mean or a deceitful way, when he'd told her how her *blood* father had died. She knew because his face could never hide the gruesomeness he must have witnessed. She never forgave her husband—she didn't need to. Hesper Griffen deserved to die for all the evil he had been.

And he never told her at whose hands the man had died. There were other things he did not tell her, and never would. She knew that, also. And she knew she did not want to hear those things. So many violent and unbelievable things had happened during those years now long gone.

Has the world gone mad? she wondered. She was comforted by knowing her beloved Uncle Em, now gone to his heavenly reward, hovered everywhere, watching over their children, *his* grandchildren. She missed the man, his love of her, and the way he had protected her when there was no one who could. She had survived a life of horror because of his devotion to her. *A life filled with contrasts*, she thought. *My husband, tortured by things he's seen. And I, relieved by things I have not seen.*

But some horrors have lives of their own. The horror of watching her father, crazed by mental illness and alcohol, kill her mother never lessened, and never would. Knowing the man would have killed her and his own grandchildren and every person she knew and loved, never faded.

"Oh God. Please protect our son," she prayed, and softly kissed her husband's forehead.

Wishing to be alone, he mumbled, "Wake me in an hour, will you?"

"Okay," she answered, knowing she had no intention of waking him.

She touched his cheek and said, "Go back to sleep." And as she closed the door to the bedroom, he began to toss and turn.

***

Entering the dining room, she greeted her daughters, giving each a motherly hug. "Your Father is the most stubborn man in the whole world. You'd think this place would fall apart if he's not out there every minute of every day . . . and at his age, humph!" she said, shaking her head. "He knows Matt can run this place. Matt's the overseer, that's why he hired him. Matt knows what needs attention on this place and what can wait. Stubborn. Stubborn, that's what he is."

The girls had heard her tirades before and knew it was her way of venting and scolding the man she loved, even if he was not present.

Samantha, the eldest, and Isabella Lynn, nicknamed Izzy by her grandfather, sat quietly. They knew their mother would continue a few more moments and then all would be quiet.

And feeling her point made, she said no more.

During breakfast, Samantha and Isabella Lynn, excited about their planned trip into Fort Harwood, said little. This was not the time for a long drawn-out conversation with their Mother. There were necessities to be seen to: hair to be brushed and coifed, dresses to be chosen and lain out, corsets and boots to be pulled tight and laced.

To them the rebellion was being fought in some far-away place and they chose to ignore that things could change in a moment's passing with war. Soon they began talking of the dresses they were wearing into town and the shops they *just had to* visit.

"Not today," their mother said. "It's not safe. There's rumors our fighting men might be getting pushed back."

"Oh, Mother, that's not fair. Besides, Holt's going with us. Please."

"No, now hush."

The girls pouted. "Mama, they said the fighting would be over in three or four months and that was almost a year ago."

They stood and stormed from the room, mad about broken promises, mad at their father, mad at Jefferson Davis, and mad at every living thing north of the Mason-Dixon line.

For now, the fighting had raged above them, mostly up in Virginia, near Washington. But rumors were spreading and had already reached as far south as Weldon. With the rumors, most exaggerated, and some not expounded upon enough, came fear and an unspoken urge of many neighboring families to flee south. Many families had already packed the barest of essentials, if indeed, they did have to leave.

Rose stood by the window overlooking the manicured lawn. In the center of the circular drive stood the gazebo in which she and Sam were married twenty-two years earlier. The gleaming white gazebo served as a reminder of everything she and her husband had accomplished. It spoke of good things and blessings. It spoke of bad things, as well.

She and Sam had built a life together, here on Swift Creek. It had been over two-and-a-half decades since he arrived from Petersburg, Virginia, to lay claim to his property, the long abandoned five-thousand acres he'd won from a dying old fool in a poker game.

Their children often played in the gazebo. The girls, pretending they were full grown—tiny debutantes gossiping and giggling, as they sat around a child-sized table, with pinkies stuck in the air, hands holding small china cups filled with imaginary tea, with frilly white napkins spread across their laps. But a fort, that was what Tad used it for. The slave children, those too young to be of any value in the fields, became the enemy, dying many times over and over so his war could continue.

Seeking its cooling and calming effects, Rose stepped onto the front porch and sat in a wing-back rattan chair. Spreading out from the porch, the lawn, bordered with old growth trees, fell gently toward the creek. As the dark green leaves of the oaks fluttered in a warm breeze, Rose absent-mindedly browsed through the Fort Harwood Graphic. The three-week old paper, worn and dog-eared from usage, its stories well read, failed to hold her attention.

The thumping of a speeding horse echoed from the direction of Weldon. Nearing the entrance to Swift Creek Plantation, the horse slowed. Rose's heart began to race—fear immobilized her. Many of her neighbors had received heartbreaking news from such riders speeding down country lanes.

As the horse raced down the mansion's drive, she stood and fled into the house, wishing to forestall the possibility of such news. She watched from behind the screened door. Her heart pounded. She willed the rider to leave, but the rider refused to abide by her wishes. He would not and could not turn away from his duty. He continued his hard ride.

Bradley Smith pulled at the horse's reins, sawing at the bit in its mouth as he jumped from the saddle. He threw the reins to the stable boy, and slapping at his trousers and shirt, he dusted them with an opened hand. He straightened his jacket and reached into his coat pocket.

He withdrew a sweat-stained brown envelope and reluctantly walked toward the front door.

Her instincts frightening her, Rose did not immediately recognized the young man, although he had been there many times before, courting Isabella Lynn, and she quickly closed and locked the French doors. If he would not ride on, she would forestall him. She knew he worked at the Post Office in Weldon. And she'd seen the brown envelopes before.

Nearly swooning with fear, she dashed up the spiral staircase, shouting, "Sam! . . . Sam!"

Holt, the house servant, seeing a young man he recognized staring through the stained-glass windows, opened the mahogany doors.

"Massa Smif," he said, with a toothy smile, "I'll go fetch the Missus." Holt turned as he heard the commotion at the top of the stairs.

Sam pulled at his boots, snapped his suspenders into place, and stepped onto the landing. He combed his tussled mass of gray hair with spread fingers. Behind him, stood his wife, clutching his sleeve in her tiny hand. Samantha and Isabella Lynn, alarmed by their mother's cries, held hands as they stared down at Bradley Smith. And together, the Biggs family descended the stairs.

***

Bradley was no stranger to the kind of grief contained inside those envelopes—he'd delivered four such brown envelopes in the last year and each had carried the worst possible of news. It seemed bad news was the contents of most of those letters, he thought.

His heart drumming, he looked at Izzy, dreading the news he suspected she and her family were about to receive. She wasn't crying, yet, and for the first time since he'd been calling on the young lady, he wanted to be gone and far away from the beautiful girl. She might see him weep. He'd admired Tad, and weeping was not a manly thing.

"Mr. Biggs," he said, extending the letter to him. "Mr. Jacobs told me to get this to you, posthaste. He wants me to wait for an answer, Sir." His arm fell to his side, and not knowing the formalities required of bad news, said, "I pray everything is alright. I'll wait outside, Sir." Giving the family privacy, he stepped onto the front porch.

Sam tore at the letter, his hands trembling. He turned away from his wife and daughter and read the note.

"Sam. What's it say?" implored Rose, with fingers pressed against pursed lips, she pleaded, "Sam. Sam. What is it?"

Samantha and Isabella Lynn hugged their mother.

He turned back to them, his face an odd mixture of fear, confusion, and relief. "It's Tad," he said, his voice cracking. "He's been hurt."